Lukas leaned hungrily forward, setting his hands on the table. "What do you see, soothsayer? Who was here three nights ago?"

"A . . . a fiend," she said breathlessly.

"A fiend?" he echoed.

"A man-fiend," she whispered, shaking her head in fear. "He was . . . wrapped in the skin of a man . . . but was truly a monster. Tall and lean . . . carried something heavy. Something cold."

"What did he carry, Madam Marosa?"

"He carried . . . he carried . . ." she began, her mouth forming silent syllables between the words. Her body went rigid, and she gasped. "He carried a little boy and a dog. Both were dead."

"What did he do with them?"

"Set them . . . there, on that window seat," the gypsy replied, pointing. "And he . . . and he . . ."

"And he changed, didn't he, Madam Marosa?" Lukas asked. "Changed from a tall, thin bard to a wolf. Am I not correct?"

The old gypsy stared back at him, stunned. Lukas could see his own wild expression in her bulging eyes.

"And that beast, Madam Marosa—that beast set to feeding, did it not?" Lukas pressed, edging savagely nearer. The woman made no response. "And it looked like me, didn't it?"

Ravenloft is a netherworld of evil, a place of darkness that can be reached from any world—escape is a different matter entirely. The unlucky who stumble into the Dark Domain find themselves trapped in lands filled with vampires, werebeasts, zombies, and worse.

Each novel in the series is a complete story in itself, revealing the chilling tales of the beleaguered heroes and powerful evil lords who populate the Dark Domain.

BOOKS

BOOKS

Heart
of
Midnight

J. Robert King

HEART OF MIDNIGHT

First Printing: December 1992
Printed in the United States of America
Library of Congress Catalog Card Number: 91-66487

9 8 7 6 5 4 3 2 1

ISBN: 1-56076-355-8

TSR, Inc.
P.O. Box 756
Lake Geneva, WI 53147
U.S.A.

TSR Ltd.
120 Church End, Cherry Hinton
Cambridge CB1 3LB
United Kingdom

To Jennie,
who has nearly cured my lycanthropy

PROLOGUE

"The city seems restless," the young guardsman mumbled to himself, filling his lungs with the nighttime air. He leaned back against the city wall and studied the oak-and-mortar houses spread out below him. Moonlight cast an icy pall over the cobbled streets, and above the city's thatched roofs, clouds drifted in uneasy swarms.

"Can't let it frighten me," he said, his face blanching.

Someone was whispering.

The guard started, shooting a glance down the wall that surrounded the city. A stone's throw away, an odd shadow hovered half-concealed in one of the limestone niches. The guard stepped forward, squinting to make out what the shadow might be.

"That wasn't there a moment ago," he thought aloud, biting his lip. "Maybe it's just a trick of the light."

Then he saw the eyes.

The form slid from the niche, its black robes billowing out on the wind. It began striding toward him. The guard stiffened. The butt of his halberd shifted uneasily on the cobblestones. The robed figure quickened its pace, beginning to run toward the guard. The cowl slipped from its shoulders, revealing a young man, lean and angular, with eyes like silver coins. He had no armor, no weapons, no clothes, but still he closed in. The guard raised his halberd, catching a toehold on the cold cobbles.

"Halt!"

Without warning, a cloud blotted out the moon, and the youth disappeared in the sudden darkness. The guard fumbled with his halberd, straining to make out the youth's form, but he couldn't. Still the relentless footfalls approached, their fevered rhythm matching the thunder of the guard's heart. He looked to the cloudy sky, praying for the moonlight to return.

As though in answer, the clouds suddenly drew back from the moon. Light washed over the youth.

But he was a youth no longer.

In the flash of moonlight that would be his last memory, the guard glimpsed a massive canine head, a silvery mane, a cavernous mouth, teeth and foam and sickle-shaped claws. . . .

Impact.

The guard hurtled backward, metal and bone smashing against the city wall. He tried to remain standing, but his legs crumpled beneath him, and he flopped like a rag doll to the street. A red tide flowed out over the cobbles. His hands pushed ineffectually against the slick stones, but he couldn't rise.

The shudder of another blow ran through him, flipping him onto his back. He dropped his head to the cold cobbles. His body shook again, but he felt no pain. He looked past the savage hackles of his slayer, looked to the stars sparkling above.

Then blackness engulfed him.

* * * * *

The werewolf gorged itself on the corpse's meaty leg, lifting its ruby muzzle only long enough to snort a breath. A growl of pleasure rumbled through its chest, punctuated by greedy gulps. Again it sank its jaws into the carcass, and again.

No one came to drive it off.

In time, the beast's breathing slowed. Blood-grisly hackles settled across its back, and its once-fiery eyes cooled to silver again. The werewolf fell back on its haunches, away from the crimson corpse. A tremor moved through its body. Slowly, beneath the lengthening shadows of the moon, the beast's limbs began to warp. Its cheekbones pressed out through balding skin; teeth blunted and shrank; snout compressed into a face; forelegs sprouted palms; pads lengthened to fingers. And everywhere, fur thinned and dissolved away into youthful skin.

The transmogrification was complete.

Now, beneath the racing sky, a young man of eighteen sat beside the corpse. He was naked except for the blood that coated him from nose to knees. His silvery eyes were cloudy, as though he had just awakened. Shaking himself, he turned to gaze at the body beside him. The guard lay motionless, his back bent at an impossible angle. Only a ragged stump remained of his right leg. The muscles of the calf and thigh were gone, and ligaments splayed from the torn joints.

The youth turned away from the corpse. "Damn," he cursed to himself. He had known he would kill a man tonight, known the moment he donned the black cape and slipped through the window. The hunger had been inexorable. But now the hunger was past, and he felt sickened. The youth winced as he glanced back at the body.

Something on the corpse moved.

Shaking, the youth leaned closer. He glimpsed movement again, movement on the guard's crimson face. An eyelid slowly opened, and the eye beneath shifted and fastened on the youth. It seemed to see through him, gazing to the clouds and stars above. And in the glossy surface of the eye, the young man saw his own frightened reflection.

The guard shuddered. His eye slowly closed, and he was still. The youth stared blankly, fearfully, at the body. He reached out, clasping the man's chill hand.

"I'm sorry," he murmured.

Then, snatching up his black robe, he disappeared into the night.

ONE

Thoris lay wide awake on his tattered cot. His pudgy fingers gripped the wooden frame beneath him as he peered toward the dormitory window. There stood Casimir, his lean form silhouetted against the late-winter sunset. The young man's long fingers picked splinters of wood from the windowsill as he gazed out on the town of Harmonia. After a few moments, he gathered up a handful of splinters and tossed them out the window onto the thatched roof below.

"Here I am, in a squalid poorhouse. . . ." Casimir muttered.

Thoris shifted his paunchy body on the cot and snorted. His voice cracked as he spoke. "And—let me guess—your mortal enemy, Zhone Clieous, watches the very same sunset from the comfort of the meistersinger's mansion."

Casimir turned toward the boy and ran his fingers through his sable hair. "Am I showing it that much, old chum?"

"More than that much," Thoris said, rolling to sit up on his cot. He filled his lungs with the stale air of the dormitory and cast a glance at the endless rows of cots around him. "Everybody's noticed. All you talk about lately is how much you hate Clieous. Whatever happened to your songs? Whatever happened to your stories? I think turning eighteen has ruined you."

Casimir withdrew from the window, folding his hands

and sitting down on his cot. He stretched once, his muscles straining against the tattered chemise he wore. "I have no more songs, no more stories. I'm worn out." He cradled his head in his hands. "Every night I pray to die in my sleep."

Thoris's eyes flashed wide. "What kind of talk is that? Look, this vendetta against Clieous is poisoning you, Casimir. Why don't you stop complaining and start acting! If you're going to get revenge, get it!"

Casimir shook his head and lay back on his cot. He drew his ragged sheet tightly about him. "You don't understand. Revenge would kill me."

Thoris pressed his lips together and harrumphed. "At least sing me one of the *Mora*, Casimir . . . for old time's sake."

The dark-complected boy gazed wearily at his friend. "I told you, Thoris, I've run out of songs. I have only dirges left."

"Then sing a dirge, for goodness' sake," Thoris said.

Sighing, Casimir clenched his jaw. Then, in a high, soft voice, he began to sing.

> *"With ev'ry wound comes quiet Death*
> *To steal away our life and breath*
> *Of youth. With ev'ry little pain—*
> *The shocks to soul or mortal flesh—*
> *An older soul takes up the rein.*
>
> *"For what is life but fleeting years*
> *Marked clearly by the scars and tears*
> *Of time? I peer across my frame,*
> *So marked and yellowed like a book*
> *That I can call each hurt by name.*
>
> *"If length of life you dearly crave,*
> *Then flee from pain and hurt to save*
> *Your soul. Or, as the vampires do,*
> *Make supplications sweet with Death*
> *To live eternal, if not true.*

"In final breaths on your death day,
You'll wonder where your youth so gay
Has fled. Yet it has never gone,
But hid beneath a mask of scars
And cares till breath is stilled and done."

The words whispered into silence. Thoris opened his mouth to speak, but nothing came forth. He fingered the canvas of his cot and peered toward Casimir. The tall boy was wrapped in his ragged sheet like a moth in a cocoon. Only his head protruded. His black hair formed a dark halo around his face.

Enough is enough, Thoris told himself. Tonight I'll discover what's plaguing him so. He's gone out that window every midnight for the past month. This time I'll follow and spy on him.

* * * * *

The hours until midnight passed torturously for Thoris. He persistently rolled over on his cot, trying to ward off sleep. At times, he would pinch himself or bend his fingers back to stay awake. Nevertheless, his eyes finally began to blink and slide closed. He could feel his mind drifting away into dreams, but he no longer had the will to stop it.

The great iron bell of Harmonic Hall cried in the distance. Thoris lurched awake, his heart suddenly pounding. He clutched the frame of the cot. The bell spoke again.

Ten more chimes to midnight.

Do I really want to do this? he asked himself. If Frau Von Matren catches us climbing out the dormitory window, we'll be thrown out on our ears. Another toll sounded. Thoris turned his eyes toward Casimir, expecting him to awaken any moment, slough off his sheet, and climb through the window. Perhaps he won't go tonight, Thoris mused with some relief. Perhaps I won't have to follow him. . . .

Again the bell rang. Casimir shifted. Thoris snapped his eyes closed and lay, feigning sleep. Then, furtively, he glanced toward Casimir, who rolled to a sitting position on his cot. His thick, black hair stood in bushy spikes around his head, and his high cheekbones bore the marks of the canvas. But his opal eyes sparkled soberly.

Casimir rose from the creaking cot, stretched, and peered through the ramshackle window. The night outside was pitch-black. As he gazed through the window, he drew a muscled hand thoughtfully to his mouth. Then the tall youth knelt, sliding a wooden box from beneath his cot. From the crate, he drew a thick, black garment, which he lifted slowly and pressed to his face. He breathed deeply and sighed. Staring long at it, he shook his head and lowered the fabric back into the crate. Then he rose and, with fluid motion, climbed into the window, filled his lungs with the night air, and slipped out.

Thoris forced himself to lie still for a count of five before he rose and peered cautiously over the sill. Below, Casimir was descending the poorhouse's oak-and-mortar wall, finding toeholds where the ancient beams had twisted. Thoris studied the older boy's descent, knowing he would follow shortly. Reaching the base of the wall, Casimir set his feet on the thatching of Cook's quarters, which lay immediately below the window. One misstep would bring him through the roof and onto Cook's stomach. Thoris gritted his teeth, his heart pounding in his ears. Sidestepping to the edge of the roof, Casimir dropped lightly to the dirt lane below. Warily he scanned the dark slum quarter. Mud-and-plank shanties spread out in a gray maze as far as the eye could see. Cautiously he stepped away from the orphanage and started down the street.

"Now or never," Thoris said to himself. He knelt beside his cot, pulling a hand-carved wooden sword from his pile of belongings. His hand ran along the keen edge of the carved blade. It was still sharp after ten years. For a moment, his mind slipped back to the hot summer day when he had first held the sword.

* * * * *

Flies buzzed noisomely in the summer air. Although the shutters of the shack stood open, the heat within was oppressive.

The heat and the stench.

But the five-year-old boy didn't notice. He sat in a corner, shivering despite the hot sunlight that poured through a nearby window and onto his back. His skin was as white as porcelain beneath his matted brown hair, and dark rings circled his sunken eyes. A fly that had been tracing zigzag lines around the room landed on the boy's cracked lips. He didn't bother to brush it away. He didn't move. He only sat, staring toward the open doorway that led to the shack's other room.

The smell came from there.

The boy shifted in the sunlight, his bony knees thudding dully on the dirt floor. He eased his body down in the patch of sunlight, cradling his head in the crook of his knobby elbow. Though his eyes remained open, he slowly fell asleep. He had slept all but a few hours of the last week, and waking or sleeping, he was always cold.

The warm beam of sunlight had moved off him when he started awake. His bony head lifted from the dirt floor, and he blinked. Someone was singing—someone outside. The voice was shrill and taunting, the voice of another boy, laughing and shouting and singing.

> "I'll kill you, you dumb dogs! Ha ha! Ha ha!
> I'll feed you to fat hogs! Ha ha! Ha ha!
> I'll stab you and slice you
> I'll chop you and dice you. Ha ha! Ha ha! Ha ha!"

The boy in the shanty rose, shivering, from the dirt floor. Placing his thin hand on the weathered window frame, he cautiously peered out. In the deep forest that surrounded the house, something flashed in the sunlight. It was the singing boy. He was playing there, dodging amongst the trees and leaping from rock to rock across the stream. His clothes were shabby and tattered. He breathlessly repeated his song, breaking the lines occasionally as he stabbed at bramble bushes with a wooden sword.

"Down, you dirty dog!" he shouted.

The boy at the window turned, hobbling quickly to the door of the shanty. He peered out, seeing the other boy slash some undergrowth with his sword.

"Take that, damn you!"

The child in the shanty covered his ears when he heard the curse. The other boy appeared to be about eight years old, but he still shouldn't swear. Dropping his hands from his ears, the younger boy cautiously stepped through the doorway of the shack. He shuffled forward slowly, watching the other child with fearful interest. The boy with the sword released another savage shout. Gasping in fear, the younger boy dropped to the ground and crawled behind a clump of ferns. He caught his breath, then slowly eased himself nearer to the eight-year-old.

Suddenly the sword-toting boy spun about, swinging his wooden blade into the ferns.

"Ha ha! Die, you dirty dog!"

Fronds flew through the air, sliced cleanly from their stalks. The sword slashed deeper into the plant, whirling inches from the boy hiding there. He screamed in terror, falling back on his bony hands. The sword stopped swinging, and the older boy leapt through the fern, leveling his blade.

"Who are you?" he demanded, placing one fist on his hip.

Wide-eyed, the younger child whimpered incomprehensibly.

A thoughtful look crossed the older boy's dark features. He ran a hand through his black hair and said. "It doesn't matter. You want to play 'hunter' with me?"

The wide-eyed boy said nothing, his lips quivering.

"Come on, I won't stab you," the black-haired child said with a cocky smile. He extended a hand. "I need a sergeant-at-arms."

Blinking nervously, the emaciated boy took the extended hand and stood.

"I'm Casimir," the older boy blurted. "What's your name?"

"Thoris," mumbled the younger one.

Casimir stowed his wooden sword in his belt and folded his arms over his chest. "So, do you want to play?"

"Play what?"

"We could play 'hunter,' or 'fight the monster,' " Casimir replied, tapping the sword at his side.

"What monster?"

"Any of 'em," Casimir said. "The big, huge, giant one or the little, tiny, puny one."

Thoris smiled shyly. "That would be fun."

" 'Course it's fun. We can fight lots of things."

Thoris's brows lowered over his sunken eyes. He shot a furtive glance back toward the shack. "Um . . . I gotta ask my mama."

Backing cautiously away from Casimir, Thoris turned and hobbled toward the shanty. The taller boy watched him, his eyes growing serious as he noted Thoris's withered arms and legs. "Something's wrong with him," he murmured warily to himself. Resting his hand on the carved hilt of his wooden sword, Casimir followed the boy.

Even a stone's throw from the shack, Casimir could smell the odor of rot. As they neared the shanty, the stench grew almost unbearable. Thoris, however, appeared to be oblivious to it, walking without hesitation toward the battered doorway. Casimir pinched his nose, nervously surveying the faded whitewash on the plank walls and the mossy thatch on the roof. The younger boy turned with a gentle smile, then stepped through the open doorway. He disappeared into the shack, its ragged door swinging partially closed behind him.

Casimir's eyes grew wide.

A crimson **X** marked the door.

It was the sign of the plague, the Kartakan pestilence.

Holding his breath, Casimir backed away several steps. He pulled the sword from his belt and turned to run, then hesitated.

That poor boy, with his sunken eyes, pallid skin, cracked lips, shy smile . . .

"Thoris?" Casimir called, turning around once more. "Come out of there." He heard no movement in the shack. "Thoris?" he shouted, his voice wavering. Cautiously he edged around to the side of the shanty, keeping his sword in front of him the whole time. Rounding the corner, he saw a splintery window, its shutters hanging loose. Taking another deep breath, Casimir peered through the window.

The boy was standing in the room, wringing his hands in front of him and staring expectantly at a woman on a cot. Casimir's eyes narrowed.

The woman was dead.

"Thoris?" he cried, the name almost choking in his throat. "Come out right now!"

Glancing out the window, Thoris turned from the bed and headed for the door. He emerged, his brow serious and his lips pressed firmly together. "Sorry. Mama said it's too dang'rous."

Unwilling to move closer, Casimir motioned the starving boy toward him. "Come here." Reluctantly Thoris stepped forward, glancing back over his shoulder and squinting through the doorway as though he expected a reprimand.

When the boy finally neared, Casimir said, "Let's go."

Thoris shook his head firmly. "No. It's too dang'rous."

Grabbing the boy's hand, Casimir said insistently, "Let's go!"

"No!" Thoris shouted, pulling free, his eyes wide with shock. "Mama said!" He pivoted around painfully and hobbled back toward the shack.

"Wait!" Casimir shouted. The boy halted, cringing as

though expecting a blow. He looked fearfully over his shoulder. Casimir shook his head, clamping his teeth together. He held his wooden sword out toward the boy. "It won't be too dangerous . . . if you have this sword."

Thoris's eyes grew wide, and a beaming smile crossed his pallid face. He turned and walked slowly toward Casimir, his hands reaching out for the blade. "Is this mine?"

"Yes," Casimir said begrudgingly, "if you come with me."

"Where are we going?"

"To the city," Casimir said, handing the blade to the boy.

"Where the big white walls are?" Thoris mumbled distractedly as he eyed the sword.

"Yeah," Casimir replied, sighing forlornly. "And the Red Porch poorhouse."

*   *   *   *   *

It is a bittersweet memory, Thoris thought, clutching the wooden hilt of the sword. And now Casimir needs me. Thoris's concern grew deeper as he followed Casimir through the dark streets of Harmonia. The black-haired youth had already led him, at a distance, from the Red Porch poorhouse, through the vast maze of slums, onto the cobbled highroad, past shops and stores and taverns—even past the meistersinger's mansion. Still he pressed onward. At last he started up a steep-sloped street that led to the crest of South Hill. Thoris gulped. South Hill was the home of Harmonia's richest people. No orphan had business there.

After countless cautious steps, Thoris also reached South Hill Street, a shiny brick avenue lined with lanterns. To either side of the road, massive walls of whitewashed stone rose, fronting the vast estates that lay beyond. Keeping a healthy distance behind Casimir, Thoris started up the road, sliding along in the shadows of the walls. Casimir walked onward, his steps weary and deliberate. Not once did he look back. Following carefully, Thoris reached the crest of South Hill. There he glimpsed one of the great manor houses of Harmonia, a rambling edifice with countless windows of leaded glass. It looked like a huge jewel box, or a castle of the gods. Surely he's not going in there! Thoris thought.

Ahead, Casimir left the road, disappearing into the mansion's stable entrance. Thoris approached cautiously. He peered around the corner just as the tall boy scaled a half-wall near the stable and dropped to the other side. Thoris followed at a distance, crouching low. His heart drummed so loudly that he was amazed Casimir hadn't heard it. Clumsily he climbed to the top of the half-wall and then froze.

Beyond the wall stretched an elegant garden. It looked like something from a dream. Stony paths wound past trees and tall shrubs, which were trimmed in the shape of cones and cylinders and spheres. In the blue-gray beams of moonlight, the place was both serene and stark. Beyond the garden, the mansion loomed like a mountain with windows.

"Where did he go?" Thoris whispered to himself. Then he spotted Casimir trudging along a hedge that ran alongside the half-wall. Regaining his breath, Thoris carefully dropped from the wall and followed after his friend. He eyed the hedge, looking for a place to hide should Casimir look back toward him. But Casimir didn't look back. He left the hedge and began to follow a snaking path leading to a broad, limestone rail.

A rail that ran along a sheer cliff.

Casimir reached the rail and sat down on it. Thoris's breath caught short as Casimir swung his legs to dangle over the cliff's edge. He peered out toward the gray heath and the thick forests that rimmed the horizon. Thoris slowed, not wanting to alert Casimir and not wanting to approach the cliff too quickly. The panorama made him queasy. He halted in the path, ducking behind a shrub. Why is Casimir here? he wondered.

A quiet melody came to his ears. It swelled, died away, then came again. It was Casimir, singing a *Mora*, one of the morality songs of Harmonia. This was another dirge, reserved for funeral processions.

> *"With sheets and shears, Dark Midwife comes*
> *To bear us from our mother's womb.*
> *Her leather hands thus bring us home*
> *Into the tombs, the catacombs.*
>
> *"The meistersinger, too, shall go*
> *Beyond his mansion's rich estate.*
> *Dark Midwife comes to lay him low*
> *With hands of fate, with hands of woe.*
>
> *"The 'ostler finds his weary way*
> *From toilsome work with guests and beds.*
> *Dark Midwife brings him 'neath her sway.*
> *He joins the dead; he flies away.*
>
> *"The watchman, too, upon the wall*
> *Awaits her face like light of dawn.*
> *Dark Midwife comes with bitt'rest gall.*
> *With watchmen gone, the cities fall.*
>
> *"The maiden comes for mother, too,*
> *Her gentle hands grown old with years.*
> *Dark Midwife swiftly bears her through*
> *Without a tear, without a rue.*
>
> *"And so, we all pass from this life*
> *To better lands, or those far worse.*
> *Our cord is severed by the knife*
> *Of death's own nurse, the Dark Midwife."*

Thoris listened closely, his hand cupped to his ear to catch the sound. Casimir's song rose gently upon the air, merging with the quiet wind. His voice had always been beautiful and haunting, but tonight it sent a cold chill down Thoris's spine.

Casimir shifted on the marble rail. He rose to his feet, standing tall above the cliff. Then he lifted his arms to each side as though surrendering to some unseen foe. His head dropped back and he stared into the starless heavens.

"Damn you!" The angry words clattered like thunder across the cliffs below. "You have haunted me my whole life! Oh, gods, how I hate you!" Casimir shouted.

Thoris's heart pounded in his ears, and his chin quivered. He stepped nearer, approaching the cliff. The stony path was cold beneath his feet. As he drew close, he saw Casimir's midnight hair thrash blackly against the blue-black sky.

"Casimir, what's wrong?" Thoris asked.

Without turning around, Casimir gasped, "Thoris?"

"What are you doing out there, Casimir?" Thoris asked.

"Getting ready to jump," Casimir said wearily

"Why, Casimir? Is it Meistersinger Clieous?"

"Good-bye, Thoris."

He stepped over the cliff's edge.

And plummeted.

Thoris gasped and rushed to the rail. Casimir was falling, turning slowly as he dropped. He neither cried out nor clutched for handholds, but instead fell silent and stiff, like a twig into a great waterfall.

"*Noooo!*" Thoris shouted.

Thoris's cry echoed from the cliff, and he wondered if Casimir heard him. For a moment, the plummeting outline appeared to reshape itself, to transform somehow. Thoris blinked and wiped his eyes.

Casimir's body struck a ledge of stone. A loud crack resounded, like a tree branch snapping. The tiny form crumpled, rolled, and fell again, tumbling from view behind an outcrop of rock. Then came the profound thud of impact.

Thoris reeled back from the rail, his breath coming shallow and fast. He couldn't stand. His knees buckled, and he fell to the velvet grass, wet with evening dew. A single phrase echoed in his brain. *Casimir is dead. Casimir is dead. Casimir is dead.* . . . With shaking hands, he covered his face. His guts had clustered into knots.

*   *   *   *   *   *

Thoris stumbled frantically down the winding path from the crest of South Hill. As he ran, he clutched unsteadily at shrubs and trees and boulders, and his pudgy hands became laced with scratches. He reached the cliff's base and halted, breathless.

There lay Casimir, draped atop a great slab of stone.

"Oh gods oh gods oh gods," Thoris breathed repeatedly, wringing his hands.

Centuries ago, the slab must have slivered from the cliff above and tumbled to this spot. Its flat top and beveled edges formed a natural dolmen for the corpse.

Casimir is dead. Casimir is dead. Casimir is dead. . . .

Thoris stared, his eyes aching as tears streamed from them. He wanted to run toward the body, but his legs felt like lead. Neither could he turn from the still form.

There was blood. Plenty of blood. Casimir's coarse tunic had wicked the dark liquid from numerous wounds across his muscled frame. His head lay limp on the rock, his eyes closed as though in peaceful sleep and his mouth rimmed with blood.

"Oh, god!" Thoris staggered forward, weaving his way among other monoliths that had fallen from the cliff above. At last he reached the boulder where Casimir lay. He placed his hands on the cold stone, which numbed his shaking fingers. Thoris reached out to touch his still friend.

Curling white wisps rose from Casimir's lips.

Thoris cringed and withdrew his hand. His brow furrowed anxiously as he glanced at the towering cliff. "He can't be alive!" Then he spotted the gentle rise and fall of Casimir's chest. "You *are* alive," he murmured breathlessly, an incredulous smile coming to his lips. "You're *alive!*" Wiping his tears away, Thoris studied the terrible wounds. Casimir's chemise was stained crimson and felt cold in Thoris's hand as he lifted it to examine the cuts. There was blood everywhere. Thoris's smile faded, and his hands began to shake violently. He turned away from the body, cupping bloodied fingers to his mouth. "Help! Help! Please!"

The cries echoed from the rocky cliff. He waited, but there was no answer. Again he shouted. Still no answer. Drawing a deep breath, he bellowed, his adolescent voice cracking, "Help us!"

A light flared in a mansion atop the cliff. Thoris strained to see the source of the light. A shutter had opened in a large bank of windows. The light flickered nervously, and Thoris thought he spotted a head peering forth.

"Help me! You up there! Please help."

The light shone only a moment longer, then the room went dark. Thoris called again, his voice edged with anger. "Please, please! You up there! Help! Please!"

In the silence that followed, Thoris heard the tiny click of a shutter lock.

The shouts died in Thoris's throat. He turned back to the stone and bowed his head, resting his brow on Casimir's warm side. Not dead yet, but soon, Thoris thought. He tugged weakly at Casimir's body, knowing he couldn't lift the boy himself and carry him up the steep path to South Hill.

A howl split the night—a wolfish howl.

Thoris froze and listened. Again the canine cry erupted, clear and melancholy like Casimir's voice. Another howl answered the first. And another. The sound came from the cliff high above. The wolves had heard his cry for help. The wolves were coming.

"What should I do? What should I do?" Thoris murmured, his heart thundering in his chest. He clutched Casimir's blood-soaked chemise and pulled. The body wouldn't move. He yanked harder, but Casimir moaned in pain. Stepping back, Thoris wrung his hands. The howls gave way to snarls and barking. Leaning against the stone, Thoris counted the baying calls. "One, two, three, four . . . might as well be twenty of 'em," he whispered to himself, wiping the cold sweat from his brow. He gazed intently at his friend's lifeless face. "Casimir, what should I do?"

Claws clicked on the stone cliff above. Gasping, Thoris gazed toward the crest. There a set of eyes glowed, staring straight toward him, smoldering like embers. Thoris's heart sank as the glowing spots began to move toward the trail.

"They've seen me," Thoris realized, pacing fearfully. "If I run now, maybe they won't catch me."

A gravel-throated growl sounded from the pack, "Down the trail, you brutes!"

"Werewolves!" Thoris said, his breath catching short. "Wolves can't speak. . . . They must be werewolves! I'd better go—they'll find Casimir, not me. . . . What am I saying?" Turning, he clasped Casimir's hand in his own and drew the wooden sword Casimir had given him. "I'll not fail you. Better to die facing them than die running away."

Thoris stooped, lifted a large stone, and set it on the dolmen beside Casimir. Frantically he bent, lifting another, and another, until a thick ring of rocks surrounded the body. Then the pudgy boy scrambled up next to his friend. He took a rock in one hand and held his sword in the other. "I'm ready."

The beasts were rushing down the trail now, their savage cries echoing against the cliff face. Thoris braced his feet and drew a deep breath. His trembling had stopped. "I'll kill as many as I can before they take me down."

The glowing eyes on the trail began to flash oddly. Peering harder, Thoris realized they were not eyes but two chinks in a tightly trimmed lantern.

"Werewolves don't carry lanterns," he whispered, breathless. "Is this the constable, with a dog pack?" He lowered himself from the rock, listening to the baying cries. "Yes, they are dogs!" he said excitedly. "Over here! Help! Over here! My friend is injured."

A resonant voice called to him across the boulder-strewn slope. "We're almost there, boy!"

"I thought your dogs were wolves!" Thoris said, laughing nervously. "Hurry! There's blood everywhere."

In moments, a pack of barking hounds closed the distance to Thoris. Their jangling harnesses towed a gaunt man with a guttering lantern. He held a set of five dogs in each hand, as though reining in a team of horses. The man leaned backward as he walked, pulling heavily on the leather harness. Each step jarred his thin legs. As soon as he caught sight of Thoris, the old man reached a withered hand to the lantern and raised the wick.

In the waxing light of the lantern, Thoris could now see the man clearly. He was an elderly fellow, bald on top, with incisive eyes, an angular nose, a thin black mustache, and a straight mouth. His clothes, though obviously tailored of fine material, looked hastily donned, and the tail of his shirt hung out from his breeches. The man stepped toward Thoris and bent down. "Now, where are you injured?"

"I'm not injured," Thoris said in shock, pointing toward the dolmen. "It's my friend."

A look of surprise swept the man's otherwise solemn face. He lifted his lantern toward the form on the rock. The light showed Casimir's wounds clearly. An angry gash ran across his forehead, passing over one eye and splitting one cheek. His chemise was mostly torn away, and his arms and legs bore deep lacerations. Wherever the skin ran without a cut, it was black with bruises or red with blood.

The man climbed onto the boulder and leaned gravely over Casimir's limp form. He wrapped his withered hands around the bloody chemise and tore it from neck to hem. Beneath, a jagged cut ran deep across the muscle of Casimir's left breast. Pulling off his own jacket and shirt, the man began ripping the shirt cloth into bandages. "Better patch the worst of these now." Wrapping the first strip across Casimir's chest, the man said grimly, "Still, he's breathing . . . that's something." Thoris watched solemnly as the man continued tearing strips from the shirt. Binding two more wounds, the man began prodding Casimir's ribs. "Doesn't look like he broke anything," he noted, his voice sounding like a growl. "Who attacked him?"

"Nobody," Thoris blurted. "He fell."

"What?" the man asked, peering up at the looming cliff. "That's impossible. He'd be dead."

"Yeah," Thoris whispered. "That's what I thought."

A smile almost formed on the man's ancient lips as he continued binding the wounds. "I'm Valsarik, a manservant. I heard your cries." He stopped to consider. "We'll carry him to my quarters, clean him up, set some plasters, and send him to bed. . . . Of course, I'll want some explanation come dawn."

"Of course."

TWO

Valsarik's bony hands wrung out the use-worn rag. Crimson water streamed from the cloth and spattered into a metal basin below. The man's fingers trembled as he once again dragged the rag across Casimir's scarred skin. A ruddy trail of drops followed in the rag's wake. Valsarik sighed, gazing up at the oil lamps that hovered above the table. Rings of concern circled his eyes. He flung the blood-soaked rag to the floor and retrieved another.

Thoris slouched in a chair beside the table. He directed his attention away from Casimir's gory form, instead scanning the cabin. The place had splintery walls of wood and plaster, with shuttered windows and a sturdy door. Beside the door stood a smoke-blackened fireplace, which held a rack of coals. Iron spits and kettles lay on the hearth. Only a couple paces from the fireplace stood the table that held Casimir. Bloody Casimir. Thoris backed his chair from the table and gazed wearily at the bed of straw, covered with real linen ticking. He clucked: countless ills can be cured by sturdy shutters, a warm fire, and linen tick.

Shaking his head, Thoris turned toward Valsarik. The manservant returned his gaze, squeezing another rag. It, too, ran red. Without looking away from Thoris, he tossed the crumpled fabric onto the floor. "You've told me your name, Thoris. Who's your friend?"

"Casimir," Thoris replied with a measure of pride.

Valsarik grunted in response. Setting down the new rag, he turned away, wandered toward the fireplace, then halted on the hearth, apparently forgetting the reason he had moved. "Did you boys know you were trespassing?"

"Yes . . . I mean no." Thoris was flustered. "We got lost . . . thought we'd take a shortcut . . . didn't know there was a cliff."

"Come now . . . he *accidentally* fell from the cliff?" Valsarik asked with a smile. He pulled a blackened kettle from atop the coals and dumped more steamy water into the basin. "The rail marks the cliff."

"Well, ah . . . yes . . . ah . . . no . . ." Thoris slumped in the creaking chair, too tired to speak. A threatening silence loomed between them. Valsarik's ink-drop eyes glistened as he returned to the table and began washing the wounds again. Thoris bit his lip. I can't tell him the truth, Thoris thought, I don't *know* the truth. Reluctantly he continued. "It was really my fault, I guess. I dared him to walk the rail. He could never turn down a dare. He did fine until he slipped."

Valsarik regarded Thoris with a dubious smile. "Which is it, then—a shortcut or a dare?"

"We took a shortcut, then I dared him," Thoris blurted.

Valsarik's eyes narrowed. "How could a boy live through such a fall? No one but a god could have survived it. Is Casimir a god, Thoris?"

"I don't know!" Thoris said, his face flushing. "You tell me how he survived! It's your cliff!"

The bloody rag stopped on Casimir's skin. The glint in Valsarik's eyes dimmed. He growled, "Take a look at him, boy! You've not taken a hard look at him yet!"

Thoris turned away from the still form.

"Look at him!"

Reluctantly Thoris faced the body. Between the swinging shadows of the lamps, Casimir lay, his naked body bruised and gashed. He looked dead. His skin was mottled black, purple, and red. Bruises ringed his eyes and covered the swollen bridge of his nose. The flesh across his brow was puffy—as pale as fine paper. The only sign of life was his constant breath. As Thoris gazed on his friend, he wondered what drove him to leap from the cliff.

"This didn't happen just because of a dare," Valsarik continued. "Your friend cried out before he jumped, didn't he? I heard something."

Thoris's eyes flicked wide, but his pudgy lips stayed shut.

Valsarik stared blankly beyond Thoris. "The cry startled me out of a dead sleep. I rose and lit a taper, but the sound didn't come again. I thought it might have been a trick of the night air on my old ears. Even so, I was too unsettled to sleep. When I heard your shouts for help, I gathered the dogs." Valsarik separated a linen strip from the pile and began wrapping Casimir's arm.

"Sorry we woke you," Thoris blurted.

Valsarik's ravenlike eyes bored into Thoris. "See here, young man. I really want to help you and Casimir. This world is filled with darkness and danger. But unless you're honest with me, I can't protect you from it. Now, what happened tonight?"

"I told you . . . he fell off a cliff!" Thoris shouted.

"I say something drove him off," the manservant replied evenly. "Either that or he threw himself over!"

Thoris rose, trembling. "I don't know what made him do it!" He flung his hand toward the corpselike body. "Ask him, but leave me alone!" Thoris stalked off, his mind whirling. He dropped wearily beside the blazing hearth and buried his face in his hands. Even there he could feel the manservant's razor-sharp gaze on his back.

"Then we'll see what the morning brings."

Thoris didn't respond. Instead, he peered sullenly into the fire. Casimir always did as he pleased, regardless of what anyone else thought. Thoris's mind returned to another cliff, five years earlier. That time, he'd been able to stop Casimir.

* * * * *

"Why go off by yourself? What's the point?" asked a
ten-year-old Thoris. He shielded his eyes from the slanting light of the sunset and wearily scanned the darken-
ing wood. "We've combed the woods all day and not
seen a single rabbit."

Casimir sighed, stepping away from a pine he'd been
leaning against. "No offense, chum, but you're just too
loud for rabbit hunting."

Irritation flashed in Thoris's eyes. "You're not gonna
find anything alone. There's not a rabbit in these
woods."

"Don't worry," Casimir said, clapping Thoris on the
back. "I'll be back before the sun sets—and with *two*
rabbits."

"But—but," Thoris stammered, "what about the
wolves?"

"Look, if you're scared of the wolves, go sit on the
cliff above the amphitheater," Casimir said, pointing to a
break in the trees behind Thoris. "There's always a show
at sunset. They'll have lanterns and guards . . . no
wolves would dare go there."

Thoris turned, looking doubtfully through the trees in
the direction Casimir had pointed. He heard footsteps
behind him and glanced back to see Casimir striding
away. Muttering, Thoris began to follow him, but Casimir
waved him off.

"Just go sit down. I'll meet you there."

Reluctantly Thoris pivoted and trudged toward the
amphitheater. It lay beyond the trees, carved into a
granite cliff that overlooked the northeastern edge of
Harmonia. The shell of the amphitheater was cut from
the face of the cliff itself, and the tiers of descending
seats were hewn from the bedrock some fifty feet
below.

Thoris approached slowly from the top of the cliff. He
could already see the lantern light glowing warmly
beyond the edge. As he neared, the murmur of the

crowd assembled in the amphitheater rose in his ears. Emerging from the trees, Thoris walked out on the lichen-encrusted stone at the top of the cliff. Down below, he could see the semicircular tiers, crowded with people. The sight made him dizzy. Cautiously, nervously, he dropped to hands and knees and approached the cliff's edge. Reaching it, he carefully lay down on his stomach and peered over.

The yawning drop almost made him sick. On the stage fifty feet below, a man stood, waving his hands to quiet the crowd. He looked minuscule atop the wide slab of gray granite.

Recognizing the man, Thoris moaned. He was Zhone Clieous, meistersinger of Harmonia and murderer of Casimir's mother.

"Casimir isn't gonna like this," Thoris said, shaking his head.

"Not gonna like what?" came Casimir's voice behind him.

Thoris started, scrambling back from the edge of the cliff. His head was spinning, and he gasped for air as he sat up. A feeble smile crossed his features. "Nothing." Only then did he notice the two dead rabbits in Casimir's hands.

"What do you mean, nothing?" asked the older boy, dropping the rabbits to the ground.

"You found some rabbits!" Thoris exclaimed, trying to change the subject. "You hunted for a few minutes and got *two?*" Ignoring his friend, Casimir strode to the cliff's edge and peered down. Thoris nervously motioned him back. "Careful. Get back!" The older boy's eyes narrowed and his face grew red. "Zhone Clieous," he said, punching his fist into his hand. "I hate him, Thoris. I really hate him."

"I know . . . I know," Thoris soothed, cold sweat dotting his brow. "Come away from there before you fall."

"I don't care," Casimir said, clenching his teeth. "Maybe I'll fall on him."

Thoris's eyes went wide. "Come on, Casimir, move

back." When the older boy didn't respond, Thoris tried a different tack. "If you promise to move back, I'll—I'll spit on him."

An incredulous smile spread across Casimir's face. "Are you serious?"

"Sure," Thoris said, gulping and turning red in embarrassment.

"I bet you wouldn't."

"Get back," the younger boy replied, his voice wavering. As Casimir withdrew from the cliff's edge, Thoris slowly knelt down and eased himself forward onto his stomach.

"We're gonna have to run like mad if it hits him," Casimir said excitedly. Then he added, "You *know* that, right?" Thoris only nodded, clearing his throat to dredge up some phlegm. Smiling fiendishly, Casimir lay down beside his friend and peered over the cliff's edge. Thoris wet his finger on his lips and held out his hand to gauge the breeze. It was blowing softly across the stage. Clieous was pacing into range. Then slowly, puckering his lips, Thoris let the spittle drop.

The bubbly glob of liquid fell, tumbling gently, peacefully in the hushed air of the amphitheater. Casimir caught his breath. He could hear his heart pounding.

The spittle struck the top of Clieous's head and spattered across his thinning hair.

Casimir blurted out a laugh that echoed through the auditorium. The meistersinger, the guards, and the audience stared up toward the top of the cliff. The boys pulled their heads back, hoping to escape notice. They were too late.

"Get those boys!" shouted the meistersinger.

"Let's get out of here!" Casimir said with a nervous laugh as he got up from the stone.

Rising, Thoris smiled triumphantly. "You owe me, Casimir."

The older boy nodded, shot his friend a grin, turned, and dashed into the deep woods. Thoris followed. The angry shouts of guards rose into the air behind them. In moments, the boys had disappeared into the woods, leaving only the dead rabbits behind.

* * * * *

Valsarik awoke before dawn and passed silently by the sleeping forms of Thoris and Casimir. He left his cabin to draw the shutters back from his master's windows, prepare and serve him breakfast, and quell the persistent queries about "those alarms last night." The sun was approaching noon before Valsarik completed his morning duties. He returned to his hovel to find the boys still asleep. After quietly unlatching the shutters, he went back outside to open them.

The sudden flash of sunlight through the window awoke Thoris instantly. He rose to his elbows, disoriented. His bones ached from sleeping on the rough plank floor. Where was he? He lay still for a moment, assimilating the smell of dormant coals and the sight of the splintery walls. Slowly he remembered the room . . . the fire . . . the old man . . . the cliff. . . . *Casimir!*

Thoris stood up, letting the thick blankets slough from his back and crumple to the floor. He surveyed the room. Valsarik was nowhere to be seen. A hammering sounded at one of the windows, and more sunlight whirled into the room. Thoris glimpsed the manservant through the window.

Peering about, Thoris spotted Casimir, lying asleep on the room's only bed. Shuffling to his friend's side, he sat down on the crackling mattress of straw.

Casimir opened his swollen eyes. Thoris winced. The wounds looked particularly brutal in the morning sunlight. He found himself momentarily wishing that Casimir hadn't survived the fall.

"You're awake," he blurted.

Casimir's brow furrowed and his swollen lips parted, but no sound emerged. His keen eyes clouded over for a moment, narrowing as they studied the unfamiliar rafters. He inhaled the ash-scented air, one hand clutching the prickly mattress beneath him. At last his eyes settled on his friend, and through puffy lips, he whispered, "What's . . . what's happened to me?"

"Don't talk," Thoris urged, setting a finger to his mouth. "We haven't much time."

"Where are we?"

"Shhhhh," Thoris insisted. His face looked grave. "Casimir, I followed you last night. Do you remember?"

"You followed me?" Casimir groaned, a spasm of fear crossing his features. He tried to pry his body up from the bed, but the wounds and bandages restrained him. After a moment of thrashing, he stilled, lifting a lacerated arm up before his face. "What's happened to me?"

Thoris wagged his head slowly. "You don't remember what happened last night?"

Casimir clamped his eyes tightly shut and cried miserably, "I don't remember a thing!"

"The cliff . . . South Hill cliff . . . don't you remember?" Thoris prodded.

Beneath the bandages and angry gashes, Casimir's face went white. "I, uh, I . . . jumped, didn't I?"

"Yeah . . . you jumped," Thoris said, a pained smile appearing for a moment on his face. "Why did you do it, Casimir? What's making you so unhappy? Is it Zhone Clieous?"

The door to the hovel rattled open, and Valsarik stepped inside. Thoris and Casimir threw startled glances toward the manservant. Valsarik closed the door, smiled civilly, and plodded toward them. "Good morning."

"Good morning," Thoris replied, a chill prickling his skin. Casimir turned a questioning stare toward Thoris.

"I am glad to see that your friend has risen . . . almost," the manservant observed, his voice nearly a growl.

"He's still too weak to talk much," Thoris declared as the man moved to the bedside and towered above Casimir. Valsarik's ravenlike eyes drew to thin slits twice before he spoke again.

"I should think so, after his evening. But maybe breakfast will revive him and loosen his tongue." With that, Valsarik turned slowly on one heel and plodded toward the pantry. "Eggs and toast, with fried mushrooms and chives?"

"Yes, please," Thoris said, eager to have the man move away.

"Very well," Valsarik replied, nodding and entering the pantry. Thoris perched nervously on the bed as Valsarik rummaged through the shelves. A moment later, he reappeared with a tray of food and an armload of wood. Kneeling at the hearth, the manservant stoked the fire and pumped the bellows. He sliced a cutting of fat into an iron pan. The fat began to pop and crackle, and the aroma of smoke tickled Thoris's nose. His stomach rumbled, and his mouth began to water.

Swallowing hard, Thoris whispered to Casimir. "He's a friend. He saved us. I didn't tell him you jumped—just that you fell, but he didn't believe me." Thoris eyed Valsarik, who was slicing a small loaf of bread. "Why did you jump, Cas?"

Casimir looked away, drawing a painful breath. "I . . . I don't know, Thoris. There's just—" he shook his head— "I don't know."

"It *is* Clieous, isn't it?" Thoris asked.

"Yes . . . no," Casimir replied. He swallowed hard, turning to face the pudgy boy. "Yes. It is Clieous, in a way. I've just run out of hope, Thoris, that's all."

Thoris leaned forward. "Don't give up, Casimir. You'll have your revenge. Clieous will pay for killing your mother."

"You don't understand." Casimir shook his head and stared into Thoris's eyes. "What can I do, Thoris? I've tried to fight it, but I'm too weak. I'm so ashamed."

"I'll help you, Casimir." Thoris gently squeezed his friend's hand. "We'll bring Clieous down."

"It's not Clieous." The lines of pain across Casimir's face softened. "No, you're right. It *is* Clieous. He's at the root of it all."

Thoris peered toward Valsarik. "He'll ask you about last night. I'll let you do the talking."

Casimir's brow dimpled. "I don't want to tell him."

"Then lie," Thoris replied. Casimir drew a long, labored breath, and his body relaxed. He sniffed the air, as though only now scenting the salty tang of fried mushrooms and chives.

Valsarik spooned some of the meal onto a wide wooden platter and plunked a couple of utensils onto it. He carried the platter to Casimir's bed, helped him to sit up gingerly against the headboard, and set the meal on his lap. Then Valsarik assembled and delivered a similar tray to Thoris.

"Your friend, Thoris, has told me your name, Casimir, and that you came from the Red Porch poorhouse. I doubt, though, that Thoris has told you my name, and so I will. Valsarik Alanov, at your service." Bowing, he stepped away from the bed for a moment and dragged a chair across the floor. Positioning it before the bed, he sat down. "I've already eaten my breakfast," he announced to no one in particular.

Thoris scooped a mass of the fluffy scrambled eggs into one hand. They were hot. He dropped the eggs again to the platter. Valsarik tapped the utensils lying next to Thoris's plate. The orphan grinned sheepishly, picked up a fork, and began to eat hungrily. Casimir did likewise.

"Doesn't the Red Porch provide flatware?" Valsarik asked.

"They give us bowls," Thoris replied simply. His mouth hung open and he puffed, trying to cool the steamy eggs on his tongue.

Casimir smiled, the pale skin clinging raggedly to his cheek and brow, and his eyes half-closed beneath blackened lids.

The sight of Casimir drew some of the savor from Thoris's eggs, but orphanage instincts drove him to clean his plate all the same. Finishing, Thoris stood up. "Maybe Casimir should go back to sleep, after all. He—"

Valsarik's hand clenched Thoris's arm. "He needs to eat. Otherwise he'll not recover." Valsarik studied Casimir's battered form. "Casimir, what drove you over the cliff last night?"

Casimir looked up, his mouth filled with mushrooms. He smiled feebly and said, "It's . . . kind of personal."

"I only want to help," the manservant said. "You can trust me. Why did you jump over the cliff last night?"

Casimir glanced briefly at Thoris and raised his eyebrows. "I was chasing a rabbit."

The manservant's visage darkened. "At midnight?"

"When else?" the orphan responded lightly. "For orphans, midnight's the best time to chase rabbits . . . the best time for half a hundred things."

Valsarik leaned back in the creaking chair, apparently sizing up the injured young man before him. "So you chased this rabbit over the railing of the cliff?"

"No," Casimir replied simply.

"Then how did you fall?" Valsarik pressed.

"The rabbit was wounded. That's why I was chasing it," Casimir said, affecting his most guileless tone. "But the more I chased, the more it ran. That's the way with rabbits. It ran to the rail. I came near and it leapt over."

"And you decided to follow?" Valsarik asked dubiously.

"No. I thought that was the end of the rabbit. But then I heard its sad little voice calling to me from beyond the rail."

Valsarik sat up, his eyes gleaming. "This was a talking rabbit?"

"Yes, in a way!" said the battered youth, his eyes wide and unblinking despite the swollen lids. He wormed himself a bit higher in the bed, the movement sending pinches of pain through his features. Then he leaned forward conspiratorially. "Haven't you ever gone on a wolf hunt?"

Impatient furrows lined Valsarik's brow. "My master is too old for such enterprises. What about the rabbit?"

Casimir smiled. "On wolf hunts, the hunters bring

along at least a dozen rabbits to serve as bait. At sunset, they wrap a wire tight around a rabbit's neck—not so tight as to kill him, but tight enough to bite into him if he struggles in the least. Then they stake him to the ground. And the choking rabbit screams. His little screams pierce the forest. The hunters stuff their ears with wool because the screams cut like cold steel.

"The wolves don't come right away. The men might torture seven or eight rabbits before they see the glowing eyes of the beasts through the trees. But eventually the wolves come. The screams of rabbits are music to the ears of wolves."

Valsarik swallowed hard, the color slowly draining from his face.

"But I heard of one batch of hunters that got their comeuppance. They attracted a werewolf. The creature ripped them apart."

"Enough of this!" Valsarik fumed, tossing his hands in the air. "I heard no rabbit screams last night. But I did hear you cry out."

"Oh, you would cry, too," Casimir said with thick naivete, "had you seen that helpless little rabbit."

"So, because you had no rope, you thought to leap down to the rabbit yourself?" the manservant blustered irritably.

"You have quite an imagination," Casimir replied with a laugh. "No. The rabbit was calling from a ledge about five feet down. I tried to reach him, but the rail was slick, and I fell."

"Thoris, here, said you were taking a shortcut. He said he dared you to walk the rail, and you fell," Valsarik countered, trying to regain control of the conversation.

Casimir shot his friend a dubious glance. "A shortcut? Ha! A shortcut to where? This place isn't on the way to anything!" He shook his head and said, "I'm embarrassed to say this, but Thoris doesn't know what he is talking about. You see, he was following me. He always follows me."

"If he was following you, then he must have seen what happened."

"All he saw was me running to a cliff, climbing over a rail, and falling," Casimir explained, as though detailing the obvious. "Do you really think a boy as fat as him could hope to keep up with me, let alone a rabbit?" After a brief tantrum of laughter, Casimir flopped back against the mattress.

Valsarik shook his head grimly. "We both know that this isn't about a rabbit, but if you won't tell me the truth, I've done all I can do. There are evil forces at work in this land. I suspect you boys have run afoul of them, but I can't help you if you won't confide in me."

"I told you the truth," Casimir said with a pained shrug.

Valsarik scowled and leaned toward Casimir. "Let me check your wounds."

The manservant carefully positioned his fingers on a bandage around Casimir's calf. He pulled back the bandage and gasped. Thoris peered over his shoulder. The night before, the laceration had penetrated nearly to the bone, but this morning it appeared to be barely more than a scratch.

Valsarik gazed coldly at the wound, then turned a piercing eye on Casimir. "Were you visited last night by healing angels?"

Casimir laughed, gesturing toward his bloody bandages. "Do I look it?"

Thoris scratched his head. "Perhaps last night the blood and the lanterns made it look worse than it was."

Valsarik released the bandage. "I've helped you all I can, unless you want to tell me the truth. . . ." Casimir's eyes fixed on the old man and he shook his head. Valsarik continued, "If, in the future, you decide you need my aid, you know where to find me. Until then, I'll leave you to return to the poorhouse. Gather up your things and dress yourselves."

Thoris objected. "Cas is too weak to walk to the Red Porch."

Valsarik turned, a toothy, unaccustomed smile spreading across his lips. "That's why we'll ride."

*   *   *   *   *

Frau Von Matren sat on a kitchen table amongst piles of dirty bowls. She watched with baleful pleasure as the round man called Cook scurried between three kettles of soup boiling on the broad hearth of the poorhouse kitchen. The steam from the kettles didn't smell of stewing meat or cabbage but merely of boiling water, for the soup was little more than that. As it was, the plump woman herself had snatched up one of the three carrots Cook had planned to divide between the pots. She bit into the root and chewed, the soiled coif on her head moving with each crunch.

"Dear Frau Matren," the round man asked, "would you be so kind as to stir the pot nearest you?"

The woman released a singular, prolonged laugh and simultaneously kicked her pudgy legs to each side. As her tattered skirt drifted back down, she croaked, "When I became a widow, I thought I'd get some rest, but instead I got a hundred poor folk instead. That's my curse. Yours is to feed 'em!" Again came the cruel laugh. "You must've made some gypsy real angry to get a curse like that!"

Cook puffed, his ruddy face showing no sign that he had even heard the lady. He muttered imprecations as he shuffled about the tiny kitchen, a room that cowered in the ominous shadow of a single, ponderous fireplace. He leaned into the hearth, adjusting the bowed spit that held the kettles over the flame.

"A clever cook would feed these useless creatures something other than soup day in and day out."

Cook turned his head as he stirred, the steam seeming to rise from his ears. "What do you want from me? To hunt the meat myself and grow my own greens?"

Frau Von Matren prepared another retort, but it died on her lips as a large, black conveyance came to a halt

outside the steamy window. The woman wriggled off the
table and drifted over to the pane, wiping the steam
from the glass. The capricious curl of her lip deepened
into a malevolent grimace. There, debarking from an
elegant two-horse hansom, were two of her ratty whelps,
the capricious Casimir and his brainless lackey, Thoris.
The woman's grimace faded as a tall, well-dressed man
of obvious breeding alighted from the hansom, sniffing
the air of the slum quarter with undisguised disdain.

Frau Von Matren raced to the door and flung it open.
The boys and their regal escort started slightly at her
abrupt appearance. She rustled toward the tall man,
curtsied awkwardly, and extended a craggy hand. "Do
you need hired hands, or perhaps slaves for your estate,
Master . . . ?"

The regal-looking man appeared not to notice the
outstretched hand or the clumsy inquiry. "No, my lady.
I'm returning these young men to you."

"Returning them?" Frau Von Matren smiled coquet-
tishly, puffs of breath wheezing through her wide-spaced
teeth. "Wouldn't you prefer to buy them?"

"No, madam," the man replied firmly. "These young
ones were injured this past night on my master's land-
holdings, and—"

"*Trespassing!*" the woman bellowed, fixing a scalding
glare on the boys.

"—and I must now return them to their proper home."

"*Trespassing*," she reiterated. "Don't worry, sir. I'll
personally oversee their beating. The jailer is a friend
of—"

"No beatings," the man stated with cold certainty. He
placed a narrow hand on Casimir and gestured at his
bandages. "This one has suffered too much abuse
already. You'll not let the jailer or anyone else touch
him, or you'll answer to me."

The woman smiled faintly, wondering whether to
press the point or forgo a good beating. "I hadn't realized he was injured. I would never lay a hand on a
wounded lad."

"Good," the man replied with some satisfaction. "If you have no other questions, then, I shall be off."

Frau Von Matren curtsied low, her bosom floating high beneath her apron. "If ever I can serve you again, Master . . . ?"

"Good day, my lady," replied the man, climbing into the hansom and flipping the reins.

*   *   *   *   *

Casimir lay on his cot, the bandages looping loosely around his limbs. He peered through the ramshackle window, watching the uneasy night descend on Harmonia. He felt exhausted.

Thoris lay on the cot beside him, studying Casimir's melancholy features. "You've got to pull yourself out of this, Casimir."

Casimir drew the sheet up to his red-streaked eyes. "You were talking about revenge this morning?"

"Yeah," replied Thoris, a glimmer of hope crossing his face. "Yeah . . . and I think I've got it. You could challenge Clieous in the meistersinger contest this Midsummers."

Casimir laughed. "Clieous is the best singer in Harmonia!"

Thoris was deadly serious as he reached out and grabbed his friend's arm. "You know the *Mora*, Casimir, and you have the most beautiful and haunting voice in all Harmonia. You can beat him."

"I can't enter the contest," Casimir declared in irritation. "I'm only an orphan. Besides, Clieous himself registers the contestants."

"Clieous won't even know who you are. You can wear a mask and costume. A lot of the participants do."

"Where will I get a mask and costume?"

"You tell me," Thoris said, with a cocky grin. "You could figure a hundred ways to pinch an outfit."

"You've gone mad," Casimir announced with a laugh.

Thoris's grip tightened on Casimir's arm. "No, I

haven't. Your hatred of Clieous nearly drove you to suicide last night. You've got to get your revenge, Casimir. It's your only hope."

Casimir sighed deeply, and his gaze became serious. "I'll need to practice" was all he said.

THREE

"How do you intend to get inside, Casimir?" Thoris asked, eyeing the ominous walls of the meistersinger's mansion. The structure was a fortification, a citadel at the heart of Harmonia. It rose from a rocky prominence in the center of town and loomed over the buildings around it. Tall walls of limestone hemmed in the estate in a huge octagon, hiding the mansion within. Only the tiled rooftop showed against the nighttime sky. The walls were fronted by a yawning archway and a cobblestone road. Beside the road ran a hedge, which currently concealed the scheming boys.

"Face it, Casimir. Those walls are easily twelve feet high."

Casimir's eyebrows lifted playfully. "I don't care whether they're twelve feet or twelve leagues high. I don't intend to climb them." He dropped one knee to the ground and peered excitedly through the hedge.

Setting a hand on the wooden sword tucked in his belt, Thoris asked, "Then how'll you get in?"

"Shhhh!"

"The masquerade is only open to bards," Thoris continued, "and we don't look much like bards."

"You worry too much," Casimir countered with a sneer. "This was *your* idea."

"I said you needed a decent costume for the contest, but I didn't tell you to steal it from someone at the masquerade!"

Casimir filled his lungs with the chill night air. "You've put me through a month of recitals to prepare for this masquerade. At least let me have fun tonight."

Thoris shook his head and muttered grimly, "Don't you—"

"Quiet! Here comes another carriage!" Casimir whispered.

The cobblestone road in front of the hedge echoed with the distant clomp of hooves. The sound grew louder and deeper until the boys couldn't even hear each other whisper. Suddenly a brace of four black horses rounded the corner. Behind the steeds, a covered carriage rumbled into view.

Across the coach's fancifully carved body danced glossy paint of red and gold and black. Below the side panels, a single fender ran from the front wheels to the back. The fender curled elegantly at both ends and dropped in the center to form an ivory-edged running board. From the tips of the fenders hung round lanterns of silver, which bobbed hypnotically. Atop the carriage sat a coachman, himself as richly adorned as any man Thoris had seen: a black, brocaded coat, a red cummerbund, black velvet breeches, woolen stockings, and a plumed hat. On the opposite side of the carriage, a footman in identical garb rode the rail.

"You see the lovely, unoccupied running board on this side of the coach?" Casimir asked, nodding toward the fender.

"Yes," Thoris gulped. "You don't mean—"

"Just such a running board will escort us into the mansion."

"What?" Thoris blurted, the pitch of his voice rising like a kettle beginning to boil. "A running board that's a finger's length from the spokes and a shin's length from the street?"

"Yes," Casimir replied smugly.

Thoris puffed in impotent rage as the carriage retreated up the road and into the arched gate of the meistersinger's mansion. "You may well be nimble enough to leap onto the running board of a moving carriage, but I'm not. You want me to run out there, clamber onto a running board, totter off, and be split in half by the rear wheel?"

"And that's not all!" Casimir pointed out with a grin. "If you don't fall off going in, you'll need to fall off once we're inside, then hide in the nearest clump of shrubs in the garden."

Thoris growled, "I refuse to go."

"Do as you wish," Casimir replied, turning his attention back toward the road.

Thoris wobbled unhappily on his aching legs. That does it, he thought. I'm not going along with this harebrained scheme, and that's final.

Before Thoris could voice his resolve to Casimir, a great, clattering carriage rumbled around the corner. A team of midnight horses led the coach, their legs churning as though they swam down the lane. The shoes of the steeds clipped harshly on the cobbles, striking sparks in the evening air. A profuse harness of leather and chain bound these brutes to the bulky coach. The black chassis listed in the curve, blood-red curtains of velvet hanging out the windows. From inside the coach emerged a haunting melody, a singer's voice, just audible over the clatter of hooves.

Thoris flung out his hand to stop Casimir, but he was too late.

Casimir was already scurrying beside the carriage, crouching to avoid the eyes within. He reached out his hand, only inches from the whirling black spokes. His fingers latched onto the ebony running board, but the horses were too fast. He held on but couldn't gain enough ground to ease his ambling weight onto the board. The road angled up, rushing suddenly toward the arched gate of Meistersinger Clieous's citadel. Above the gate hung the spearheads of a hovering portcullis.

Now or never, Casimir thought.

With an awkward leap, Casimir landed askew on the board. He struggled to pull his feet away from the whirling spokes—one foot to safety, and now the next. He sighed deeply and glanced up toward the coach's window. His landing had jolted the carriage considerably; he hoped the occupant wouldn't think to look for stowaways.

Casimir froze.

There, in a corner of darkness beside a curtain, an eye seemed to peer out at him—not a fearful eye, not an angry eye, but an eye of malevolent interest. The longer Casimir stared at it, the more certain he became that someone was staring back.

Suddenly the carriage was swallowed in clattering darkness. They had passed beneath the portcullis, into the gateway tunnel. They hadn't even slowed for the gate guard as the other carriages had. Either the driver is a fool or this guest of Meistersinger Clieous must be a personage of some honor, Casimir thought with dread. If the guest saw me, surely he'll tell Clieous and I'll be clapped in irons.

Suddenly the darkness was gone. Casimir almost forgot to leap from the carriage as it emerged from the tunnel into a leafy garden. Luckily an overgrown holly bough reminded him, its branches scratching heavily across his legs. He rolled from the running board, eluding the track of the rear wheel by inches. As the coach rumbled on, he scrambled between the holly bush and the vine-strewn wall. There, in the darkness of his prickly hideout, he caught his breath, rubbing the stinging scratches on his legs. He raised his head to survey the scene.

The meistersinger's garden surpassed all words. Its diamond-shaped collection of lawns, paths, founts, and flower beds filled one quadrant of the octagonal citadel. Along two sides of the garden stood the fortress's high outer walls. Though these limestone bulwarks looked imposing from the outside, within the garden, they were decked in strands of ivy. Lanterns snaked in merry chains across the tops of the walls. The lantern light masked the occasional glint of mail-clad guards on the parapets above. On the opposite sides of the garden stood inner walls of red brick—the mansion proper. The windows and doors of the mansion were grand, serviced by prodigious ba!conies. Trellises bore trailing vines up to these balconies, or cast ivy in leafy canopies over them.

As for the garden itself, the grass was verdantly green and trimmed with amazing precision. Every lawn was ringed by lush beds of exotic flowers and shrubs. Around these beds ran numerous stone paths, leading variously to doorways or benches or balconies. All the paths eventually wandered to a great fountain, set like a jewel in the garden's center.

This wonderland of light and greenery was peopled by all manner of exotic folk. Many wore simple black masks across their eyes, their capes and dresses otherwise unadorned. Others wore full-face masks with fanciful images painted on them. One man's mask held leering eyes and a twisted beak, and his cape shimmered with bird feathers. Another wore a fish-head mask, his cape rimmed with glistening scale mail. A third was draped all in black and wore an ebony death mask. Even the musicians wore masks as they piped their flutes, pattered their drums, and plucked their lyres.

All of this Casimir took in within moments—the lantern light, the fragrant food and wine, the music and laughter and song. But the setting's beauty only hardened his hatred toward the meistersinger. While Casimir had spent years decked in lice-ridden clothes, his nemesis had lounged in this garden, had made conversation with elegant folk, had feasted on the bounty of the land. Casimir shook his head grimly. This garden, this mansion, will be mine someday. I will be revenged.

The black carriage that Casimir had ridden on rolled to a stop some twenty yards from where he crouched. Casimir heard the sound of voices beside the carriage, and he strained to listen to them over the babble of the masquerade.

"How kind you were to come, good sir, and all the way from Skald!" came the refined voice of a richly garbed attendant.

The carriage's leaf springs flexed gently as a sable-robed figure alighted. Removing his gloves, the man spoke in a darkly musical tone. "Now that your guards have learned to recognize my carriage, trips to your little borough take less toll on me."

Apparently uncertain of whether the word *toll* was meant as a pun, the other man laughed nervously and added with feigned enthusiasm, "I'll not soon forget the time those green-eared guards stopped your coach and ordered it searched." He broke off into chortles, but his levity was not shared by his guest. The titters died away like a tin cup reaching the bottom of a staircase. "Now guardsman training begins with the lesson,'No toll for Master Lukas!' "

The man called Lukas still refused to laugh. He answered with dry sarcasm, "A good bit of training, that. Easier on the families that way."

A knot formed in Casimir's stomach as he realized who the two men were. "Master Lukas" was clearly Harkon Lukas, the fabled bard of Kartakass. He was reputed to be the land's greatest musician, but he had never won a meistersinger contest. Casimir even vaguely remembered the bard being a friend of his mother's. Yes, Casimir looked forward to meeting Harkon Lukas, looked forward to singing before him.

But the bard's companion was no mere attendant. He was, in fact, Zhone Clieous himself, meistersinger of Harmonia and the man Casimir had sworn to take vengeance on. The orphan boy peered hard toward his nemesis, fascinated by the man's brutal face. He had a crinkled brow, oversize eyes, a muzzlelike nose, and a straight gash where his mouth should have been. Casimir had been only six when he had last seen this man up close. The decade had been kind to Clieous, aging him little. Still, Casimir noted the lines of depravity that ringed his eyes.

The man's a monster, Casimir thought darkly. He killed my mother and left me with nothing, but there he stands, haughty and self-important. I'll have my revenge. . . . It begins tonight.

" . . . I little suspect," Meistersinger Clieous was saying, "that you will join our contest this year, though you are certainly welcome if you wish."

Lukas waved a dismissal. "I hunger for your power no more than for your blood, Clieous."

Despite the veiled threat, Clieous's tightly strung body appeared to ease with Lukas's reply. "You're perfectly welcome, either way."

"Of course," Harkon Lukas said with an icy laugh.

Clieous set a hand on Lukas's back and said, "Let your horseman take the carriage to the stables. Come, follow me to the richest food, the stoutest *meekulbrau*, and the fairest maids."

"I approve of your tastes, Clieous, though you have the order quite backward," Lukas said as he strolled away beside him.

Casimir watched them go, then shook the phantoms of memory from his mind. He'd come here for a costume, not for revenge. Not yet. Slicing Clieous's head from his shoulders would be satisfying, yes, but the guards would only summarily execute him afterward. Better stick to the plan, he thought.

He glanced about the shadowy garden and checked the moon in the sky. Should I wait for Thoris or not? he wondered. I don't want him to blunder in after my plan is set in motion, nor can I wait for someone who said he wouldn't come. "Thoris be damned," he whispered. "He's probably crawling into his cot just about now."

The next step was to acquire a costume. He needed to find a drunkard—someone deep enough into his cups that he'd hardly notice being gagged and stripped, but not so deep that he'd have soiled his costume already. Casimir scanned the garden for likely candidates. A knot of guests clustered about the fountain, their laughter lubricated with wine—but not nearly enough wine. I need a lone celebrant, Casimir thought, someone whose disappearance will go unnoticed. A nodding youth sat in the last row of chairs before the musicians. Casimir began crawling toward him but spotted an alert flautist and held back.

Then his eyes settled on a mark—a tall, meatless man wearing a leering mask. The man hovered near the *meekulbrau* barrel. His reckless stance and skewed limbs assured Casimir that he was indeed drunk. Casimir smiled and began to crawl toward him between flowering shrubs and the outer wall. The drunkard didn't move from the barrel. He pushed the mask up onto his forehead and downed the red liquid in his stein. Sliding the mask back into place, he pitched precariously toward the barrel and filled his tankard again. Casimir's mouth watered, but not from thirst. On hands and knees, he closed on the man.

The garden fell quickly away before Casimir. He soon found himself crouched behind a heady rosebush, in front of which stood the gaunt man. Casimir's heart pounded, and a familiar ache spread wonderfully through his muscles.

Should I clamp my hand over the man's mouth and nose and drag him behind the bush? he thought. Or should I snap his neck first?

No, Casimir told himself, I mustn't lose control. I don't need to kill him to take his costume. I'll save that sort of revenge for Zhone Clieous . . . after the contest.

Even through the roses, Casimir could smell his prey—not the salty, natural tang of a commoner, but the sweet, liquor-tainted scent of a nobleman. His mouth was watering again. The man's odor brought a savory taste to his tongue. His heart felt suddenly hot in his rib cage. The blood welled in his eyes, coloring everything red. His jaw was shaking, and he drew a breath through ragged teeth. His hand raised and snaked through the rosebush, reaching toward the man's head. The muscles across his lower arm began to spasm. He could almost feel the soft strands of the man's hair in his fingers. He need only clutch quickly and wrench the head to one side. Then would come the wonderful snap and . . .

No! he thought, biting back the desire with jagged teeth. No! I'm not a monster! He withdrew his hand through the rosebush, sinking his nails deep in his palms. The gouging pain tempered the blaze that had sprung up in his chest. He raised his hand to cradle a rosebud and forced his eyes to study the complex beauty of the flower. Then he buried his nose in the petals and drew the sweet fragrance into his lungs.

Slowly Casimir's heart cooled; his breathing calmed. He released his clenched hand. His fingernails were rimmed with blood, and his palms were scarred with four crescent-shaped wounds.

That was too close. The hunger within him was strong. Too strong. But he would not give in to it. He would perform this task quickly and impassively, as though he were being paid—not as though he enjoyed it. He needn't kill the man to take his costume.

Casimir stood on tiptoe behind the roses and quickly surveyed the garden. No one seemed to be watching. Quickly Casimir slipped his bleeding hand between the man's mask and his mouth and dragged him back behind the bush. Pushing him to the ground, Casimir swung his legs over the man's narrow chest. He stripped back the mask. Beneath it, frantic eyes stared upward. Casimir's fist fell, solidly striking the man's jaw. The nobleman's eyes snapped shut. Twelve years in the poorhouse had taught Casimir how to end a fight quickly, but never before had he been assisted by *meek-ulbrau*.

The costume fit Casimir perfectly. Its ruffled shirt of silk was topped by a red doublet, a fringed baldric, and a long cape. White cannons covered Casimir's muscled legs, and long-toed shoes clung to his feet. Wearing the costume, Casimir felt like a new man, divorced from the squalor of the poorhouse.

Lastly Casimir picked up the mask. It was exquisite. Two long feathers topped it, one sky-blue and the other blood-red. The mask itself was carefully carved of thick wood and painted a shiny white. The face it depicted leered maniacally, a grimace lined with suffering. Casimir's fingers followed the fine contours of its manic smile. With slow reverence, he lifted the mask to his face and slipped the band over his head. Despite its weight and inflexibility, it felt comfortable.

A dry laugh rose to his lips as he stepped from behind the roses. He had half-expected to be met by shouts of accusation and anger, but no one appeared to take notice of him. He took a stiff step forward, and his foot settled onto something round. Bending over in an exaggerated attempt to see through the thick mask, he saw an empty stein lying beneath his foot. The nobleman must have dropped it. Stooping, Casimir recovered the skin, then shuffled to the keg of *meekulbrau* and filled it. The red liquor, thin though it was, felt heavy in the stein. Seeing no one near, Casimir tipped the mask back on his forehead and eagerly drained the glass. The liquid stung angrily in his throat, but he refused to choke on it. Tears welled in his eyes.

As he lowered the stein, he saw with shock that Harkon Lukas stood before him. Hurriedly he dropped the mask into place over his face and swallowed the last of the bitter drink.

"They say that the first time a man drinks *meekulbrau* his tongue can tell nothing but truth," the jet-haired bard said.

"This isn't my first time," Casimir lied.

As Lukas laughed humorlessly, Casimir studied the bard's sharp features. He wore a broad-brimmed hat, beneath which spilled locks of curly black hair. He had a tightly trimmed beard, equally black, a long mustache with waxed tips, and a monocle ensconced in his left eye.

The monocled eye locked on Casimir. "I thought I recognized you when your mask was up. Have we met?"

Casimir's face flushed, and he was suddenly glad for the weighty mask. "I don't think so. I know you from your fame, Master Lukas. My fame, however, offers you no such advantage," he said, stiffly affecting a schooled tone.

This time Lukas's laugh was genuine. "So do you come just to get drunk, or are you one of those ambitious lads who seeks to yank the seat of Harmonia from under Zhone Clieous?"

"If I yank the seat away and he's stupid enough to sit down, nature will take its course," Casimir observed. Lukas had kept the meistersinger tripping in conversation, and Casimir was determined not to prove as easy to bait. "Besides, claim to the seat of Harmonia is the birthright of all who live here."

"You've a bold tongue! You might guard it more carefully. What is your name, lad?" Harkon growled.

Casimir shook his head slowly. "No, sir. I'll not tell my real name. After all, this is a masquerade."

Harkon's eyes narrowed, and an amused smile curled about his lips. "I don't like the smell of you, lad. You smell of darkness and stale blood. But you mask your greater ills beneath a pleasant aroma of ambition." He stopped, licking his lips slowly. "I hope you lose this contest. If your ambition is real, your powers would be wasted in the meistersinger's seat."

"I hope the same for Zhone Clieous," Casimir said wryly.

Lukas took a long, languorous yawn and stretched widely as he scanned the garden. His modest smile grew to a sinister grin. "Look there—Gaston's preparing his parody of the Dark Midwife. I saw it only last year. It's really quite good. He casts her as the strumpet of Death."

"I have never had an appetite for that song."

Harkon turned, regarding Casimir with calculated interest. "Your appetites appear to run hot and cold."

"So they do," Casimir said, setting his stein down beside the barrel and stalking away. He had no wish to mingle. He wanted only to register for the meistersinger contest and steal away. The longer he tarried, the more likely his victim would rise from behind the roses and show him to be an imposter. He should sign the registry book and then make his escape.

The book lay on a lectern across the garden. Casimir strode toward it, weaving his way through clusters of chattering guests. A compact man in black robes guarded the registry, his balding head shiny in the lamplight. The man's features were drawn together like the mouth of a drawstring purse. Atop an upturned nose perched an odd pair of round spectacles.

Steeling his nerve, Casimir strode to the lectern.

He arrived just before noticing the man's dog. The large, lanky beast had broad jaws and a cropped tail, and lay wound about the robed man's feet. Casimir winced, stepping back as the beast rose and drew his scent into its lungs. Casimir stepped back again. The dog lunged forward. A thick-linked chain played out from the creature's harness. *Clink, clink, clink.* Casimir stumbled backward.

The dog was upon him.

Casimir's leg drew back. Teeth clamped solidly around his calf as servants converged on the dog and youth. Casimir shouted, trying to wrench his leg from the clamped jaws. Finally servants managed to pry the dog loose and dragged it, scrabbling, away. A collection of unseen hands eased the boy to the ground, and a servant brought a white towel to wrap his leg.

The balding man in black suddenly appeared beside Casimir. Over his shoulder hovered Zhone Clieous himself. Servants pushed back the gathering crowd of guests as the man in black began to speak.

"*How tuerna thou baeren?*"

Despite the pain lacing his calf, Casimir puzzled out the old speech. "Born of woman I was."

"*Tuerna thou sires ofen lupawigten?*"

"No, of a mortal man," Casimir moaned weakly.

"*Sufferna thou wit allbeflossen, by beaste ofen nigten?*"

"No, this bite is the first."

Zhone Clieous leaned over abruptly, pulling the mask from Casimir's face. Casimir threw his hands up to guard his features from the probing eyes. The man in black, with surprising strength, forced his hands away from his face. Meistersinger Clieous studied the youth closely, but Clieous's ratlike features didn't betray whether he recognized the young man. Slowly he spoke, his voice emotionless.

"You cannot perform in the meistersinger contest."

Casimir seized Clieous's tunic and pulled him down toward him. "Have I trained so long at the foot of Harkon Lukas, only to be denied by you now?"

Zhone Clieous went white. His eyes darted nervously behind the small black mask he wore. He bit his lip. "I apologize, young master. Allow me to help you to your feet."

Lowering his mask over his face again, Casimir struggled to rise, assisted by numerous hands. A pair of them belonged to a young and beautiful woman. Her hair was deep black, quite rare among the fair folk of Kartakass. Quite rare and quite striking, thought Casimir. She wore an equally black eye mask, and her eyes beneath the mask were emerald green. Her skin was white, like pure linen, and the elegant lines of her lips drew into an expression of worry as she eyed Casimir.

Her small hands pressed gently on his arm. "How is your leg, young sir?"

Casimir's eyes wouldn't leave her. "My leg?"

"Come, sign the book," Clieous directed, pulling Casimir to the lectern and setting the quill pen in his hand.

Smelling Clieous's fear, Casimir replied, "I'm not a Harmonic Hall lackey, Master Clieous. I have therefore not learned the perverse art of the scribe."

"Forgive me, young sir," Clieous said, taking the quill back. "What name shall I put down for you?"

A pang clenched Casimir's heart. He didn't dare tell his true name, not after Clieous saw his face. The orphan boy returned his gaze to the black-haired maiden and a song entered his thoughts, a song called "Sundered Heart."

"Sundered Heart," Casimir murmured distractedly. "I am Sundered Heart."

Clieous stared blankly toward the youth, his eyes prying at the grotesquely leering mask. For a moment, Casimir feared he had been discovered. Then the meistersinger turned his prodigious nose toward the page and wrote, *Master Sundered Heart, ward of Harkon Lukas.*

As Clieous inscribed the final letters, Casimir asked, "Who is this beautiful nursemaid on my arm?"

Zhone's skin went white a second time. He licked his dry lips and said civilly, "This is my grandniece, my eldest sister's grandchild, Julianna Estovina."

A relation of Clieous's? Casimir wondered. How could this spotless creature share his foul blood? He stared, dumbfounded, at her. Except for her jet-black hair, she seemed Clieous's exact opposite: light to his dark, purity to his depravity.

Casimir dropped to his healthy knee, slipped the mask from his face, and kissed the silky back of her hand. "How lucky I am, Julianna Estovina, that your great-uncle has such an unruly dog. Otherwise I wouldn't have met you."

As Casimir rose, the meistersinger began to speak nervously. "My deepest apologies, dear Harkon. I'd no notion that this remarkable young lad was your ward."

Casimir stiffened. Harkon Lukas released a hollow, ringing laugh. "He is indeed remarkable," Lukas noted sarcastically. "I only hope his talent proves equal to his ambition."

Casimir stole a glance toward Lukas, who wore a darkly knowing smile. Then he returned his eyes to Julianna.

"We'll know of his talent soon enough," Meistersinger Clieous said, gesturing toward the book. "He's registered for the contest. Now he must sing a prelude, like all the others." He tugged on Casimir's arm, pulling him away from Julianna. "Come, Sundered Heart. Come to the stage for a song. The players await."

Casimir pulled free from the meistersinger's grip and stared at the snow-skinned beauty. "I sing this song for you, Lady Julianna." Then Casimir lowered his grimacing mask, rose to his feet, and began to limp toward the stage. Lukas and Clieous escorted him, one on each side.

"If your voice isn't as sweet as your lies," Lukas whispered savagely, "I'll disown you publicly and kill you privately."

Casimir didn't respond, conveying himself with all the dignity he could muster despite his wounded leg. He finally gained the stage, and Lukas and Clieous settled together in the front seats like a pair of ravens. One of the instrumentalists, a man with a rebec, leaned over to Casimir. "What shall we play?"

Casimir waved him off. "I don't sing to the moan of rebecs." The man's eyes narrowed and he shook his head. Lukas fixed Casimir with a killing stare. Ignoring his "mentor," Casimir stepped to stage front and cleared his voice. "I am Sundered Heart."

Whispers and chuckles ran through the crowd. "Is he a singer or a song?" "Looks more like Sundered Leg to me." "Obviously not a Harmonic Hall man." "Get ready for 'Alley Cat Serenade.' "

Casimir coughed to halt the comments. Oddly, in the wake of his meeting with Julianna, he couldn't feel anger toward these people—only irritation. "I am Sundered Heart, and I will sing 'Sundered Heart' to the beautiful lady, Julianna Estovina."

The cruel banter began again. One Hall apprentice even whispered consolation to Julianna. Casimir ignored them, closing his eyes and beginning to sing. His clear, haunting voice rose above the murmur of the crowd.

> "Hold now, dear love. I cannot let
> Thee sleep in crimson death's dark stain.
> For look, I am too weak to set

A stone to mark thy resting place
In heart and thought and ground. Thy pain
I feel as mine. I'll ne'er forget
Thy will to live as life doth wane—
Thy sundered heart and spring-touched face.

"Beneath these high-arched boughs we went
Like young loves, hand in hand were we.
Till goblin scout an arrow sent
To sink its shaft into thy heart:
It sundered, too, the heart of me.
I cradled thee, thy strength full spent,
While that foul goblin turned to flee;
Into his back I shot a dart.

"A goblin's death does nothing to
Restore to me my pierced love.
That cursed shaft, so foreign through
Thy blessed heart, doth make me mad
With grief. I curse the gods above
And those below whose works can do
Such foul injustice to a dove
Like thee. To me 'tis hopeless sad.

"Oh, now thine eyes close! Love so sweet,
Thy fight with death is done. But mine
Begins, for as I live, I'll never meet
Again thy matchless, restless soul.
My sundered heart should be like thine,
Not cleft entire by passion's heat
But also by a blade. The wine
Of blood springs from my dirk and soul."

The barbed ridicules had ceased; Casimir's voice had silenced them. His melancholy, pure tone, uncompromised by the vibrato taught in the hall, carried the song through the crowd to Julianna. He had imagined her struck by an arrow, slowly dying, cradled in his mournful arms.

"He's like a creature born to sing." "More nightingale than alley cat in this one." "Three hundred gold a month, and still you can't sing as well." As conversation welled up in the garden; a man seated in front began to clap. Casimir turned toward the sound. It was Harkon Lukas. Others in the crowd turned to see who was clapping. Astonishment enveloped their faces.

"Harkon Lukas . . . clapping?"

One by one, they joined in the applause. Even Zhone Clieous, whose face had turned to a greenish hue, reluctantly clapped twice in token show.

Suddenly another sound rang through the crowd. For a moment, the applause mingled with gasps and shouts of dismay. The clapping faltered and died away entirely. Shocked guests scrambled back from their seats to clear a path. Casimir strained to see the source of the commotion. Lukas and Clieous gained their feet as a manservant approached through the crowd, dragging behind him the struggling form of a pudgy peasant boy.

"Thoris!" Casimir gasped.

The manservant hauled Thoris up to Meistersinger Clieous. "Master, this—this urchin tried to stow aboard a coach to sneak into the party."

The meistersinger's face reddened, his lips twitching with anger. "Need you drag this whelp through my masquerade? Haven't you brain enough to whip him and throw him into the moat?"

Bowing fearfully, the manservant stammered, "My humblest apologies, my—"

"This man shouldn't apologize for something that's my fault," Casimir interrupted. He stepped down from the stage and approached Lukas and Clieous. "This is my dear servant. His father was slain by a werewolf some years ago, and I've taken charge of him." Casimir set his trembling hand on Clieous's shoulder. "Do forgive him, Clieous. He loves me so. Indeed, he would risk life and limb to hear me sing. I charged him to stay outside, but he couldn't resist."

The fury hadn't left Clieous's features. Struggling to contain his wrath, the meistersinger turned toward Harkon Lukas. Lukas merely shrugged. Exasperated, Clieous blurted, "He cannot stay."

"Oh, no," Casimir replied hastily. "I never dreamt he could. We will leave now."

The meistersinger appeared pleased by the idea. "Most certainly, young master. Don't let us detain you."

Casimir slipped his hand beneath Thoris's arm. The stocky boy was quivering pitifully, and sweat streamed down his white face.

"All is well, good servant," Casimir said, patting Thoris's hand gently. "We'll be going now." Before they could depart, though, another shout erupted.

A man standing behind a rosebush cried out, "I've found another—a naked drunkard lying here in the flowers."

Meistersinger Clieous drew a breath through clenched teeth. "Another of your friends, Sundered Heart?"

Casimir turned slowly, his grimacing mask hiding a glib smile. "Why, I'm certain he isn't!"

Clieous threw his hands into the air and bellowed, "What sort of fortress is this? Take the intruder out and flog him, then throw him in the deepest cell in the jail-house. While you're at it, call in the gate guard and do the same to him!"

FOUR

Dusk deepened over the stonework amphitheater as Casimir entered for the meistersinger contest. His gaze traced the timeworn stairs leading to the stage below. It was dark granite, carved into the very cliff that overshadowed Harmonia. As a child, Casimir had spent many afternoons playing on the stone seats that ringed the stage. Tonight, though, the seats were jammed with people. Their echoing voices rose into the stony shell above like the disquieted voice of the world.

Casimir began his descent into the amphitheater. The stairs were flanked by a mossy wall of stone, covered by a sheen of moisture that drained from the field above. Jaundiced lanterns and thick banners of state hung on the wall, their banners casting ghostlike shadows across the stairs. After descending past a clump of patrons, Casimir reached a cave mouth that opened in the wall. This was the entrance to the Crystal Club, an expensive tavern for Harmonia's elite. From the cave mouth drifted the enticing aromas of meat and *meekulbrau*—and money. Casimir didn't pause at the entrance, continuing his descent toward the stone stage.

"Hello, Sundered Heart," came the voice of a young woman.

Julianna Estovina stood before Casimir. She had risen from a seat beside the stair. The light of the failing day glimmered softly on her sable hair, and an elegant gown of white silk draped from her shoulders. Her eyes shone like jade, and her lips curved in perfect crimson beauty on her face.

"I had hoped to see you here tonight, Sundered Heart," Julianna said. The pleasant fragrance of her skin filled his nose, dispelling the earthy odors of the amphitheater.

"I had hoped to see you here as well."

She moved toward him, her eyes fastened on his. "It's so cold in this place." With casual ease, she lifted his hand and twirled slowly into his arms. She nestled against his chest.

The air was indeed chill, but the soft press of Julianna's body felt anything but cold. Clumsily Casimir ran his fingers through her hair. Her delicate hand slid around his waist. Looking up at him, she said, "Do you want to kiss me, Sundered Heart?"

Casimir was speechless. He stared stupidly into her dazzling eyes. Again she pressed lightly against him, raising herself slowly to tiptoe. Her lips settled onto his.

The kiss felt painfully hot, but Casimir didn't pull back. Her breath was sweet and intoxicating. Her small hands pressed him mercilessly against her, as though she hoped to cut him open and crawl inside. Casimir trembled. Her very soul seemed to force its way into him. The sensation was wonderful. He could smell the hot blood rushing through her lips. Rushing through her face. Through her neck. Through her shoulders. Rushing. Rushing.

He was hungry.

His teeth fastened on her lip. Blood gushed into his mouth. She pushed back from the kiss, but his arms held her fast. His ruby fangs sank into her struggling neck. A scarlet tide poured across her collarbone and stained her dress red. The white-hot flesh of her throat melted away in his mouth. It burned as it slid down his gullet.

More. He wanted more.

He bit deeply. Another bite—teeth sinking into her soft flesh. And another. Vaguely, he knew she was dying, but the hunger was heedless. And with each taste, the hunger grew.

Then he felt his teeth lodge in bone.

* * * * *

Casimir bolted upright in his cot. His lungs raked breaths from the steamy air. He felt he was suffocating. His heart clattered in his ribs, and dream images flitted before his eyes.

"Damn!" he murmured. "How I hate this curse."

Julianna hovered like a shadow just beyond his cot. Her eyes were wide with horror and her face was paper-white. He reached his hand out toward the shadow. Her lip ruptured. A crimson line wormed down from it onto her chin. Casimir withdrew his hand. Her white neck burst open like a blossoming rose. He mopped his sweat-beaded forehead. His fingernails felt razor-sharp on his brow, and the knuckles were coarse with hair.

Thoris stirred.

Casimir buried his warped hands in the sheet. He wrenched the ragged linen up to hide behind. Thoris raised up on one elbow and rubbed a hand across his face. He swung leaden legs over his cot's edge and sat up. His eyes were clouded with sleep.

"Nightmare?" he slurred through pasty lips.

Casimir kept the sheet pulled up around him. "Yeah."

Thoris forced his eyes wide, as though to break cob-webs across their corners. Leaning into the white-blue shaft of moonlight that fell through the window, he squinted. "Had a nightmare myself," he said, studying his friend's face. "Hard to sleep with the contest tomorrow and everything."

Casimir didn't respond. He remained motionless in the moonlight. Thoris shrugged, swung his legs back onto the cot, and dropped his head to the canvas. Silence settled. Only the crickets spoke.

* * * * *

The next day passed in a blur for Casimir. He felt he had hardly woken up before the sun was setting and the meistersinger contest had arrived. The moon hung full over the amphitheater, and Casimir's blood curdled at the sight of it. "Why tonight?" he wondered aloud. Running a gloved hand over his brocaded satin doublet, he stepped to the edge of the stone theater and surveyed the crowd through his leering mask. "Why tonight?"

Thoris's hand settled warmly on his shoulder. "The attendants won't let me go any farther, Casimir—not without money." He smiled sheepishly. "But I'll find a spot along the back and watch from there." Casimir was oblivious, intent on the stage. Thoris tapped his shoulder again, and Casimir swung about irritably. Thoris smiled, staring intently over Casimir's shoulder. "Say, Casimir, wouldn't that be the maiden you met at the party?"

"What maiden?" Casimir asked, following Thoris's gaze.

"The one you've spoken of practically every moment since," Thoris clarified. "Julianna."

It *was* Julianna.

She sat a number of tiers below them, facing the stage. Even so, Casimir knew her immediately. Her flowing hair, black as Casimir's own, shone with dusky highlights amid the fair-haired folk around her. The backless seat where she sat allowed him to see most of her body. A silky white dress of lace draped from her smooth shoulders, gathered about her slim waist, and clung to the graceful contours of her legs.

The dream flashed into his mind. The mask felt suddenly suffocating on his face, and hunger prickled along his jaw.

"Go ahead—go talk to her," Thoris said, pushing his stone-faced friend down the steps. "Surely you want to see her again."

Casimir plodded reluctantly down one flight of stairs before he balked. Thoris gestured him onward. Another step down. Then another. He looked at Julianna. The moonlight washed cool over her silken hair and down across her sculpted legs. He descended another flight. Casimir's muscles began to ache, a feeling he knew all too well. Clenching his jaw beneath the grinning mask, Casimir planted his feet on the stair and pulled up short. I cannot talk to her, he decided.

As though she sensed his thoughts, Julianna turned her head. Her eyes fixed on him. She rose from her seat with slow, natural grace. The folds of her dress tumbled across her legs.

"Hello, Sundered Heart," she called.

Casimir retreated a step up the stairs. Julianna motioned toward him, her brow lowering in puzzlement. Casimir sighed. I must go speak with her now. He resumed the descent. A magnificent smile spread across her lips as the young singer approached. Reaching her row, Casimir pushed past a plump merchant and his wife, who sat at the end. Arriving at last, he clasped her slim hands in his white-gloved palms.

"I see by your healthy strides that your leg has healed since our last meeting," she said.

Casimir's blush was hidden by the mask. "Yes, it's fine now." Recovering himself, he dropped to one knee, raised the mask from his face, and kissed her hand. "I have you to thank."

She laughed easily. "Many others helped you to your feet."

"Helping me to my feet and inspiring me to health are two quite different things," Casimir said, rising. He left his mask up.

"Let me see that leg," she said. With a shy smile, Casimir set his curly-toed shoe on the stone seat. Julianna sat down beside it. She ran her slender fingers along the silken cannons, pressing gently around the tooth marks in the fabric. "You heal very quickly, Sundered Heart. And I'm surprised at how well the bloodstain came out of the stocking."

"I hoped the lantern light would mask the stain."

"I'm also surprised the wound didn't fester," she continued, relief apparent in her voice. "My uncle's dogs have cost more than one man his leg."

"Strange that our meistersinger keeps such fierce dogs," Casimir noted bitterly. He lowered his foot again.

"Most times the dogs attack only thieves," Julianna offered. "Otherwise they are friendly . . . except to uncle," she added with a laugh. "They absolutely hate him." She paused, her smile fading. "I wonder why the dog attacked you."

"Perhaps it thought I was a thief. After all, I plan to steal Clieous's rule."

"Do you really?" she asked, curious.

"Yes, I do. But if my singing wins only your applause tonight, I'll be happy."

She smiled. "It is strange to find another person with black hair in Harmonia. I haven't seen more than two families with dark hair."

"It's as if we are blood kin," Casimir ventured cryptically.

"Or somehow destined to meet," Julianna responded.

A hand tapped Casimir roughly on the shoulder. It was one of the Harmonic Hall attendants.

"The singers have gathered in the Crystal Club for the precontest toast. They await you."

Casimir didn't turn away from Julianna. "I hope to see you in *my* meistersinger's mansion when this evening ends."

"We'll see," she said.

Casimir leaned impulsively forward and kissed her on the lips. "Yes . . . we'll see."

Julianna flushed, her eyes wide with shock. Casimir stepped back. Was I wrong to kiss her? he wondered. She bit her lip as he retreated another step. He turned, unsure what to do. Feeling foolish, Casimir began to shoulder his way past the pudgy merchant. A slender hand caught his shoulder. Julianna pulled him back toward her and whispered softly, "Don't drink the toast." She leaned forward, her lips brushing his cheek.

Casimir stumbled back from her as the attendant again tapped his shoulder. Julianna's eyes followed him. The noise of his heart rose above the murmur of the crowd. He retreated up the stairs, taking a final, inquisitive glance back toward Julianna before lowering his leering mask.

*   *   *   *   *

Dark rumors of the Crystal Club had reached even the ears of Casimir, but he had never ventured there before. Taking a deep breath, he stepped into the cave mouth that served as the club's entrance. The passage looked like no cave he had ever seen. The walls and ceiling were packed with glimmering quartz: clear, red, and green. Their facets glowed with the ambience of the lanterns without, producing a diffuse and cloudy light. As Casimir proceeded, the stones echoed his swishing footfalls and the murmuring sound of the crowd outside. If they ring like this from such slight cause, Casimir thought, I wonder what music does to them.

Fragrances of wine and perfume hung in the air ahead of him. He followed the aromas to the far end of the entryway. There a pair of plate mail suits guarded a broad iron gate. Just beyond the gate stood two smiling maidens. The perfume was unmistakably theirs. Their skin seemed to be painted with the stuff.

"Name?" asked the one on Casimir's left.

"Sundered Heart," Casimir responded.

"Ah, here it is," she said, consulting the broad register from the masquerade. "Welcome to the Crystal Club, Master Heart."

Casimir nodded, passing between the women and into the club. The establishment spread through a small, mazelike cave. Numerous tables stood amongst a forest of natural rock columns. Each table held a flickering candle, hemmed in by a thick circle of patrons. Platters of pheasant, duck, or lamb occupied the center of most tables. From the meat rose fragrant steam that circled above the heads of the feasters. The murmur of the crowd filled the chill air.

Scanning the room, Casimir caught sight of the main bar, a circular counter surrounding a column of crystal. Above the bar hovered goblets in glittering rows, and around the bar stood many finely attired bards. Casimir headed toward the crowd, weaving past the burgeoning tables. As he approached, he glimpsed a row of glass steins on the bar, each foaming with reddish-brown *meekulbrau*. Zhone Clieous, red-faced with exuberance, stood atop a short stool and lifted a full stein of the liquor.

"May I have your attention?" he shouted. The huddled bards grew suddenly silent. Clieous took a sip and continued. "Thank you. The hostesses inform me that the final contestant has arrived. And so, singers, please grab a tankard for the toast!"

The crowd converged thirstily on the bar, each grabbing a tankard. Casimir waited, Julianna's warning echoing in his ears. Perhaps the barman miscounted the steins—barmen are notoriously bad with numbers, he thought. Slowly the other bards stepped back from the bar, leaving one stein unclaimed.

The meistersinger peered about hawkishly. "Come now. One of you hasn't a glass for the toast. Who is it? I'll need to see empty steins all around before anyone sings."

Casimir stepped forward, sliding his hand around the sweating tankard.

"Ah . . . it was you, then, Sundered Heart," Clieous said, his voice edged with derision. "Let's have none of that nonsense you pulled at the masquerade! Now for the toast!" Clieous raised his glass high and spoke the traditional words: "Oh, let us sing with joyful tones a song that stirs us to our bones. And should we fail to win the crown, oh, let us willingly step down."

The room rang with the merry clink of glasses and calls of "Hear, hear!" Casimir watched as the bards set the drinks to their lips and tilted their heads back.

The sweating stein slipped easily from Casimir's fingers.

The sound of shattering glass and splashing liquor echoed through the room. Faces turned in dismay toward Casimir. Zhone Clieous looked livid.

Casimir shrugged. "Please forgive my clumsiness."

He stepped around the pool of ale as servants scurried to clean up the mess. Reaching the bar, Casimir pushed his way between stunned bards. "Barman, kindly draw me another pint."

The barman's brow was stormy as he drew a new glass. Clieous watched with thinly veiled dismay. The contestants to either side of Casimir began to chuckle, and any who hadn't drained his pint did so now. The barman set the newly filled pint stein down and Casimir snatched it up. With a lusty smile, he drained it.

Up went the cry, "To the contest! To the contest!" Raising his empty stein with the others, Casimir added his voice to the shouts.

*   *   *   *   *

In the field above the amphitheater, Thoris pushed through the peasant throng. He had quickly learned that only those along the front rail could see, and they had staked their positions well before sundown. Determined to gain a view of the stage, Thoris set his shoulder to the task.

"Watch where you're going, boy!"

"Get in back!"

"Off my foot!"

He ignored the cries, worming his way through a wall of laborers whose clothes reeked of soil and sweat. Beyond them stood a pair in funeral garb, doubtless the only finery they owned. He squeezed rudely between them, and then caught a glimpse of the thick stone railing. Villagers stood three deep between him and the rail. Those farthest forward leaned on the rail, while the next row peered over the shoulders of the first and the next over the shoulders of the second.

After scouting for a moment, Thoris spotted an opening. A greengrocer leaned heavily against the rail, his large backside clearing out a space sufficient for two people. More importantly, though, the man's bowed legs left a fair-sized opening near the ground. Thoris scrambled for the opening. When he was settled beside the rail, his face peered through the squat stone spindles—a perfect view, as long as the greengrocer kept his balance.

He had arrived just in time: the contest was about to begin. From the shadowy recesses of the backstage, a solitary man slowly emerged. Lantern light gradually revealed unwavering eyes, heavy black brows, flattened cheekbones, a muzzlelike nose, and a leering grin.

Zhone Clieous.

A chill ran through Thoris as he eyed Casimir's nemesis. The audience fell silent. His eyes glinting orange in the lantern light, Clieous swept his hands out to each side. The cape he wore fluttered behind him like a looming shadow. His lips parted, revealing a yellowed forest of teeth, and he began to speak.

"*Nostoremak, sprictdesdemis, schtilla erschta nictevact!*"

Though Thoris wasn't conversant in the old speech, the phrase was common enough: "Winter's death, death of spring, midsummer's night eternal!"

Clieous continued, now speaking in the common tongue. "Ours is a land of heroes. Ours is a land of songs. This midsummer's night, witnessed by the wind in the pines and sealed by the full moon, we sing songs, we find heroes!" Clieous motioned for applause, and the crowd responded eagerly. His ratlike nose twitched with delight as he listened to the ovation. In time it quieted, and he resumed. "Who shall rule us? Who among us is most virtuous in song? Who among us is most virtuous in life? Tonight will tell!" Again on cue, the clapping rang out. This time Clieous motioned the crowd into premature silence. He gazed about imperiously before shouting, "Let the songs begin!"

A riotous clamor erupted behind Zhone. At first, the cacophony sounded like the shouts of an angry crowd. After listening more closely, Thoris realized the voices weren't shouting but singing, a host of voices singing a host of songs. One by one, bards emerged from the shadowy backstage into the wavering light, each singing a different song. They strode out toward the audience, lining the front of the stage and marching up the stairs to mingle with the crowd.

A man garbed in red sang in a deep bass from his post above a fat woman. Another, wearing the regalia of a troubadour, gestured wildly as she bounded from stair to stair. A third, dressed in a feathery cape, kissed young maidens and old maids as he forged his noisy way along. Each singer sung toward a section of the audience, virtually shouting to be heard above the others. To Thoris, it sounded more like the din of beggars than the music of masters. All the contestants had now emerged, and many were climbing like mountain rams through the seats. Thoris could make out the songs only of those who had reached the top tier. Their voices were rough and strained. Nothing like Casimir's voice, Thoris thought. "Where *is* Casimir?"

Then Thoris spotted his friend among the final singers to emerge. Casimir stood quietly on the stage, heels together, hands at his sides. Thoris strained his ears to hear the clarion voice of his friend, but he couldn't. Casimir hardly seemed to be breathing, let alone singing.

Thoris bit his lip and whispered, "Open your mouth, Casimir!"

Casimir simply stood in rigid silence. He didn't sing. He didn't move. Thoris's heart felt like lead in his chest. The people sitting directly in front of Casimir had turned around to listen to the bards behind them.

Sudden anger boiled up in Thoris. He filled his lungs with air and, before he could stop himself, bellowed, "Revenge, Casimir! *Revenge!*"

The greengrocer shot a shocked glare down toward the scrubby orphan, but Thoris was too intent on his friend to notice.

The words appeared to stir Casimir. He lifted his hands to each side and drew a deep breath. Then he sang. His voice cut clear and sweet through the chaos of the amphitheater. Those who sat below him began to turn around again. Nearby competitors, noticing that hardly anyone was listening to them anymore, edged nearer to the young bard. Even so, more folk turned to listen to Casimir. The dark-haired youth stepped toward the audience, his wildly mournful voice rising like the cry of a wolf. A cold chill ran through Thoris as the people near Casimir began to applaud.

During the next half hour, Casimir made his way through the people, garnering more listeners with each step. Some of the less talented singers, unable to secure an audience, retreated into the Crystal Club. Others retired in fits of coughing. At last, Meistersinger Clieous signaled the remaining bards to line up along the dark wall backstage.

Reading from his roster, Clieous called the name of the first competitor. The young singer emerged from the darkness and was greeted by smatterings of applause. As the clapping died down, Clieous scribbled a notation in the margin of his book. Then he summoned the next singer, who received his applause. So it went until, almost last on the list, Casimir was called.

"Sundered Heart, ward of Master Lukas!"

A long, silent pause followed. Slowly Casimir emerged from the darkness. Tepid fingers of lantern light began to trace out the lines of his mask. He took another step forward, and his full form entered the light.

A hush followed.

Thoris shut his eyes and began clapping violently. Casimir had obviously had the most beautiful voice among the bards, and now the crowd repaid him with silence. Thoris continued to clap, tears welling up in his closed eyes. His palms began to sting, and his arms grew heavy with despair. As his applause slowed, he noticed that the greengrocer was also clapping. So, too, were many others below—indeed, most of the auditorium! Thoris was ecstatic. After two more names, the wondrous news was confirmed.

"The final five—one of whom may succeed me and rule over Harmonia—are . . . Gaston Olyava . . . Eldon Comistev . . . Ravenik Oltavic . . . Heindle Brahg . . . and Sundered Heart."

FIVE

Thoris could hardly contain his excitement as Casimir and the other bards retired to the Crystal Club. "It's working!" he whispered to himself. "I can't believe it! It's working! It's working!" In a wave of joy, he found himself hugging the thick ankles of the greengrocer above him.

A pillowy but benevolent face stared down past a flapping apron. "Hello down there."

Gritting his teeth, Thoris cautiously withdrew his arms and waited for the fist to fall. A meaty hand clamped around the collar of his tunic. Then came a strangling yank. Thoris's stomach slid across the ground, and his head nearly struck the stone rail. Abruptly he was on his feet, standing between the railing and the grocer's ponderous belly.

The huge man spoke, "I'm growing tired of straddling you like a bridge. Stay in front; you're small enough."

"Th-thank you," Thoris replied dubiously, rubbing his neck.

"Who're you backing, boy?" the greengrocer boomed.

"Backing?" Thoris asked, confused.

"Who're you cheering for?"

"Oh, Casi—uh, Sundered Heart."

"Hope he's good at insults, 'cause that's the next round."

"Next round?"

"It's s'posed to test what they call rhet'ric, but it's just a pack of insults," the man said. "Insults is something meistersingers've gotta be good at."

"Oh, Sundered Heart is good at insults," Thoris said. "If he wins the insult contest, will he be meistersinger?"

"No, not yet. Then he's got to beat Clieous on the bal-lads."

Thoris shook his head. "Will this contest never end?"

*   *   *   *   *

Another quarter of an hour passed before the singers emerged once more. They fanned out along the stage front behind newly filled lanterns. Casimir was the last of the five to emerge. He moved to the stairs and stood, heels touching and hands at his sides. Zhone Clieous remained behind the line of bards, his face hovering ghostlike near the back of the stage.

The crowd hushed to silence.

Clieous imperiously scanned the audience, then began the second round. "Gaston Olyava, what makes you fit to rule?"

A green-clad, muscular bard stepped forward. "My days as Lord High of Harmonic Hall prepared me to rule."

"They were many days indeed," shouted a rotund singer named Heindle. "Nearly a fortnight!"

"I spent two years as Lord High!" Gaston snapped.

Eldon, a barrel-chested bard, laughed. "Tell them why, my Lord High, you were removed from your lofty post."

"I'll tell them why," interrupted Casimir, apparently grasping the object of the competition. "Because you were too fond of lording it high over the ladies!"

The audience began to chuckle. Gaston bellowed, "I governed with unimpeachable honor!"

"You denounced not a single strumpet that wanted governing!" Casimir added. The crowd broke into hoots of laughter.

"How have you any knowledge of this, outsider?" Gaston shot back, wringing a cheer from the audience.

"Even outsiders have heard of your exploits, Gaston!" Casimir replied.

Thoris sniggered into his hands.

Gaston's aspect changed. "Well, then let me receive credit where it's due. If a man can govern womankind— the most mysterious, complex, and lovely creations of the gods—who could challenge his ability to govern the lady Harmonia?"

"But you are hardly the marrying kind! Do you want Harmonia for a mistress or wife?" asked an effeminate bard named Ravenik.

"I would care for this city as a loving husband!"

"Yes—as a husband loving a tart!" Casimir corrected.

"I would faithfully serve her," insisted Gaston.

"Faithfully serve her to the hounds," finished Casimir.

Gaston's eyes had grown fiery. "You know nothing of Harmonia or of me, Splintered Brain."

"On the contrary," Casimir replied, "I know everything of Harmonia and you. You want to dominate Harmonia like a husband, you say. But I say Harmonia is a woman you must not dominate! Harmonia is no whore you pay to ride. She is no wanton barmaid! No. Harmonia is a washerwoman and mother of many, a healer of festered wounds and a comfort to every barefoot boy and girl. Look around you at these quiet, strong ladies. *They* are Harmonia. Do you truly wish to dominate them? It would be better—far better—if they dominated you!"

Laughter and applause rang out from the crowd. Casimir bowed low before the audience, seeing a number of stout women stand as they clapped. The wealthy ones applauded with gloved hands while the bawdy ones along the upper rail whistled unabashedly.

Zhone Clieous quieted the applause with a wave of his hands. Anger was apparent on his shadowy face. His vulture eyes swept the crowd as he waited for silence. At last he cleared his throat and began the next set of questions.

"Eldon Comistev, what makes you fit to rule?"

The broad-chested bard stepped forward. A toothy

grin spread across his face. "I am a merchant in this city of merchants, and therefore I can bring prosperity to every corner of Harmonia."

"No doubt! Your slum shacks wring prosperity even from the poor!" spat Casimir.

"I'll give work to every poor man of the city," Eldon replied, his smile beginning to slip.

"You already give them work," Casimir laughed. "Now how about paying them?"

Gaston leapt in. "He thinks a liberal lash payment enough."

Eldon waved his hands for a chance to speak. "The work I offer will pay well—in coin. Our city has treasure for all."

"The treasure of Harmonia is people, not coins," Casimir said indignantly. "What is the market value of a soul these days, Eldon? Surely you know!"

"I offer prosperity, Sundered Heart, not money," Eldon replied. "In my Harmonia, neighbor will help neighbor and rich will help poor."

"All on pain of death," Ravenik interjected.

"My Harmonia will be a happy family," said the shaken man.

"Gaston would be a dominating husband and you an oppressive father," Casimir shouted. "Shouldn't the people be served, not oppressed?" More applause erupted in the amphitheater.

Before the clapping died away, the banter continued. As the pasty moon rose in the sky, Casimir's snide rebuttals grew more incisive. Always he led the attack, to the laughter and applause of the audience. The other bards became increasingly resentful toward the indomitable and merciless Sundered Heart. With every dart he landed, they charged their fangs with venom, waiting for the questions to turn on him.

"Sundered Heart, what makes you fit to rule?"

Casimir paused, waiting for the crowd's full attention.

"I have the heart of my people."

Gaston was first to the attack. "Did the sundering of

your heart split your head also?"

"A split head is better than none at all . . . but you wouldn't know."

Gaston shouted over the laughter, "Split-headed rulers make split-headed decisions."

"Our own Zhone Clieous is the master of split-headed decisions. He makes the rich richer and the poor poorer. Perhaps with my split-headedness, I can remember the rich without forgetting the poor."

Eldon jabbed, "How came you by this split head? Did it cushion your fall once too often?"

"What cuts my heart deeply also cuts my head," Casimir countered. "If you fellows had hearts rather than lumps of coal in your breasts, you might feel the same."

"Why do you hide behind a mask?" Heindle sneered.

"Faces tell lies, good Heindle, but hearts speak truth. I hope your face has lied well for you tonight . . . as well as my heart has spoken for me."

Ravenik broke in. "You hate our beloved Clieous, don't you?"

Casimir hesitated, raising his gloved hand to cover his heart. "I love . . . " he began, his voice breaking for a moment. He cleared his throat and continued. "I love Zhone Clieous as much as an only son would. And as for you, Ravenik, if you love our lord so well, why do you plot to steal his office?"

"Enough!" Zhone Clieous's deep voice echoed through the amphitheater. He motioned the competitors to retreat from stage front and line up in the shadows at the rear. Then, one by one as before, he called them forward. The crowd, trained from years of such contests, followed each name with their applause. As the ovation died away, Clieous scribbled notes in his book. The applause had spread evenly among the first four singers. Only Casimir remained. The crowd was filled with unsettled murmurs.

"Master Sundered Heart."

The resulting roar left no doubt: Sundered Heart had won the second round.

*   *   *   *   *

Casimir was sitting alone at a corner table of the Crystal Club when a familiar voice spoke.

"Best damned bard I never trained."

Casimir raised his masked face to see a dark-haired man. His waxed mustache twitched with a smile, and candlelight reflected from his monocle.

"Good evening, Master Lukas. I hope I've made you proud."

Harkon Lukas's eyes gleamed fiendishly in the dusky room. "I reserve judgment until tomorrow, when you are meistersinger."

When you are meistersinger. The phrase echoed dizzily in Casimir's head. He had planned for revenge, not rulership. He never dreamed it would come this far.

"Perhaps I should deliberately lose the contest. You said being meistersinger would be a waste of my talent," Casimir noted.

"*If,* Master Heart," Lukas began, sliding into a chair. "*If* you win the contest, honestly or not, the office would waste your talent. But if you lose, you haven't any talent to waste."

"Well, win or lose, my performance reflects on my teacher. Perhaps if you had rigorously pursued my education, the title would already be mine."

Instead of the banter Casimir expected, the legendary bard was initially silent. The gleam in his eyes intensified, and a curious smile curved his lip. "If you win, Master Heart, we will talk about your education." Then he sighed and motioned toward Casimir's empty hand. "Not drinking tonight?"

Casimir clutched his neck. "Bad for the throat."

"Bad indeed," Lukas replied with a knowing smile. "Well, I must be off. And you, young apprentice, must save your voice." Rising, he stalked away into the club's dark recesses.

A thickly attired man suddenly loomed up before Casimir's table. Huge in the candlelight, he dropped into the seat beside Casimir. The man smelled of sweat and oil, some mixture of which glistened on his rough-cut beard. Beneath the woolen coat he wore, his lungs filled and emptied like massive bellows.

Casimir's hand clutched his mask. "There are other tables."

"Refusin' drink, are ye?" the man asked, his breath putrid.

"If you will excuse me," Casimir said, beginning to rise.

The man's tree-trunk arm slung around him, and a meaty hand clutched Casimir's shoulder. "Clieous says ye wouldn't toast the boys." He motioned toward the tavernkeep, who brought a stein toward them. "Let's hear ye sing with a swaller o' this in ye."

The tavernkeep set the reddish-brown brew on the table, then disappeared. Casimir struggled to rise. The man's corpulent arm tightened around his neck. "Ye'll be goin' nowhere till ye've drained this." The brute's free hand pushed the mask up on Casimir's forehead, gouging a line across his brow. Casimir gasped. He lurched to break free, his fists pounding on the man's chest. The ruffian's hold only tightened. His hand dropped from the mask and lifted the stein to Casimir's lips.

Red-hot rods of anger shot through Casimir's arms. He willed his nails to harden beneath the silken gloves. His spine jolted and twisted. The tankard was at his lips. He hissed violently, spraying reddish foam onto the man's fat-creased face. A massive hand fastened over his nose, and the stein was thrust deep into his mouth. Choking, Casimir knew he must drink or drown. The liquor coursed bitter down his throat, leaving an unusual grit. Casimir gasped for air as his warping bones and muscles hardened.

Suddenly his hand broke free. With extended claws, it buried itself into the bovine stomach of the astonished man. Through the tightly strung shell of muscle, past the hot viscera, between the shuddering lungs, his fingers passed. His hand fastened quickly on the man's ponderous heart. He wrenched the convulsing muscle free and dropped it to the floor.

The arm across his shoulder went limp. Casimir sloughed it off. He pulled the mask down over his panting face and stared stupidly at the oily giant. The man didn't even slump forward on the table. His sightless eyes bulged as though he had eaten too much. Casimir's attention shifted to the stained arm of his doublet. Thank the gods it was already red, he thought. Picking up the stein with his other hand, he poured what little remained of the brew across the jacket arm. With a measure of disgust, he pulled the sloppy gloves from his hands.

"Third round begins momentarily," called out a server.

Casimir allowed the tingling to dissipate from his fingers before he stood up. Scanning the dark corner, he decided the man wouldn't be discovered soon unless someone slipped on the puddle.

*   *   *   *   *

Thoris watched nervously as Casimir and Clieous emerged on the stage. In the first two rounds, Thoris had cheered Casimir's success, but now he hoped for failure. How can Casimir rule Harmonia? Thoris wondered. He's only eighteen. What if he can't control the guardsmen? What if Harmonic Hall rebels? What if the people discover he's an orphan?

Casimir remained in the shadows as Zhone Clieous stepped to stage front. The audience greeted him with healthy applause. Clieous took a long bow, waiting for the ovation to die down. For all his fine clothes and elegant manners, he looked frail now to Thoris. Frail and fearful and mortal—not the villainous demigod Casimir had depicted. As the applause died away, the meistersinger began to sing "The Ballad of Nunieve." The crowd responded with more applause. The song was among their favorites.

> *"In Halliel fair, beneath the trees,*
> *Before the world had learned of hate,*

There lived Nunieve, who from the seas
Had risen pure with eyes of gold
And walked the garden with a gait
Of love. Her heart could bend the trees,
It's told, but not the heavy fate
That 'tombed her deep in waters cold.

"In meadows soft, she wandered 'round,
With creatures crawling by her feet.
The birds would flock to hear the sound
Of winds that filled her silken veils
And sang her praises mild and sweet.
Her shadow often graced the ground
With blooming flowers by her feet,
For flowers by her face would pale.

"This selfsame shadow followed her,
To gaze in waters still and clear.
But when she spied her shadow there,
Gazing toward her from the pool,
She spoke into the misty mirror,
'Who are you that sees me there?
Your face is boyish, it appears,
Yet I'm a girl, or I'm a fool.'

"For in the pool's reflective face
A boy gazed forth with curling locks.
He said, 'Your image I replace.
I live below in nether worlds,
In obverse space beneath your docks.
But you I'm longing to embrace,
To bring you down beneath these rocks
And hold you as the day unfurls.'

"But Nunieve cried, 'Forbid such things!
Your world would tear this world of mine,
For up is down and legs are wings,
Sky is earth and earth is sky.
It is not love but hate that pines

Within the praises that you sing.
But I lie safe behind this line
Of water where you'll always lie.'

"The boy cried thus, 'You soon forget
That I your lifelong shadow be.
When night draws close, when sunlight sets,
I'll slip this liquid rim right through
As shadow-roaming-shadow me.
And in your womb, I'll quick beget
My shadow children—set them free
To bring me ever unto you.'

"But Nunieve answered, 'Shadow boy,
You never yet shall know my love,
For candlelight I shall employ
To keep you shadow, nothing more.
Ev'n at night, this world above
Can rest in all its steadfast joy,
For Nunieve's heart is fearless of
The shadow boy and shadow shore.'

"Indeed, that night, 'neath candlelight,
Nunieve slept soundly. Shadows stayed
Beneath her form and out of sight.
And when the morning sun awoke
O'er Halliel fair where Nunieve laid
Her head, the woods were warm and bright,
And creatures slept within the shade,
Forgetting words the shadow spoke.

"And so the days passed fair and warm
Until one night's capricious breeze
Blew from the lake a raging storm
That doused the candle's timid life,
And set the boy to roam with ease
Through Halliel fair in fiendish form.
He wreaked what ruin he would please,
And pierced Nunieve with shadow knife.

"Next day in Halliel, Nunieve woke
And mourned the death of bird and beast.
Remembering words her shadow spoke
She gazed into the turgid lake
And said, 'Oh, what a wretched feast
You've made of all my world's dear folk.
But you, unholy, wholly beast
Never more shall ever wake.'

"The shadow boy then said, 'I will,
For I'm immortal through your life.
Yes, there is nothing that can kill
Me while you live. And while the breeze
Blows, I will call you yet my wife.
For by your womb my children will
Be born, will tear their minds with strife.
But unlike me, you will love these.'

"The time did come when two were born,
The children of the night and day.
Her son Nunieve named Midithorn,
Her daughter Maldi of the Wood.
She loved them more than she could say,
But these small ones inside were torn
With warring natures to obey.
They could not hold to only good.

"Each night by candlelight she slept,
Each night she held her children there.
For them and for herself she wept,
And for their father's evil hate.
Come morning, she would stroke their hair
And think how shadows might be kept
From crawling from their darksome lair.
She plotted to escape her fate.

"When Midithorn had grown of age,
She charged him to his sister's care
And left her clothes upon the sage

That bordered on that mirror pool.
And Nunieve called her husband there,
'I've come here bearing mother's rage.'
She dived. He raped that mother fair.
She drowned herself, and drowned that fool.

"From Halliel passed that lady kind
Whose face could pale that of a flower.
Embracing death, she killed the mind
That filled the woodland with such dread.
But ever from that very hour
No peace can humans ever find.
For in us struggle two great powers,
Our comfort, great, good mother, is dead.

"In Halliel fair, beneath the trees,
Before the world had learned of hate,
There lived Nunieve, who from the seas
Had risen pure with eyes of gold
And walked the garden with a gait
Of love. Her heart could bend the trees,
It's told, but not the heavy fate
That 'tombed her deep in waters cold."

As the meistersinger's rich voice trailed off, the crowd
sighed and began to clap. The sound was like the slow
onset of summer rain—tentative, unwilling to disturb the
quiet that preceded it, and yet inevitable. When finally
the ovation reached its peak, the amphitheater roared
with applause.

Casimir now approached stage front. The silken
gloves were gone from his hands. His shoulders were
rounded. His shuffling steps belied the mocking smile of
his mask. The crowd hushed. Casimir slowly raised his
hands to sing. Only a rasping cry emerged. Then silence
fell. He lowered his hands and clutched his throat. Once
again, the rasping sound came. His hands dropped to
his sides.

A worried murmur rolled through the crowd. Casimir

slowly lifted the mask from his face and cast it to the ground. The granite stage received the wooden mask with a haunting rattle. The crowd gasped. A band of blood crossed Casimir's forehead. His eyes fumed black beneath his blood-caked brow. He fixed a killing gaze on Zhone Clieous and began to speak. His hoarse whisper sliced through the shocked silence.

"In a village much like this one, there lived a most wicked and stupid meistersinger. Through debauched deeds, he wronged every citizen in his fair lands. When his vile and lecherous hand soiled a beautiful gypsy girl, however, he earned the dreadful curse of the Vistana matriarch. It was a fitting curse, transforming him into a foul beast that feasted on the blood of innocents." Here Casimir's voice thinned and he began to cough. He caught his breath, peering toward Zhone Clieous, whose face was red with bottled fury. A wicked smile broke over Casimir's face, and he continued.

"His beautiful wife innocently loved him, despite his well-deserved curse. But the curse was undeserving when it fell on his first and only son. Upon the boy's birth, the meistersinger, foul beast that he was, told his loving wife to slay the child if he showed signs of the curse. His wife reluctantly agreed, but when she discovered that the son also bore the damnable mark, she loved him too much to kill him. Fearing for her son's life, she masked the boy's depravity and kept it from his father. But treachery and duplicity were so native to the meistersinger's heart that he couldn't trust his wife. He watched the child constantly, waiting for a sign.

"When the boy was but six, the meistersinger saw the sign. Too cowardly to kill the child himself, he sent a guard to slay the mother and child by fire in the nursery. The woman died, thrashing in flames before the eyes of her child, but not before exhorting her son to use his power to flee. And so, by virtue of the curse that had undone them, he escaped the flames." Casimir stopped again, not to cough this time but to let the full hatred in his gaze settle on Zhone Clieous. Slowly the meistersinger's expression changed from fury, to recognition, to horror.

"Long the boy spent living among the fleas and rats of an orphanage, plotting sweet revenge on his evil father. In time, he mastered the curse that plagued him, honed his dark powers, and set his plan in motion." The meistersinger had edged to the other side of the stage and motioned a troop of guardsmen to move quietly between the two of them. Casimir only smiled. "On a moon-bright midsummer's eve, much as this one, the boy returned to face his father and right these wrongs. On that night, he summoned the curse's power, slew the meistersinger, and freed the people from their twenty-year curse."

Casimir's voice trailed away to silence; it could clearly stand no more. Picking up the mask, he bowed grace-fully toward the audience. Only a reluctant smattering of bewildered applause greeted him. Not even Thoris clapped. Instead, he shivered as he studied the slim, silent form of his friend. The horror was suddenly plain.

Zhone Clieous was Casimir's father.

He had killed Casimir's mother by fire, but the child had escaped, and now Casimir had returned for revenge. Thoris gazed dumbfounded at the pair of them. Zhone Clieous stood fearfully behind a wall of guards as Casimir leered at him with bloodied lips.

A man in the third tier began to shout "Clieous! Clieous! Clieous! Clieous!" A handful of others joined him, and soon the whole stadium was chanting it.

All but Thoris.

Casimir bowed one last time toward the shouting audience, then slowly crossed the stage. The smile never left his lips as he reached the stairs and began his ascent. The chants of the throng grew louder, but Casimir didn't avert his eyes. Rather, he gazed upward, searching for Thoris.

SIX

"Don't be an idiot. Let me see your forehead!" Thoris demanded as he and Casimir wandered the slum street.

The raven-haired orphan halted in the center of the dried-mud road. Defiantly he set his hands on his hips. Moonlight glinted from his spreading smile, and his teeth glowed like pearls. "There—have another look at the wound, Nurse Thoris!"

Despite the darkness of the early morning, Thoris stood on tiptoe and squinted at the oozing gouges. "Would you recognize the man who did this?"

Casimir laughed, throwing his hands resignedly into the air. "First you become a nursemaid and now a guardsman! I've no interest in who did it, Thoris. I reserve my anger for Clieous." He turned from Thoris's examining fingers and set out again. Reluctantly Thoris followed.

Casimir cast a smile toward his sullen friend. "Did you see how furious Zhone Clieous was?"

Thoris didn't respond.

"Did you?" he reiterated.

Thoris looked up blankly. "Huh? Oh, yes, of course," he blurted. Once again he averted his eyes. "Everyone saw, Casimir. You frightened him. I doubt he's been that scared in twenty years. And you ran him a close second."

"I would have been first if he hadn't cheated," Casimir said. He sighed. "I'm not looking forward to changing back into my orphan clothes. These make me feel like a prince, but those—"

"Casimir," Thoris broke in. The sudden interruption quieted him immediately. "How much of that story you told was true?"

"Which story?"

"The one about Zhone Clieous killing his wife, and his son running away and becoming an, um, orphan and, ah . . ." Thoris stammered into silence. He nibbled his lower lip and appeared to collect his thoughts. Then he looked up with glistening eyes. "You say you hate the meistersinger because he killed your mother—I mean, made you an orphan. It sounds like—"

"Let's just say," Casimir countered, draping his arm over his friend's paunchy shoulders, "whether or not the story was true, it worked. You saw how angry it made Clieous."

"Yes," Thoris murmured, tugging on his lower lip. "So then, um, if the story *is* true, are you the son of Zhone Clieous?"

Casimir stopped in his tracks. "What do *you* think, Thoris?"

The younger boy's eyes were flecked with moonlight. "I think you might be."

"I am," Casimir said, his teeth gleaming darkly.

"You are?" Thoris's face went white with shock. "What is the curse that you spoke of?"

Casimir cannily eyed his friend. "Nothing to bother with."

"Tell me!" Thoris blurted, his brow furrowed with concern.

Beneath his coal-black hair, Casimir's forehead knotted. He studied Thoris's face and his eyes darkened. Then Casimir spoke. "A typical Vistana curse it was—to go dark-headed among a fair-haired folk—a curse that marks one as a lustful adulterer."

"That's it?" Thoris asked, incredulous. "But you said it caused him to eat babies or something like that."

"I exaggerated," Casimir answered with cold finality.

Thoris studied his friend's face a moment longer, then released Casimir's collar and vented a heavy sigh. "Good." He began to laugh, his voice suddenly playful. "I thought for a moment you were a werewolf."

A reluctant smile split Casimir's blanched face. He joined Thoris in laughter, chuckling dryly. "For a moment, I did, too."

Thoris's eyebrow cocked oddly, but he continued to laugh.

Casimir licked his cracked lips. "Look, we're almost home. Let's go."

The Red Porch poorhouse loomed ahead, the single structure in the slums that rose to a second story. Reaching the poorhouse, Casimir laced his fingers together and offered Thoris a boost to the thatched roof of Cook's wing. The pudgy boy accepted the help gratefully. He wriggled up to the straw-strewn roof, threaded his tottering way to its peak, and struggled through the window. Only then did Casimir follow, climbing the half-timber wall to reach the thatching. He paced to the peak of Cook's roof and, before passing through the window, gazed out over the wide city.

Casimir shook his head and sighed. His revenge was complete, but the world remained the same. He'd accomplished precisely nothing. He hadn't brought his mother back, nor lifted the curse from his shoulders. Tonight he wore brocade, but tomorrow he would wear rags. He felt more alone than ever.

"Casimir," Thoris whispered. "Come inside."

Casimir turned away from the darksome city and climbed through the window.

* * * * *

Hooded figures watched from an abandoned shanty as Sundered Heart slid through the window. The foremost man ran callused fingers along the splintery doorframe where they stood. He turned slowly to his companions. Their whispers barely carried beyond their thick-hooded cloaks. The second and third men nodded. Then, one by one, they emerged from the weathered shack. After a few paces, they each blended with fluid ease into the maze of shadows in the street.

*   *   *   *   *

Thoris and Casimir spent the next day in their cots. Despite the oppressive heat in the upstairs dormitory, Casimir slept like a dead man. Thoris wasn't as lucky. He tossed and turned, feeling sweat run down his temples and across his back. The noise of the slum street poured in through the window, and the heat of the sun made his heart pound in his head. He hardly slept at all. When the sun finally set and the air cooled, Thoris dropped immediately into sleep. Casimir, on the other hand, rose and began to pace.

"It was a fairly decent revenge, as revenges go, don't you think, Thoris?" he asked. "I might even have won the thing but for that gritty drink." Thoris offered no response except long, sonorous breaths. *Who am I trying to kid?* Casimir asked himself. *I want to kill my father, not just frighten him.*

He knelt down and slid the wooden box from beneath his cot. Wrenching the tattered shirt from his shoulders, he donned the silken one. Then, reverently, he lifted the brocaded doublet from the box. "My revenge isn't complete," he murmured. He donned the coat and cannons. A smile crossed his lips as he remembered Julianna's soft hand on those hose. He knelt anxiously beside Thoris's bed and shook him.

"Wake up, Thoris. Tonight we celebrate my victory." The whispered words felt stale in his mouth.

Thoris's sleepy eyes opened slowly.

"Come on, Thoris. Harmonia beckons. Let me teach you the wonders of *meekulbrau!*" Casimir hissed.

The boy fixed Casimir with a withering gaze. "Go away."

Casimir flung Thoris's sheet back and began to pull

the boy from the cot. "Come, or I'll throw myself from South Hill."

With a savage yank, Thoris slipped from Casimir's grasp and wrapped himself in his sheet. "Say hello to Valsarik for me."

Standing straight-backed with hands on his hips, Casimir studied his slumbering friend. "I suppose you need the sleep," he said flatly.

With that, Casimir slipped through the window and out into the night. He dropped noiselessly to the ground below. Glad now that Thoris was too tired to join him, Casimir darted along the shadows and raced from the slum.

*　*　*　*　*　*

Beside the slum road, within a leaning pile of wood that even vagrants wouldn't call home, the hooded figures had returned. Moonlight passed through the hovel's rickety frame, falling in knifelike triangles across the floor. At the shanty's center hovered the cowled figures. Their breathing came long and labored.

One cleared his throat. "You sure you saw 'em go in?"

Both of the others nodded. One spoke, "Yes, Kavik. Every light's been out for at least an hour, and none've gone in or out since. They're asleep."

"Good," Kavik responded simply. He stooped in the corner of the shack and raised a burlap sack to his shoulder. The others did the same. Kavik spoke again, his voice little more than a growl, "Wedges 'neath the doors what swings out, ropes on 'em what swings in. If a window's got shutters, tie 'em off; if it don't, be waitin' for any of 'em to scamper out. Don't bother with 'em what ain't Sundered Heart, but if it is 'im, slit his throat. Use the special daggers if you need to, but don't let 'im get out.

"Use the oil on anythin' wood, not on thatch. It's doors, then windows, then oil, then torches. Don't worry if they rattle the doors before the place is flamin'. Nobody'll come help."

*   *   *   *   *

Although he was dressed like a courtier, Casimir felt like a pauper as he trudged the cobbled highroad. The waning moon hadn't yet risen over the city, and Casimir's spirits felt equally low. Sighing, he kicked a loose stone. It skidded across the time-smoothed street and clattered into the distance. A lackluster celebration at best.

"So that's the purpose of *meekulbrau* and music," Casimir mused aloud, "to force festivity on unfestive hearts."

Sullenly he halted in the street. "*Meekulbrau.*" He thought for a moment of blood and felt the tingle begin between his shoulderblades. It spread deliciously through him. He wouldn't give over to it entirely, only enough to heighten his senses. He sniffed the pollen-heavy air, sifting out the heady scent of the distant heath. He wanted *meekulbrau*, not heather. But the air in his nostrils smelled more of summer than of liquor. Three more sniffs and he gave up. His shoulders slumped. Perhaps he should head back to the poorhouse.

As he turned to go, a faint sound came to him on the wind. Listening more closely, he made out notes of festive music. A smile broke across his face. "A celebration . . . surely they would welcome the bard who placed second in the meistersinger contest." He turned to gauge the song's source, then set out toward it.

As he passed down the night-veiled lanes, the music grew louder. The intertwining melodies became mixed with sounds of laughter and conversation. "I'm glad I dressed decently," he said to himself as he passed rows of shuttered houses. The sound was very near now, just beyond a small estate to the right. A few paces later, he rounded the corner and caught sight of the festival house.

His heart sank.

It was Harmonic Hall, the bastion of Zhone Clieous and all his bards-to-be. The building's stately walls of limestone rose above billowy rhododendrons that fronted the lot. Ivy climbed the walls, rising past the second story to clutch at the gently sloped roof above. Around the roof stood castlelike spires that seemed to support the starry heavens. At the roof's center sat a belfry, which harbored the melancholy bell that tolled the hours.

A flash of whirling dresses in the windows below shifted Casimir's attention from the bell. The windows spilled golden light into the darkness. Through them, Casimir glimpsed bright dresses and tailored coats. He smiled grimly. "Well, I suppose I'm not welcome here. This is Clieous's celebration, not mine."

Just then Julianna appeared at the window. An elegant dress of deep ruby hung from her lovely shoulders. Her black hair shone upon a lacy gorget. Across her ivory brow draped a golden-chained *ferronniere* with a ruby amulet. Casimir's eyes grew wide and his mouth dropped slowly open. He could have happily stood in the street all night gazing at her. That would have been celebration enough. He would have been happy, that is, but for the blond-haired youth who stood beside her, basking in her dazzling smile.

The guards clustered in front of the Hall noticed Casimir. With practiced nonchalance, they wandered back to their posts at the building's four corners. Casimir smiled. I could easily get past these dull-witted dolts, he thought. He paced confidently toward the front door. The impeccably suited guard there, who a moment before had been joking with colleagues, wore a solemn expression.

"Your name, please, sir?"

"Sundered Heart," Casimir replied distractedly as he peered toward the window.

The man skimmed the scroll he held, then droned, "This party is for Harmonic Hall members only, Master Heart."

Casimir's eyes settled on the man. He smiled impressively. "How silly of me. Clieous has me down as Gaston Olyava."

The guard primly rolled up the scroll and said, "Master Heart, you should leave this place with no further incident." He emphasized the statement by nodding toward the street.

Casimir turned without comment and stalked off. He walked in the precise direction the guard had indicated. Without casting a backward glance, he knew the guards were gathering again in front of the main entry. As he rounded the street corner and slipped from sight, their muffled laughter broke the stillness.

Edging a modest estate that stood beside Harmonic Hall, Casimir allowed himself a toothy grin. These guards were indeed useless. He circled the estate, reaching its back corner. Once there, he peered toward the rear of Harmonic Hall. A series of glass-paneled doors opened out onto a broad balcony, which overlooked a garden. Banks of flowering brush circled the garden in tidy rows, and flower beds striped the ground between.

The garden was unguarded, just as Casimir had expected. He moved forward through the shadows, using the natural cover of the shrubs. After slogging through muddy flower beds, he crept to a point beneath one of the glowing windows. A few feet away, a vine-laden trellis rose to the broad balcony. Casimir eased himself onto the trellis and climbed it. In moments, his eyes were even with the windowsill.

Hiding himself in the thick ivy on the wall, Casimir gazed through the window, waiting for a glimpse of Julianna. Many people came to the window, revealing faces to the dark night that they would never show to their fellow revelers, but not Julianna. The moon had cleared the treetops long before she happened by the window.

As fate would have it, she stood alone, watching the dancers float about the room. A smile hung half-forgotten on her lips. Her eyes held a faraway look. Casimir secured a handhold among the thick-veined ivy. Leaning cautiously toward the window, he rapped on the pane and raised his face into the light. Julianna turned, more from reflex than curiosity. Peering out, she gave a small start. Her delicate hand dropped the flower she held and fanned perfectly across her chest. Casimir motioned her toward the balcony door. Her brow creased, and she peered warily to each side. Then a gleam entered her eyes, and before moving from the window, she winked at him.

A grin split Casimir's face. He nimbly descended the trellis and plucked a full-blossomed rose. Bearing the beautiful flower, he climbed again. The latch on the balcony's central door clicked quietly in the night. The door swung open, spilling music and light across the stone balcony. Julianna slipped through the door, her billowing dress ruffling on the frame as she passed. Then she closed the door behind her.

"Julianna . . . over here!" Casimir hissed.

Her head turned toward him and, smiling, she stepped in his direction. Hearing a guard approach from the front of the building, Casimir ducked into the ivy.

"Is everything all right?" the guard asked.

Startled by the voice, Julianna gasped, "Just out for a breath of air."

A smile grew on the guard's aged face. "You needn't fear beasts, dear lady. I've been a guardsman for thirty-three years, and—"

"Oh, I don't fear beasts," Julianna broke in. "And if they would want me, I'm sure you couldn't stop them."

The man's face went slack, but he held his ground.

"Good guardsman, let me be alone, please," she said.

The man bowed twice and slinked away behind the hall.

Casimir emerged from the ivy, climbed smoothly over the balcony's rail, and, without a word, presented the rose. Julianna's delicate hand extended in reflex. "Why did you come here? You must be insane. My uncle . . . ouch!" Her fingers had fastened for a moment on the stem, then let the crimson bud flutter to the ground.

Casimir gently took her hand and turned it over. A drop of blood had formed—a beautiful, scarlet ball—on her fingertip. With natural grace, Casimir lifted her hand and kissed the spot. The blood spread red across his lips. He turned her palm down and kissed the back of her hand. She smiled warmly.

"I've come tonight," he said, "because your face is the loveliest in Harmonia."

She blushed and pulled back her hand. "Flatter all you like, but if you're caught, my uncle will have you flogged to death."

"Whose death . . . his or mine?" asked Casimir, smiling. "Oh, Julianna, why do you dance in there to celebrate his victory when you can dance out here to celebrate mine! Come with me tonight!"

Her voice was both indignant and regretful. "I can't leave here with you. You'd be hunted down within the hour and your head put on a pikestaff."

Casimir feigned incredulity. "If you'll not leave with me, I'll stay here until I am caught and slain. Either way, my life is at its end. Don't deny me your company in this last hour of my life."

She retrieved the rose and flipped its blossom in his face. "You aren't safe here!"

"Neither are you," Casimir countered. "I've watched through this window and seen numerous wolves."

"They are gentlemen."

"They are fools."

"I am not going with you," she said flatly, turning away.

"Then you care nothing for me?" Casimir asked.

"Of course I care for—"

"And you aren't in the least sorry that your uncle stole my voice last night?" Casimir pursued.

"Hold your tongue and you'll hear how sorry I—"

"Come with me!" Casimir implored.

"You know I cannot," she said sadly. "If I were but—"

Her words were cut off by the sudden swell of music in the garden. The door had opened behind her, and a trim gentleman stood gaping into the dark. "Why, there you are, Julianna. Won't you come inside?"

Casimir leapt nimbly over the balcony rail and clung to the vines above the trellises. She answered smoothly, "One moment, Gaston."

The silhouette stepped forward. "Are you ill, my dear?"

"No," she said. "Please go back inside. I'll join you shortly."

Reaching through the railing, Casimir tugged on her lacy dress. "Come with me!"

Gaston called out, "I'll wait here for you."

Julianna shot a glance toward Casimir and hissed, "I can't!"

Still at the door, Gaston asked, "Did you say something, Julianna, or do my ears play tricks?"

Casimir whispered, "Tell me you love me and I'll go."

"It's only your ears, Gaston!" Julianna called, irritated. Her voice dropped to a whisper. "I do love you, Sundered Heart."

Casimir was stunned. Then, before his incredulous eyes, the rose fell to the ground again. He looked up, and Julianna knelt down beside the rail. Her lips pressed full on his as her hand fastened on the rose.

"Is something wrong?" Gaston asked, marching forward.

Julianna stood up and lifted the rose. She spun about to face Gaston. Casimir huddled, as still and breathless as a corpse, behind the rail. Julianna slid her arm into Gaston's. Quietly she led him back toward the door.

"Where did you get that rose?" Gaston asked in amazement.

She laughed musically. "There *is* a garden out there."

"But what happened to the flower I gave you?" Gaston asked dramatically. He closed the door behind him.

Slowly Casimir rose. He touched his tingling lips. His mouth dropped open, a disbelieving smile pulling at its corners. He slid along the rail to the balcony's edge. Through the window, he spotted Julianna. She stood there in scarlet splendor, pretending to talk with Gaston. Every few moments, though, her eyes darted to the window and her smile widened.

This was cause for celebration.

With sudden abandon, Casimir leapt to the ivy-covered wall and began to climb. His fingers and toes sought out holds—on the vines, in the recesses between stones, on the edges of moldings. A new toehold, another pull, a higher purchase . . . clawing and clambering, he ascended the wall. The familiar ache of frenzy had entered his muscles. It stung, it burned luxuriantly. In moments, he had gained the second story of the hall. He scrambled onto a turret that jutted from the dark upper floor. Then he scaled to the shallow-sloped roof above. He climbed onto the tile and kicked off his long-toed shoes.

Releasing a laugh, he ran across the broad rooftop to the belfry perched at its center. His hands clutched the wooden rail of the belfry, and he vaulted into it. There hung the great iron bell. Stripping off his doublet and shirt, he sat back on the rail and set his feet on the bell. With a rail-cracking heave, Casimir's feet swung the cold iron. Before the broad clapper even struck, the rail split beneath him, and he fell, laughing, onto the shallow roof.

DROOoommm . . . loom-DROOoommmm . . . loom-DROOoommm . . .

The bell's baleful tone contrasted starkly to Casimir's mad outburst. From below, he heard the sound of latches clicking open. Then music flooded the night. The guards began to scurry and shout. Voices rang out from the crowd.

Casimir merely laughed. "This is better than music or *meekulbrau*," he shouted. "This is immortality!"

He howled at the star-brilliant heavens, the manicured gardens, the far-flung clutter of Harmonia. He shrieked, oblivious to the guards and guests shouting from the garden below. In time, the bell's tolling quieted. His stomach was knotted with giggles as he ambled stiffly toward the belfry.

Only then did he scent the smoke.

Turning his nose toward the smell, he glimpsed a distant fire. The leer on his face slowly eased as his eyes traced out the fire-engulfed building. It lay in the center of the slums, the only two-story structure in that quarter.

Casimir's heart shifted uneasily. His eyes wouldn't move from the blazing spot. The laughter had fled his lips. A solitary word escaped his mouth.

"Thoris!"

A tingling ache spread through his muscles. Casimir consciously deepened the pain, forcing it to the tips of his fingers and the ends of his feet. Bones grew ember-hot. Muscles shifted beneath his skin. Jagged teeth clamped together, forcing down a scream that rose from every tissue. His flesh was boiling. The front of his face lengthened and darkened into a muzzle. His silvery eyes began to glow red as he studied the rooftop. Toenails caught a firm grip on the thick-laid tile. Then, with a blood-chilling wail, Casimir charged the roof's edge.

The celebrants below—those who hadn't retreated when they heard the unearthly cry—now fell back with horrified gasps. For a moment, the moon went black, eclipsed by the shrieking shadow. Gaston cowered behind Julianna, who had swooned into his arms. The whole sky seemed filled with the wolf. Its moon-shadow moved with evil speed over the crowd. Then, with horrifying suddenness, the black sky again became a field of blooming stars.

*   *   *   *   *

Winds rushed down the abandoned slum streets, drawing leaves toward the inferno . . . toward the Red Porch. It burned like a second sun. Despite the spectacle of it, the poor folk remained in their hovels. They feared the robed men who had set the blaze, the men who now moved with malice among those who had escaped. Only twelve orphans—the inhabitants of one wing—had gotten out alive. Those twelve now stood before the holocaust, soot-blackened and shivering, covered with burns and cold sweat. The cowled men inspected them, seizing a child by his chin, tipping his head back, and gaping into his fearful eyes.

"It's not him, Kavik," one man growled into a boy's burnt face.

"Not any of 'em," barked Kavik with certainty. He turned toward the blaze, the sweat illumined on his stubbled face. "Looks like 'im an' 'is little chum died in the fire."

The other man, shorter than his companion by several inches, turned his back on the children and sidled up to his comrade. "Where's Meslik?"

"On the other side, makin' sure no one else 'scapes," Kavik droned over the roar of the flames.

The shorter man ventured, "This might be kinda late to ask, but, ah, what good is fire against him? I mean if it's true he's—"

"If 'e never woke up, what's the difference?"

"But what if he *did* wake up?"

"Don't be an ass," Kavik snapped. "That bus'ness about silver an' magic blades don't mean nothin' next to total destruction."

"What are you talking about?" the shorter man asked.

The stubbled face split into a mocking smile. "You think if you dropped a mountain on 'im 'e'd still come after you? Think for a second! They just seem like you can't hurt 'em cause 'e heals so fast. But if you trap 'im in an oven, like we done here, and make 'im get hurt continuous, 'e gets hurt faster than 'e can heal. If 'e wasn't trapped in there, that'd be different, but since 'e is . . . " Kavik didn't finish the thought. He scratched his chin and added, " 'Sides, they gots to breathe to live, and there ain't nothin' but smoke to breathe in there."

The shorter man shot a glance behind him. His expression soured. The children were gone. Solemnly he tapped Kavik on the shoulder and motioned with his thumb.

"Let 'em go. They're not the ones we care about. Anyways, who they gonna tell?"

The shorter man nodded and smiled.

He was turning back around when the thing hit him. His joints pulled apart and blood gushed through his nose. The world was suddenly flipping over. The edges of buildings stretched into broad circles. He saw the fire and he knew he was tumbling toward it. The ground spun overhead for a moment, then crashed down on him with the weight of the world behind it.

He felt his bones shatter like glass.

His limbs lay in an odd pile beneath him. He tried to get up, but his body wouldn't move. It formed a jagged, uneven pillow beneath his head.

Red teeth and black jowls . . . fiery eyes and streaming gums . . . Had he lived a moment more, he might have ascribed a name to his slayer. But the claws sunk home.

Oblivion.

The beast rose from the still form. Despite its towering height, it looked almost spidery. Sinewy arms and legs hung at odd angles from its hunched body. Coarse hair sprouted everywhere. Its head was canine, taut with muscles and bristling teeth. The beast's eyes glowed in its massive head. Its body was more manlike, with knobby hands and fingers tipped with wicked claws.

Kavik staggered backward, the cowl falling from his terror-stricken face. He wanted to run, but the beast's eyes held him in place. The creature bounded forward, its rancid breath billowing over him. Stumbling back toward the fire, Kavik remembered the dagger at his waist. Fumbling in his robes, he produced it—smooth and shiny, red with the inferno.

"Back, beast-man!" the man croaked. "This blade is silver!"

The creature appeared to smile. Then it spoke, its voice raspy and seething. "*Where is he?*"

The blood rushed from Kavik's face. If it could speak, it could think. He kept the blade well before him. "Where is who?"

"Where is my friend?" the creature roared, its breath

as hot as the fire behind it.

"He's safe. He got out. We let him go."

"Liar!" the creature bellowed.

It sprang forward, wrapping a clawed hand about Kavik's belt. Kavik brought the silver blade down. It glanced off the creature's arm. With a howl of rage, the beast hefted the burly man into the air, held him aloft with one arm, and hurled him, writhing, into the blaze. The inferno hungrily swallowed Kavik. He thrashed for a moment, mantled in flame, then lay still.

"Thoris!"

Gathering his strength, Casimir bounded atop the flaming shell of Cook's wing. The thatch had burned away, leaving only flaming rafters and beams. The fire seared his feet, and the hair all across his body curled into acrid knots. Another leap brought him through the dormitory window. Much of the floor had burned through or crumbled away, but the section below the window still stood. The room was blistering. In the wreck of bodies and embers inside, Casimir found Thoris, facedown and motionless beside the window. A pile of debris lay atop him, sheltering him from the flames.

But he wasn't breathing.

Casimir lifted the lifeless form, careful not to cut the boy's arm with his claws. Thoris seemed boneless, save that in one hand, he clutched the charred mask of Sundered Heart, and in the other, the wooden sword Casimir had given him years before. Casimir pressed the pallid body against him and leapt through the blazing window. They careened into the sizzling night air. Casimir twisted to land feetfirst on the fire-laced main beam below the window. His feet struck the red-hot embers atop the beam. Flesh fried instantly to the wood. He bundled his muscles to spring clear, but the timber cracked beneath his feet. He plummeted onto the kitchen floor, showered by sparks and coals.

Landing on the charred rubble of a table, Casimir leapt through the room. He rushed the flame-licked door and, with a cry of pain, rammed the portal. The wedge beneath the door held, but the frame didn't. Fiery splinters of wood swarmed into the night. An orphan on the street screamed as the charred beast emerged. It was like a nightmare: gaunt, powerful, reeking of smoke and singed flesh, with teeth of black and yellow and red. A gray-faced youth was cradled to the monster's side.

Then suddenly it was gone.

* * * * *

Thoris awoke, feeling both hot and cold at the same time. His legs felt cast in lead—cold and numb and immovable. His arms and back, however, blazed with heat. Breathing came with difficulty; his lungs felt full of sand. Every muscle in his body cried out.

Against the starry sky above him, Thoris could just barely make out the face of Casimir. An undulating light shone on his blistered features, and his eyes were wide with concern. He wore a strange frock that wasn't his.

A chaos of memories flashed through Thoris's mind, but he pushed them aside and struggled to sit up. Casimir helped him, and only then did Thoris hear the lapping sounds of water.

"Where . . . where are we?" he choked out through parched lips.

"Beside the river, good Thoris," Casimir said, his voice rough. "Or I should say, you are half in the river. The burns don't seem too deep. How do you feel?"

"I don't," Thoris replied with a sad smile. He drew a shallow breath. "Casimir, what happened?"

Although he spoke quietly, Casimir's voice was filled with fury. "Zhone Clieous happened. He was offended by my revenge."

Thoris looked away and moaned softly. "I remember the fire. . . ."

"The Red Porch is destroyed. Only a few escaped."

Coughing deeply, Thoris said, "He's a monster."

"Yes, a monster indeed. My revenge has failed," Casimir said coldly.

Thoris took a number of short, strained breaths. His raspy voice came with deadly calm. "No. Your revenge isn't complete yet, Casimir. You must bring him down."

Casimir fell back on scratched palms. "What?"

"I have a plan, Casimir," Thoris rasped.

Casimir shook his head grimly. "A plan will do us little good, Thoris. We must rest and heal."

"There's a large abandoned building just outside the slums. We can rest there."

SEVEN

The doors of the abandoned temple towered above Casimir and the motley assortment of orphans. He shot a dubious glance at Thoris, whom he half-dragged, half-carried. "Do you really think we should go in there?" The burn-covered boy merely nodded. Casimir took a deep breath and tried the latch. The hinges creaked open. Fetid air billowed from the passage beyond. Casimir stepped into the archway and motioned his wards inside.

It was a ragged bunch. Minor burns and cuts covered their faces and bodies. None of them had slept, and their worry-wrung eyes showed it. Casimir sighed as he surveyed them. Thoris had asked him to gather the children from the flea-infested shacks where they hid. He had said they were part of his plan. Casimir was already doubting this plan. The tattered mob wandered reluctantly through the archway into a cavelike narthex. As the orphans' shuffling feet whispered to a halt, Casimir closed the creaking door behind them.

Beyond the narthex stood a chamber filled with a murky glow. From the chamber drifted a high, lilting melody. The sound was thin and smooth. Quieting the orphans, Casimir listened. "A flute," he whispered. The instrument sobbed soberly like a mourning dove. Following the sound, Casimir stalked through the narthex and set his hand on the embossed stone doorway at the other end. He stared through it into the echoing nave beyond.

The nave was a cavernous, circular room ringed by stout pillars. Above it hovered an ornately ribbed vault. The ceiling of the vault was lost in darkness. At the chamber's center, a sprawling, cobweb-strewn organ lay like the skeleton of some mythical beast. Decaying seats perched on the concentric tiers that rose above the silent instrument.

Still the song came.

"The music isn't coming from the organ," Casimir thought aloud. "The sound echoes through this room from the passages beyond."

He moved forward, carrying Thoris and motioning for the ragtag orphans to follow cautiously. Casimir led them through the pillar-lined passage that circled the nave, his ear cocked toward the haunting song. He studied the dusty floor, noting where footprints had worn a path clean. Following the path, Casimir led the straggling band around the curving edge of the sanctuary to an arched doorway beyond.

Passing through the doorway, they left the nave and entered a small chapel that seemed to be of later design. The air within smelled of old books and oiled wood rather than musty decay. The chapel reminded Casimir of an autumnal glade. Slender columns of black marble rose to the roof, where they sprouted into elegant branches. Tall lancets of stained glass allowed warm sunlight to cascade into the room. Dark bookcases lined the walls, here and there supporting a rack of musical instruments. Benches stood in neat rows along the floor.

Then Casimir saw the flautist. He had ceased playing, and slouched silently beneath the glowing windows. Staring with apparent suspicion, he clutched the red collar of his gold-embroidered vestments and scratched the thin gold netting over his white hair. Then, setting the end of his flute on the stone floor, he leaned on it like a cane.

"No services today," he said.

"My good sir," Casimir began, affecting a diplomatic tone, "these poor orphans lost their home and friends last night, and some are in danger of losing their lives from their grievous burns."

"Milil is not a god of healing, boy," the man croaked.

"True enough. Milil is a god of song. And what better salve to the aching heart is there than song?" Casimir asked. Thoris, despite his pain, smiled appreciatively.

"In these dark days, Milil's church is peopled with ghosts," said the man bitterly. "The organ is ruined by neglect, the sanctuary fallen to rubble, and I can count the faithful on one hand. I haven't the means to care for you."

"How can Milil turn away from these children—from these young voices that might sing for him?"

The priest rose, carefully laying the flute on the floor. He tottered toward the children, spreading his arms hopelessly. "If Milil can forsake his priest," he murmured darkly, "he can forsake you."

Casimir bit his lip and stood silent for a moment. The priest reached one of the children and began examining his burns. He shook his head sadly and moved on to the next. "You shall have to return the way you came."

Casimir cast a glance toward the ruined sanctuary. "Has Milil forsaken Harmonia, the land of song?"

The priest's brow raised, drawing back folds of flesh. "This is no land of song, lad. Here men use songs like swords, to kill, to maim. They care nothing for Milil's truth, his beauty. They want only his power. So Milil abandoned Harmonia." He opened his withered hand as though scattering dust.

"Good master, look at these burned and blistered faces," Casimir implored.

The priest dropped his hands from the orphan he was examining. He fixed Casimir with a cold stare before he turned and plodded away.

Casimir set Thoris on one of the benches, then followed the priest, dropping to his knees behind the old man. "Let us stay, master. Let us bind our wounds. Teach us of beauty and truth, and you will have your sanctuary back."

"How can orphans bring back my sanctuary?" the man snorted.

"Milil may forsake us," Casimir said, "but will you?"

"What obligation do I owe you?"

"You're a good man, master," Casimir said, "or once were. Why should I pile up reasons for you to do what your heart tells you is right?"

The man muttered to himself and shook his head. He turned around slowly, his eyes fixing on the children, and sighed shallowly. At last he motioned with one hand toward the benches. "Those of you who are hobbled, please take a seat. The rest of you, come with me to fetch water and linens."

Casimir bowed low. "Your congregation has just trebled, Master . . . ?"

"Gustav," the man replied as he headed toward the hall. Casimir followed close behind, a queue of orphans forming in his wake. Gustav continued, "I cannot offer you new clothes. I have only my vestments and those of the choir."

"How long has it been since you had a children's choir, Master Gustav?" Casimir asked with coy interest.

Passing beneath the arch, the man snorted. "You think this bundle of bantlings have suitable voices?"

"Their voices may well bring back Milil."

"More likely they'll summon fiends from hell."

*   *   *   *   *

The week passed slowly. While the orphans were recovering, Gustav taught them stories and songs of Milil. Of the twelve, only three had natural singing voices, though seven others could distinguish pitches. The last two were tone-deaf, and Gustav told them so. But even they received choir robes to wear, robes they hiked up around their waists to keep from tripping.

Of all the voices Gustav heard, Casimir's was by far his favorite. While the others rested and healed, Casimir spent hours in song. He didn't mind humoring the old priest, for the chapel echoed his voice like no other place—not even the amphitheater.

Between choir practices, Casimir tended to Thoris. His friend's burns were painful but not serious. "You're lucky you were shielded by that rubble," Casimir said, "otherwise you'd've been ash by now." Thoris only smiled in response, then turned over to fall asleep again. After the fourth day, he began to walk, and after the sixth, his pain gradually subsided. All the while, though, he plotted and planned their mutual revenge.

Thoris's scheme quickly grew from simplicity to elaboration. At first, it involved only Casimir and a few others, but in the end, all the orphans were enlisted. Thoris and Casimir repeatedly gathered the burnt children together to rehearse the plan. By week's end, the plot seemed flawless. Still, Casimir had doubts.

"But will it work, Thoris?" he asked, pulling him aside.

"Of course. None of them have missed a cue."

"No . . . I don't mean that," Casimir replied. "I mean, will it do all we hope it will?"

"It will topple Clieous from power. It will make him despised and hunted," Thoris said with conviction. "What more is there?"

"Yes," Casimir mused aloud, "what more?"

At last the time arrived to enact Thoris's plan, the night of Clieous's first Primae Consularae, a public forum to be held at the amphitheater. The sun hovered low on the horizon as Casimir and the robed orphans stole silently from Milil's temple.

*   *   *   *   *

Clieous's deep baritone voice lingered in the amphitheater long moments after his song was finished. The crowd responded with respectful applause. Clieous smiled and bowed low. As the applause died, Clieous straightened and cleared his throat.

"Welcome tonight to this first city meeting of my twentieth year as meistersinger." More applause rang out. Clieous's rodentlike nose dipped as his smile broadened. "As always, all citizens of Harmonia are welcome to these meetings free of charge. Afterward, for this week's performance, students of Harmonic Hall will circulate among the rows and collect donations."

The smile on Clieous's lips faltered as he spotted the robed figures sprinkled throughout the crowd. They looked like members of a children's choir. A muscle in his cheek spasmed nervously. "Tonight's performance should be truly a pleasure," Zhone Clieous continued. "Harkon Lukas has brought with him from Skald a talented troupe of bards, acrobats, and actors." Clieous eyed the children suspiciously. "Let us keep the meeting short so that our friends from Skald may begin before they drink all the Crystal Club's wine!"

Laughter rippled through the auditorium, and Clieous relaxed slightly. As the chuckles subsided, he raised his arms.

"Has anyone an item for discussion?" he asked with thinly veiled disinterest.

A voice called out from the crowd. "Tell us what happened at the Red Porch."

Clieous squinted, trying to make out the speaker. No one in the crowd acknowledged the statement. He shook his head and clucked loudly. "A great tragedy indeed. I am told not a single creature survived the blaze that razed the building. Already my officers search for another site where we can locate a new poorhouse. A tragedy indeed. But let us not dwell on despair. Because of the fire, undeniably a horrible disaster, many miserable folk escaped their impossible burdens. In the midst of our sorrow for their loss, Harmonia can be glad these citizens found rest. And we, in the aftermath, are a city whose walls are untroubled by the helpless cries of the destitute."

Clieous scanned the crowd for another question. An anonymous voice shouted, "Who set the fire?"

The meistersinger bristled for a moment, then flashed his most winning smile. "My officers are investigating the affair. If anyone set the fire deliberately, he will be found out."

"I saw three men run from the burning building."

Clieous's eyes darted through the stands and settled on one of the robed figures, a mere boy. A toothy smile stretched across the meistersinger's features. "Your testimony will prove helpful to my officers. After the meeting, the stage guards will bring you to me." His eyes were intense as he spoke the words. "Any other concerns?"

"Was Sundered Heart killed in the blaze?"

Irritated, Clieous shook his head. "Stand and identify yourself if you have a question!"

One of the robed figures stood.

Clieous staggered backward.

The young man wore the leering mask of Sundered Heart, and he was moving forward.

"I am Sundered Heart," came the unmistakable voice. "My death, you see, was greatly exaggerated."

The people's eyes turned to follow the young man. Murmurs of surprise swept in waves throughout the assemblage. Clieous stood like a fencepost on the stage as Casimir descended the stairs with stately confidence. "I hadn't had a chance to congratulate you, dear Clieous, on your amazing victory in the meistersinger competition."

Zhone's face blanched and his eyes grew wide as Casimir reached the stage. "I'm glad you're here to prove the rumors false. Some had falsely suspected me of wishing you dead."

"I should apologize, Meistersinger Clieous," Casimir said as he gained the stage, "for I was among the people who thought so." The crowd laughed nervously.

Stripping off his mask, Casimir strode to the meistersinger. He dropped the mask, letting it clatter to the stone stage. Then, flinging his arms wide, he wrapped Clieous in a bear hug and kissed him once on each cheek. With the second kiss, Casimir bit lightly into the meistersinger's cheek. Clieous tried to push away, but

Casimir's arms remained clamped around him like iron bands.

"Hello, Father," he whispered. "To celebrate our reunion, I plan to kill you tonight, as I have dreamt of doing for a thousand nights."

The crowd began to applaud nervously. Casimir released the meistersinger, but fastened a viselike grip on one of his hands. Zhone Clieous smiled uneasily as he faced the crowd, his free hand cradling the side of his face. Casimir bowed, pulling his father into a bow also. The halfhearted applause now swelled to a full ovation, and Casimir flashed a smile at the meistersinger.

"Your death has begun," he said quietly.

"Guards, please remove him!" Clieous shouted.

Casimir grinned disarmingly and waved them off. "Please, good guards. I plan to honor our ruler, not injure him." Pulling his captive to the front of the stage, Casimir shouted flamboyantly, "As prelude to this evening's performance, might I honor our meistersinger with my own performance?"

The applause rose to a roar that drowned out Clieous's protests. Bowing once more, Casimir motioned toward the audience. Twelve robed figures rose from their seats and scurried toward the stage. The meistersinger, visibly rattled, pulled free from his son's grasp. Casimir made a game of it, leaping after Clieous and grappling him around the waist.

"He's so humble," Casimir shouted gleefully. The crowd laughed. "But he won't get away that easily! Shouldn't Master Clieous participate in his own tribute?"

Bawdy hoots and more applause answered Casimir's question.

"Guards, order him to release me!" repeated Clieous.

"Guards, order Zhone Clieous to enjoy himself," Casimir cried mirthfully, "unless you would let him ruin this tribute!"

The guards smiled mutinously at their master and remained at their posts. Meanwhile, the audience laughed as the robed forms tripped their way down to the stage. Reaching the stage, they shed their robes. Gasps filled the amphitheater as the sooty, ragged children were revealed.

They walked to the center of the stage and lay down in four neat rows. As the orphans settled, Casimir dragged the struggling meistersinger offstage. Nervous laughter accompanied their exit.

"He's so eager!" Casimir shouted.

The audience hushed as the tribute began. One of the children lying on the stage cried out, "Oh, how lonely it is to be an orphan in Harmonia!"

Another crowed, "Yes, and on such a fearfully dark night!"

"And on one so cold!" shouted Thoris, who lay near the back corner of the stage.

Casimir strode into the lantern light, pushing the meistersinger before him like a huge puppet. "Hello, young orphans!"

"Hello, Meistersinger Clieous!" the children chimed.

"You said you were lonely?" Casimir asked.

A child called out, "Very lonely!"

"You said you were afraid of the dark?"

A heavily bandaged girl answered, "Quite afraid!"

"You said you were cold?"

All the children shouted, "Most cold, most cold!"

"Then allow me to help you, children," Casimir cried out, forcing Clieous into a grossly exaggerated bow.

"How will you help us, Meistersinger Zhone Clieous?" came the raucous response.

"By giving you something!"

"What do you have for us?"

"Something to make you less lonely!"

"What?"

"Something to make you less fearful!"

"*What?*"

"Something to make you less cold!"

"WHAT? WHAT? WHAT DO YOU HAVE FOR US?!"

Casimir pulled the meistersinger over to the children and lifted him from his feet. Zhone Clieous hovered over the orphans, kicking helplessly. "I've brought you *fire!*"

The orphans began writhing about on the stage, their voices screaming shrilly. The meistersinger's protests were lost in the gale of feigned agony.

But the guards read his lips.

As the guards rushed the stage, their steel-tipped boots thundering, the crowd gasped with horror and leapt to their feet. The guards converged on Casimir, and the audience flowed out onto the stairs. Casimir produced a dagger from his robe and held it over the meistersinger's heaving chest.

"Come no farther, or this dagger sinks home!" The guards continued their advance. Casimir set the dagger's tip between his father's ribs and let the steel tooth bite lightly through his silken shirt. Crimson liquid curled onto the blade.

"Back, you idiots!" The meistersinger shouted, his face streaming with sweat. "Can't you see he's mad enough to do it?"

The guards fell back, leaving their swords unsheathed. The crowd hesitated in the stands. The other orphans had sat up in shock. Some even crawled fearfully toward the edge of the stage. Thoris's face had gone white.

Casimir withdrew the knife, allowing the meistersinger's tunic to close over the wound. His temples pounded furiously as he gazed out at the hostile crowd. "For those of you unskilled in theatrics, our little play was performed to illustrate the murder of the Red Porch poor and orphaned!" Casimir pushed the meistersinger to center stage and held him just behind a blazing lantern. "And here is your murderer . . . Zhone Clieous himself!"

"Murderer?" came a shout from the crowd. "How does he know these things?" "Why believe Sundered Heart?" "Listen to him!" "Let the meistersinger go!"

Casimir cried above the cacophony, "I know Zhone Clieous is the murderer because these friends of mine were orphans at that very site. They all saw Zhone Clieous's henchmen set the place ablaze!"

"You lie to us!" "I saw Clieous in Harmonic Hall that very night!" "Give over the meistersinger!" "Listen to the youth!" "He only hungers for Clieous's power!"

Guards seized the orphans who had retreated to the edge of the stage. Casimir set his jaw. The guards now had hostages of their own. The knife in Casimir's hand was slick with blood, and he struggled to tighten his hold. As he pulled his father back from the lantern, a wicked smile spread across Zhone Clieous's face. Clieous sneered. "I could kill you in broad daylight, and the fools would cheer me!"

The guards had begun to advance again onto the stage, holding orphan hostages before them. The angry mob filled the stairs and moved down toward the stage.

"Wait!" came a bold cry from the crowd. The guards halted in their tracks. A tall figure, mantled in black and red, pushed his way through the moiling crowd. "Wait, citizens of Harmonia!"

It was Harkon Lukas.

"Don't be so quick to condemn this friend of widows and orphans. Half of you are just as impoverished under Clieous's rule." Lukas waded through the stunned crowd and at last gained the stage. He approached a guard and gestured for him to leave the stage. The guard stood unmoving. Lukas set his boot firmly on the man's gut and kicked him back off the stage. The giggles that circulated among the crowd mixed oddly with growls of anger. Lukas bowed grandly, sweeping his plumed hat over the spot where the man had stood. He peered at the other guards, noting with pleasure that they had relinquished the stage.

Straightening, Lukas continued. "But perhaps, if the word of an orphan isn't enough for you, the word of a legendary bard will be. While visiting your meistersinger last week, I personally overheard him order the poorhouse to be set ablaze!"

Shock ran through the crowd. Casimir gazed dizzily up at the boiling audience. He edged toward Harkon Lukas, listening to the shouts of the crowd.

"Do you hear what Lukas says?" "He lies, and the orphan, too!" "Lukas wants his puppet to rule!" "Clieous is a monster!" "That boy is the monster!" "And Lukas, too!" "Kill them both! Save Clieous!"

Casimir's fear suddenly melted away and anger flared hot within him. He shifted his arm to Clieous's throat. With bold steps, he pushed the meistersinger toward the crowd.

"You speak of monsters? You call *me* a monster? Do these burns across my body make me a monster? Does my poverty? My mad rage? My resolve for vengeance? All of these I have received from this foul man! If you seek a monster, here he is!"

The steel dagger sank with sudden violence into the meistersinger's chest.

Clieous went rigid.

Blood poured hot across Casimir's hand. He whispered into his father's ear, "If you don't transform, this blade will kill you." A shuddering spasm ran through the meistersinger. He lurched against his son's arms. The crowd stared, unbreathing. Harkon Lukas stumbled back from the stage. Tears of confusion filled Thoris's eyes as Clieous slipped on the blood-smeared stone. He fell, tearing loose from his killer's hands and dropping to the stage with a wrenching thud.

The sound ignited the crowd. Guards poured onto the stage and swarmed Casimir. They dragged his blood-smeared form away from the meistersinger. Their spittle rained down on the young traitor, spittle along with fierce kicks, but Casimir was numb to it all.

"Change or die, Clieous . . . change or die, Clieous . . . change or die, Clieous . . . " Casimir chanted over and over to himself.

A furious mob enclosed Casimir and the ring of guards. Although a moment before the guards had been kicking Casimir, now they were forced to keep the crowd from doing the same. Despite their efforts, many of the mob's kicks and punches still struck the young orphan, now a true orphan at last.

A blood-chilling cry suddenly erupted from the meistersinger. "Are you waking up, Clieous?" Casimir called with a grin. The citizens who had clustered around Zhone Clieous fell back. Casimir's guards peered hawkishly toward the meistersinger. Another cry split through the murmurs, and the riot quickly stilled. Dismay rippled through the crowd. A fat woman ran toward the stairs while others turned, their eyes bulging with terror. Panicked screams filled the stands.

A beast rose from the blood-smeared spot where Zhone Clieous had lain. It rose on its hind legs, towering above the scarlet stage. Teeth crowded the creature's jaws, and its eyes glowed malevolently. Its massive head hungrily surveyed the villagers. With a low growl, it wrapped clawed fingers around the dagger in its chest and yanked the blade out. The oozing wound quickly sealed. The beast inhaled deeply, its ribs splaying beneath the dark fur. Then it roared.

The once-frozen audience began to shift and move like an ice floe. The masses lining the stairs turned and clambered for the exit. The guardsmen fell away from Casimir and backed toward the stairs. Casimir stumbled to his feet. The beast roared again, its razor-tipped hand slashing the throat of a stammering guard. With a laughing howl, it scrambled across the stage and gleefully blocked the stairs. Casimir edged toward the stage's rear exit.

The thing sighted him. Casimir turned, his feet slipping on the cold granite stage. He began to run. The beast lunged after him, its enormous nails scrabbling across the smooth stone. In three surging bounds, it reached the youth. Hearing the clicking of its claws, Casimir dived to the stage. Five razor-tipped fingers sliced the air above his head. Casimir rolled rapidly to one side as the creature slid past him, its claws raking the stone floor.

Casimir scrambled to his feet, training his eyes on the stairwell for the rear exit. He knew he couldn't reach it in time, but he had no choice but to try. The beast roared, its nails striking sparks on the stage as it thundered toward him. Hot breath spewed over Casimir's back. The werewolf's claws again arced through the air, this time finding flesh. The nails sunk in. Casimir gasped, pulling free. His robe was torn in ribbons and blood striped his back. The beast vaulted after him again, drawing the heady scent of blood into its quivering nostrils.

The stairwell opened up before Casimir. He had approached it from the wrong side! The stairs descended from the other end, and a ten-foot drop lay before him. The claws whistled again in his ears. With a scream, Casimir flung his body across the smooth stone of the stage and slid into the gaping stairwell. Darkness opened up beneath him. The next moment, he smashed into the wall on the opposite side of the stairwell and dropped to the ground.

The beast filled the air above.

Casimir scrambled through the iron gateway at the bottom of the stairs and into the Crystal Club, slamming the massive gate shut behind him. The creature landed and sprang against the bars. Casimir clutched the key in the lock and turned it. Clawed fingers seized his arm, but he yanked free, the claws raking furrows through his skin. Key in hand, he stumbled backward as the beast howled, its angry claws spinning only inches from him. The creature pulled back from the gate and rammed the rusted iron bars, bending one of them. Eyeing the gate warily, Casimir retreated into the Crystal Club.

"Run!" he shouted to the few patrons in the place. "Run! It's a werewolf!"

The diners glanced up dubiously from their meals.

"Look at my back, my arm!" Casimir shouted, displaying his ruby flesh. In the silence that fell, the werewolf's seething roar echoed through the club. Lurching up from their seats, the diners ran for the front entrance. Even the servers and barman hurried out. Casimir sniffed the air to be sure that no one remained. Only the scent of food and wine lingered. The place seemed empty.

Sloughing off his robe, he willed the beast to enter his blood. The transformation began. His blood grew thick. A tingle spread through him, and the bones in his legs and arms grew ember-hot. His muscles sizzled. Slowly his forearms lengthened, stretching skin and tendons. Then fingers melted into pads, and palms narrowed and elongated. Fingernails twisted into long, curving claws, and stringy hair sprouted feverishly from every pore of his skin. His legs twisted out from under him, and he fell to the floor, his lower limbs warping and reshaping. Sinews popped. Muscles boiled. The delicate bones of his face shuddered and split beneath the skin, then rapidly reshaped into a stout muzzle with piercing fangs. His mouth stretched painfully across the new teeth, and his lips darkened into black jowls.

Finally the transformation reached his brain. Reason evaporated, and sensation rose to dominate his mind. The smell of food on the tables became simply *hunger*; the sight of fire at the hearth became simply *danger*; the sound of Clieous ramming the gate became simply *hatred*. At last the dividing line between desire and action dissolved as well. To want was to act. Casimir had ceased to be a man or even a creature, and had become only a hunger.

He was no longer Casimir. He was neither man nor wolf. He had become nothing. And everything.

*   *   *   *   *

In half-wolf form, Zhone Clieous hurled himself a final time at the ancient iron door. The bars shattered, spraying shards of metal into the passage beyond. He stalked inside, his nostrils flaring as he smelled another were-beast. Growling, Clieous moved forward on his hind legs, scanning the dark Crystal Club. He listened intently. From a distance came the telltale click of claws on stone.

His son was hiding in a cave that branched to the left.

Turning toward the sound, Clieous advanced. He sniffed the food-rich air. Strange. Casimir's lupine smell was strong, but he didn't smell of fear. The beast-man's dark-seeing eyes searched the lightless chamber ahead. Nothing.

Hesitant, he moved into the cave branch and spoke in a raspy whisper. "Come, Casimir. Let us be like father and son again." The words echoed from the stony walls. No answer came. "Change back to human form and I will, too. We'll rule together as father and son!"

Not a sound came in return. Clieous halted, wondering if his son had assumed a fully lupine form, changing entirely to a wolf rather than retaining his fingers, humanlike legs, and ability to think. No, he thought, Casimir would want to keep his human wits about him.

"Son," he hissed, moving deeper into the darkness, "forgive me. I was afraid of you before, when I burned the nursery and the poorhouse. But let us be reconciled now." He plodded on, sniffing heavily. "You cannot hide from me forever, you know."

He barely glimpsed the eyes as a black shadow dropped from the ceiling. Needle-tipped fangs sank into his throat, and steamy blood sprayed the passage. Clieous fell backward; a dire wolf, its jaw clenched on his throat, followed him down. Deeper the teeth sank, meeting in the center of the meistersinger's throat. He landed heavily on his back, the dire wolf on top of him. Screaming, he raked vicious claws across the wolf's mouth. Still the jaws clamped. He pried at the dire wolf's teeth and ripped the flesh along its muzzle. Still it held on.

Reeling, Clieous dragged himself across the blood-slick floor, pulling the dire wolf behind him. With a mighty effort, he rose, lifting the wolf with the sinews of his neck. His bloodied hand reached over the nearby bar, pulling open a drawer. Knives gleamed coldly in the darkness within. Clieous slid his hand back and forth frantically through the drawer. One of the knives—a silver one—sliced open his palm. He clutched the knife, but the cold silver slid from his bleeding hand. He made another grab, but his fingers would no longer clench.

He knew he was dying.

Zhone Clieous, werewolf and one-time meistersinger of Harmonia, sank slowly beneath the massive weight of his killer. The dire wolf hungrily dragged the body to the floor and began to gorge on his neck.

*   *   *   *   *

By the time Sundered Heart emerged into the chaotic amphitheater, half the patrons had fled, and the remaining folk frantically crowded the stairs or climbed from level to level. The roar in the place was deafening. Casimir tightened his grip on the silver knife he carried and raised the head of Zhone Clieous high for the crowd to see.

"People of Harmonia!" he shouted. "Turn and heed me!"

Those pressing at the lower end of the amphitheater spun about and gasped, seeing the head of Zhone Clieous lifted in the hands of the crimson bard.

Casimir continued. "I have slain the foul beast with this very knife of silver, and I have severed his head that you might see!" A profound silence fell over the people as they turned and gazed. Horror and relief strangely mixed on their faces.

A dark form was moving down the stairs. Casimir lifted his eyes, hoping it would be Thoris. Instead, the gleaming smile of Harkon Lukas greeted him. The tall and elegant bard swung about as he descended, raising his arms to address the people.

"Behold the new meistersinger of Harmonia!" shouted the black-haired bard. "He stood alone against a creature that you wouldn't face together! With a simple knife of silver, he has undone twenty years of treachery and evil in Harmonia! Single-handed, he discovered the meistersinger's secret and revealed it to the world. And there is no better singer in all your lands, for he placed second only to Clieous in your contest a week ago. Let every man among you hail Sundered Heart!"

The amphitheater remained silent.

Lukas raised Casimir's scarred arms and shouted, "Hail to Sundered Heart."

A man near the exit returned the cry: "Hail to Sundered Heart!"

Then came a woman's voice: "Hail! Hail to the young lord!"

Another cry came, and another, until the whole place rang with the shouts. Lukas lifted Casimir to his shoulder and started up the stairs. The masses joyously crowded to touch the young ruler. Their shouts solidified into a single voice.

"Hail, Sundered Heart! Hail, Sundered Heart!"

The people began to fall in line behind Lukas. Even Zhone Clieous's guards joined the euphoric throng.

"Off to the meistersinger's mansion!" cried Harkon Lukas.

Casimir shouted, "No. Take me to the Temple of Milil!"

Lukas cocked an eyebrow at the new ruler.

"To the temple!" cried Casimir, ignoring Lukas. Others took up the cry from their new meistersinger.

"To the temple! To the temple!"

*   *   *   *   *

Long after the crowd had departed, a lone youth stumbled from the Crystal Club. He lurched across the granite stairs to the row of seats beyond the club's entrance. There he fell on his stomach. Wild images flashed through his mind, images of blood and fangs and death. The stone seat felt cool against his fevered brow and the aching burns on his body.

"Oh, my friend! You *are* a monster!" Thoris moaned.

EIGHT

Gustav slept amongst a sprawl of books, a flute clutched in his hand. Beside the white-haired priest rested a guttering candle, burnt to its nub. The flame peered out between spindly columns of tallow. Typically, Gustav was miserly with his candles, but tonight sleep had taken him unawares; he had expected the children to return sooner. After the first several hours of his vigil, Gustav sank into slumber.

A low roar began in the distance and slowly swelled until it filled the temple. Gustav cracked his eyelids with halfhearted interest. A fiery light spattered through the chapel's stained glass. Gustav opened his eyes fully and listened. The noise sounded like the tread of a throng on the street. The priest sat up, color draining from his cheeks.

Thoooom, thoooom, thoooom.

Something massive was pounding on the temple doors. The sound rumbled profoundly through the sanctuary, rolling into the chapel: *thoooom, thoooom, thoooom.*

"They've come for me," the withered old man said, using his battered flute to raise himself from the floor. "The children have done something horrible, and—"

Thoooom, thoooom, thoooom.

"Why don't they just open the blasted door?" Gustav wondered aloud. Straightening his stiff back, he snatched up the guttering candle, made his way through the chapel, and entered the sanctuary. His embroidered robe dragged through the dust as he studied the stubby candle. "Waste of wax," he said.

The old man reached the door just as the blows began to fall again. With a capricious grin, he swung the door wide. Five grubby villagers sprawled heavily across the threshold. Outside was a mob, their faces lit by glaring torchlight. There Gustav glimpsed a familiar face. It was Casimir, and he was smiling broadly.

"As promised, I've brought your temple back, Master Gustav," Casimir shouted from his perch atop the villagers' shoulders.

The priest gazed suspiciously at the boy, whose face in the fiery light appeared to be mantled in blood. "What are you raving about, boy?"

Casimir gestured widely, "These folk! These good folk are your new congregation and the rebuilders of your sanctuary. They have had their earful of dirges. Now they want dances!"

The smiling faces around Casimir confirmed his unlikely story. Even the five who had prostrated themselves across the threshold now stood, beaming.

"They haven't come here to lynch me?"

The crowd laughed, and Casimir, slipping from the shoulders of two stout yeomen, turned to address them.

"Beyond these doors lies the new heart of our city, the temple of song! It is all but dead now and has long been so. But tonight marks its rebirth! No longer shall folk look with longing eyes to the meistersinger's citadel, wishing to hear the songs of rich men. Now, every man and every woman shall come to this place and sing the songs themselves! Come see the house of our god!"

Casimir spun on his heels and waved the crowd to follow. He marched proudly through the ancient portal. Gustav fell back against the stony walls, his heart laboring strangely. In marched the throng. The clatter of their feet filled the hall, and fierce torchlight danced across the pillars. Gustav followed the procession into the sanctuary. The bobbing line of torches had already traced halfway around the temple.

"What has Casimir done?" Gustav whispered, incredulous.

The ribbon of people continued to circle the sanctuary. The long-silent temple rang with laughter and gasps of awe. Soon the laughter infected even Gustav, and he merged with the tide of revelers. Torchlight flowed over the stone columns, splashing on the metal corpse of the organ below. At last the ring of torches was complete. Casimir cried out, "Behold, people of Harmonia, the temple of your faith! Though it now stands in ruin, it will rise from decay to be a place of unceasing songs of praise!"

A cheer rang out from the throng. The cry echoed through the massive structure as though the building itself assented.

"Let it so be decreed in this, my first proclamation," Casimir shouted, "that in five days, no man will labor, be it in his fields, at his shop, or with his stack of money. All will instead come here with buckets and hammers and rags. Let each man bring the tools of his trade—the shopkeeper his fabric and glass, the joiner his hammer and saw, the scrivener his parchment and pen. Even your meistersinger will join you. Side by side we'll labor! On the last day of each week, we will work until the sanctuary is rebuilt!"

A shout arose from the people and whirled through the sanctuary.

"Let it be so! Now, on to the mansion!"

*   *   *   *   *

A coach with four black horses pulled to a stop before a mansion on South Hill. A cloaked figure alighted and strode to the gatehouse, his cape flapping darkly behind him. The attendant at the gatehouse stepped forward for a moment, but the dark man waved him back. The guard nodded, fearful recognition flashing in his eyes, and withdrew to the gatehouse. Without altering his pace, the man pushed past the creaking iron gate and walked down the marble path that led to the mansion. Reaching the estate's thick door, the man rapped twice.

In time, a servant woman came to the door and cautiously cracked it open. She peered out suspiciously. "Master Olyava is in bed. Come again tomor—"

The stranger thrust the door open, pushing the woman into the room and stepping across the threshold. He strode to the center of the receiving hall and said civilly, "He will want to see me now. The matter is urgent."

"Urgent?" squawked the servant woman as she adjusted her apron. "What could be so urgent that you have to barge—?"

"The meistersinger is dead," the man replied curtly. "He was murdered only half an hour ago, and his murderer has ascended to Harmonia's seat." Pulling a scarlet kerchief from his pocket, the man dabbed his brow. "I wish to speak to Gaston. This very night, he must stage a rebellion and a coup."

*　*　*　*　*

The walls outside the meistersinger's mansion glowed beneath the steely moon. A black mass of villagers lined the base of the wall, their torches shining like stars and their voices rumbling in the still night. Noblemen in nearby estates watched the scene with growing fear. Over the crowd's chant rose the elegant voice of a young man.

"Once again I order you to stand off, guardsman. I am your meistersinger now!" Casimir demanded.

The glaive-armed soldier stubbornly barred the entrance, standing like a human portcullis. His massive frame was densely stacked with armor, and his low-slanted brow showed no lack of determination.

"Back, all of you," he growled, "or to the stockade with you!"

Casimir sized up the human bulwark. "Zhone Clieous, the werewolf, is dead. I am the new meistersinger."

Anger flashed across the guard's features. He swung his polearm to bear on the new meistersinger. Casimir left his hands at his sides and smiled with icy confidence.

"I just killed a werewolf. Do you really want to take me on?" Casimir snarled.

Before the guard could respond, a large man jostled through the crowd. Although Casimir didn't take his eyes off the polearm, he knew the approaching man was a soldier by his jangling armor.

"Put away that glaive, you rock-brained fool," the soldier barked. Frowning, the guard lowered the polearm. The soldier continued, "Don't you recognize Clieous's men? Don't you see our helmets glinting there, and there, and there? I tell you, Meistersinger Casimir speaks the truth: Clieous was a fiend, and this young man has saved us all. Now stand down, you lump of lead, or I'll wrench that stubborn head from your thick neck!"

With a precise lockstep, the guard moved aside. Casimir bowed graciously and strode forward. The soldier stepped in beside him and shouted, "Raise the gates!"

Iron links clattered on a metal drum. Slowly the massive portcullis lurched upward. The chains creaked in complaint as the gate rose into the archway. Casimir reached the gate and, bending slightly, passed beneath it into the tunnel entrance. The crowd flooded through at his heels. The clatter of iron and stomping of leather shoes filled the stony passage. Casimir gazed appreciatively at the arch overhead: He had last entered this place as a stowaway, but this time he came as lord.

Casimir tapped the clanking armor of the soldier beside him. "Run ahead and inform the servants."

The warrior squinted for a moment at Casimir. Then he nodded and rushed off. Casimir spun about, motioning a set of grubby boys toward him. "You fellows know what a pantry is, don't you?"

They nodded seriously.

"Go find the pantry. There'll be big barrels there. No . . . on second thought, you're too small for the barrels.

There'll be great blocks of cheese and other foods. Bring them!" As the boys ran off, Casimir snagged a burly farmer. "Follow them to the pantry and bring back every cask of *meekulbrau* you find there."

The farmer's eyes grew wide with disbelief as he hurried to obey.

The throng swept into the meistersinger's magnificent garden, spreading out with exclamations of wonder. In a sudden burst of joy, Casimir raced toward the fountain, leapt over its watery well, and clambered up the broad statue at its center. Flinging his hands in a gesture of welcome, he cried, "Come! Enter into this place built by your hands and bought by your taxes! Sit or lie down! Take rest. This garden is yours. Wine is coming, and *meekulbrau*, and the finest cheese in Harmonia. Join my victor's feast tonight. Tomorrow dawns a new era for Harmonia!"

A scattered cheer rang through the garden as the people wandered about. Astounded guards stared down at the odd collection of people, poor and rich, warrior and baker, greengrocer and undertaker. Barrels of *meekulbrau* were rolled into the garden, and boys carried in bundled wheels of cheese. Casimir laughed, leaping from the top of the fountain, landing on the grass, and rolling to a stop below. As he stood up, the people steadily drifted across the garden to where the broad barrels were being tapped and the blocks of cheese sliced open. Casimir's stomach began to growl. He started toward the food.

"What's all this?" came a familiar voice.

It was Julianna. Her eyes were sleepy, and she wore a robe wrapped hastily about her silken nightgown. A smile filling his lips, Casimir strode like a young conqueror to meet her.

"Sundered Heart!" she gasped, her bleary eyes suddenly wide with shock. "You must leave immediately! If my uncle finds—"

"Enough of your protests," Casimir interrupted. "Are you glad to see me or not?"

"Of course I'm glad," she said, rubbing her eyes.

"Then come have a drink with me," Casimir replied. He slipped his hand behind her slender waist and directed her toward the tapped barrels. As they pushed through the motley crowd of celebrants, the strangeness of this midnight celebration sank in on Julianna. She planted her feet, refusing to go farther.

"What is happening here?" Julianna asked accusingly.

Casimir stared at her with mock incredulity. He extended a hand toward the man at the barrel. "You mean you don't know?" The portly man placed a sloshing stein of the maroon *meekulbrau* in his open hand. He passed it to Julianna.

"I am quite sure I don't," Julianna replied curtly.

"What is happening?" Casimir took a stein for himself and quickly drained it. "Why, you are toasting me, just as everyone else is." He filled the tankard again, nodded with a sardonic smile, and downed the bitter, stinging brew.

Julianna's serious eyes pinned him. She set her tankard on a nearby table. "Toast you? Toast you for what?"

The *meekulbrau* sloshed in Casimir's eyes. "Dance with me!"

"Dance?" Julianna stomped. "To what music? And why?"

Casimir set his stein down and clapped his foamy hands together. "Music, everyone! Sing for the first lady of the realm!"

Julianna stepped forward angrily, her delicate hands clasping Casimir's. She peered disapprovingly at his stained robes. "Look at you! Your cloak is covered with mud!"

"That's not all," Casimir said, grinning and spinning around clumsily to show a vertical gash in his robe. "It has rear exits, too."

Gasping, Julianna turned him about and fixed him with a deadly stare. "That's not mud. It's blood. Tell me what has happened."

Casimir gazed back, struggling to remain serious. "Your uncle was a werewolf."

"What?" she said, her eyes probing his.

"It's the truth," Casimir responded. He extended his lower lip to suppress a belch. "He tried to kill me tonight."

She dropped his hands and backed away from him. "Don't lie to me, Sundered Heart," she said, but her quivering voice belied her uncertainty.

The man at the tap caught Julianna's shoulders as she backed into him. "He speaks the truth, miss. We all saw Clieous change and go after the young lad—uh, the meistersinger. 'Course, you needn't worry. Master Heart killed 'im."

The confusion in Julianna's features had deepened with each word. As the man finished, she twisted free from him and rushed away toward one of the mansion's doors. Casimir gazed after her in surprise. Setting down his stein, he hurried after her, his legs feeling heavy with *meekulbrau*. Julianna pulled the door open, slipped lithely inside, and closed it behind her. Casimir reached the door and found it unlocked. Turning the brassy handle, he stepped cautiously across the threshold into the hallway beyond.

She was gone.

Sighing, he set his weary shoulder against the doorframe. She could have gone in either direction through the mazelike hall. "Nothing to do but look for her," he muttered.

*   *   *   *   *

At last Casimir found Julianna in a small upper room. It was an awkward, unfinished space hidden beneath a slanting roof. The attic was so cluttered with crates and so draped in dust that at first Casimir didn't see her. But as his eyes grew used to the dim light, he heard the sound of sobs.

"It's me, Julianna," Casimir said, his voice weighted with concern. "I won't harm you."

No response came except for the quiet sobs. Rounding a pile of crates, Casimir caught sight of her. She was slumped against a wall of dusty lath and plaster. Moonlight slanted through a vent in the eaves and cut across her disheveled form. Casimir knelt beside her and slid his arm gently about her shoulder.

"I'm sorry," he said.

She tried to speak but couldn't; irregular sobs choked back her words. Casimir waited patiently, content to encircle her in his arm. At length she spoke. "Then . . . then he is dead, isn't he?"

"I'm sorry," Casimir repeated simply.

Julianna shook her head and swallowed. "I thought werewolves were mere fictions . . . the stuff of huntsmen's tales."

"How I wish they were," Casimir responded sincerely. He dropped from his knee to sit on the planks, his arm still wrapped about her. He forgot his wounds, feeling only Julianna's warmth beside him.

A new wave of sobbing had begun. Only after repeated attempts to speak did Julianna succeed. "To have known someone . . . who was . . . If I think back, I can remember signs," she thought aloud. Casimir eyed her with sober concern. "Those tunics of his must have been stained with blood. . . . He always healed quickly. . . . He was polished, but cynical and savage, too. . . ."

Casimir paled. She might as easily have been describing him with those words. He pulled her closer to him.

". . . even if I had known," she continued tearfully, "even if I had read the signs, I couldn't have . . ." She turned her sorrowful eyes toward Casimir before speaking again. "I loved my uncle, Sundered Heart. Despite his faults—and this . . . abomination—I loved him. But if he was a monster . . . "

Casimir felt as if there were an iron band around his chest. "Sundered Heart is only a stage name. My true name is Casimir."

Julianna's teary face brightened, "Casimir . . . ?"

He smiled in spite of himself.

"Casimir . . . a handsome name," she said, testing the name on her lips. "How was it that you killed a werewolf, Casimir?"

A lump formed in his throat. Yes, Casimir, he thought, how could you have killed a werewolf? "Werewolves have their weaknesses," he replied unconvincingly.

"Oh, I don't want to hear all the bloody particulars," she said, a weary disregard entering her voice. "I only want to know how you came out of the battle still alive."

The iron band tightened. "You make it sound as though I suffered no injuries, and I did, you know," he said, sliding his arm into the moonlight to show the lacerations.

Julianna gasped and struggled to her feet. Her eyes swelled with fear. "They say it's contagious—werewolfism, I mean. They say the curse is in the blood. If any of his blood mixed with any of yours . . ."

She left the sentence unfinished, dragging Casimir up from the floor and out of the narrow attic. Speechless, he plodded along behind her. They rushed through the mansion's snaking hallways, rounding countless corners. At last they descended a short flight of stairs and reached a small room below. Outside the room, Julianna took a lantern from the wall and said, "We've got to clean those cuts."

She entered the room, pulling him behind her. The walls within were lined with deep scarlet paper and cluttered with many dark shelves and porcelain-knobbed cabinets. Lamplight glinted off the countless jars that lined the shelves. Strange implements of ceramic and tarnished brass lay across the countertops. At the room's center, a small, stocky table stood. Beneath it, a stained rug covered the cold stone floor. In one corner, an odd metal barrel sat embedded in a brick column.

"What *is* this?" Casimir asked. "Was your uncle a warlock, too?"

Julianna smiled. "No. This is a healer's room. It belongs to Richter, the alchemist." As she spoke, Julianna directed Casimir to sit down on the stout table.

"Alchemist?" Casimir repeated, his suspicion growing.

"Yes," she said, stoking a fire in the strange metallic barrel. "Alchemists believe that bits of dried plant or parts of animals help people heal. They aren't real healers, as priests are, but Uncle didn't much like priests." Casimir smiled nervously from his perch atop the table. Julianna lit more lamps and then turned toward him. "Don't worry. I just want to wash and bandage your wounds." She became suddenly grave. "Especially if you've got any of that bad blood. We'll have to keep watch over you come next full moon." She puttered a bit more, then added mischievously, "We might even have to put you in shackles."

Though Casimir laughed, a chill ran through him. Julianna poured water into a kettle and set it on the iron barrel. She then approached him. "Now show me where your wounds are."

"Only on my arms and back," Casimir replied.

"Then I'll need to see them," Julianna said, gently pulling the torn robe from his blood-encrusted shoulders. The robe fell back, and Casimir gathered the garment about his waist. His skin prickled in the cool air. Julianna's warm fingers traced around the first of five long scratches that ran from his shoulder blades to his hip bones. With her free hand, she lifted a lantern toward the wounds.

"For all the blood here, the wounds look strangely shallow."

Again Casimir shivered. Of course they're shallow. I healed some when I changed back, he thought. I need to distract her. "What do you think I should do with this land of mine?"

Julianna didn't look up from her work. "What do you mean?"

"To start with, I need to build a new poorhouse," Casimir elaborated. "And I've already declared Milil the state religion."

"Oh," Julianna said, preoccupied. "You mean what improvements should you make?" She turned away, fetching the kettle of water. She set a shallow basin on the table behind Casimir and poured the water from the kettle. Casimir sighed as the cloud of steam billowed up his back.

"Yes," he responded. "Like how can I help the poor?"

Lifting a steamy rag to Casimir's back, Julianna replied, "Good question. The slums of Harmonia aren't fit for dogs."

"Hmmm," Casimir responded, suddenly sitting straighter. "I think I have an idea. We'll help the poor through song!"

"What?"

Casimir glanced over his shoulder at Julianna. "What if I were to decree that Reaptide this year wouldn't take place between the amphitheater and Harmonic Hall, but in the streets of the slums."

The scalding rag stopped its advance across Casimir's back. Julianna circled around before him, her face quizzical. "Who would want a festival there?"

"Precisely," Casimir answered, smiling. "By proclamation, I will divide the slums into quarters or sixths—however many lords we have—and tell each that he must make his sector clean enough for the festival! Come Reaptide, I'll inspect the place, meting out punishment for each broken window and piece of filth I see."

Now Julianna smiled. "There'll be lampposts and fences, proper doors and proper hinges, and whitewash on every wall."

"They'll hunt down the rats, burn the refuse, hand out clean tunics, shovel the sewage, and cart it to the fields."

"Yes," Julianna replied excitedly, "but how can we keep the rats away after the festival? And how can we teach the folk to clean themselves and care for their homes?"

"You said 'we,' didn't you?" Casimir asked, leveling his gaze toward her. Julianna didn't respond, taking hold of Casimir's wounded arm and washing the gash. At length, she said, "When I first met you, Casimir, you were cunning and witty and strong." She stopped washing and peered into his eyes. "But now you seem to be kind, too."

*   *   *   *   *

"Master Casimir," came the voice of a servant boy.

"What?" Casimir shouted in alarm, sitting bolt upright in the meistersinger's feather bed. The afternoon sun shone bright through the bedroom window. His head swirled with dreams.

"Master Casimir," repeated the servant boy at the door. "Some jurisconsults are here to see you."

"Some what?" Casimir asked, rubbing his eyes and steadying himself on the whirling bed.

"Jurists . . . fellows what deals with the law."

Casimir leaned back against the pile of downy pillows and drew the thick blankets up to his neck. "What do they want?"

"They have a docket of business," the boy replied simply.

"Unless they want to see me naked," Casimir sighed resignedly, "they'll have to wait till I'm dressed."

"I'll tell them so, sir, and send someone to dress you."

Casimir's brow darkened. "I haven't needed help dressing for sixteen years. I doubt I'll need it now."

"But Master Clieous used to—"

"I care little what Master Clieous once did. Now run along."

The servant boy complied wordlessly. Casimir sighed, gazing languidly beyond the bed's canopy to the ornate bosses on the ceiling. "Quite a change from waking up beneath the rafters of the Red Porch," he noted. "Bosses on the ceiling and jurists in the hall." He fastened stiff fingers around the finely carved wood of the bed frame and stretched languorously. Muscles pulled taut within their gauzy bandages. A smile came to Casimir's lips as he remembered Julianna from the night before.

He sat up again, swinging his legs over the bedside. Where's Thoris? he wondered suddenly. What could have happened to him? Was he in the crowd last night? No. He'd have made himself known. Perhaps he's returned to the temple. Casimir rose from the bed, intending to get dressed and go to the temple.

The jurists.

His shoulders slumped. "I suppose, as meistersinger, I should attend to them." He pulled back the closet doors.

Clothing had never made him dizzy before. Gazing dumbfounded at the vast assortment of strange garb, Casimir wished someone *were* coming to dress him.

*   *   *   *   *

The new meistersinger descended the stairs. He wore a red cowl, yellow tunic, and orange tabard. A leather belt-girdle strapped down the tabard's ends, and a baldric fouled the tabard's fringe. Beneath these, he wore bunchy red breeches with stockings that almost matched. Black horseman's boots covered most of his calf, and spurs clicked across the stone floor as he walked.

He blustered importantly into the book-lined study where the jurisconsults were waiting. They rose as Casimir swept in. He dropped with despotic flair into a chair and said, "What is it, then?"

The most severe-looking of the three bowed with gracious solemnity and said, "Master Casimir, I am called Ausler."

"And I am Shelzen," said the second, bowing.

"And I, Machen," said the third.

"Yes, yes," Casimir sighed. "What do you want?"

Ausler spoke up, "There are a number of pressing concerns this afternoon, meistersinger."

"And they are . . . ?" Casimir gestured impatiently.

"To start, there is the matter of your succession to rule. Then there is the funeral that must be held for the departed meistersinger. There is also the matter of the will."

"As to my succession, I have done so by right of law. I was second in the contest only to Clieous, who is now dead."

Ausler smiled hesitantly. "That is understood. Even so, you must admit that your ascension is irregular—no, unique—in the history of Harmonia. For twenty years, one man has ruled Harmonia. That man's death and your irregular installation make your reign shaky in the minds of the nobles."

"Which are more important, nobles or laws?" Casimir asked.

"Laws, of course, but—"

"And what does the law say about a meistersinger's death?"

"That his seat should go to the second in the contest."

"Precisely," Casimir said shortly. "I know that, you know that, and so do the nobles."

"If you will forgive me," Machen broke in, "what we speak of here isn't law but power. In Harmonia, laws have no effect unless the powerful citizens support them. What is true for laws is true for meistersingers as well."

"Your job is law," Casimir replied. "My job is power. Understood? Now, on to the funeral. Shelzen, do I employ you?"

"Yes, meistersinger."

"Then please arrange a suitable funeral of state and tell me when services will be held," Casimir said. He added with an odd smile, "I don't wish to miss the burial."

"Yes sir."

"Finally, we have the business of the will."

"I have it here," Machen offered, producing an oddly crumpled scroll and passing it toward the meistersinger.

Casimir waved him off. "You read it to me."

Drawing back in amazement, Machen unrolled the crinkling paper. He paused, peering at Casimir through the tops of his eyes. "The document is lengthy."

"Then just answer a few of my questions. How many of the mansion's furnishings belonged to Zhone Clieous?"

"All of them," the jurist replied dryly.

Apparently unsurprised by this response, Casimir continued. "And does the will leave anything to immediate family?"

"The meistersinger had no family," Machen responded.

"Indeed he d—" Casimir began, but he thought better of it. Surely the people would realize that a werewolf's son may also be a werewolf. "Well, then, is anything earmarked to remain in the mansion?"

"No."

"Hmmm," he replied, considering the quandary. At length he announced, "I'll have to declare the will void."

"You cannot do that, sir," Machen protested cautiously. "The will of a freeman—if demonstrably a genuine article in accord with the law—cannot be nullified by any agency or personage."

"Ausler, tell me: Do I have the right as meistersinger to declare a man a criminal of the state?" Casimir asked.

"Well, of course, but—"

"Then Zhone Clieous was a criminal of the state," Casimir said, "charged with the wanton destruction of the Red Porch and the murder of all those who perished within. Now, Machen, does a criminal of the state have right to a will?"

"No," Machen replied, dejectedly rolling the will back up, "but neither does he have the right to a full state funeral."

"Quite right." Casimir nodded. "Shelzen, cancel that funeral. Let Zhone Clieous be buried among the paupers in the common grave." Casimir gazed about the room with satisfaction. None of the jurists dared to move. Finally he asked, "Does anything remain undone?"

Machen was reluctant to speak up. "Well, there is the matter of what to do with this." He tilted the rolled will, letting a small dagger slide out from its center. "The will was wrapped around this. I plan to destroy the will, insofar as it is now void, but I doubt the knife would burn." He handed the blade, handle first, to Casimir.

The dagger was unmistakably silver. "What is this?"

Slowly Machen unrolled the will. "There's a cryptic note at the bottom here. Let's see. Yes, here it is: *And if my son still lives, the dagger enclosed is for him. May he use it well.*"

Casimir calmly passed the dagger back to the jurist. "Bury Clieous with this in his heart."

* * * * *

Later that day, after flagging down a servant to help him dress properly, Casimir went to the temple of Milil. He had hoped to find Thoris, but instead found only Gustav. Next he searched the amphitheater and the Crystal Club, where Harmonic Hall students were cleaning up after the previous night's grim events. Still no sign of Thoris. Finally he wandered the streets, asking citizens. Wherever he went, people pointed and whispered, "There he is—the new meistersinger." The poor said it with awe, and the rich with shock. But all people said it. Everyone knew of him, but no one knew of Thoris.

Night fell, and Casimir still hadn't found a clue to the whereabouts of his friend.

"He must be somewhere in this city," Casimir thought aloud as he wandered the slums. As the darkness deepened around him, he gazed at the gibbous moon. It was vast and round and seductive, riding high on savage breezes from the heath, and it infused Casimir with desire.

"I'm hungry," he murmured, the words rising unbidden to his lips. Perhaps I can transform just enough to sniff out Thoris, he thought. Just enough to heighten my senses, but not enough to change my appearance.

Beneath the inexorable pull of the moon, the delicious transformation began. Casimir sniffed the wind. It brimmed with exotic odors: the fetid heath, the fearful hare, the aromatic pine, the churning water. Fragrances rolled in from the corners of the world. Still he caught no scent of Thoris. The transformation deepened. Impotent human sight gave way to the sharp gray tones of lupine vision. The wind, which before sounded merely restless, now spoke vividly in his ears. The change reached his mind, awakening in it a chaos of desire—hunger, lust, hatred.

Blood.

*　　*　　*　　*　　*

When his mind returned, Casimir found himself feasting on a corpse. The dead man lay, eyes open, in a hovel near the slums. Casimir drew back from the gory body, horror playing over his now-human features. Blood covered his hands and coated his clothes. He hadn't even disrobed before assuming his half-wolf form. He spat the blood from his mouth.

Then he scented something chilling.

Thoris.

He rose from the body and headed into the slums, following the smell. In a short time, he sniffed out the boy in a warren of shanties. Thoris lay against one of the shacks, his eyes closed, his face battered black and blue. Casimir knelt and touched his friend; the boy's skin felt ice cold. The wooden sword, which Thoris had always worn beneath his rope belt, was gone. Falling to both knees, Casimir shook Thoris.

He didn't move.

"No!" Casimir gasped, breathless. He slipped his arms beneath Thoris's body. "Wake up. You've got to wake up!" he demanded through gritted teeth. Casimir raised his hand to slap the boy's face, but drew short, noticing the sharp claws that still lingered on his fingertips. He lowered his hand, balling it into a fist. "I did this to you, didn't I?" he whispered.

Casimir sat back, staring into the starry sky. "Oh, my friend," he said sadly, "if Clieous is to be buried with paupers, then you will be buried with lords."

NINE

As Casimir knelt beside the shanty, clasping the still form of Thoris, he felt the boy shudder slightly. Gasping, Casimir flattened his hand on the boy's chest. "His heart is beating," he said excitedly, "but for how long?" He tightened his grip around him and stood up.

"I seen it all," came a ragged voice behind Casimir. He glanced over his shoulder to see a withered old man, his bony frame draped in rags. "He come shufflin' in last night, eyes empty an' hopeless, mutt'rin' 'bout monsters. These three hoodlums sees his robes and rolls him, thinkin' he's got coin. He doesn't fight back or nothin'."

Nodding wordlessly, Casimir pushed past the old man. He charged out into the street, heading for the mansion. The old man shouted after him, "When they finds he's got nothin', they beats him ev'n more. I could 'dentify 'em . . . for a price!"

Casimir was already gone.

* * * * *

Thoris's battered body lay atop the healing room's table amidst a flurry of action. Julianna bustled around the room, trimming lamps and stoking a fire in the odd metal barrel. Richter, the alchemical healer, wandered among the shelves, his bald head bobbing eagerly as he eyed the jars. Occasionally he opened a container and snuffed a pinch of its contents into his nostrils. Then he continued along the shelf, loading jars under his bony arm.

Only Casimir was still. He stood in a dark corner of the healing room, apparently oblivious to the proceedings. His fevered gaze had a sole focus—Thoris. Thoris still breathed, but how long would he continue to? Casimir's unblinking eyes ached.

Finally stopping in another corner of the room, Richter dumped foul herbs into a basin of steaming water. The liquid became an unhealthy orange-red, which stained the white basin and clung eagerly to the withered man's fingers. Turning, Richter ladled the steaming pulp thickly onto Thoris's chest. He was careful to cover every inch. The red concoction contrasted sharply to the boy's bruises and his otherwise pallid skin. When all the salve had been applied, Richter stepped back, holding crimson fingers high. Seizing the boy's flaccid arms, he raised and lowered them.

Casimir watched the procedure with disciplined silence. He didn't look away when Richter performed his other odd rites: cutting the boy, burning him, setting leeches. Casimir trained his eyes only on Thoris's slowly pulsing chest. Hours passed. No change came, for better or ill. At last Richter pulled the leeches away, washed his hands, and set the wounds.

"Is that it?" Casimir asked angrily, jerking away from the wall.

"Come, Casimir." The voice was Julianna's. She took his arm and steered him from the cringing alchemist. "Let's get Thoris to bed and get some sleep ourselves."

Wearily Casimir turned away from the alchemist. He tenderly lifted Thoris—scarlet and bandaged—and followed Julianna up the stairs. She led him to a moderately appointed bedroom and turned down the sheets. Casimir arrayed Thoris's cold limbs on the bed, then piled the covers high.

Julianna's hand rested warm on his shoulder. "We can do nothing more for him." Her hand pulled away.

She moved toward the door. "Let him sleep now."

Casimir nodded distractedly and sank into a high-backed chair. His weary eyes settled again on Thoris.

Julianna sighed. "Casimir, you need some rest. Tomorrow you are once again meistersinger of Harmonia."

"Let Harmonia go on without me," Casimir muttered bitterly.

"The city can't go on without you."

He turned from the pale form of his friend. His eyes were twin pits in his skull. "And I can't go on without him."

* * * * *

The morning sunlight shone on Casimir, still awake and propped in the chair. Deep rings of worry traced his eyes. Thoris's rest had appeared to help the boy little. Scorched and cut and starved, only his stubborn lungs held on. Julianna had visited once that morning, but the ashen meistersinger paid her no heed. The messenger who announced the jurists and petitioners met with more success: Casimir flung a shoe at him.

By midmorning, the messages had stopped.

By afternoon, Casimir had surrendered to sleep.

* * * * *

"You've much to learn," came a deep voice, rumbling dreamlike through Casimir's sleeping mind, "and sleep is not the best tutor."

An attenuate hand jiggled Casimir's numb shoulder. Suddenly realizing he had fallen asleep, Casimir lurched awake. A self-deprecating scowl crossed his face. Ignoring the hand on his shoulder, he peered toward Thoris. Still the boy slept. The world had gone dark, Casimir realized. Beyond the open window hung velvety night. A cool breeze spilled through.

The hand left Casimir's shoulder, and the hollow thud of boots sounded. A candle rounded the high-backed chair, its eye of flame making Casimir wince. In the fiery glow, he made out the monocled face of a man.

"Master Lukas!" Casimir gasped.

The bard lowered his candle to a nearby table, and the light cast sinister shadows across his face. A wry smile formed there as Lukas seated himself on Thoris's bed. His piercing eyes fixed on the meistersinger.

"Not Master Lukas . . . Call me Harkon . . . a pupil's privilege."

"Pupils have tutors," Casimir murmured sleepily, "and tutors are hired. Who hired you, Lukas?"

"The folk of Harmonia, who want a ruler," Lukas replied with lighthearted malice. "Instead, they have a child in their mansion."

Shaking the sleep from his head, Casimir replied, "All rulers are children—impatient children. So leave now!"

Harkon dropped the monocle from his eye and rubbed it distractedly with his handkerchief. "I left you too quickly when you lost the contest. Your dismantling of Zhone Clieous and his rule proved me too hasty. I won't forsake you now, even though you're turning out to be quite hopeless as a ruler."

Casimir slid forward on his high-backed chair. His eyes bored into Lukas and his voice became a growl. "I've secured my succession, founded a state religion, collected Clieous's holdings, declared him an outlaw, and ordered a pauper's burial for him, all in two days. I wouldn't call that hopeless."

Where the monocle had once been, a calloused ring of flesh circled Lukas's eye. He lifted the glass circle back in place, and his eyelids cut a skeptical line across his pupils. "In two days, you've enraged Harmonic Hall and the nobles, confused the people, ignored your duties, and—" he paused, gesturing toward Thoris—"left your dearest friend for dead."

Casimir gritted his teeth. "I searched long for him and remained at his side from the moment I found him! And I care nothing for Harmonic Hall or the rich men. They're only a spoiled handful next to the hundreds of poor."

"The rich are everything, you fool! You've much to learn, Casimir," Lukas said wearily. "It *is* Casimir, is it not?"

"What right have you, a simple bard, to lecture me?"

"Stupid men choose tutors by their papers," Lukas replied calmly, picking up his broad-rimmed hat and running his fingers along the brim. "But wise men choose tutors by their lessons." Rising, the bard donned the hat. "Come with me. You may as well begin your lessons now."

Casimir sank back into his chair. "I'll not leave Thoris."

"Unwilling to leave but willing to sleep?" Lukas replied coldly. Casimir flung his arms over his chest and looked away. Lukas continued, his voice suddenly devoid of malice. "He won't awaken tonight, Casimir. I can assure you of that. And if he awakens tomorrow and the people have revolted, he's lost everything."

"Revolted?" Casimir said, sitting up.

"You've much to learn. Come with me."

Taking a last glance at Thoris's steadily breathing form, Casimir arose from the high-backed chair.

"I've had the housemaid ready your boots and cloak," Lukas said.

*   *   *   *   *

In contrast to the damp air within the stony mansion, the woodlands northeast of Harmonia were dry and heavy with the scent of life. A thick canopy of broadleaf trees crowded above the tall bard and his young apprentice as they moved along a deer path. Harkon Lukas led the hike, his broad-brimmed hat passing with odd ease through the thick growth. Marching in his footsteps, Casimir surveyed Lukas curiously. The man was sure-footed in the dark forest and appeared little afraid of nighttime beasts. Everyone in Harmonia knew the stories of werewolves haunting the wilds beyond the city walls, but Lukas plodded along with unconcerned ease.

Indeed, perhaps I should show this arrogant man a were-wolf myself, Casimir thought with a capricious smile.

As soon as the thought found shape, though, Casimir knew he would never attack Lukas. He little liked the black-mustachioed bard, true, but greatly respected him all the same. He carried himself like no other man Casimir had seen. Vulnerability and fear had distinct odors to Casimir's lupine nose, and every creature he had ever met—Clieous, Gustav, Julianna, Thoris—bore at least a taint of these smells, but Lukas was different. The scent that came from him was jaded, confident, sober. He was the first man Casimir had met who was perfectly at home in his own skin.

Reaching a small, leaf-strewn clearing, Harkon halted. Casimir pushed a fern branch from the path and stepped beside the tall bard. Apparently oblivious to his ward, Lukas listened to the quiet rustling of the nighttime forest.

After a moment of silence, Casimir asked, "What are you listening for?"

"Hush," the bard said, raising a finger to his lips. His eyes wandered aimlessly about the dark canopy above. A grin jagged across his face, as though some inaudible voice had whispered a joke in the bard's ear. He straightened, drawing the dry air noisily into his lungs. Then his gaze fell on Casimir's shadowed face. He began to speak. "The stories of your incompetent rule have reached even Skald."

"Why need we stand in the woodlands for you tell me that?" Casimir snapped angrily. "I have consolidated my—"

"Casimir, Casimir," the bard interrupted, patting the young man's back. "Your rule is fated in every regard— *what* you decree, *how* you decree, and *why* you decree! Julianna told me about your plans for the slums. You plan to rule your people with paternal kindness, like a father caring for his sons!"

"I doubt I'll rule like a father. I am, after all, an orphan," Casimir said derisively. "But even if I grant your comparison, what's wrong with ruling like a father?"

"A father raises his sons to overthrow him," Lukas said without hesitation. "Most sons do so passively, enduring years of discontent in order to claim inheritance. Some sons do so actively, killing their fathers and seizing their lands." Lukas paused, fixing Casimir in a speculative gaze. "Either way, sons rise up and overthrow their fathers. Is that what you plan for the folk of Harmonia to do to you?"

"That's stupid."

"Is it?" Lukas asked. "Don't you see, Casimir? You want to treat the poor like little children, improve their lot, arm them with money, knowledge, and hope. Meanwhile, you ignore the nobles and Harmonic Hall, treating them like gangly teens and pushing them toward independence. And you've apprenticed all your children to Milil's temple, giving them a priest to rival you in power, a priest who is more than a match for you. If the rich don't kill you, the poor will rise up and do so. And if, by some impossible contrivance of the gods, the rich and poor both stay loyal, the temple will slay you and bury you with the saints."

Casimir responded acidly, "So I shouldn't rule as a father, but as a mother, or mother's brother, or next-door neighbor—perhaps a fishmonger, a haberdasher, a jester—"

"Silence!" Lukas cried, shaking his head in irritation, "No. Rule your folk as a predator rules its prey."

"Ha!" Casimir laughed. "I should hunt down my folk and eat them?"

"Precisely," the bard responded brutally. "A predator is never overthrown by his prey as a father is by his sons. A ruler, like a predator, must hem in his people and feast on those who stray."

Drawing a sharp breath, Casimir said, "Any ruler who acted as you say would be overthrown and killed by his subjects."

"Does the hare slay the wolf?" Lukas asked, his teeth gleaming darkly. "It might if it had the wolf's teeth and claws, or the wolf's thirst for blood and battle. But rabbits love to flee, not fight." The tall bard clamped his hands on Casimir's shoulders, and a wild glow spilled from his eyes. "Don't you see, Casimir? The guardsmen are yours, and the jails and the laws, too! You have the teeth and claws to kill them. Now you need only the thirst for the hunt and for blood."

Shivering despite the cloak about him, Casimir said, "I have no wish to slay my people."

"Unless you feast on them, as wolf on hare, your good people will rise up and kill you. Take a lesson from Zhone Clieous, who ruled for twenty years: Keep them in their warrens, keep them in their clustered fear, keep from them the claws and fangs of power, or you will fall."

"I would rather fall," Casimir said unconvincingly, "than rule so unjustly."

Now Lukas laughed, and the sound of it echoed through the trees. "What is evil or unjust about living true to your nature? Men are predators. Each day we savor the flesh of slain beasts. Why not of humans? What are they but beasts?"

Pausing, he gestured grandly at the moiling blackness of the forest around them. "The feasting of predator on prey is the way of all things: grass devours the dead; caterpillars devour the grass; shrews hunt caterpillars; cats hunt shrews; wolves hunt cats; men hunt wolves; kings hunt men; gods hunt kings. Casimir, you must rule as a hunter, or live among the hunted." Turning away, the bard filled his lungs with the night air and began to sing. His voice rang somber through the woods, like the lonely tolling of a great bell.

> "Now come to me, O wayward beast
> who roams this world in splendor.
> I call you here to heed my will,
> To search among the world and kill
> A feast for thine own pleasure.
>
> "Oh, come and pay me fealty, thus;
> come heed your master's singing.

In woodlands deep, you'll find your prey,
A sumptuous beast for you to slay
With rushing claws and gnashing."

The bard's lips had hardly closed when a massive dire wolf stepped soundlessly from the undergrowth. Lukas folded his arms with satisfaction as Casimir's eyes narrowed and he stepped back toward a nearby tree. The wolf stood easily four feet tall at its shoulders and bore itself with a loping gait. Its eyes glowed with hunger, and its pelt emitted an oily tang that permeated the air.

Despite—or perhaps because of—the blood Casimir shared with the creature, it repulsed him. Bristling, he set off the transformation in his muscles. Blunt rods of pain began to push through his arms and legs.

Lukas held a hand up disinterestedly before the creature and ordered it to sit. It immediately did so. Casimir halted his transformation, but didn't allow the tingling to slip from his muscles. Lukas's smile faded to a smirk. He threw a glance at Casimir and gestured casually toward the dire wolf.

"Wise folk select their tutors by lessons. . . ." The bard fixed his calm eyes on the beast. "Go find a hare. Bring it alive to me without the slightest wound on it." The beast regarded the bard intently. Casimir studied its witless eyes and wondered how the creature could possibly obey. Lukas lifted his hand into the still air and gestured angrily. "Go!"

As silently as it had come, the creature lifted its massive body and slipped away into the nighttime forest.

Letting the tingle drain from his limbs, Casimir eyed Lukas suspiciously. "How did you summon him?"

The bard didn't return the boy's gaze. "Even common bards marshal the hearts of men. Superlative singers can marshal the hearts of beasts."

"That's no answer," Casimir stated.

"Perhaps not for you," Lukas said flatly.

"You're wrong, by the way, about a ruler and his people."

"How so?" Lukas asked in a tone that discouraged response.

Casimir replied anyway. "You assume it's wrong for the old to give way to the new. But I've freed Harmonia by ridding it of my . . . my predecessor. In turn, when I grow old and incapable, a young ruler should succeed me."

"He should kill you?" Lukas asked.

"If I'm corrupt enough, yes; if I'm so entrenched that I can be removed in no other way; if I'm Zhone Clieous— yes, someone should kill me," Casimir said, swallowing hard.

"If you are truly willing to forfeit your life for the freedom of others, you're a fool," Lukas said derisively.

"Each of us must die sometime," Casimir countered. "You said yourself that men die and feed the grass with their bodies."

"Men die, yes, but gods don't."

"What does that matter?"

"The belief that all men must die is a peasant myth," Lukas responded matter-of-factly.

Casimir laughed. "What?"

"Common men know only a fragment of their true nature, and unless I judge wrongly, you are no common man," Lukas replied.

Before Casimir could respond, the dire wolf had once again emerged from the brush. In its black and panting jowls, a white hare dangled by the nape of its neck. Lukas motioned the wolf to approach. The beast came and relinquished the wriggling hare into Lukas's gloved hand. The bard held the quivering rabbit up before him, examining it in the moonlight.

"You see, Casimir? Despite its unquenchable hunger, this wolf has brought the hare to me unharmed. Why? Because I am a god to him. He bows to me not out of love, but fear. I am a wielder of fire, a slinger of arrows, a bringer of death. You must be the same to the folk of Harmonia if you wish to keep life and rule."

Lukas held his free palm before the dire wolf to keep

it in place, then gently lowered the hare to the ground. The moment the creature's scrabbling claws touched earth, it bolted frantically into the underbrush and disappeared. The dire wolf didn't give chase, staring dutifully at Harkon's palm. Nodding, Lukas removed his hand and turned toward his pupil. "Easy enough."

On one fingertip of the bard's gloved hands, Casimir glimpsed a dark spot of blood. Noting the shift of his student's attention, Lukas dropped his gaze to the offending spot. Pressing the fingertip to his thumb, Lukas felt the sticky liquid wick across on the clean fabric. He lifted his hand and sniffed the dark spot. His jaw clenched. Stepping toward the dire wolf, Lukas extended the stained finger in front of the beast's nose. Fear welled up in the wolf's dull eyes.

"I said *unharmed*," Lukas hissed. Seizing the muzzle and mane of the wolf, he wrenched suddenly. The massive head turned at an impossible angle to the body. A splitting crack echoed among the trees. The creature's joints folded beneath it. Trembling, the body collapsed to the earth.

Casimir staggered back, eyes bulging with shock.

Lukas eyed him calmly. "I hunt wolves, and gods hunt me."

Biting his lip, Casimir muttered, "I've learned enough."

"No," Lukas replied, stepping over the shuddering body and gesturing for Casimir to leave the clearing. "Now *you* have some hunting to do."

*   *   *   *   *

"He cannot stand over Harmonia! He's never set foot in this hallowed hall!" The shouts of Gaston Olyava met with thunderous applause and foot stomping from those gathered in Harmonic Hall's great room. Rarely had this chamber filled so fully—not even for the seasonal dances held here. Tonight, in addition to current students, the great room held alumni noblemen, jurisconsults, guardsmen, merchants, officials of all sorts, and countless scribes.

"A man who kills a meistersinger is no hero! A boy who kills a meistersinger must be born of fiends! I'll not have such a ruler over my fair city!" Once again the ovation rang out. The bard stepped back from the podium, shielding the smile that crossed his face. Still the shouts of support filled the room. Stoking his anger again to full boil, Gaston shouted, "We must remove Casimir as he removed our beloved Clieous!"

"Let *me* remove your treasonous tongue!" came a furious shout from the back of the room. Gaston's mouth snapped tight in indignation as the seated listeners pivoted noisily in their chairs to catch sight of the speaker.

"The meistersinger! It's the meistersinger!"

Meistersinger Casimir stepped boldly into the room, his face scarlet with rage. Beside him towered the black-mustachioed Harkon Lukas, whose steely eyes scanned the assembled folk with cold malice. Casimir strode toward the podium.

Gaston's face went white with shock as he struggled to regain his voice. Before he could speak, however, Casimir continued. "My friend and mentor, Harkon Lukas, was kind enough to inform me of this meeting. My name must have slipped your roster of invitations . . . a fatal oversight."

Gaston eyed the audience to gauge their mood. Each face he saw regarded the young meistersinger with disdain, if not hatred. He spat venomously, "It was no oversight, Master Casimir. You neither belong to nor support the hall, and the hall neither belongs to nor supports you."

An approving murmur stirred through the crowd.

Casimir marched forward, stepped onto the low platform, and brushed Gaston away from the lectern. "Though I have had no association with this hall, you would best invite me to do so now. I am meistersinger! I have outsung, outargued, outwitted, and outfought all of you in the meistersinger contest."

"Outfought? Ha!" Gaston shouted, pushing his way back to the podium. "You mean outbrawled and out-back-stabbed."

"Disperse from here, by order of the meistersinger," Casimir ordered, glossing over the insult. "I will summon the guard to—"

"You've little need to call the guard, meistersinger," Gaston interrupted wryly. "The captain of the guard is here among us, along with his three lieutenants. Do you intend to fight us all?"

Casimir stared into the masses that filled the chamber. They stared back with a predatory lust he knew all too well. Surely they smelled the fear in him, the fear and the weakness. Thoughts of the wolf hunt flooded into Casimir's mind—the dull eyes, the crimson spot, the cracking spine, the homage the wolf paid Lukas. Suddenly Casimir knew what he must do.

"No, I'll not fight all of you," he shouted, silencing the crowd's growing murmur. "But because you seem to be the speaker for the crowd, Gaston Olyava, I *will* fight you."

Gaston blanched. He shook his head and released a rattling laugh. "I'll not take part in a street brawl with you, orphan lord."

"Name the means, then," Casimir challenged.

Sweat beaded across Gaston's incredulous brow. He laughed once. "How ludicrous this is!" Sighing with dramatic disinterest he said, "Rapiers then."

"Fine," Casimir growled, "and because you named the means of our battle, I shall name the end: Rapiers to the death."

A thrill traveled through the crowd.

Turning disdainfully away from Casimir, Gaston called out, "Clear a space here. Someone bring us a pair of rapiers." Whirling about, he whispered over the clatter of chairs, "I must warn you, I'm the hall's best swords-man."

Casimir replied with a nod. "I must warn you, I've single-handedly killed a werewolf."

"You won't win by treachery as you did before."

"Neither will I lose by it."

As their banter continued, the crowd rearranged the chairs in a large crescent that pulled away from the stage. Most of the noblemen sat in the center of the crescent, but a few stragglers remained along the side walls. Among them sat Harkon Lukas.

The crowd quieted as two wards of the hall came through the entryway bearing rapiers. Gaston turned toward Casimir with a wicked smile. "Choose your blade."

Stepping forward to meet the bearers, Casimir selected a sword. He'd never before wielded a blade larger than a dagger, and despite the rapier's fine balance, it felt slow and awkward in his hand. Distractedly whirling the sword in figure eights before his face, Casimir began to wonder if any of his skill with a dagger would translate to this weapon. Gaston selected his weapon, and the blade bearers retreated quickly from the open circle. Executing a few impressive sweeps with the sword, Gaston turned his back on Casimir and walked toward the opposite wall. Taking the cue, Casimir turned and did the same. When the duelers reached opposite sides of the room, they turned and faced each other gravely. The audience fell silent.

Gaston raised the rapier slowly from his side, pointing its tip toward Casimir. In ritual motion, he gradually rotated the hilt until his wrist lay downward. Casimir mimicked the motion. Now Gaston turned the blade in a quick arc and leveled it, flat side up, across his midsection. Casimir did the same. Then Gaston assumed his combat stance: sword angled upward to the front above his forward leg; free hand held high in back above his rear leg; knees bent and head back. Casimir studied the awkward position and tried to effect a similar stance. The crowd chuckled.

Gaston charged him. The bard's movements were at once graceful and powerful as he crossed the floor. Casimir raised his blade. Gaston closed the gap. Desperately

Casimir swung his sword in front of him. Gaston's rapier struck with a solid clang, its edge raking across Casimir's sword and forcing it to the floor. The swords tangled. Gaston buried his charging shoulder in the young meistersinger's stomach. Casimir sprawled onto his back, and a mirthful shout rang up from the crowd.

Gaston took no pause for the ovation, lunging at the scrambling form. Casimir rolled and gasped. His shoulder grew warm and slick with blood. Swinging his sword wide, he knocked the blade away from the wound. Scrambling to his feet on the bloodstained floor, he assumed the wiry crouch he used in dagger fights. With shallow sweeps of his blade, Casimir jabbed at Gaston's stomach. The rapier moved in sluggish, innocuous swipes, unable to pass Gaston's whirling steel. Deflecting a dozen weak jabs, Gaston drove forward, flipping Casimir's blade back as though it were a buzzing fly. With the sharp ringing of steel on steel, he rushed Casimir and sliced him deeply across one cheek.

Casimir leapt back, his free hand pressing on the cut. His sweaty palm stung in the open wound.

"Perhaps, orphan lord, I'll kill you this way, one wound after another until you're a bleeding lump," Gaston said with a sneer.

Ignoring the hoots of the crowd, Casimir lunged forward, his blade whistling. Gaston canted his rapier slightly to deflect the attack, and the razor edges ground against each other. Thrusting the blow to his side, the bard slashed into Casimir's bony hip. Whirling, Casimir pulled away from the blade and stepped back, holding his sword before him. A scarlet wave slowly rolled down his leg as he circled outside the swordsman's reach.

"What will happen if I slay you, meistersinger?" Gaston taunted. "Surely I'd be meistersinger myself by right of slaughter, ascending the seat of power as you yourself did."

Casimir's eyes narrowed. Should I transform and kill him? he wondered. No, not in this crowd. They'd hunt me down and kill me.

Swinging his bloodied blade high, Gaston approached with a series of aggressive feints. He charged Casimir, batting his sword aside with casual strokes. Another gash striped the boy-meistersinger's stomach. Casimir stumbled weakly backward, but couldn't regain his footing. He fell to the floor, slipping on his own blood. Gaston advanced, towering over him. A look of hatred crossed his face. He set his sharp-tipped sword on the helpless young man's throat.

"I think you've had enough," he spat. "Enough of humiliation, enough of injury, enough of life."

The blade pressed into Casimir's neck, then stopped and withdrew. Hands fastened on Gaston's shoulders, and he stepped back. A baritone voice boomed, "Surely you wouldn't slay a man on his back, would you?"

Harkon Lukas.

Gaston withdrew, smiling broadly and bowing to the cheers of the crowd. With Harkon's help, Casimir rose and steadied himself. Weak, breathless, and battered, he half-wished Gaston had sunk the blade home.

The tall bard's voice whispered in his ear, "Devour him, Casimir. You have the fangs and claws. You need only the lust for the hunt and for blood."

Casimir shook his head. "He's too strong. I can't do it."

"Take the wounds. Take the wounds and drive him into my lap. I'll do the rest."

Nodding, though he little understood, Casimir stepped away from the supporting hands. His body felt loose-jointed and weary. His head slumped forward as he peered at Gaston through half-closed eyes. Slowly he circled. Twice Gaston lunged toward him, landing blows. The crowd ceased its laughter. Mantled in blood, Casimir shambled around the room, gasping for air like a punctured bellows.

Gritting his teeth, Casimir suddenly threw himself at Gaston. The bard's rapier hit once, and again, and again, but still Casimir came on. By sheer force, he drove the singer back on his heels, stumbling in retreat across the clear space. Casimir's blade struck its first blow, glancing though it was, on his enemy's side. Gaston hissed, clutching the wound. He tumbled back. Casimir directed the retreat, pursuing still with flashing sword. Gaston lanced Casimir's sword arm one last time before he sprawled onto Harkon Lukas's lap.

Suddenly pain striped his features.

Harkon pushed the rigid man off him and onto Casimir's extended blade. The metal slid easily through the heaving chest, as though it were cutting through water. With a final gasp, Gaston slumped to the floor and lay still.

Casimir drew forth the blood-sheathed rapier, his eyes growing wide. He set the sword's tip on the floor. Leaning on the blade, he shouted, "Flee now from here, you vermin! If any one of you ever rises against me again, I'll hunt you down and kill you myself. I've already noted many of your faces! Now go!"

As the crowd began its hurried retreat, Casimir once more felt hands on his shoulders. "So ends the first lesson."

Without answering, Casimir pulled dizzily away and wandered into the adjoining kitchen. He pushed past the creaking pantry door and closed it behind him. The cool darkness worked into his sizzling wounds. Must transform. Must heal these cuts, he thought, triggering the transformation.

TEN

Julianna leaned back in the creaking chair. Sighing, she set her low-burning candle on the bedstand and drew a shaking hand across her perspiration-beaded brow. The night was hot. Pulling the sticky chemise away from her chest, she propped her throbbing feet on the bedframe. It, too, creaked. The fringed canopy above swayed slightly.

The bed's slumbering inhabitant was Meistersinger Casimir. He lay dressed in a nightshirt, the last of his bandages poking out through the sleeves. During the past week, each of the sword wounds on his body had closed without infection, thanks to Julianna's ministrations. She allowed herself a weary smile.

"I wish Thoris were doing as well," she thought aloud, peering through the dark doorway that stood beside the bed. In the room beyond the doorway, Thoris lay asleep on a similar bed. Though some of the color had returned to his face, his eyes had remained closed for over a week. As Julianna stared into the dark room where he lay, her worried fingers distractedly tugged at the linen collar of her chemise.

The sultry air pressed heavily on her. She undid the top buttons of her chemise and fanned her perspiration-slick neck. "Better head to bed," she decided. Rising from the chair, she stretched, and her tired muscles pulled lazily against the seams of her shirt. Before leaving, she bent over Casimir's bedside one last time to check his wounds.

His eyes blinked slowly open, and a smile spread over his face. "Hi."

"Hi," she replied softly, pulling away from him.

"It's good of you to stop by," Casimir said sleepily.

Biting her lip, she said, "I never left."

Casimir's brow furrowed. "When I was awake last time, you said you were going to bed."

"A week ago you said you were going for a walk," she snapped sarcastically, "and you came back looking like this."

"Thanks for your help." He rubbed his bandaged shoulder.

"It works out well," she said wryly. "You dismember yourself, and I re-member you." She studied the lacerations on his forearm. "You're almost well."

"Yeah," Casimir said, watching her closely, "but I've been having nightmares."

Julianna began to fan herself. "Nightmares?"

"I've been dreaming about werewolves."

"I can think of better things to dream about," Julianna observed, setting the candle back on the bedside stand.

"Actually," Casimir said tentatively, "I dreamt about being a werewolf."

"Your wounds from Uncle weren't infected, were they?" she asked.

"No," Casimir responded, gazing beyond the bed's velvet canopy. "But I still dream. I dream I'm a good man trapped in a wolf's body."

"What do you do?" Julianna asked curiously. "Can you do good things, or only evil?"

"Only evil," Casimir replied, staring blankly ahead. "No matter what I try to do, it always comes out evil."

"I wonder why," Julianna mused.

Casimir dropped his hand on hers. His eyes traced the slender curve of her arm. "I don't know."

Peering furtively at their hands, Julianna blinked. "You should stop having these dreams."

"Perhaps being a wolf frightens me less than being

meistersinger," Casimir said, his eyes still fixed on hers.

"Afraid of being meistersinger?" Julianna asked, her voice growing more confident. She looked toward the window and drew a deep breath. "You'll do fine. You've begun the restoration of the temple of Milil, you've started preparations for a new Reaptide, and you've put down a rebellion. When you're well, no one will stop you."

Casimir raised her hand to his lips and kissed it. Then he smiled, peering into her eyes. "Do you remember our first real kiss?"

"Yes," she said, pulling her hand back. "On Harmonic Hall balcony, the night the poorhouse burned."

"Funny . . . I can't seem to remember it," Casimir replied. "Could we try it again?"

Wordlessly she bent over him. Resting a delicate hand on his uninjured shoulder, she set her lips to his in a light kiss. The touch of his flesh felt hot in the steamy room. He slid one hand into her cascading hair, kissing her earlobe and caressing the lines of her neck. She raised her head, breathing deeply.

A ghostlike form hovered in the doorway.

Julianna gasped, pushing away from Casimir. The form simply stood there, staring with black, sunken eyes. Casimir sat up, turning his head toward the figure. It was Thoris, cadaverous and cold despite the blistering night. His face glowed dimly beyond the candlelight, and his eyes looked damnably sober.

"Casimir," Thoris whispered simply. Then his eyes slowly closed, and he began to collapse.

With a surge of strength he didn't know he had, Casimir leapt to his feet and rushed to Thoris. Julianna joined him, and together they dragged the boy back to his bed. While Casimir arrayed Thoris's limp body on the linen, Julianna fetched the candle. Breathless, they pulled chairs up to sit at the bedside.

"Wake up, Thoris," Casimir said, jiggling the boy's leg. "Wake up." He shot a questioning gaze toward Julianna.

"Thoris, wake up," she said, gently patting his hand.

The color slowly returned to Thoris's drawn cheeks. His eyelids began to flutter, then drew slowly open. The pupils beneath were abnormally wide.

Thoris's voice was a croaking moan. "Casimir?"

"Yes, Thoris," Casimir answered, leaning forward.

A shudder ran through the boy's body. He caught a few shallow breaths, then spoke. "Send her away."

Quizzically Casimir studied his friend's face. "This is Julianna, Thoris. She's our friend."

"Send her away."

Julianna had already risen, the backs of her legs pushing the chair away from the bed. "I'll go. . . . It's best to humor him," she said. Confusion showed on her pale features as she circled around the bed and swept silently from the room.

Casimir watched her go, his heart lodged in his throat. He listened for her footsteps retreating in the hall, then turned intently toward his ailing friend.

"Thoris, it's good to have you back."

"Close the door," Thoris said coldly.

Not wanting to upset his friend, Casimir rose and secured the door. His heart pounded unevenly as he made his way back toward the bed. He lowered himself to one of the wooden chairs and waited for Thoris to speak.

The boy's voice was dry and craggy. "How dare you kiss her?"

Casimir stared at him, smiling incredulously. "Is that what this is all about—jealousy?"

"How dare you kiss her, knowing what you are?"

The smile on Casimir's face went slack. "What are you talking about?"

"I saw you in the Crystal Club," Thoris said, his voice gaining an angry pitch. "I saw what you did. I saw what you are."

Casimir could feel the blood draining from his face. His hands were suddenly clammy and cold. "What did you see, Thoris?"

The pallid boy pushed himself up on his elbows, compressing the pillow behind him into a wedge. Easing his head back, he leveled a deadly gaze at his friend and spoke:

"You are a beast-man, Casimir . . . a werewolf."

The sentence struck Casimir like a fist, almost knocking him from his seat. He rose, wide-eyed, and began to pace the room. His feet felt numb, and sweat streamed down his fevered brow.

"You're an abomination," Thoris said quietly, coughing. "A murderer . . . a monster."

Now Thoris knows, thought Casimir, and he hates me. Now he'll tell Julianna, tell all of Harmonia. . . .

"You lied to me, your only friend," Thoris said sadly. "You lied to me, and now to Julianna."

Casimir stopped pacing and eased himself into one of the chairs beside the bed. He stared at Thoris, his eyes narrowing. "So . . . you know my secret."

"You're not even human," Thoris blurted, miserable.

"Yes, I am," Casimir said quietly. Then, dropping his head into his hands, he muttered. "No, perhaps you're right. Perhaps I'm not human. I've fought this thing all my life and never won. I can't stop it, Thoris. That's why I threw myself from South Hill. I wish you'd never rescued me."

"How many men have you killed, Casimir?" Thoris whispered, his eyes staring hollowly. "One for each night you left the poorhouse?"

"Yes!" Casimir admitted through clenched teeth.

"How long did you plan to hide this from me?" Thoris snapped. "Or did you plan to kill me before I found out?"

Enough was enough.

Casimir rose, indignation reddening his face. The transformation had begun. "How dare you presume to be so important to me! Struggle beneath your own curse for eighteen years before you judge me! Yes, perhaps I should kill you. There'd be one less orphan in Harmonia."

Thoris cast back the blankets Casimir had drawn over him and struggled to a sitting position on the bedside. He threw his arms wide and said quietly, "Then kill me now, beast-man! I'd rather be dead than befriend a monster."

Fury worked across Casimir's flushed face, and a raucous jangling filled his muscles. His teeth proliferated evilly, forcing cracked lips into a leer. Beneath the bandages, his flesh rippled and flexed, stretching across the warping bones of his frame. As his back began its reshaping, he peered with blazing eyes at the huddled boy.

Yes, my power will be the last thing he ever sees.

Thoris's head slumped forward on his chest, though he kept his arms out to each side. He was trembling. Slowly the ashen boy raised his face to gaze on the beast forming before him. His voice was gentle against the bone-snapping transformation. "Kill me. You should have done it years ago."

Casimir's mind reeled. If I kill him, I really will be an inhuman monster. But if Thoris divulges my secret to anyone, I'll be hunted down and killed myself.

The half-formed beast-man tottered unevenly on his warped legs. Turning, he scrambled away from Thoris and disappeared into the adjoining room. In moments, he emerged again with something shiny in his hand.

"Kill me, Thoris! *Kill me!*"

The werewolf's massive claw flung a letter opener onto the bed beside Thoris. The blade was long and keen, and its cold slickness was unmistakably silver.

Thoris latched onto the blade. He looked from the shining silver in his palm to the panting beast before him. The beast was slowly reorienting itself. Its hatchet chest grew more shallow; its misaligned limbs straightened; its muzzle contracted into its face; its hair slid into its flesh. Just as Thoris had done, the creature spread its arms to its side, inviting the dagger. With each heartbeat, the beast looked less like a monster and more like Casimir.

The silver blade slipped from Thoris's fingers and clattered to the bare floor. Pushing himself up from the bed, Thoris stepped forward weakly. He laid his trembling palms on the sides of Casimir's face just as the jagging jawbone released its last tremor. Weak and shaky, Thoris's knees buckled, and he slumped to the floor. Now fully human, Casimir knelt over him, wrapping his friend in his arms.

"What can we do, Thoris?" Casimir said. "I won't kill you, and you won't kill me."

"Perhaps . . . perhaps Gustav can cure you."

Casimir gazed toward the ceiling, thinking of Lukas's warning about the priest. "Yes . . . perhaps he can."

Visibly mustering his strength, Thoris said, "Let's go tonight."

* * * * *

Meistersinger Casimir, his face overhung by a dark cloak, stepped from his black carriage. Drawing the hood from his head, he cast back his shock of midnight hair and gazed into the night sky. It was the dark of the moon, when Casimir felt more human than any other time. He turned and lifted a hand to help the weak-bodied Thoris down from the carriage. As Thoris alighted, Casimir breathed the sultry air. "So tonight I will be free," he said dubiously under his breath.

With Thoris on his arm, Casimir stepped slowly up to the door of the temple. It was the same door that had greeted him weeks before—ancient, iron-banded, and thick-set, with forbidding bolts. But one structure on that aged frame had a sharp-edged newness to it: a massive lock set deep in the wood.

"I see my reforms are going well for the church," he observed wryly, indicating the lock. "I've been told that the church might try to lock me out."

"Perhaps it isn't locked," Thoris ventured.

The black-haired ruler gazed doubtfully at Thoris as he tried the latch. The door swung silently open on newly cast hinges. With mild surprise, Casimir stared into the moiling darkness within. A faint light glowed in the sanctuary.

"I doubted Gustav would lock out the people," Thoris said.

"Perhaps not," Casimir replied, crossing his arms over his chest, "now that the poorhouse alm-seekers are dead."

Without a word, Thoris pulled his arm from Casimir's and tottered across the threshold. Regretting his sarcasm, the meistersinger followed and presented his arm for Thoris to lean on. After a few more shaky steps, Thoris accepted the help and the boys entered the sanctuary.

They little recognized the place—only the dark gloom of it looked familiar. The grime that once lined the stone passageways had been scoured away, and the floor beneath their feet was dry and shiny. The musty, cave-like odor was also gone. As they approached the faintly glowing pit where the organ lay, Casimir noted the broad and beautiful banners that ringed the sanctuary. Below them sat rows of repaired and polished seats. But the heart of the sanctuary, the organ, still slouched in disrepair. In the midst of the organ's skeleton, a stooped figure moved.

Gustav.

"Has Milil returned to his sanctuary?" Casimir cried.

Startled, Gustav spun about to face them. He clutched a nearby organ pipe to keep from falling to the floor. "If Milil has returned, he'll surely punish you for frightening me!"

With Thoris on his arm, Casimir started slowly down the stairs. "The wrath of the god of music . . . forgive me if I don't tremble. What would Milil do, torture me with trumpets?"

Gustav's smile belied his angry words. "Don't mock the power of music, lad. Were this organ working, I could play a melody so plaintive as to steal your very soul."

"You wouldn't want my soul," Casimir said soberly.

The old man shrugged off the comment, his watery eyes greeting them and lingering sadly on their wounds.

"Your rulership appears to be treating you lads poorly." He reached out, tentatively setting one hand on each one's arm.

"You, however, appear to profit from my rule," Casimir noted, peering about at the polished wood and new fabrics.

"Not only I, but Milil as well," Gustav said. A mild smile formed on the craggy lips. He sighed and said distractedly, "I even have parishioners now." He gestured wearily toward the organ behind him and his smile faded. "I'd proclaim Milil's return, except that his heart—the organ—is still silent."

"It's a shame, really," Casimir responded dryly. His expression changed and he said, "I understand a master organ builder dwells in Skald. I'll send for him tomorrow."

"The whole thing's in ruins. It needs new stops and plates and dampers, and half the pipes have gone bad."

"I'll send for him tomorrow," Casimir repeated flatly.

Gustav shook his head as though to clear it. "Forgive me. This organ's filled my thoughts for a week now. I've not even been able to sleep, as you well see. But enough about my failings. What urgent business has brought you here tonight?"

"Well, it's rather difficult . . ." Casimir's words trailed off as Thoris stepped forward and spoke.

"We need your help, Gustav," Thoris said.

The old priest's eyes narrowed. "What could you need from me? I could bless these wounds of yours. . . ."

"Perhaps," Casimir responded. "But the wound we need healed is far deeper than these."

"What wound do you mean?" Gustav asked, growing curious.

"Can Milil cure . . . lycanthropy?" Casimir responded, the words feeling flat on his lips.

Gustav's hand strayed to his heart. He stumbled backward, catching his weight on a pew behind him. His bulging eyes looked glossy in the lantern's dim light. "*Now* I know why you came at night . . . why at the dark of the moon . . . why with such foul cuts and scars across your body."

Casimir strode with steely deliberateness toward the priest. "You must heal me, master. I brought back your god. Bring back my soul."

Gustav averted his eyes as he spoke. "It's been a long time since I've practiced such rites."

"Please, Gustav," Casimir said. "If you don't save me from this monster, he'll unmake me, and unmake you as well."

"I'll need to consult many dark, tattered volumes to remember what I must do," Gustav observed to no one in particular. "Even so, my powers are meaningless unless you've indeed brought back Milil." He cast a dubious glance toward the pipe organ, then turned again toward Casimir. "Come . . . let's go to the temple library and my books."

* * * * *

Thoris and Casimir sat quietly at a table in the temple library, the cool air soaking like a salve into their angry wounds. As they watched, Gustav moved among his countless books, pulling down broad tomes and stacking them in his feeble arms. At last Gustav set his stack on a table and began poring over the cryptic texts. He'd thoroughly searched through three books before he spoke, but even then he didn't look up from the text. "How long have you been . . . afflicted?"

Startled after the long silence, Casimir replied, "As long as I can remember."

Gustav looked up. "Then you have killed before?"

"Yes." The answer rang cold on the stone.

Gustav sighed heavily, closing the thick tome. "Before we can even think about healing your lycanthropy, you'll need to be purified of the murders. How many have you committed, boy?"

"I'm no longer a boy, Master Gustav," Casimir said, mildly irritated. "And I've committed many."

Gustav rose, holding the book under his arm and moving toward the library's door. "To the altar," he said, motioning for them to follow. Casimir assisted Thoris in standing, and together they followed the priest. He led them to the chapel altar, a broad dolmen of cut and polished stone. As they arrived, Gustav began paging through the book. His eyes roved over the symbol-laden page, then found the passage he sought. He translated aloud:

> "Our lord Milil harbors not wrath for us, as does Helm for his folk, nor heaps law upon law that we may confuse our right hand with our left. Instead, Milil calls us to harmony, not law, a harmony that holds but three acts in contempt: blasphemy, for this is denying Milil's song. Milil denies his song to no one. Self-slaughter, for this is putting an end to one's own song. Milil alone can say when your song must end. And murder, for this is ending the song of another. Only Milil knows when another's song must end.
>
> "These three contempts were the first creations of Kakaphon, bastard brother to Milil. It is written: 'And as our lord Milil wandered through the garden, Kakaphon opposed him, saying, "My brother, thy sweet songs have slain me: the sun and earth turn to thee as, too, the beasts and men. They call thee Song and seek thee, but call me Discord and flee my face. Thy song thus has brought me to nought." And so saying, Kakaphon of Discord fell dead.
>
> " 'In grief for his brother, Milil repented of his beautiful song and would not sing. The sun darkened the firmament, the earth leapt in fear, the beasts burrowed and would not rise, and the men hid their despairing eyes. Seeing these things, Milil wept and said, "My song brought this brother of mine to nought, but my silence might end the whole world. It is blasphemy that I have denied my

world its song; it is murder that I have slain my kin with my singing; and it is self-slaughter that I have caused in Kakaphon."

"'To heal the triune wrong, Milil clove a notch from his ear in memory of Kakaphon of Discord. That notch marred the music that entered our lord's ear, and so brought discord into Milil's sweet hymns. By that discord, Milil then sang his song and restored the world, rectifying to himself all those who dwell in discord.'

"So even if a man should bear the guilt of blasphemy, self-slaughter, or murder, Milil will forgive, and his song will grow richer through the discord. Let those who seek mercy come forward now."

As the priest droned on, Casimir studied the solid stone altar before him. A silken stole lay upon it, twined about a delicate wooden bowl and a small ceremonial knife of tarnished silver. Casimir clenched his teeth: how fitting that the blade was silver, he thought. Gustav finally closed the book, setting its dusty bulk on a stand beside the altar. Rising, he lifted the stole in his trembling hands, kissed it, and looped it like a yoke around his neck. Then, setting a hand on Casimir's shoulder, he began the ritual.

"Casimir, have you drawn near in full knowledge of your contempts, wishing thus to be freed of them?"

"I have."

"And of the three contempts—blasphemy, self-slaughter, and murder—for which of these do you seek pardon?"

"For mur—" Casimir began, but remembered the night on South Hill. "For all of these, good priest."

"Milil has pardoned and purified you, Casimir," Gustav continued, "and because your ear is untouched by the outward mark of this inward healing, your pardon awaits its seal in flesh." He reached to the altar, retrieving the silver blade without even glancing at it. Holding the knife before Casimir, the priest continued gravely.

"This blade, blessed by the hands of Milil's priest, has become the very edge by which Milil clove his own ear. Touch this point to the tip of your tongue."

Casimir did so, and Gustav continued, "You have thus touched the blade, signifying that these contempts arose from your mouth and entered your ear as discords in conflict with the song of Milil. Before you forsake that song, remember your blasphemies, your self-slaughters, your murders. Then think ahead to belief, commitment to the song, and enhancement of the lives of others."

Gustav stepped toward Casimir and slid his free hand behind the youth's earlobe. Lifting the knife high into the air, Gustav said, "Casimir, before I sink this blade, remember the faces of those you have slain. And let this mark seal that memory."

With two clean strokes of the keen blade, Gustav sliced a small triangular wedge of flesh from Casimir's earlobe. Picking up the bowl, he caught the blood that poured from the ear. Placing the bit of flesh and the rubied knife on the altar, he lifted a bleached cloth from his pocket and stanched the blood flow.

"Milil has pardoned your contempts, good Casimir. Henceforth sing his song with duty," Gustav said, motioning for Casimir to hold the cloth in place. Lifting his hand to the reddening rag, Casimir noticed that Thoris had approached and now stood beside him. The ashen boy said nothing, but a feeble smile was on his lips. Meanwhile, Gustav took the knife and bowl from the altar, removed the stole from his shoulders and folded it, and turned toward the two young men.

"This is but the first step, Casimir," Gustav said. "You are pardoned, but not healed. You cannot be healed until the night of the full moon, a fortnight from now, when you must return here for the rites."

The smile faded from Thoris's face, and Casimir went white. "So I must stay clear of these—these contempts until then?"

"Yes," Gustav said simply.

"Why didn't you say so before the ceremony?"

"To have any hope of this working, Casimir, you must remain faithful to the song of Milil from now to the next full moon. You must commit no blasphemy, no self-slaughter, and no murder." The old priest's eyes were cold and calculating. "That's why I didn't tell you."

Breathing deeply, Casimir said, "Despite your lack of faith in me, good Gustav, I'll remain pure this fortnight." Then, turning angrily, the raven-haired meistersinger headed with Thoris from the altar.

"That mark on your ear makes you a child of Milil," Gustav cried out as the boys retreated into the vast darkness of the chapel.

Without turning around, Casimir snarled, "If Milil won't save me, I will damn him."

Gustav called after them, "Avoid the contempts and Milil will save you! It isn't *he* who will be damned if you fail."

The words rang hollowly through the chamber as Casimir and Thoris disappeared into the inky dark. Weakly Gustav wandered from the altar and slumped onto the front pew. Closing his eyes and running a hand through his frazzled hair, the old man began to sing an ancient hymn.

> *"So, too, Milil, the dark ones cry to thee,*
> *The ones who dwell among the dead,*
> *Whose steps are laid in troubled ways,*
> *In paths where darkness lives.*
> *They cry to thee as night to day,*
> *As Fear's dark child, bent on hope.*

> *"These midnight ones are born in blood*
> *And nurtured on the bones of men.*
> *Their crooked paths lead to the grave,*
> *Their passions to the pangs of death.*
> *Still they cry to thee, Milil,*
> *They cry in hopes that thou wilt hear,*
> *Wilt hear and change them utterly."*

ELEVEN

Casimir surveyed the bustling marketplace. Its canvas stalls and wooden booths shone brightly beneath the early autumn sun. Shouts of merchants mixed with the melodic piping of street musicians. Despite the festive banners and brisk air of the market, Casimir felt dead. Tonight the full moon would rise, bringing his last chance to be cured of lycanthropy. "Very little chance indeed," he muttered to himself. Although he had committed no further murders since his purification, he suspected Milil either wouldn't or couldn't save him. Casimir sighed, his eyes wandering to the leather-worker's stall at the market's edge. There Thoris was dutifully trying on an enormous studded belt while Julianna laughed uproariously. A faint smile formed on Casimir's lips, then faded. "If the rite fails, Gustav and Thoris will put me to death."

"Death . . . life . . . metamorphosis," came a rich voice behind Casimir as a long-fingered hand settled on his shoulder. Turning, Casimir saw Harkon Lukas. The bard cut a dark silhouette against the pale, autumnal sky. Lukas smiled broadly and extended his hand. In his open palm rested a necklace with a pendant of yellow glass. "I bought something for you." Casimir squinted, peering into the translucent oval. The glass held a butterfly, its thin legs and membranous wings crushed against its body. "Metamorphosis—the dance of death unto life unto death," Harkon explained.

"Feeling philosophical today, are we?" Casimir observed humorlessly, taking the pendant from the bard.

"And why not?" Lukas asked. Setting his hand on Casimir's back, Lukas directed him down the market lane. "The air smells of autumn, tonight is the full moon, and you've reined in your rebel state." Again Lukas flashed a toothy grin.

Depositing the pendant in his pocket, Casimir peered down at the rugged cobbles of the marketplace. "Do you really think so, Master Lukas? Do you really think I've done well?"

"You killed Gaston the traitor, seized control of the hall, cowed the nobles, and filled the jail with dissidents," the bard observed. "You've become quite a predatory ruler, Casimir, and almost overnight."

Raising his narrowed eyes toward Lukas, Casimir asked, "Did *I* kill Gaston, or did *you?*"

"Does it matter?" Lukas asked flatly.

Casimir averted his eyes again toward the cobbles. "Even though I hated Gaston, I wish I hadn't killed him." Kicking a loose stone across the road, he added, "My predations are over."

Stepping squarely in front of Casimir, Harkon Lukas clamped his hands on the young ruler's shoulders. Lukas's eyes had grown serious. "How near to death must you wander before you learn from the lessons I have for you? If you hadn't killed Gaston that night, he would have killed you. You must prey on them, Casimir, prey on them and keep preying."

"Enough," Casimir replied, stepping around Lukas and setting off through the market. "If I can only rule through viciousness and cruelty, perhaps I *should* be killed."

Lukas's smile faded and the monocle dropped from his eye into his gloved palm. He stared incredulously at Casimir, then started after him, wiping the lens on a silk kerchief. "Cruelty is inherent to rulership, Casimir. The corruption lies not in you, but in humanity."

"You know nothing of my corruptions," Casimir growled.

Lifting the monocle to his eye and putting it in place, the tall bard said, "Perhaps you need another lesson. Meet me tonight in the woods just beyond the river."

"I have a prior engagement tonight," Casimir said. "Besides, you'd only be wasting your time. As you yourself said, I'll be dead in a fortnight."

"Meet me at midnight," Lukas repeated sternly, then turned with a whirl of his cloak and slipped away through the crowded market.

*　*　*　*　*

The day's final light lingered in the stained glass of Milil's temple. For long hours, the only sound in the temple had come from Gustav's creaking wrench as the old priest labored on his tedious resurrection of the long-dead organ. But now, as the sun set, a high, clear, and beautiful sound quietly vibrated within the ancient walls. Craning over the dismantled shell of the organ, Gustav stopped his repairs. The ratchet cradled in his trembling hand slipped loose, clattering onto the age-yellowed ivory of the keyboard. Gustav cocked his ear and listened.

The sound was pure and soft, a solitary note, thin and yet rich in tone. It filled the entire sanctuary. Gustav's brow furrowed as he gazed toward the piccolo pipes before him. "Perhaps the organ's venting," he speculated. With his knobby hand, he removed the wrench from the keyboard, then depressed a number of the high-octave keys. The tone didn't change. "It's not from the organ." He scooted the rattling bench backward and rose, stepping into the sanctuary.

The tone lowered in pitch. Gustav eyed the vast gray walls of the temple. The wind sometimes whistled in the lancets, but this sound was different. "Who's playing . . . ?" he murmured, but the words trailed off as an ancient hymn rose in his mind:

*Milil's bright angel chorus sings loud in every ear
To bring unto the people his glad celestial Song.*

They sing in chords so lofty that mortal folk won't hear
Until the hour that Death's regretful work is done.

"The Song of Milil! After all these years, I hear it,"
Gustav said wonderingly. A chill prickled along his
spine. "Does it mean I will die tonight?" Dropping heavily to the nearest pew, the holy man steadied himself.
His had been a long life, if not a particularly easy one.
He studied his aged hands, tracing the multitude of lines
and scars there. His palms seemed like scrolls where his
life lay written. "But the temple isn't finished; the faithful
are not yet gathered . . . "

The sound suddenly ceased. Gustav sat still and
cocked his ear toward the high-vaulted ceiling. Silence.
Only the priest's thudding heart disturbed the hush. His
aged eyes traced the stone vault above.

The soft padding of leather-soled feet sounded at the
top of the stairs. Someone was coming. Gustav rose
slowly from his seat and turned toward the footfalls. He
peered into the darkness beyond the stairs, half-know-
ing who would emerge. First came the silhouette of a
regal young man with icy eyes, then the rounded
shadow of a youth. As the dark figures began to
descend, the stained glass of the sanctuary cast blood-
hued light over them.

"My lord Casimir and Master Thoris, how good to see
you again," Gustav said, his eyes narrowing beneath
frazzled brows.

Casimir replied solemnly, "It's the first night of the full
moon."

"I know," the old man responded.

The darkness deepened on Casimir's face as he
neared. "I thought you'd want to start before sunset."

Gustav started up the stairs. "Come . . . I've prepared
a small altar for the ceremony. The sanctuary of Milil is
no place for such rites."

*   *   *   *   *   *

Casimir bristled, pulling on the thick iron bands around his ankles and wrists. "I didn't know Milil believed in shackles."

"He doesn't," Gustav replied soberly, passing the broad-linked chains through the base of the stone altar. "I borrowed these from the jailers, who said they were strong enough to hold even a rampaging werewolf." The old man shot a piercing gaze toward Casimir. "Are the jailers accustomed to werewolves?"

Ignoring the question, Casimir scanned the room. It was small and windowless, with walls of thick stone. The massive oaken door was shut and locked. This isn't a chapel, Casimir thought. It's a redoubt. Gustav couldn't have found a more fitting place for the ritual. "I take it this is an all-or-nothing proposition," Casimir noted wryly. "You plan to cure me or kill me, don't you."

"Yes," Gustav said simply. His tone softened. "Whatever the result, it will be for the best." He finished his preparations and stood, brushing dust from his hands. "The ceremony cannot begin until you transform."

Casimir regarded the priest dubiously. "I am . . . different when I transform. My desires, my hungers . . . I can't promise how I'll act if—"

"That's what the shackles are for. Please begin the transformation now."

Casimir nodded solemnly. He touched off the transformation and his arms began to shudder. The thick chains jangled against the stone floor. Gustav gazed intently at Casimir, awe and revulsion mixing on his features. Through proliferating teeth, Casimir gasped out, "Get back! It's started!" Gustav slowly staggered backward.

Hair sprouted across Casimir's spasming form, and bones twisted and snapped. His eyes changed from silver to blood-red, and blackening lips stretched across his jutting muzzle. The tunic he wore split as his shoulders skewed and realigned and his chest grew deeper and narrower. His legs bowed and reshaped and his flesh boiled. Gustav took another step back and Thoris pressed into a corner as the transformation was completed. Casimir had assumed his half-wolf form, his body a cross between man and beast.

He lunged out from the altar, his shackles paying out link by link. Suddenly the chains yanked taut, jerking the giant creature from his hind legs and sending him sprawling to the floor. The thick shackles bit angrily into Casimir's ankles, now grown too thick for the constricting iron. But the metal held firm. He rose, snarling, and lunged again. The broad chains whipped violently through the air, then drew tight. Yanking short of the priest, Casimir fell again to the floor. This time he rose more slowly, clasping the chains in his clawed hands and tugging, trying to wrench them from the altar.

Breathless, Thoris clung to the corner as Gustav stepped cautiously toward the man-beast. He took another step forward, reaching into his robe pocket and producing a large silver medallion that bore a leafy harp, the holy symbol of Milil. Raising the medallion, Gustav approached the snarling creature.

"O mighty lord, Milil of all songs . . . " the priest began.

At the mention of Milil, the seething man-wolf sprayed foam from his muzzle toward the withered priest. Although he was struck by the spittle, Gustav stood firm, continuing the ritual. "Thou who makes symphony of cacophony, who dwells in the hiding place of sound and robes thyself in song, I call to thee!"

"Milil is dead, priest!" the man-creature rasped.

"This one have I brought to you, Milil, having cleansed him of all wrong. He comes desiring freedom from his curse."

"I'll kill you, Gustav, and you, too, Thoris. I'll kill you . . . eat you . . . stash your bodies in a well somewhere!"

"Mighty Milil, hear my call."

Flinging himself forward against the chains, Casimir roared, "Come closer!" He swung his claws just short of the priest.

"Remove this curse from our meistersinger, good Milil. Free him from the power of the moon. Lift his doom!" Gustav shouted, swinging the medallion so that it struck Casimir in the face.

Abruptly Casimir stilled. A sober confusion entered his lupine face, and the blood-red color of his eyes subtly dimmed. Thoris gasped, covering his mouth. Gustav pulled back his medallion and eyed the man-beast suspiciously. Casimir tottered momentarily, then staggered backward in his clanking shackles. He stumbled against the blocky altar and slid awkwardly to the floor. His body convulsed, and his muscles and bones began to reshape.

"See how it passes now?" a breathless Gustav whispered to Thoris, peering intently at the creature before them.

Thoris moved from the corner, his face hopeful. "I see."

Gustav's expression brightened. "If he is healed, then it is proof that Milil has returned."

Thoris needed no further word. He rushed forward, well within the length of the chains. He knelt beside Casimir and laid a hand on his convulsing shoulder. Slowly the thick fur that covered Casimir melted away, and his shuddering spasms eased. His normal face formed again, his chest grew shallow, and his limbs reshaped. In mere moments, the human Casimir had returned. He lay limp and cadaverous in the shredded rags that had been his clothes. His wrists and ankles bled where the shackles had cut into them, and spots of saliva flecked his chest.

"You're healed, Casimir!" Thoris said excitedly. "Really healed!"

Casimir's eyes were sunken. "I'm . . . healed?" he asked in a sickly, uncertain voice.

"Yes you are," Thoris assured his friend, rubbing his hands together. The old priest's hand settled on Thoris's shoulder, and Thoris pulled back. Now Gustav knelt, his eyes slitted suspiciously as he examined Casimir. The leathery wrinkles on the priest's temples pulled into tight lines of worry.

"Are you truly healed?" came his croaking voice.

Casimir searched the inscrutable face. "I hope so."

Gustav stared icily at Casimir. Then the priest raised his knobby hand beside his ear and clenched a fist.

With a sudden grimace, he struck Casimir. The stinging blow had hardly landed before another fell, reddening the cheek with a fist-shaped splotch. Gustav punched him again; then a fourth time. He towered above Casimir, his eyes blazing and his fist twitching beside his ear. He raised his hand to strike again, but Thoris grabbed his arm.

"Let me loose!" Gustav roared, throwing Thoris to the floor. "Don't you see?" he shouted, his twisted finger pointing toward Casimir. "He's lying! He hasn't been cured! Look at him!" With that, Gustav balled his hand into a fist and swung again. His time-scarred knuckles cracked against Casimir's jaw. The blow knocked Casimir back, and his head struck against the dolmen. Gustav flipped Casimir over and knelt on his back. He slipped a knife from his belt and ran its razor edge along the veins of Casimir's neck.

"Now, werewolf, this is your last chance to transform. This steel dagger cannot harm you in wolf form, but it will kill you as you are. Change, or you will die!"

Casimir thrashed helplessly. He could scarcely breathe. Gustav's bony knee compressed his bruised back. Helpless, Casimir looked up at Thoris, who had backed into the corner.

Casimir rasped, "I can't . . . I can't do it anymore."

"I'll slice your neck, as you did your father's, and see how fast you heal," the priest snapped.

"Do it!" Casimir blurted through clenched teeth. "Kill me!"

Sweat ran down the old man's face as he studied Casimir. Not a sign of the beast returned. He counted twenty heartbeats before he eased the knife blade back from Casimir's neck.

The priest rose. "You *are* healed," he whispered incredulously, extending a hand to help the battered boy get up. "You've passed every test, Casimir." The old man paused, slipping the knife beneath the belt of his robe. "Milil *has* returned, and you are his first miracle."

Casimir stood up shakily. Thoris came forward, steadying his friend. "Please, Master Gustav, remove the shackles."

Nodding, the wizened man retrieved the keys from a hook on the wall. Casimir turned his bruised wrists, presenting the keyholes to Gustav. The priest fit the iron key into each lock. Rubbing his wounds, the rag-garbed meistersinger coldly studied the old man.

"You must forgive my fists, Casimir," Gustav said as he loosened the leg shackles. "But I had to be certain of your healing."

The final chain clattered to the floor. The old man rose, straightening his crooked back. His tired eyes settled on Casimir's face just long enough to see the malice there.

Craaack!

Casimir's fist smashed into the aged face. In a twisting convulsion, the priest lurched backward and crumpled to the floor, where he lay, trembling, not even a moan escaping his lips. Casimir peered dispassionately at him. "I accept your apology. Cross me again and I'll have your head on a pikestaff." Stepping from the clutter of chains, Casimir took the keys from Gustav's twitching hand and strode to the door.

The key clicked in the lock, and the massive door creaked open. Wordlessly the two young men slipped across the threshold. Thoris took a fleeting glimpse back, his compassionate eyes resting on the crumpled priest. Then he, too, was gone.

Gustav lay long in that dim and silent room, the cold hardness of the stone beneath him soothing his weary wounds. He couldn't move, couldn't feel his legs or his arms. Even breathing was a struggle, for his neck was bent oddly to one side.

Then, sweet and clarion clear, the song returned.

Gustav's breath eased as he listened to the strange tone. As the sound deepened, a tear worked across the priest's half-paralyzed face. His eyes were wide and glossy. Gustav breathed his last, and shuddered to stillness on the cold stone.

* * * * *

"I knew it wouldn't work," Casimir murmured as he pulled a tunic over his shoulders. He gazed sullenly into the tall dressing mirror in his room. Lifting a candle up to the mirror, he lightly traced the faint bruises on his face.

"Thoris said you had a good visit with Gustav tonight," Julianna commented from the doorway behind him.

Casimir stiffened, pulling the candle away from his face. "Yes . . . I suppose so." He turned slowly toward her.

She wore a festive dress of gypsy fabric with a shawl draped over her shoulders. "It's a beautiful night. The winds are cool, the moon is full. Would you like to go for a walk?"

Casimir set the candle down and shuffled toward her. "I—I would, but . . ." he bit his lip. "I can't, Julianna. Not tonight."

He tried to push past her to reach the doorway, but she latched onto his arm. "What's wrong, Casimir? You seem . . . fearful." Casimir looked away, hiding his bruised cheek. She reached out, turning his face toward her. "I wish you'd confide in me."

Casimir glanced into her deep green eyes. His jaw clenched, and he suddenly felt short of breath. Reaching out, he drew Julianna to him and embraced her passionately. She felt small and fragile in his arms. The warm softness of her body pressed against him, and he breathed deeply the fragrance of her hair.

Suddenly he realized his fingernails were sharpening into claws. Stepping back, he grabbed his cloak and stalked off into the hall.

*   *   *   *   *

"Your other engagement then . . . it was canceled?" asked Harkon Lukas, his teeth gleaming in the moonlight.

Casimir breathed the pine-scented air deep into his lungs and thrust his hands into the warm pockets of his cloak. "Yes . . . canceled." He gazed wearily at the moonlit treetops in the thick forest around them.

The dark bard sniffed the air. "You've been hurt. By whom?"

Casimir pulled his hands from his pockets and displayed his gouged wrists. "How did you know I had been injured?"

"I'm a man of many talents, Casimir," he said with an odd laugh. "Were those cuts . . . self-inflicted?"

"No," Casimir replied, shifting his feet on the needle-strewn forest floor. "A bit of trouble at the temple."

"Ah, yes . . . the temple." Lukas sighed knowingly. "That cantankerous old priest enjoys giving you trouble."

"Tonight I whipped him into line," said Casimir.

Removing his broad-brimmed hat, the bard shook his head and clucked, "No more trouble from him."

Casimir sighed heavily and sank his bandaged hands into his pockets again. "I didn't come for prattle, Lukas. You promised me another lesson."

Lukas laughed. "Two weeks ago you cared little for my lessons. Why the change of heart?"

"Survival," Casimir said, gingerly touching his cheek.

Lukas only nodded. "On to the lesson, then. Beasts walk on four legs, while men walk on two. Men thus set their hearts above their stomachs and their heads above their hearts. But for beasts, head and heart and stomach are equal."

Casimir shook his head. "More riddles?"

"Yes, more riddles," Lukas replied. "But the answer to this riddle is simple. You'll be a better ruler when you cease to set your head above your heart and stomach."

"Why should I?" Casimir asked. "You just said that's the way of humans."

"Yes . . . of humans," Lukas responded. "But you're a werebeast."

Casimir stepped back from the bard, catching a foothold and bracing himself for attack. He prepared the transformation in his bones. "What makes you think that?"

"I don't think it, I know it," Lukas said coolly. "We are kin, you see."

Casimir gasped. Looping lines of hair were emerging across Lukas's cheekbones. With a hollow laugh, Lukas sloughed off his long cape. It fell from his shoulders and fluttered like a shadow to the ground. The light of the full moon washed over his transforming body: long, sinewy arms and legs, a massive torso, a canine head, and eyes that flickered like candles. Steam rose from the half-wolf skin, and breath curled white in the moonlight.

Casimir fell back another step, touching off his own transformation. Muscles boiled; coarse shafts of hair sprouted; bones snapped apart and realigned; limbs twisted; teeth multiplied. His red-hot heart fueled the metamorphosis. All the while, Casimir focused his blurred eyes on the towering beast that had once been Harkon Lukas.

"I knew of your curse from the moment I met you," Lukas rasped. "I could smell your wolf's blood." As he spoke, a shadowy creature emerged from the thick stands of trees around them and loped to Lukas's side. Then another shadow entered the clearing, and another. Casimir's blackening nose picked up the scent.

More wolves.

"Come, Casimir," Harkon Lukas beckoned. "Come take your place among the kindred of wolves. You belong among us, not among humans."

Now also in half-wolf form, Casimir growled, "What do you want from me?"

Lukas hissed his reply, "Don't you see, Casimir? I'm apprenticing you . . . teaching you your true nature . . .

empowering you."

"Apprenticing me?" Casimir rasped through dagger teeth. "Why should you apprentice me?"

"Because, Casimir," Lukas replied with a fiendish grin, "because you are a fetal god!"

Casimir stared in mute shock at Lukas.

"Come, weak one," Lukas snarled, "the high moon leaves us few hours for the hunt."

Casimir's wolfish brows lowered. "I've committed enough murders already. I won't go with you."

"We're predators, Casimir, not murderers," Lukas sneered. "We hunt stag. Accept yourself for what you are. Come with us!"

The cold light of the moon flickered for a moment in Casimir's eyes. Lukas gestured toward him with his sickle-shaped claws. Casimir moved cautiously toward the group. With a leering grin, Lukas dropped to his hands and knees and assumed his full-wolf form. Casimir did likewise.

Just then Casimir's nose picked up the sweet smell of prey a mile or so distant. He drew the scent into his lungs, letting it perfuse every tissue of his body.

He was hungry.

In unspoken unison, the wolf pack set out after the scent. Casimir shouldered his way forward amongst the bustling beasts. For a moment, the smell of stag was masked by the savage odor of the wolves themselves: dried blood, greasy jowls, damp fur, dust and rain and urine. Casimir's hackles rose in excitement, and saliva wet his black jowls. Moving forward, the pack began to spread out. Casimir kept pace with them, his gaze darting from one loping form to the next.

Through the deep forest they passed, the rhythm of their feet keeping time with their quickening heartbeats. The world slid effortlessly away with each of Casimir's graceful strides. He weaved his way among the stout tree trunks, digging his feet into the damp soil. The scent of deer returned to his nose, stronger and nearer. It was a scent tinged with fear.

Suddenly the ground before them dropped away into a sharp vale. The wolves surged over the edge and ran down the slope, gaining speed as they went. Leaping from stone to stone, Casimir pushed past the pack, coming stride for stride alongside Harkon Lukas. Vaulting a narrow creek at the base of the vale, Lukas and Casimir began their climb up the slope on the other side. Casimir's legs tingled with blood, his claws biting into the rock-strewn hillside. Lukas remained at his shoulder, matching his pace. Moonlight washed over their rippling pelts.

Reaching the top of the hill, they sighted the hart in the next valley. The beast was magnificent. A broad tangle of antlers rose above its attentive ears, and its eyes were wide with fright. It stood poised to run, its narrow hooves wedged in the rocky soil.

Leaping onto a stony ledge, Casimir lifted his head toward the glaring moon and unleashed a piercing howl. The sound rent the night, and another howl rose to join it—this one from Harkon Lukas. Then came a third cry, and a fourth, until the woods echoed with the sound.

The stag stood motionless for a moment, then bounded off frantically into the woods. Casimir leapt from the rocky outcrop, soaring easily through the night air. With a spray of dead leaves, his paws struck the earth. Pushing off again, he rushed down the lengthy slope, his wolfish brothers at his heels. With graceful, arching strides, Lukas gained on Casimir. Pouring like a fierce river down the embankment, the pack surged into the valley and spread out along the retreating hart's trail.

Topping a slight rise, Casimir caught sight of the stag's white tail as it rushed away. He plunged after it, his claws tearing the ground and his lungs pumping like bellows. Closer he came, the scent wild and sweet on the wind. The hart darted frantically through the forest, kicking up clods of moist earth. It bounded left, then right, its eyes welling with fear. Casimir charged straight toward the clattering hooves of the creature. Lukas surged forward, hemming the stag in on one flank as

Casimir thundered up on the other. The hart turned its narrow muzzle to look on the snapping jaws.

Casimir leapt for the creature's throat, sinking his teeth through the white fur and into the salty flesh beneath. The hart pitched forward, dragged down by Casimir's weight. Its sharp-tipped hooves struck painfully against Casimir as the beast toppled. Flopping and skidding on the rough ground, the struggling stag floundered to a halt. Casimir bit again into the blood-soaked neck. In snarling frenzy, the rest of the pack fell on the beast, tearing at the legs and flank. In moments, its convulsive kicks stopped.

Only after he had eaten his fill did Casimir turn from the carcass. Soundlessly he withdrew from the snarling wolves and loped away into the woods.

Harkon Lukas's wolf form raised his head from the kill and watched as Casimir retreated. When Casimir was finally gone, Lukas lowered his dripping mouth again to the still beast.

TWELVE

Next morning the rising sun found Casimir awake, sitting on his bedroom balcony, his hands pillowing his head against the high-backed chair where he sat and his feet resting easily on the balcony rail. Below him, sunlight glinted off the dewy rooftops of Harmonia. Casimir surveyed the drowsy town, watching sparrows flit from rooftop to rooftop.

A sparrow winged up to the ivy-laden balcony and landed soundlessly on the rail, mere inches from Casimir's feet. He gazed intently at the bird, noting the fluttering shiver in its feathers. "Better fly south, little bird," he murmured quietly. "Winter's coming." The bird hopped distractedly along the rail until it reached a gold-leafed ivy vine. Its furtive beak pecked a fermented berry from one of the dry branches; then it turned and leapt into the sky.

As Casimir's eyes followed the bird, he thought of the previous night. The midnight air had been intoxicating in his lungs, and his pounding legs had seemed to shake the forest. No one could have stood before him last night—not even Harkon Lukas. And what a kill the stag had been. To bend its antlered head, to sink teeth into its pillowy neck and drag it down, to feast without pangs of guilt . . .

And now, with the fresh autumn air pouring into his lungs, Casimir wanted nothing more than to hunt again—not alone, as he had done for eighteen long years, but with the pack, with the kindred of wolves. He was no longer alone.

A telltale click sounded in the room behind him. Then came the tentative tread of a bald leather sole.

" 'Morning, Master Casimir," came the hesitant voice of a servant boy.

Sighing loudly, Casimir motioned the boy toward him. "What's so important that you find it necessary to break in like this?"

The smooth leather shoes found their shuffling way across the hardwood floor, bringing a wide-eyed page to the meistersinger's side.

"Let's have it, then," Casimir said.

"Master Casimir, the good priest Gustav is dead."

Casimir's throat clenched and his face darkened. Gustav? Dead?

A chill ran down Casimir's neck, and he drew a long breath. Turning away from the boy, he peered down at silent Harmonia. The sparrows continued their flitting dance over the rooftops, oblivious to the folk below. After a few moments, Casimir reached a hand out to the messenger's arm and said, "Go fetch Thoris."

Without a moment's pause, the boy rushed from the room. Casimir buried his face in his hands.

"The wolf has struck again," he mused, lowering his feet from the rail and folding his arms over his chest. He felt suddenly cold. "I can't stop it, can't be cured of it, can't kill it." He rose slowly and paced into the inner chamber. A knock sounded at the door.

"Yes, Thoris. Please enter."

The door swung wide, and Thoris, darkly silhouetted, moved slowly across the threshold. "What is it, Casimir?" he asked.

Casimir weakly motioned his friend toward him. Thoris came fearfully forward. "Tell me, Casimir . . . what's wrong?"

"Gustav is dead, Thoris," Casimir said coldly.

"Dead?" Thoris gasped.

"I must have killed him when I hit him last night."

Thoris placed his fingers on his friend's slack arms. "Don't do this to yourself, Casimir. You didn't mean to kill him."

"I meant to hurt him, though."

Flattening the fear from his voice, Thoris said, "At least he cured you before he died."

"He cured me and I killed him," Casimir said heavily.

Sitting down slowly on the bedside, Thoris said, "There's nothing we can do about it now."

"We can plan a funeral," Casimir replied, stalking to the balcony and staring out over Harmonia. "I want a service at the temple, with every freeman of Harmonia attending. The organ must be repaired before the service. I myself will deliver the eulogy and decree that henceforth all Harmonians must worship at the temple."

"Should I summon a jurist to arrange the details?" Thoris asked.

Without turning around, Casimir said gently, "No. I want you to handle it. Plan a funeral march from the temple to South Hill. I want Gustav buried on the same spot where I leapt from the cliff. Commission a sculptor to carve a granite statue of Gustav and set it at the head of the grave. Then go to Harmonic Hall and find me a choirmaster and an organist for the temple."

Thoris's head was spinning. He rubbed his brow and asked, "A choirmaster and organist? But what about a priest?"

Casimir turned around slowly. "The priest's power is second only to my own, and a corrupt priest could overthrow me. I can trust no one else but you."

"What?" Thoris gasped, incredulous.

"The choirmaster will sing for you, and the organist will play. I'll deliver your homilies," Casimir said simply. "You need only learn to pray and perhaps to read so that you'll know the tales of Milil."

"But I'm only sixteen!" Thoris protested.

"I was only eighteen when I became meistersinger."

"No one will listen to me."

"They'll listen to me," Casimir replied quietly.

"Don't do this, Casimir," Thoris pleaded.

"It's already done, Thoris," came the unhesitant reply.

*   *   *   *   *

Thoris stood shivering in the stone-walled vestibule that stood between the temple and the chapter house. Through the closed temple door, organ music blared into the vestibule, mixing with the moan of the winter wind. Thoris bundled more tightly in his baggy robe of embroidered silk and gazed through the window beside him. The age-warped glass showed a swirling blizzard, which blanketed the half-timber houses with snow. "Four solid months," Thoris observed dismally. "When will this blasted winter end?"

Still, he preferred the cold and the whistling wind to the howl of the great organ. Ever since he had arranged the organ's repairing for Gustav's funeral, he wished he hadn't. Thoris pitied the congregation, whose unfailing presence Casimir demanded at each of these ear-splitting services.

The organ bellowed its final chords, then rumbled into silence. Casting a glance toward the vault above, Thoris hummed a tuneless thanks to Milil. He still hadn't decided whether he believed in this pasty-faced god of song, but the office of priesthood had its demands.

Gathering up his trailing robes, Thoris pulled the vestibule door open and moved into the warm, incense-laden air of the sanctuary. He always returned to the sanctuary when Casimir's homilies began. In the six months since Gustav's death, Casimir had grown into a passionate and eloquent speaker. His messages warmed the hearts of poor and rich alike, even during the chill winter. Reaching the edge of the nave, Thoris caught sight of Casimir. Lately he looked as white and drawn as a man in his grave, but the pallor belied the passion in him.

Casimir set his graceful hands on the lectern's edges and drew a deep breath. A frigid wind rushed across the temple's roof, plucking savagely at its age-loosened slates.

"These winters . . . " he paused, shaking his head, "these winters with their ruthless cold and pounding wind drive us from the streets, from the tepid sunlight to tiny hearth fires whose heat and light are mere travesties of summer. And when we bundle ourselves beside the hearth and wrap our shawls about us, we wonder about our savage world. Does Milil indeed hear our songs? Does Milil indeed care for us? How far does his song reach in such a cold and heartless place?"

Casimir took another long pause, listening to the wind moan in the lancets. "Among Milil's celestial choirs sung the voice of the peasant man Olya. Throughout his short life, Olya's hands bore the scars of the bondsman, and his shoulders carried the loads of his master. Hard and bitter and sad was his life, but he bore through it, dreaming of heaven. And soon came the merciful slip of the axe that killed him, that cleft his soul from his body. So came Olya to join Milil's choirs. There his voice rang purer and sweeter than all the voices of the saints. The dull bondsman had died, but a matchless voice had been born.

"Milil came often to hear Olya sing, crying out in plaintive tones that broke the god's heart. And as our god wept, so moved was he by his servant's songs, he neglected the world, and the first winter came. Beneath the firmament, ice and hail descended, slaying many people. Wailing women and weeping men raised their tearful cry to Milil, yet he heard naught but the song of Olya. Only when the leviathan and the nightingales joined their voices did Milil hear. Rousing from his grief, he turned his sorrowing eyes on the world and awoke the sun again.

"Then to Olya he said, 'How has thy rough and graceless life given birth to so flawless a voice?'

"And Olya said, 'My voice is not flawless, as thou sayst.'

" 'Though it may not be perfect in meter, tone, or

pitch,' said Milil, 'it strikes chords of perfect sorrow in me.'

" 'Then flawless in sorrow it is,' Olya said.

" 'But why dost thou mourn in this happy choir, Olya?'

" 'I mourn my life long past, for I squandered it in hopes of your heavens, Milil,' Olya said.

" 'But aside from hopes of my heavens, thy life was short and sad,' Milil said. 'So did not hope for my heavens enrich your impoverished life?'

" 'Oh, but life is not impoverished, as you say, my lord,' Olya replied, 'for nestled amongst the cruelest barbs lies a singular rose, whose fleeting scents and withering hues are more precious to me than all your angel choirs. The man who has tasted honey finds it richer for the bee's bitter sting. A soul that treads but once along the trail of time feels itself a king for its solitary privilege.

" 'But all of that mortal beauty I discounted in reverent hope for this endless place of song.'

"Hearing these things, Milil was deeply grieved. And so the god of song said to his greatest voice, 'If I give thee thy life back, returning thee to those fleeting things, Olya, thou wilt have spent thy deathless soul. When thy fainting flesh has run its course and laid itself in death's dark couch, thy soul will sink and spread like rain into the earth and be gone forever.'

"The singer's faceless voice was filled with sorrow. 'My lord Milil, I had not dreamt I could reclaim what has been lost to me. I care not for my deathless soul, but for that lifeless flesh of mine. If I can but taste joy again for one brief span in endless time, thou wilt have blessed me beyond degree.'

"These sad words brought tears once more to Lord Milil. And with these tears, he touched the voice, anointing it again to live, and sent Olya into a husk of flesh, much like the one he left entombed. Rising in a virgin glade, Olya wiped death from his eyes and drew into his soul the incense of pine. Between the trees passed golden shafts of sun, which melted warm on his muscled arms—the warm embrace of joy.

"Peering down on his singer, Lord Milil then smiled and dabbed away his perfect tears. But as Milil tended his tears, a shadow rose at Olya's back—a bear whose belly groaned in want of meat after the winter of Milil. The beast then raised its razor claws and felled Olya. It sunk its teeth into his dying form. When Milil saw the massive beast, with Olya beneath its bulk, his face grew dark with wrath to kill the bear. But Olya, with his dying breath, said, 'Hold, my lord Milil, for I have had my joy, and this beast wants only to feast as I have feasted, too. Slay him not. His life is gone soon enough.' And saying so, he died.

"With tears anew, Milil waylaid his wrath and spared the hungry beast. But still our lord of song doth mourn the voice who was called Olya. And in his grief, Milil has made the winters come with every year, sending all to hearth and home and sending all bears to their winter dens to sleep a little death."

The homily was at an end, and the oppressive wail of the wind returned to the sanctuary. The worshipers shifted in reverent silence. Thoris quietly withdrew from the rim of the sanctuary to sit along the outer colonnade. A tone sounded from the organ, filling the temple with its clarion call to prayer. Picking up the tone, Casimir began the melodic chant:

O lord, Milil, we sing to thee.

The full-bellied response rang up from the congregation:

> **We sing thy song of praise.**
> *From wintery tombs of ice and snow*
> **We sing thy song of praise.**
> *From souls beset with crudest flesh*
> **We sing thy song of praise.**

O cure us of our wayward hearts
In hope we cry to thee.
O slay the beast that in us dwells
In hope we cry to thee.
Now heed our supplication song
We sing to thee a song of hope.
O hear thy song of praise.

The bold unison of the chant splintered now into a multitude of songs, each rising from a different singer. Thoris also sang out petitions: for the health of the church, for his service as surrogate priest, for the rule of Meistersinger Casimir, for the happiness of Julianna. . . .

Faint through the chaotic chorus of voices, a thin, high tone came to Thoris. It sounded like a flute—or longhorn, as the old texts of Milil called it. Thoris ceased his chanting prayers to listen to the sound. The tone was too steady and ceaseless to come from any human voice. Now it intensified, droning with painful edge in Thoris's ear.

What's that sound? Thoris asked himself, listening intently. Milil is said to play a longhorn pipe.

Thoris.

The word formed out of the chorus of chanted prayers.

Thoris.

The sound was unmistakable. Dread settled over Thoris.

Thoris.

A chill ran down his back as he whispered, "What?"

Do not be lulled, Thoris.

Swallowing hard, Thoris murmured, "Who are you?"

The beast still lives.

"What beast?"

Casimir.

Thoris blanched. He set his clammy, trembling hands on the cold seat beneath him and steadied himself. Mustering his strength, he blurted once again, "Who are you?"

Slay the beast, Thoris.

Despite the trembling in his legs, Thoris pushed himself up from his seat and tottered along the colonnade wall. Perhaps he could escape this voice. Perhaps it was merely the wind and the songs and his weary mind. He stumbled farther along the wall, the directive echoing in his ears: *Slay the beast, Thoris. Slay the beast.* Sinking to his knees, he clutched his hands over his ears. The voice only grew louder. Gasping, he fainted away into blackness.

*   *   *   *   *

The last snow of winter fell in swirling flakes from leaden clouds as the old farmer trudged through his muddy field. He halted, craning his neck to gauge the sky. Behind him, the guardsmen and the young cleric came to a stop.

The barrel-chested guardsman eyed him impatiently, his hand on the pommel of his sword. "So where's this reservoir you're talking about?"

The farmer scratched his forehead. "Jus' worried 'bout the snow. Sorry t' drag you 'long, priest Thoris, but I thoughtcha should see it."

Thoris nodded silently, pulling the robes of his priesthood tighter against the biting wind.

Glancing at the sky again, the farmer strode forward. The guardsman fell reluctantly in line behind him, and Thoris followed. " 'S up here—'side o' the city wall." Crossing his arms over his chest, the farmer plodded on toward the spot where his property abutted the city wall. "Some o' the stone fer the wall was quarried from here. The hole filled up wi' water, an' we all on this stretch used it fer our 'stock an' fields. Till recent."

The farmer's words trailed away as they reached the hedge that bounded his field. Beyond it lay a deep reservoir, carved into an outcropping of granite. The banks of the pool still bore scars from the quarriers' chisels and saws. The pool itself looked oddly red beneath the gray sky.

"Rust in the water?" the barrel-chested guard asked.

" 'Tain't rust."

Thoris leaned farther over the hedge, peering into the reservoir. Then he saw the bodies. The broad basin of the pool was littered with them. And they were human.

*   *   *   *   *

Thoris sat nervously in the library of the meister-singer's mansion. He was cold, even though he had positioned his chair in a patch of sunlight that fell from the stained-glass windows. His eyes scanned the dark bookshelves lining the walls and the thick tapestries that hung from the hammer-beam ceiling above.

What's taking her so long? he wondered worriedly.

The stained glass went dark as a cloud obscured the sun. The patch of warmth that had bathed Thoris disappeared. He shivered, glancing toward the window. Only now, without the dazzling sun behind it, could Thoris see what the stained glass depicted—a chorus of Milil's angels hovering over a hilltop, casting giant shadows in the grass below. As Thoris studied the image, he saw that the shadows formed another choir, a choir of wolves covering the hilltop and howling to the moon. Was his mind playing tricks on him? Thoris's breath caught short. The longer he looked, the more certain he was that the angels were, in fact, the shadows of the wolves.

"You wanted to see me?" came Julianna's voice from behind him.

Thoris started, then gestured for her to sit in the chair opposite him. "Yes . . . it's a pressing matter of the church."

Julianna's face looked grave as she took the seat across from him. Her fingers tugged at her long dress of charcoal-colored wool, and she drew her cloak tighter about her shoulders. "It's rather cold in here, isn't it?"

Thoris nodded, smiling weakly. Then his face grew solemn. "I know this wouldn't normally be any of my business," he began, his voice trembling slightly, "but I need to ask, for the sake of Casimir and Harmonia and the church. . . ."

Julianna's emerald eyes didn't waver. "Go on."

Thoris shifted in his seat and wrung his shaking hands. "Ah . . . this is difficult to ask. How are . . . things between you and Casimir?"

"Things?"

"Yes . . ." Thoris responded, smiling nervously. "Has he been . . . acting well toward you?"

Julianna's brow furrowed. "Of course. He's always perfectly mannered. Why?"

"Ah . . . has he ever been too forceful? Has he ever struck you?"

"Certainly not," Julianna said, looking indignant.

Thoris nodded, pursing his lips. He scratched the side of his face, where downy whiskers were beginning to show. "This next question is purely for the good of the church. Are you and he . . . intimate?"

Julianna stood up, her hands knotting together over her midsection. "How is that information for the good of the church?"

Nervously Thoris gestured for her to sit. "Please . . . please sit down, Julianna. I can't tell you why at this point, but you must trust me. It's essential that I know."

Slowly she sat back down, her hands clutching the armrests. She averted her eyes and breathed deeply. "Yes, we are," she said softly.

Thoris paled and he, too, looked away. Sunlight suddenly cascaded through the stained glass again, spreading its blanket of warmth over them both. Even so, Thoris shivered. "This news is not good," he said seriously.

Julianna looked up at him, her eyes narrowing. "What's wrong? We've done nothing to break the law of Milil."

"It's not that," Thoris said, swallowing hard. "Casimir's . . . not well."

"Not well?"

"You've seen how pale he's become. Richter, the alchemist, doesn't know what's wrong with him, and

neither do I. We're afraid, though, that you might catch
the ill humor from him."

Now Julianna also paled. "If he's ill, I want to nurse
him back to health."

Thoris smiled uneasily. "Before you can help heal
him, you need to be completely free of the illness yourself."

"What do you mean?"

"Richter and I believe you may have already contracted the disease," Thoris replied evenly, reddening at
the slight lie. "But don't worry. I know of a priest in Gundarak, the country just north of us. If I take you to him,
he can heal you, and he can send a balm for Casimir."

"Why doesn't Casimir go along?" Julianna asked.

"The trip might kill him."

Julianna bit her lip and glanced away. "When do we
leave?"

"Tonight."

                    *   *   *   *   *

Casimir trudged wearily up the muddy hillside.
Moonlight illumined the melting clumps of snow at his
feet, and the trickle of springtime runoff filled the air.
Casimir halted, planting his mud-clogged boots. He gritted his teeth and grumbled, "Spring."

"Greetings, O matchless meistersinger!" came a
familiar voice from the peak of the knoll. Sighing,
Casimir looked up to see Harkon Lukas towering in dark
silhouette against the blue-black sky. The bard removed
his broad-brimmed hat and bowed grandly. "What shall
we hunt tonight, my liege? Man or beast?"

Prying his boots from the sucking mud, Casimir
approached the bard and spoke irritably. "Why should I
care which we hunt? They both have blood. But I think
we've killed enough men in the past month. Wouldn't
you agree?"

Hanging his hat on a dead tree stump, Lukas sighed.
"I suppose so, though hunting stag is less challenging."

"If it's challenge you want," Casimir snapped, "men aren't your quarry. Despite their reputation, men are as a rule helpless, yammering, grovelling kills."

"You *are* in a foul mood tonight," Lukas noted with delight. "Is it perhaps that ludicrous temple you continue to fund, against every warning of mine?"

"No, it isn't," Casimir replied curtly.

"I've heard that the bumbling illiterate you installed as priest has laid plots against you," Lukas said casually.

"You've heard wrong," Casimir growled.

"Then what *is* causing this foul humor, Casimir?" Lukas asked, his knifelike teeth gleaming in the moonlight. "Why have you, the silver-tongued orator of Milil's burgeoning temple, become so sad and dispossessed in the very heart of your empire?"

"I don't know."

"So," the bard sang out, "you concede your discomfort?"

Casimir vented the stale air from his lungs. "How about hunting bear tonight?"

Apparently caught off guard by the sudden shift in topic, Lukas paused before replying. "We would need to travel very far afield to find a wakeful bear. I haven't seen a bear in ages. Perhaps if we head toward Gundarak in the north . . . ?"

Only now removing his robe and hanging it on a tree, Casimir said, "Perhaps." And with that one word, he touched off the transformation in his tired bones.

*   *   *   *   *

The two dire wolves rushed through the dense maze of trees, their broad, powerful feet pounding on the muddy path. Lukas led the hunt, his hackles raised in excited anticipation. Casimir followed behind, clumps of muddy earth flying from Harkon's feet and clinging to Casimir's coarse pelt. He cared little. This was Lukas's hunt, not his. Though they often caught the sweet scent of deer, Lukas never turned toward it. He seemed utterly invested in their hunt for bear. He never strayed beyond a half-mile of the Gundarak road, never stopped to sniff the black mud or listen to the nervous shifting of creatures among the trees. His unrelenting run slowed only once, when he caught scent of a wanderer on the road. Even then, Lukas stopped merely long enough to kill the man.

They had run easily fifteen miles past the nearby town of Skald when Casimir scented some men on horseback. Though he had no appetite for killing humans tonight, he preferred such a kill to this ceaseless and pointless running. Casimir doubled the thunderous rhythm of his paws and nosed past Lukas. Now in the lead, he rushed down a rocky vale that lay between them and the road. Turning into the wind, his twitching nose caught the unmistakable odor of horses and men. Leaping the watery gorge at the base of the vale, Casimir dashed up the slope on its other side. His claws dug hungrily into the water-soaked humus, sending up sprays with his every footfall. Lukas came right behind him, matching his pace stride for stride.

Casimir rose to the bald summit of the hill. Below lay the Gundarak road, like a deep knife slit in the forest. The road's muddy expanse was pocked with watery troughs. Two horsemen picked their way among the puddles, the hooves of their mounts thudding dully on the road. Lukas pulled up beside Casimir just as the latter prepared to charge down the hill toward the riders. Then a familiar fragrance entered Casimir's nose.

It was Julianna.

The soft scent of her flesh came first, followed by the sweaty tang of Thoris. Casimir drew another breath, hoping he had been mistaken. The odors were undeniable.

"Your priest friend suspects you," Lukas said. Casimir cast a startled glance at the bard, who had, unnoticed, returned to his human form. "It is as I said, Casimir. He plots against you but fears first for the life of Julianna."

Casimir looked again toward the road.

Lukas continued. "He hasn't yet told her of your curse. He's not certain he believes it himself. Even so, Casimir, your priest is bearing her to safety before he raises the knife against you."

Casimir shuddered, his heart boiling with anger. He willed the transformation to half-wolf form. In moments, he rose on his hind legs and hissed, "I'll kill him before he takes her from me!"

Lukas grasped Casimir's hand. "Hold, Casimir. If you attack your priest, Julianna will spur her steed into Gundarak and escape you forever. There's another way. This is your next lesson." Turning solemnly, Lukas raised his hands toward the road like a choirmaster before a great chorus. Then, sweeping his hands together, he brought them down in a line before him.

A song began in the nearby woods. It began as a soft, subtle, rhythmic sound, like water pattering from the tree branches. Slowly, then, a low rumble joined the percussive sound. The drone was so deep and seamless that Casimir felt it more than he heard it. Next, above the low tone, a cautious melody arose, borne on the wind. The melody seemed to emanate from the very trees and stalks of grass.

On the road below, Julianna reined in her steed, stopping to listen to the earthy song from the woods. Thoris's beast clomped on a few paces before he, too, halted. Now both of them sat still, in perfect attention on their steeds, their ears trained to the sound and the reins gone limp in their hands.

Casimir turned toward Harkon Lukas, who wore a narrow smile. Lukas spoke, his voice small against the tapestrial music. "You see, Casimir, until you accepted the powerful beast within you, you were impotent to act, and miserable. But now you are empowered. The full extent of that power you have yet to realize, but here is a mere foretaste."

A chill ran through Casimir, and he cast a glance at the road. Julianna and Thoris lay slumped on the necks of their steeds. Casimir shot a concerned glare at Lukas.

The bard waved him off. "They aren't harmed. I'll magically spirit them away to their beds. They'll awaken in the morning, thinking it all a dream. But they won't soon wish to try another escape."

The song filled the silence that followed. Casimir grew quiet and calm, letting the beast slip from his blood. Slowly his body reworked itself into the shape of a man. Once the transformation was complete, Casimir folded to his knees on the spongy grass. Some ten feet away, Lukas stood, staring down at the road. Casimir followed his gaze, seeing the riderless horses wandering the brink of the forest.

His voice trembling, Casimir asked, "What other powers have you, Master Lukas?"

"The lesson is ended," the bard said coldly. "You've heard the song, too. You'll awaken as will they, meistersinger. But you'll know, most definitely, that this was not a dream."

THIRTEEN

Through leaden eyes, Casimir gazed at Julianna's sleeping form. Her black hair lay in graceful curves about her ivory face, and beneath the sheet, her chest rose and fell gently. With each silent breath, a tremble gently moved through her. She seemed cold. Rising, Casimir pulled another blanket over her.

Looking away from Julianna, Casimir stared out the window beside her bed. Beyond the glass, the white heavens stretched on endlessly and sparrows chased each other through the sky. Only last night, Casimir thought, his eyes following the flitting birds, she tried to escape me. A sparrow landed on the sill outside. It scuttled awkwardly on the cold stone as though the chill pained its twiglike feet. He touched the pane of glass lightly. Perhaps I should have let her escape, now that I'm . . . irredeemable.

Dropping his attention from the sparrow, Casimir's face darkened. He knew he'd never let her go. Only Julianna stood between his present torment and his final damnation. As long as I have her, he mused, staring at Julianna, I can bear to live.

He sat for a long while at her bedside, his attenuate fingers woven coarsely together about his knee. He wanted to wake her, to touch her, to assure himself that she wouldn't slip away again. At last Julianna turned her head on the pillow. Her broad-lashed eyes slowly opened, and the sun's rays touched her emerald eyes.

She blinked with shock at seeing Casimir. Edging up in the bed, she pulled the blankets up to her collarbone and granted Casimir a furtive smile. His narrow eyes rested, immovable, on her.

"Master Casimir," she said, coyly shrugging off his intrusion, "to what do I owe the honor of this visit?"

"You've been dreaming," Casimir replied flatly.

"Have I?" she asked, a dimple forming in her brow.

"Yes," Casimir said.

She eyed him oddly. "I suppose I have."

"Tell me of your dream, Julianna," he said.

The sound of her name on his lips produced goose-flesh on her shoulders. She pulled the blankets over her shoulders and looked away. "Let me see. . . . It's all kind of . . . unclear," she said, leveling her eyes with his again. "I think I dreamt of a journey."

"Where were you going?" Casimir asked pointedly.

"I don't know," she said with a pout, then added as an afterthought, "The dream was unclear on that, too."

"Where did your journey begin?"

"From here."

"Why were you leaving?"

She nestled into her pillow. "It was only a dream."

Now Casimir's hard stare softened. Unlacing his hands from his knee, he leaned forward on the chair. "Why would you leave me, Julianna?"

She pulled back from him, the outer blanket tumbling away between them. Her eyes grew wide despite her struggle to appear calm. "Casimir, I think you put too much stock in dreams."

Seizing her shoulders, he said, "Tell me!"

Now fear showed plainly on her face. Seeing it, Casimir released her and sat angrily back in his chair. She glared at him, her eyes displaying an odd mixture of shock and concern. "Casimir, you're ill. You've grown pale and weak and distant and angry all the time. There's a priest in Gundarak—"

"No more priests," Casimir snapped. He leaned forward, burying his face in his hands.

"What's wrong with you?" she asked, suddenly indignant. "Don't you want to be well? I first knew something was wrong last autumn, but you wouldn't confide in me then, and not now either."

"I'm sorry," Casimir said dejectedly.

Now the desperation in Julianna's eyes verged on anger. "Thoris and Richter think its some ill-humor, but I think its because of being meistersinger, or maybe because of Gustav's death—or maybe because of me!"

"No!" Casimir shouted. "Never say that! Yes, being meistersinger is difficult, and so, too, was Gustav's death, and a thousand other things—but not you. Never you. Over and over you've sealed my wounds and healed my heart, Julianna. If you ever leave me, you will kill me."

"No more of your flattery!" Julianna said angrily.

"This isn't flattery," Casimir said. He tried to finish his thought, but the words refused to form on his lips. In frustration, he dropped from the chair and knelt beside the bed. "Marry me, Julianna. I can't risk losing you again."

She gasped, her flushed face suddenly going white. She stared for long moments at him, then lowered her trembling hand into his. "Of course I will," she said quietly.

Casimir lifted her hand to his lips and kissed it. Then, leaning forward, he wrapped her in his arms. She laid her hands on his shoulders and clung to him. Casimir could smell her blood, coursing fast and hot within her spotless neck. He strengthened his hold on her, feeling her body tremble. The sweet incense of fear began to rise from her breath and skin, swirling seductively in his nose. He grew suddenly aware of the thinness of the sheet that lay between them. The exotic rhythm of her heart welled up in his ears. He wanted to sink his teeth into her lovely neck and . . .

No!

Releasing Julianna, Casimir pulled back suddenly and stumbled to his feet. Sweat streaked his blanched face.

Julianna sat up, holding the sheet up before her. The morning sunlight traced her fragile and sensual silhouette on the sheet.

The transformation began in Casimir's aching bones. Biting his lip, he clambered backward toward the door.

Julianna rose from the bed. "Casimir, are you all right?"

He halted at the door. "Julianna, I love you." Then he flung the door wide and rushed out.

*   *   *   *   *

"Casimir, please, you must listen to me," Thoris implored a week later. He pulled his gold-embroidered robe up at the knees and scuttled across the marble-floored stateroom. The meistersinger, a dark silhouette against the broad bank of garden windows, stood on the chamber's far side. "It's urgent," Thoris said.

Casimir made no move to acknowledge Thoris, contenting himself to watch the gardener beyond the glass. Only when the young priest reached him and tugged on his sleeve did Casimir speak. "Nothing is urgent anymore, Thoris."

Dropping the hem of his baggy robe to the carpet, Thoris put his hand reassuringly on Casimir's shoulder. "You've always made time for me, Casimir. Please don't ignore me now."

The meistersinger turned irritably from the window. He raised his thin fingers to stroke his chin. "Well, what's this urgent business you have for me?"

Motioning toward a cluster of chairs beside the window, Thoris said, "Sit down, at least."

Nodding, Casimir strode curtly to the nearest chair and dropped into it. Thoris sat gravely in the next seat. "You see, it comes down to this. I've heard voices in the temple."

Casimir's silver gaze was profound, and his voice was almost a growl. "And you wish to lock the doors after nightfall?"

"No," Thoris said with a fleeting smile. "I've heard voices speak to me."

The meistersinger sat silently, considering the statement. Finally he repeated, "You've heard voices speak to you?"

"Yes," Thoris responded simply. Then he added, "Or perhaps I should say I've heard one specific voice speak to me."

"And, pray, what did this singular voice say?" Casimir asked in clipped tones.

"It said—or, I should say, *he* said—" before continuing, Thoris averted his eyes to the richly-hued tapestry beneath their feet—"he said you lied to me."

The meistersinger's raven hair shadowed his gaze. "Lied to you? Who is this *he* who calls me a liar, and what does *he* say I've lied about?"

"I don't know who he is," Thoris responded, his tone hardening against Casimir's sarcasm. "But I know this much: The voice said you're still a werewolf."

Casimir's lips spread in a thin, angry smile, and he released a grating laugh. The mirthless sound arced up through the room and rattled faintly in the aged glass of the windows. Thoris waited in silence. His face remained as humorless as the laugh itself. Casimir gasped, "What would ever make you think such a thing, my friend?"

"The voice, of course," Thoris responded coldly.

Quieting his laughter, Casimir leaned toward Thoris and smiled. "A lunatic voice is your source?"

Thoris rose from his seat, clasping hands behind his back and stepping pensively away from the cluster of chairs. "Whether or not that curse still inhabits your blood, Casimir, it clings to you. I can see the beast even now in your face and your eyes. It's like a poison that began in your skin and is working inward toward your heart."

"What about my speeches in the temple?" Casimir asked dramatically, rising from his chair. "Don't they count for something? What about my work on behalf of the poor? What about my festivals, my edicts? Are they nothing?"

"You're trying to use the blessings to excuse the curse," Thoris said. He stopped and pivoted toward Casimir. "But why excuse the curse unless it still remains with you?"

"It doesn't!" Casimir shouted.

"Even Julianna says something's wrong."

Casimir's eyes flared. "You stay clear of Julianna. *Never* tell her about the curse and *never* try to take her away from me. If anyone gets between me and her, I'll kill him."

"This is what I mean!" Thoris said. "Listen to yourself!"

Striding defiantly toward Thoris, Casimir growled, "My curse is gone. But if it weren't, what would you do, priest Thoris?"

Struggling to remain calm, Thoris searched his friend's anger-reddened face. Swallowing once, he said, "As priest of Milil, I'd perform again the rites of purification."

"What a waste of time!" Casimir shouted, whirling around and stalking off toward the windows. "If the first rite failed me, Milil is either a false god or a dead one. Or perhaps he lives, but extends no hope to me. What sort of god would he be, then? What sort of merciless and cruel master? Even you, Thoris—you who are as petty and mortal as any of us—even you had mercy on me! You wouldn't deny me salvation! Is Milil less than you?"

Thoris hummed a penance for the blasphemy. "Are you saying Milil is dead?"

"Perhaps."

"Why would you say that," Thoris asked, striding toward him, "unless Milil didn't remove your curse?"

"And what curse might that be?" came an elegant baritone voice from the stateroom's door.

Harkon Lukas.

The bard wore his customarily wicked smile. He stepped into the room, his black cloak hanging like a set of wings behind him. Sweeping the broad-brimmed hat from his head, he bowed low. Thoris scuttled uneasily back toward Casimir, his face reddening. Harkon Lukas rose from his bow and paced into the room. "Must I put the question again? What curse are you speaking of?"

Thoris opened his mouth, but Casimir spoke first, "The curse of being continually interrupted by folk of no account."

Lukas shrugged off the comment. "That *would* be troublesome."

"May I ask to what I owe this honor?" Casimir said curtly.

Lukas cast a theatrical glance of confidentiality toward Thoris. "It's a rather private matter, meistersinger."

"My priest and I stand as one," Casimir responded evenly.

The corners of Lukas's lips turned down in a capricious expression of indulgence. "Perhaps I should leave this matter to a time of more privacy."

Thoris spoke up. "No, Casimir. I've gotten my answer. It'd be a shame for Master Lukas to travel all the way from Skald only to be turned away now." Thoris passed between the two and, nearly tripping, lifted his robe up away from his feet. Casimir watched in silence as Thoris left, swinging the door softly closed behind him.

The meistersinger turned stiffly toward the tall bard and said, "I hope your business is important."

The cunning smile melted from Lukas's features. "My business is always important." Reaching into his coat, Lukas pulled out a blackened lump of wood. "While passing through the market today, I noticed a grubby man hawking grubby things. Among them was this." Carelessly Lukas flung the black mass onto a small reading table. The rough edges of the wood left thin claw marks on the tabletop as they slid across it.

It was the mask of Sundered Heart—the mask Casimir had worn in the meistersinger contest.

"The aforementioned grubby man said he found this bauble in a firepit beside the amphitheater. He said I could have it for six coppers," Lukas continued. Casimir stared at the sooty mask as though mesmerized by it.

The feathers that had once graced its top now curled in black balls above the charred face. The brow above one eye had been broken away, creating a wild and ludicrous leer on that side of the mask. Lines of smoke traced over the silent features, and cracks webbed the surface. Lukas's voice came again, breaking into Casimir's reverie. "I bargained the old bugger down to three coppers: a fitting sum, in remembrance of your past."

Raising his eyes from the mask, Casimir said flatly, "What do you know of my past?"

Lukas's expression grew deadly serious. "I know this: The wolf saved you from the poorhouse, the wolf saved you from Zhone Clieous, the wolf delivered you onto this throne and killed those who would overthrow you. Don't you see, Casimir? Your salvation has always come from the beast within you, not from your human side. When you deny that beast, you are nothing. Only by embracing it do you live!"

"What has occasioned this diatribe?" Casimir hissed.

"Only this," Lukas growled. "I heard yesterday of your ridiculous betrothal to Julianna. What is wrong with you? Do you want to shackle yourself to your human side? Do you want to die and bring her down to death with you?"

Casimir snatched the mask from the tabletop and studied its charred edges. "This isn't my past. You point to my shadow and say it is me." He pulled his soot-smeared hand from the mask and presented it to the bard. "Look how the shadow dirties my hands. I can't wash it away—I've tried. But maybe Julianna can. She is pure and strong, untouched by—"

Lukas seized Casimir's black hair and roared angrily into his face, "Forget Julianna! *You* are the shadow, Casimir! The shadow holds your power. The shadow grants you life! Call off the wedding! Discipline your priest! Denounce your humanity. You are a beast and nothing more."

Casimir's fist cracked heavily on the bard's jaw, knocking him to the floor. Standing over him, Casimir demanded, "How dare you order me about in my own mansion?"

"Remember my power, Casimir!" Lukas growled as he stood up.

"Your power be damned, and you as well!" Casimir raged, lifting the blackened mask above his head. He shouted, "This isn't me!" He flung the mask to the stony floor. With a sound like thick glass shattering, the charred wood broke into countless splinters, each rushing from the point of impact in swirling, chaotic lines.

As the last pieces slid into the far wall, Casimir pointed his sooty finger toward the door. "Get out, Lukas. You're no longer welcome in this hall, or in my councils, my amphitheater, or any building of state in Harmonia. I spit on your life of darkness, and I denounce the wolf in me!"

The bard's eyes were expressionless. He turned from the meistersinger, placed his broad-brimmed hat on his head, and strolled easily toward the door. Nearing the threshold, he set his heel on one of the rough shards of Casimir's mask and pivoted slowly. The grinding of the boot filled the still air.

"The gods can't exorcise this monster from you, Casimir. You say you've denounced your life of darkness, but that choice isn't yours to make. You can pretend not to be a monster, but you'll be living a lie. The hunger will awaken again, Casimir. You'll kill again, and when you do, your rule in Harmonia will be over." With calm deliberateness, Lukas turned, opened the door, and strode from the room.

*   *   *   *   *

"Good day, dogman," Harkon Lukas said, shading his narrowed eyes against the white afternoon sky. He leaned back on the garden bench, watching the thin manservant rein in the mob of hunting dogs around him. Despite the man's efforts, the canines pulled him across the garden to the bench where Lukas sat. The hounds crowded up to the dark bard, sniffing his clothing.

The man eyed Lukas suspiciously. "Did you say 'dog-man'?"

Lukas motioned toward the nuzzling pack. "These are dogs, are they not?"

The gray lines of distrust deepened on the man's face. "I prefer my given name—Valsarik—to the title 'dog-man.'"

"Oh," Lukas responded with feigned surprise and an unapologizing grin. "If we're to be on a name basis, mine is Harkon Lukas."

"Yes, I know," replied the solemn-faced servant. He pulled ineffectually at the host of dogs, but they continued their aggressive sniffing of Lukas's pant legs.

"Beautiful hounds," Lukas noted offhandedly.

Dragging on the leashes with more insistence, Valsarik pulled the wet noses from Lukas's pant legs. "I apologize. They're not usually so aggressive toward people."

"Not toward people," Lukas echoed, "but toward other creatures, yes?"

"Obviously," Valsarik replied stiffly. "These are hunting dogs—*wolf*-hunting dogs."

"Is that so?" Lukas asked without interest. He stretched his arms in the warm sunlight and yawned. His gaze settled on the small boy playing at the other end of the garden. "Rather a nice garden for such fierce dogs to be wandering through."

"I've just had them out in the woods to the east." Valsarik cast a distracted glance around the finely manicured garden. A few tugs on the leashes brought his attention sharply back to the dogs. "Beasts such as these need to run."

"I know the feeling," Lukas replied with a disarming smile. He leaned over, scratching the velvety coat of one of the dogs with his long, thin fingers and murmuring cheerfully in the creature's attentive ear. Valsarik stared hawkishly at this exchange, his voice sharpening.

"The kennels adjoin this garden." With a nod, he indicated a squat building that lay half hidden behind the garden wall. But all the while his eyes remained on the whispering bard. Valsarik's features darkened, and he added absently, "No other way in or out but through the garden."

Sitting up again, Lukas studied the old man's uninviting expression. "My dear Valsarik, you needn't be so fearful to find me here in your master's garden."

"Needn't I?" Valsarik asked bluntly.

"Your master and I have been friends for many years."

"Yes, I know," the old man noted, tugging heavily on the leashes. Turning decidedly away from Lukas, he pulled the panting hounds from the bard and led them toward the kennels.

"Good day, then, good Valsarik," Lukas said wryly.

"And to you as well," Valsarik replied, emotionless. Then, redirecting his voice to the hounds around him, the old man led the pack down the garden path, around the short wall that surrounded it, and into the kennels.

Filling his lungs with the springtime air, Lukas turned his attention from the dogs to his real interest—the boy playing beside the mansion. The innocent child could have been no more than four years old—perfect in age and station for Lukas's plan. Indeed, when he had spotted the boy from the road, the tall bard had known immediately he must have him. He had made his way through the garden gate, unopposed by the lord of the estate, and sat down on the garden bench in full view of the child. For an hour now, the boy had been running, tumbling, and screaming with delight as his imagined foes pursued him across the cleanly cut grass. The screams sent a thrill of pleasure through Lukas.

His eyes shifted from the child when the boy's mother came to the tall window and gazed with loving concern at her son.

Through lips twisted in a mirthless leer, Lukas whispered to himself, "Every trap needs suitable bait, bait that one would reach for by mere instinct." His gaze alternated hungrily between the mother and her child.

Slowly the smile wilted on his lips and he mumbled, "You'll do nicely, my boy. Nicely indeed."

Rising, Lukas strolled toward the garden gateway.

A hundred feet away, the woman glimpsed the dark bard leaving the garden. She forced the heavy window open and shouted shrilly: "Johannes, come inside this instant!"

*   *   *   *   *

The hunting kennels stood silent beneath the gibbous moon. Across rough, hay-strewn floorboards lay dogs in sleep. Their sawlike breathing filled the small wooden shack, drowning out even the aggressive chittering of the crickets outside. Occasionally a dog yelped in dreamt pain or scraped the planking with its fidgeting toenails. Soon, though, these dreamers sank again into fitful sleep.

Aside from the dogs' snoring, the air was thick with the mingled smells of urine, feces, pelts, and straw. The stifling odor found only occasional relief when gusts of springtime air ventured into the kennel through high-set wooden vents. Such a breeze now wafted over a slumbering bitch.

The breeze carried the smell of man.

Instantly the creature awoke, sniffing the thick air. She recognized the scent of this man. Not Valsarik, but another. Pushing herself up on stiff legs, the dog took another lungful of air. Yes. An unmistakable scent. The perfumed man. The forest-clothed man. The dark man with the shiny eyes.

Stretching her tired muscles, the hound peered curiously toward the narrow-slatted vent above her head. Through the thin bars of wood, she could see the black sky and its fiercely sparkling stars, but no silhouette of man. Still, the scent was sure. The man stood just beyond the vent, very close—perhaps leaning on the wall. The dog's claws clicked on the rough kennel floor as she moved toward the wall. She reared up, setting her forelegs just below the vent. The odor came so strong, her probing nose could almost taste the stranger. Her ears pivoted toward the wooden slats.

The man was whispering.

The strange sibilance of human speech struck the dog's ear, much as it had countless times before. Now, though, the speech flowed with commands the bitch didn't know. She recognized not a single word.

But a fire awoke in her bones.

Bundling her muscles, the dog leapt violently at the vent. Her muzzle and forelegs struck on the wooden slats, which flung her back on her tail. Without a moment's pause, the beast hurled herself again at the barred opening and again tumbled awkwardly back from the collision. Dogs lying beneath the vent awoke and scurried with tucked tails from the spot. The bitch leapt a third time; her forefeet and muzzle struck the central slats, which emitted a snapping sound, but the wood held. She tumbled to the rough planking, then scrambled to her feet. Blood oozed from the abrasions across her nose as she charged the vent again. One bar snapped. Beneath the staring moon, a nose print, moist with blood, glimmered on the wooden rails. Her claws raked the floor; she rose into the air; two more slats cracked. With awkward and weary leaps, the frenzied creature threw herself again and again at the wooden frame until all the slats had finally snapped. With the last blow, fragments of wood showered the night air outside. The bitch leapt for the opening. Her belly slid over the jagged sill, and she yelped in pain. Then she dropped to the chill ground beside the kennel.

The man was gone.

As though unaware of the long gashes in her stomach, the hound turned her nose to the wild scents on the wind, searching for the forest man's scent.

He truly was gone.

Again those thick, foreign whispers echoed through her ears. She found her limbs moving beneath her, carrying her across the dew-soaked grass of the garden.

Instinctively her nose dropped to the fetid earth, leaving a
faint trail on the dewy lawn as she passed. Reaching the
shrubs that lined the mansion's base, the hound followed
a path along the wall. Panting breaths whirled in spectral
circles before her as her feet drove her along the building's foundation. Across her scratched pelt, hackles
stood in savage spikes. Her whiskers bristled. She didn't
smell her prey, nor know what she was hunting.

But she *was* hunting.

As the bitch rounded a corner of the mansion, light
from the huge moon struck her full in the face. She
turned her eyes toward the mansion wall before her.
Banks of tall windows stood empty and dark. Her stare
was drawn to one particular window. It lay unopened
and curtainless like the others, and in the vast blackness
of the room, the dog spotted something. Her pads fid-
geted on the sweating grass.

It was small, unmoving, lifeless.

Its eyes stared at her unblinkingly.

She had seen the small one carry it, talk to it as
though it could hear. But it never spoke a word.

Her legs pushed her toward the window: walking, trot-
ting, running. The black window loomed larger as she
approached. The silent one stared unblinkingly at her.
She neared the house. Just below the window, the bitch
thrust her forelegs against the ground, and her rear legs
followed through. She leapt. Her body hurtled upward,
sliding silently through the night air. The black, rectangular window soared toward her. For a instant, she saw
her own reflection.

Her nose struck the pane.

A magnificent explosion of glass cracked the night as
the window ruptured, spraying knifelike slivers into the
dark room. The bloodied bitch arced smoothly through
the glass-filled air. Her forepaws struck the room's thick
tapestry. Glass fell like hail around her. She pushed off
from the carpet, pulling her hind paws to the floor.
Another bound. She traced a looping path toward the
dark corner of the room.

Toward the bed and its shivering occupant.

Leaping from the slick floor, the bitch vaulted onto the feather mattress. The child huddled there, clutching sheets to his chin in mute terror. Teeth shiny with her own blood, the bitch clamped down on the boy. The scream never passed his throat. Spinning about, the hound pulled the limp body from its covers. The beast leapt from the bed and bounded toward the window. With each footfall, glass shards rammed into her pads. Still the dog ran. Dragging the lifeless child along the floor, the hound reached the window. Her muscles bundled beneath her ribboned pelt, and she leapt through the jagged pane into the night.

In the doorway to the room appeared a woman. Horror laced her face. She had reached the threshold just in time to hear her child's foot strike dully against the windowsill.

                    *   *   *   *   *

Harkon Lukas stepped out on the running board of his unlighted coach. With gloved hands, he gracefully lifted the two lifeless forms into the carriage. Drawing the door closed, he signaled the dark-cloaked driver. A whip cracked in the night, and the carriage lurched forward. Lukas settled back comfortably on the seat, crossing his legs above the still forms. The smell of blood was strong in the coach, and Lukas inhaled it with deep satisfaction. For a long while, he sat listening to the clatter of the horses' hooves and allowing the sinister plan to circulate through his mind. At length, Lukas lit the small lantern within the carriage.

The bodies were a gruesome sight, carved up wickedly by fragments of glass. Lukas stared with some disgust at the broken creatures, but a sardonic smile crossed his face: The blood conveniently matched the scarlet lining of the carriage.

Reaching into an inner pocket of his satin waistcoat, the dark bard produced a small piece of paper, folded neatly across its center. He set the paper on his knee and began unfolding it with one hand while the other produced a pen and a jar of ink from a small compartment. Pivoting a silver tray from the carriage wall, Lukas spread the blank paper onto the tray. Then he paused and murmured, "How shall I phrase this?" Setting the pen's end to his lip, he said, "I have the bait, but I must tell the woman I have it, and must somehow link it to Casimir." At last, the words fell together in his head. Setting the pen into the open ink jar, he began to write:

Dear Lady,

If ever you wish to hold again in your arms this child of yours, wait for me outside the meistersinger's mansion on the three nights of the full moon. On one of the said nights, I will appear from the mansion, tall and elegant and cowled in a dark robe. Meet me and accompany me where I will lead. Make no struggle, and there I will show you your child.

Lukas paused before setting the last dark strokes to the page.

Sincerely Yours,
Heart of Midnight

FOURTEEN

"I assure you, bard Lukas," came the craggy voice of the Vistana crone, "I wouldn't agree to read outside my wagon for just any inquirer. But your repute soothes my distrust."

The bard sat on the floridly carved window seat of the inn room. His thin fingers were crossed elegantly in his lap, and his merciless eyes watched the street below. Periodically his gaze wandered to the full moon, which labored slowly up from the roof-lined horizon. But always his eyes returned to the vacant street fronting the meistersinger's mansion.

The gypsy eyed Lukas with suspicion. She emptied a silken pouch of bones onto the small night table. The bones, dry and polished, tumbled musically against the green marble tabletop. Sorting them, the gypsy said offhandedly, "Something else presses more heavily on your mind than the reading, perhaps?"

Slowly Lukas sat upright. He stretched and stared blankly at the gangly crone. A capricious light entered his eyes. "Forgive me, dear Marosa. I fear my thinking of late has grown muddled. I do appreciate your willingness to perform the reading here. After all, my concern lies in the events of this room. Scrying in any other place would turn up nothing."

The gypsy's cataract-frosted eyes regarded him coldly, but her ancient voice was hospitable. "This room may be older than either of us, Master Lukas. It has many stories to tell. What stories, then, do you require of this place, mmmmmm?"

Casting a final glance through the rippled window, Lukas rose from the window seat and paced forward. He stroked his goatee thoughtfully and said, "I'd like to know who stayed here, what they did, why they came, where they went . . ."

Gathering the bones in her knobby hand, Madam Marosa asked, "Shall I look for any person in particular?"

Lukas slid into a seat beside the table. His wicked smile had returned. "You know me well enough to realize I'm not a fool, Madam Marosa. No, I'll not tell you whom I seek. Tell me whom you find, and I'll indicate whether you are correct."

"I'm no fool either," the gnarled gypsy retorted, laying her empty hand out before her. "Ten gold . . . now."

Reaching into his luxuriant vest, Lukas produced a handful of coins and dropped them singly into the gypsy's craggy hand. "Here's twenty gold, dear lady. Now kindly begin your reading."

Slipping the warm coins into a belt pouch, Madam Marosa said, "Twenty-one gold, but who counts such trifles?"

"Let that extra gold inspire your lips to truth."

The cunning look faded from the gypsy's face. Her eyes darkened as she turned to the task. Mixing the bones dexterously in her hand, she said, "Though I cast and read the bones, I truly read the room tonight. The bones will channel and clarify the voices of the room."

"Begin."

She closed her papery eyelids and began to hum. Unclenching her fist, she dropped the bones onto the table. Her eyes fluttered open, and she peered intently toward the pile of bones. Lukas also examined them. They lay in a chaotic mound on the green marble.

The gypsy pursed her lips and began to speak, "Last night this room held . . . an odd man. He had a man's head and body, but . . . a child's limbs. From Darkon, he was."

"I have no interest in dwarfs," Lukas said in a half-growl, "nor other carnival creatures. Who was here the night before?"

She glared hostilely at him, and once again her hand gathered the bones. She closed her eyes, raised her face toward the room's ceiling, and let the bones drop. Opening her eyes, she began the second reading. "The night before last . . . forbidden lovers shared that bed. The room . . . is rainbowed with their lust. I—"

"The night before that."

Sighing irately, Madam Marosa lifted the bones again and let them fall. This time when she glanced at the pattern, she reeled as though struck by a fist. Lukas studied the old woman's face. Her features had gone white, and a line of sweat beaded on her craggy brow. Clutching the table, she steadied herself on the chair.

Lukas leaned hungrily forward, setting his hands on the table. "What do you see, woman? Who was here three nights ago?"

"A . . . a fiend," she said breathlessly.

"A fiend?" he echoed.

"A man-fiend," she whispered. Her eyes turned in slow circles, focusing fearfully beyond the room's walls.

The bard smiled deeply. "What do you mean, 'a man-fiend'?"

The wizened woman shook her head in fear. "He was . . . wrapped in the skin of a man . . . but was truly a monster. Tall and lean . . . carried something heavy. Something cold."

"What did he carry, Madam Marosa?"

"He carried . . . he carried—" she began, her mouth forming silent syllables between the words. Her body went rigid, and she gasped. "He carried a little boy and a dog. Both were dead."

"What did he do with them?"

"Set them . . . there, on that window seat," the gypsy replied, pointing. "And he . . . and he . . ."

"And he changed, didn't he, Madam Marosa?" Lukas asked. "Changed from a tall, thin bard to a wolf. Am I not correct?"

The old gypsy stared back at him, stunned. Lukas could see his own wild expression in her bulging eyes.

"And that beast, Madam Marosa—that beast set to feeding, did it not?" Lukas pressed, edging savagely nearer. The woman made no response. "And it looked like me, didn't it?"

With a dexterous motion that belied her swollen joints, she seized the bones from the table, flung them in Lukas's face, and lurched frantically backward. A vise-like hand clamped around her throat. She struggled violently to escape.

A grisly snap echoed through the room.

Her body went limp, slumping downward. Lukas retained his grip on her neck and breathed deeply. He strode toward the window, dragging the lifeless form of the gypsy woman. Pushing back the window curtain, he peered out. A monstrous grin crossed his features.

Down below, on the road that fronted the meistersinger's mansion, a solitary woman stood. She wrung her hands and gazed continually down the intersecting streets. Lukas leaned closer to the glass. Turning a small bar on the casement, he cautiously opened a section of the window. A cool nighttime breeze wafted in. Lukas's nose drew in the fragrant air.

The wind was stiff with fear.

He turned from the window, a strange transformation taking place across his body. He was growing smaller; his shock of black hair lengthened down his back, halting just above his waist; the mustache and beard disappeared; the time-rumpled skin of his brow smoothed; his monocle dropped to an awaiting hand; the angular edges of his face rounded into curves. Slowly the transformation swept his entire form until an alluring, black-haired woman stood in his stead. The bard's finery hung loose on her as she looked down at the dead gypsy.

"Her clothes should fit me nicely."

* * * * *

Julianna prodded distractedly at her food. Plumes of steam rose from the fine venison and danced in the cold air of the dining hall. The scrape of her knife on the porcelain plate was the only sound in the vast room. She shifted uncomfortably in the high-backed chair, her gaze wandering across the table to Casimir. He sat opposite her, picking unenthusiastically at his plate. His complexion had grown only grayer since their betrothal, and daily he became quieter and more withdrawn.

Setting her knife down, Julianna said, "Why won't you go to the priest in Gundarak? He can heal you."

Casimir looked up blankly. "Heal me of what?"

"Look at you," she replied, anger edging her voice. "You look like a corpse."

"There's nothing wrong with me," Casimir said sullenly.

"Well, then there's something wrong with me," Julianna replied, standing up and throwing her napkin on her plate. She strode to the door and opened it. "A year ago you were so full of life. Now you're just full of death. And it's affecting me as well." Turning, she marched out the door.

Casimir watched her go. He slid his fork beneath the venison on his plate and turned the meat over slowly. Sighing, he dropped his fork and stared into the candelabra at the center of the table. Twice the thought occurred to him that he should get up and go after Julianna, but neither time did he move.

"What's happened to me?" he wondered aloud. "I haven't hunted in three weeks—not even transformed. But instead of feeling better, I feel worse." Pushing the plate out of the way, he folded his arms on the table and laid his head down. "I'm just so tired." He shut his eyes for a moment.

Casimir awoke as a manservant cautiously lifted the plate from before him. Wrinkling his pallid brow, Casimir blinked. The servant winced and bit his lip. "Are you finished, sir?"

Casimir stared dazedly at the man. "Yes. Take it."

The man nodded obsequiously and, lifting the plate, backed away toward the kitchen.

"Oh . . . ah, before you go," Casimir said. "Could you please summon Julianna to me?"

The servant cringed. "Begging your forgiveness, sir, but the lady Julianna left the citadel about half an hour ago."

Casimir's face hardened. "What? Where did she go?"

"She didn't say, sir," the servant replied, "but she wore a traveling cloak and carried a bag. I believe the priest had sent for her."

Casimir's fist clenched and he pounded it on the table. "Damn it, not again! I warned him not to do this."

The servant bowed nervously and said, "Also, the priest sent some lay elders from the temple to speak with you. They're in the library." Wincing noticeably, the servant disappeared into the kitchen.

"I've no time for church mice." Casimir rose from his seat and strode out the dining hall door. His heart pounded heavily in his chest, and he could feel the color coming back into his cheeks. As he paced down the main hall, he thought, I've got to stop Thoris from taking her away. Lukas was right. He's trying to get her safely out of the way before he turns on me. Casimir slammed his fist against his palm.

As he passed the library doors, a sudden chill swept over him. He halted, turning back toward the library. Cautiously cracking the doors, he peered inside. Five robed elders of Milil sat within, two reading books and the other three glancing nervously about the room. Casimir's breath caught. Beneath the long robes of one of the lay elders, he glimpsed a boot sheath that held a large dagger. The dagger shone like silver. Sweat broke out on Casimir's brow as he studied the others. At least three of the five carried identical knives.

Pulling back from the door, Casimir leaned breathlessly against the wall. "He was going to kill me tonight," he whispered, wide-eyed. "Not even he, but a set of assassins."

Stepping away from the wall, he staggered down the hallway, his hand clutched to his heart. "He wants to kill me." Eyes glowing like embers in his skull, Casimir entered his quarters and shut the door behind him. Dragging a hand across his sweating brow, he gazed out the window at the full moon. Its cold light seemed to drive the quivering from his body, seemed to harden his resolve. He breathed deeply, calming his mind. Pulling a black cloak from the wall, he turned about and headed for the door. "We'll see who does the killing. Tonight Thoris dies."

* * * * *

"Where's Madam Marosa?" Thoris asked the caravan driver. He veiled his face with his robes and scanned the dark slum street.

The young, black-haired gypsy woman atop the caravan tied off the reins and leapt down before the priest. "She's busy. I'm her daughter, Donya. I'll be taking you to Gundarak."

Thoris frowned, noting that the young woman's clothes were identical to those of Madam Marosa, the Vistana matriarch he'd booked passage with. Eyeing the brightly painted caravan, he said, "The other passenger will be here any moment."

The gypsy woman laid a slender hand on his shoulder and said, "I'm in no hurry. I already have your gold."

"Remember, secrecy is critical," Thoris said. "Once we get into the caravan, don't let anyone but the gate guards stop you until we reach Gundarak. Tell the guards you're alone. Drive quickly, but don't look like you're in a hurry."

"Yes, yes, *giorgio*," she said, patting his head mockingly.

Ducking out from under her hand, Thoris said, "Now listen to me: This is important. Three weeks ago when we tried to go to Gundarak, a song rose up as we reached the border—"

"And it lulled you to sleep. I know, I know," Donya said. "Don't worry. Gypsies are immune to the sleep song of Kartakass."

"That's what I'd heard. It's why I hired you," Thoris said. Footsteps approached on the street. Thoris gasped. Pressing himself against the side of the *vardo*, he held his breath. I hope that's not Casimir, he thought.

"Sorry I'm late," Julianna said as she rounded the corner of the caravan.

Motioning her into the coach, Thoris said, "Everything's arranged. I sent some temple elders to talk with Casimir to try to convince him of his illness."

Stepping through the *vardo*'s door, Julianna said, "He became angry when I mentioned it. I hope the elders can handle a fight."

"I made sure they could defend themselves."

*   *   *   *   *

Casimir stepped from the terrace of the dining hall. He drew his long black cloak tightly about his neck; the night was unseasonably chill. Raising the hood of his cloak, Casimir eyed the blue-black heavens. The full moon hovered white like an eye in the eastern sky.

Casimir stepped onto the garden path and followed it past the fountain and the budding racks of *meekulbrau*. He gained the cobbled carriage track and marched on into the black entryway. The click of his steel-tipped boots echoed in the cavernous passage. He passed under the portcullis, between the gate guards, and out beneath the starry sky. After descending the rampway from the mansion, he drifted to the right edge of the road. The elegant Longpipe Inn stood on that side. Walking next to it, Casimir let his fingertips skim over the edifice's rough wall as he approached a lamp-lit intersection.

"Tonight I kill Thoris."

With heavy strides, he rounded the corner of the Long-pipe. A woman was standing in his path. He halted too late, knocking her heavily to the stone pavement. Casimir gasped, kneeling immediately beside her and offering his hand. "Forgive me, my dear, I didn't see you."

She peered up toward him, studying his shadowed features. Aside from the fear in her eyes, the woman was stunningly beautiful. Her golden-blond hair framed a finely shaped face, with a small nose and full, ruby lips. Casimir gazed, incredulous, at her. Slowly she reached out an exquisitely small hand, placing it in his. He set his other hand on her shoulder and raised her to her feet. The lacy gorget she wore settled against her chest, and the ruffles in her gown arrayed themselves about her trim waist.

Casimir ventured, "It's a dangerous night to be out alone."

"I'll go with you," she said, her deep voice belying the childlike innocence of her features.

I'll go with you? Casimir wondered quizzically. "But you don't know where I'm going."

"Yes," she said, her voice quivering. "I don't know."

He peered dubiously at her. "Shouldn't you go home?"

"Please," the woman said, becoming suddenly upset. "I'm so afraid. Don't play games with me. I won't return without my son."

She's drunken or mad, thought Casimir. Even so, he was drawn to her. She had awakened the hunger in him. His eyes traced over the slender lines of her neck, and he willingly breathed in the seductive scent of her body. "I'll gladly escort you wherever you're going."

She fit her trembling hand to his arm and leaned her head against his shoulder. "Please . . . tell me, where are we going?"

Casimir's throat tightened, and the desire in him grew sharper. He murmured, "The temple of Milil."

"Take me there, meistersinger," she said sadly.

The sound of his title on her lips sent gooseflesh across his spine, and her melancholy voice heightened the tingle that had already begun in his bones. He could smell her blood, could imagine sinking his razor-tipped claws one by one into her skin and exposing the fragrant muscle beneath. He closed his eyes, pushing back the horrible images. The tingling advance of the beast had spread through much of his body already, but he halted it. Halted it for a time.

"Please, Master Casimir," the woman begged, "if we are going, let us be on our way."

He nodded, cupping his fingers reluctantly over her icy hand. Then he set out for the temple. Neither of them spoke as they walked, though Casimir felt sure she could hear the pounding of his heart.

*   *   *   *   *

Three shadowy figures watched from the dark alley as Casimir led the woman off toward the temple. Waiting for a full minute after the meistersinger had passed, one of the figures whispered hoarsely to the other two. They responded, then all the voices fell silent. The first figure moved away from its fellows and peered out into the lamp-lit street. Casimir and the woman were nowhere in sight. Slipping cautiously around the corner, the shadowy man gathered his cloak around him and dashed silently past the Longhorn Inn. Crossing the cobbled street, he opened the front door of an estate.

The door closed silently behind him. He stepped into the foyer, a grave expression on his mustachioed face. At the foyer's end stood a thin, well-dressed woman, silhouetted in candlelight. She motioned the man urgently toward the kitchen. Nodding wordlessly, he strode across the luxuriant parlor, through a dining hall, and to the broad-banded door beyond.

In nervous haste, he threw the door wide. A score of dogs who had been resting on the other side scuttled in panic about the slick stone floor. One by one they began to bark. An aged man grappled with their leashes, giving a surprisingly powerful yank that pulled many of the hounds to their seats.

"Silence!" Valsarik shouted, and the command, ringing off the stony walls, accomplished its aim.

The shadowy man, now revealed as a warrior by the kitchen lanterns, waded amongst the dogs to reach Valsarik. He began to speak in confidential tones. "It's Meistersinger Casimir, not Lukas, as you suspected."

Lines of grief formed on the servant's otherwise reticent face. "Master Casimir, is it?"

"Yes," the guardsman responded evenly. "Elyana asked where he would take her, and he said to the temple of Milil."

"I'll circle around with the dogs and arrive before he does," Valsarik said.

"Good," the warrior replied. "Have your beasts ready. Casimir is rumored to be a cunning and ruthless foe."

The old man set piercing eyes on the warrior. "Yes, indeed."

*   *   *   *   *

Casimir and the woman threaded their way through the slum streets, heading toward the temple, which rose ominously in the distance. The shacks and shanties looked much as they had a year before, despite Casimir's reforms. Moonlight shone bright on the deserted street, and a cold wind had begun to blow. Wrapping the woman in his cloak, Casimir led her to the burned-out shell of the Red Porch poorhouse.

"You're not taking me to the temple, are you?" she asked, biting her lip.

Casimir turned to face her, running a trembling finger along the curving line of her jaw. "No, I am not."

Tears filled her eyes. "I'll do anything you ask, just please, please, tell me where my—"

Casimir stopped the words with a kiss. Her lips felt warm and magnificent beneath his. The transformation had begun in him. He kissed her again, biting lightly into her lip. She struggled to break free, prying against his warping bones. With an angry slap, she jarred his hands loose and backed away, catching a foothold on the ash-strewn ground. Blood was running from her lower lip, across her chin, and down her neck. The fear had left her eyes, replaced by an angry light. "Where is my son?"

Casimir didn't even hear the question; his transformation to half-wolf form was nearly complete. The full moon had sped the change as, too, had the woman's fear and her blood. Casting his cloak to the ground, Casimir leapt toward her. His wiry arms wrapped about her, and lethal claws sprouted from his fingertips. She struggled to break free, striking his black-lipped muzzle. She reached out to tear at the glowing eyes before her, but the beastman caught her arm in his scissoring jaws.

Then he heard the dogs.

He pulled back and listened, ignoring the volley of fists on his chest.

They were hounds . . . wolf-hunting hounds, and they were approaching.

Casimir released the woman. She stumbled back away from him. He pivoted on his half-wolf legs, his ears swiveling to locate the source of the baying. The woman, cradling her lacerated arm, scrambled to her feet and dashed away into the slums.

Now he saw them.

A pack of twenty baying beasts poured down the slum street, heading straight for the ruins of the Red Porch. Their strong scent rode heavy on the wind. Casimir pivoted and ripped the shirt from his back. The transmogrification stirred again in his bones; he needed the speed of his full-wolf form. Clawed toes shortened and blunted, biting into the ash below. He leapt from the ruins as his legs reshaped. Muscles knotted painfully beneath his roiling hide as he landed on all fours. His angular arms thinned, and his fingers blunted into pads. Stepping from his breeches, Casimir lunged away from the poorhouse. A furious rhythm took hold of his feet, and the mud street began to speed dizzily away with each lunging stride.

He was now fully a wolf.

The hounds' throaty calls grew loud behind him, loud even over the thunder of his feet. He turned down another street, heading out of the slums. The pack of dogs closed, turning after him. Casimir's claws scraped savagely at the cobblestones as the tide of dogs swelled quick on his heels. Turning sharply, Casimir leapt a half-wall between two houses. Clearing it, he plunged into the dark alcove beyond. The hounds followed, flooding over the wall. Casimir toppled a pair of rubbish bins in the alcove and cut behind one of the houses. The dogs leapt nimbly over the bins. The wolf vaulted a thick shrub and landed in the adjacent street, but the hounds followed.

They surged forward, nipping at his flank. With each step, they clawed away the tiny lead he held. He cursed his failing lungs, already wringing the air for all their worth. He couldn't outrun them, and he couldn't outfight them.

But he *could* out-think them.

Casimir drove his shrieking muscles onward. With slow agony, he gained precious inches on the pack. Before him lay a two-story home, fronted by a shuttered window. The shutters looked poorly built, and old, and rotten.

The pack of hounds welled up behind Casimir, and he quickened his pace. The window neared: ten more strides. A fang tore savagely through his heel. Five more strides . . . two more. He flung himself into the air.

The shutters sailed up to meet him.

His legs and teeth struck the rotten wood. It splintered, and Casimir plummeted headlong into the glass window beyond. The pane cracked instantly. Glass erupted into the interior of the warm room as Casimir's lupine body passed through the window, glass shards filling the air around him. The fragments pelted the walls and the terror-stricken man clinging to the mantel.

Casimir landed heavily on the plank floor, glass raining down to each side. With another bound, he reached the stairs that led to the second floor. Hounds began hurtling in through the shattered window. Casimir clambered up the stairs, again summoning the transformation in his bones: Now he needed his half-wolf form again. The feral howl of the hounds below mixed with the man's shouts of terror. Casimir was heedless. With each lunging step of his ascent, the change advanced, warping his frame and reworking his joints. The dogs were right behind him. He gained the second floor, his pads stretching into fingers.

Rising on his hind legs, he sunk his newly formed claws into the lath-and-plaster wall. He began to climb, his claws carving out palm-deep handholds in the wall. He pulled himself higher as the dogs leapt at his heels. Soon he was out of their reach, clinging near the ceiling. With a swing of his muscled forearm, Casimir raked a hole through the plaster ceiling and into the attic above. He pulled down chunks of plaster, creating a choking haze. Latching onto the rafters, he climbed through the hole and into the attic above.

Once there, he loped across the rough-hewn beams toward a small gabled window cluttered with cobwebs. Setting his claws to the window frame, he ripped the entire frame from the gable. He gazed out toward the skyline of Harmonia, seeing to his delight that he could leap to the roof of the adjacent house, a one-story building that lay twenty feet away. He pulled back from the window, then charged it and soared easily through.

With a crash, Casimir landed on the tile roof of the adjacent house. His claws clittered furiously across the clay tiles as he rose to the roof's peak. Gathering speed again, he leapt toward another house. There he landed more easily.

Turning a wicked leer back the way he came, he listened for the distant bellowing of the dogs. Instead, he heard shouting.

"Kill the meistersinger!" "Kill the wolf-man!" "Kill Casimir! Kill the wolf-man." The cries rose up from a throng gathering in the streets, waving torches and flails.

Harmonia was his no longer.

*   *   *   *   *

Thoris sat amid the florid silks and satins of the caravan. So far, the escape had gone flawlessly. The gypsy must have worked magic on the Harmonian guards, for they didn't even stop the *vardo* at the city gates.

Thoris's eyes wandered to Julianna. She was sleeping on a short bed on the caravan's opposite side. "At last she'll be safe," Thoris said to himself. He still wasn't sure whether Casimir was a werewolf or not, but removing Julianna from harm's way would give him the chance to find out.

The rocking motion of the aged carriage worked its spell on Thoris. He grew sleepy. In time, his ears dulled to the squeak of the carriage's springs, and his vision became thick in the yellow lantern light. At last he, like Julianna, surrendered to sleep.

He awoke suddenly. The carriage had stopped. He peered irritably out the caravan's window, seeing it was night and they were still in the forest. Pushing his cramped body up from the short bed, Thoris set his feet on the carriage floor and listened. Outside, above the loud violining of crickets, he could hear hushed voices speaking. One he recognized as the alluring gypsy driver. The other voice was indistinguishable—a resonant rumble, obviously that of a man. Thoris sat silent, a chill passing through him. The voices stopped speaking. The coach's springs complained as the gypsy woman climbed back onto the driver's board.

Perhaps it was just a beggar or wanderer, Thoris thought.

The door handle began to move. Thoris watched in horror as the knob made a quarter turn and the latch slipped back from the doorpost. Slowly the door opened. Cold, black air rolled into the coach, and then a man stepped aboard.

It was Casimir, a dark blue cloak drawn tight about him.

"Going to Gundarak, young Thoris?" the meistersinger asked, smiling with daggerlike teeth. "I think not."

FIFTEEN

"Please, Casimir, I beg of you," Thoris said as the caravan began rolling forward again. "There's a true priest in Gundarak—not a priest of Milil, but a *true* priest." Thoris swallowed hard and hummed a penance for his blasphemy. "If any taint of the wolf still remains in you, let us go to Gundarak so he can heal you."

Glaring, Casimir gestured for Thoris to make less noise. He nodded toward the sleeping Julianna. "We can speak more freely, just the two of us," he spat, leaning back on the stool where he sat.

"Will you come with us to Gundarak?" Thoris asked in a low voice.

"Don't be an idiot," Casimir replied, his nostrils flaring, "and don't expect me to be one, either. There's no priest in Gundarak. You're trying to spirit Julianna away from me." His jaw clenched and his eyes narrowed. "I can't believe you'd stab me in the back like this. And what about those assassins you sent?"

"Assassins?" Thoris whispered incredulously. "Those were elders from the laity. You've got this all wrong."

"Have I?" the meistersinger snapped. "You send dagger-bearing elders to kill me while you take Julianna away!"

"The daggers were for their protection in case you went wild. I don't know if you're still a monster," Thoris said, his eyes growing wide. "Casimir, you've got to under—"

"You do believe I'm a monster, don't you? Well, I

haven't killed *you* yet, even though you've been planning to kill me." Casimir rose from the stool and clutched the lantern bracket of the swaying *vardo*. He loomed menacingly over Thoris, his lamp-lit shadow covering the priest. "I ought to kill you right now."

Julianna turned over on the cramped bed. Casimir froze, peering down at her through the corners of his eyes. She yawned and opened her eyes.

"Casimir!" she gasped, sitting up. "You're going with us to Gundarak?"

The meistersinger backed away from Thoris, lowering himself to the stool again. He smiled stiffly and said, "We aren't going to Gundarak."

Thoris said flatly, "He's turned the caravan around. We're heading back to Harmonia."

"No, we're not," Casimir said curtly. "We're going to Skald to spend some time with my mentor, Harkon Lukas."

"What?" Thoris and Julianna blurted in unison.

Small beads of sweat dotted Casimir's brow. "Yes . . . we're going to Skald. You've both been worried about my health. I think Harkon Lukas holds the key to it."

Julianna bit her lip, and Thoris paled. He asked, "But tales say Harkon Lukas doesn't have a home—he just drifts. How're you going to find him?"

"We'll inquire at the Kartakan Inn, beside the river," Casimir said brusquely. He sighed, crossing his arms over his chest. "Now you two should get some rest."

"What about you?" Julianna said, yawning and rubbing her temples. "You're the one who's sick."

Casimir waved her off. "I can't sleep in this pitching contraption."

Julianna scooted back on the bed. "Well, at least come lie down beside me. The night is cold."

* * * * *

Dawn arrived before the caravan reached Skald. Julianna and Casimir had fallen asleep on the short bed, but Thoris had remained up all night, his eyes trained on the meistersinger. With dawn, Thoris's vigil eased. Leaning forward on sleep-numbed legs, he swung open the small window in the carriage's side and pushed his head through the opening, peering ahead. On the gray northern horizon lay the walls of Skald, harsh and looming. "We should have been here long before dawn. What kind of Vistana magic . . ." Thoris pulled his head back into the cart and closed the window. Casimir, awake now, stared coldly at his friend.

"We're not going back to Harmonia . . . ever," he said flatly.

"Why the sudden move?" Thoris asked, his nerves raw from sleeplessness. "Did your secret get out?"

Casimir's eyes narrowed, fuming, and he glanced down at Julianna to make sure she was asleep.

"Did they exile you, wolf-boy?" Thoris snapped.

Casimir leveled a finger at his former friend and whispered, "If you betray me to her, Thoris, I swear I'll kill you."

His mouth clamping shut, Thoris turned away and peered out the window. The *vardo* was entering Skald. A deep rumble began outside the caravan, distinguishable despite the shuddering toil of the wheels. The sound was quiet but powerful, like distant thunder. Holding his breath, Thoris listened more closely. The rumble only grew louder as they rattled forward. The wagon rolled deeper into Skald, passing rows of tidy houses decked with blue or green shutters. With each laborious turn of the wheel, the rumble grew.

"What's that sound?" Julianna murmured, turning over on the bed. Swinging her legs down to the caravan's floor, she leaned her graceful body forward and peered out the *vardo*'s window. "Perhaps a storm is coming."

Casimir sniffed the air that poured through the window. "It's not a storm," he noted, setting his hand on her back.

The rumble by now had grown quite loud, and the

golden sunlight that had once shone warmly in the curtains faded to a silvery glow. Thoris knelt beside the round window and peered out. They had entered a thick fog. The city outside was steeped in it. Whitewashed houses towered beside the road, casting vast shadows in the whirling mist. Their roofs were invisible in the fog, making the stark walls appear infinitely tall. The caravan passed the last such structure, which rolled silently away into the mist. Then Thoris could see nothing. Still the roar grew louder.

The sound of wooden wheels on wooden planks told Thoris the *vardo* was crossing a bridge. Peering down, he could see the bridge, but not the water below. The fog grew denser, shutting out what little sunlight prickled through the mist. A small lurch signaled the end of the bridge, and through the fog, Thoris glimpsed coarse, twisted grass on the roadside. The blades were yellow-white and spongy like heather.

The *vardo* came to a halt. A faint line of dark rectangles hovered in the mist beside the caravan. Thoris could only guess they were windows.

"The inn," he mused, but the words were lost beneath the churning roar outside. He glanced back, seeing that Julianna and Casimir were moving toward the *vardo*'s door. Rising, Thoris followed. He stepped from the wagon into the swirling mist. Here the roar was deafening, coming from only a stone's throw away. Squinting, Thoris saw, vaguely silhouetted through the fog, a massive wall of rock and a rushing cascade of water. A wide, rocky pool lay at the base of the waterfall, and from the pool poured a broad river. "Quite a waterfall!" Thoris shouted, turning toward Casimir. He stood beside the coach, staring quizzically up at the empty driver's seat. The gypsy was gone, as though she had leapt straight up into the mist and disappeared.

Casimir turned toward Thoris, setting his attenuate hand on the vestments of Milil. "Let's get inside!"

Thoris gazed up at the sprawling, mist-shrouded edifice before him . . . the Kartakan Inn. It looked immense.

He nodded once at Casimir, and they headed toward the dark-stained doors. Aged hinges complained as the doors swung open and Casimir and Thoris stepped inside. They entered a dimly lit foyer, mist swirling about their heels. As the doors swung closed behind them, the mist slumped dispiritedly to the floor.

Julianna shivered at the foyer's other end, standing beside another set of doors. Her lovely face was creased and weary. Casimir moved toward her, opening his dewlapped robe and wrapping her in it. Speaking a word of comfort, he pushed through the doors into the long hall beyond. On the left opened a large dining area, dark now and silent; through a curtained doorway to the right came the pleasant chatter of conversation and smell of food.

"First we need a room," Casimir said, pacing forward.

At the other end of the lantern-lit hall, a clerk sat quietly behind a desk. Casimir led the way toward him, the metal toes of his boots clattering on the stone floor.

The clerk was a young and colorless thing. He raised his squinting eyes toward Casimir—eyes visibly thickened by long hours of labor with books. Drawing a wan hand distractedly across his cheek, the man said, "No rooms till noon."

Casimir studied the clerk, irritation dripping from his forced grin. "Perhaps, then, we'll just sit here on your desk till you're ready to check us in."

"No sitting on the desk," the young man replied flatly, as though more than one guest had suggested such to him. "You can sit in the taproom, as long as you buy breakfast."

"What about sitting in the dining hall?" Casimir asked.

"I'm sorry, sir," the clerk said, turning back to his books. "Dining hall's only for dinner and supper."

Casimir clenched his fist. "Perhaps I'll—"

"Perhaps we'll have breakfast," Thoris said, pulling Casimir back.

The man nodded in dismissal as Thoris and Julianna drew the red-faced Casimir down the hall. Casimir's gaze remained on the attendant until they reached the doorway to the taproom. Thoris pulled back the curtain and forced Casimir inside.

The taproom was small and crowded, with thick-paneled walls and misty windows. The patrons, clustered about a number of round tables, looked up from their steaming eggs and stared at the newcomers. Casimir was in no mood to be stared at. Scowling, he descended the short flight of stairs that led to the taproom floor. To his left lay three curtained alcoves. The closest one stood empty. Casimir plodded heavily toward it, towing Julianna behind. Thoris, meanwhile, scanned the rough-looking clientele. Folding the symbol of Milil under his vestments, he scuttled after his companions.

As they seated themselves around the alcove table, the tavernkeep, a rotund man with a rash about his lips, appeared, a scrap of parchment in hand. He leaned his corpulent body over the dark, wooden tabletop and wiped it once with a soiled rag.

"What'll it be, then?"

"Steak and eggs—poached," Casimir said without hesitation.

"The same," Thoris said wearily, his eyes fastened on an ulcerous mole on the man's forehead.

"Only tea for me," Julianna said quietly.

Casimir glanced with concern toward her. "Only tea? Are you well, Julianna? Aren't you hungry?"

She shrugged weakly and said, "No, not really."

The tavernkeep nodded and backed out of the alcove, pulling the drapes closed. Thoris seemed about to speak, but Casimir shot a squelching glare his way. Thoris closed his mouth, his eyes settling on an unremarkable knot in the tabletop. With the curtain drawn, the nook was ominously dark, lighted only by a stout candle in the center of the table. Thoris's eyes strayed momentarily from the knot to his companions. They looked like inquirers at a scrying table, their heads cast down and silent, their eyes fixed on the hypnotic flame.

There was nothing to say.

"Ho, there, Master Lukas!" came a shout outside the alcove.

Casimir slowly drew the curtain back. In the tavern's center stood the legendary bard, Harkon Lukas, framed black against the misty windows. He wore a dark cloak of silk that draped to the folds of his leathery boots. The bard pulled gloves from his hands, swept the hat from his head, and bowed grandly.

"Sing us a song, Harkon!" cried out a barmaid, leaning over the bar. She was as voluptuous as the tavern-keep was corpulent. Lukas strode over to her, clutched her hand across the bar, bowed low, and kissed her work-stiffened fingers.

"My dear, the air is full of songs. Reach up and pull one down." He swung his long-fingered hand gracefully above the woman's head and produced a crimson rose. A glib smirk crossed his lips as he handed the rose to the woman. She took the flower and held it beneath her nostrils, then inhaled deeply, making sure her hand didn't block the swell of her breast. Lukas, meanwhile, spun to face the gathered folk.

"What should I sing?" he asked with a sycophantic grin.

Numerous cries rang out. Lukas raised his eyebrows attentively and cupped a hand behind his ear. The petitioners shouted louder. Lukas held up a hand to halt the noise, his eyes turning inquisitively toward the first alcove. He stepped from the bar and began moving toward the alcove. Reaching it, he flung the curtains wide and said, "What have we here! The meistersinger of Harmonia!"

The crowd behind Lukas turned for a second look at Casimir.

"Even the priest of Milil has come . . . and the fair Julianna." Lukas scooped Julianna's hand from the table and kissed it lightly. "The sight of you, Casimir, brings a special song to mind."

The other patrons scooted their chairs around in anticipation of the song. Casimir's eyes settled coldly on

Lukas. The scraping of chairs died down, and the song began.

"Beneath the bright sun, the exile wanders.
His heart is turned in; his spirit ponders
What sins he has done to deserve his fate.
Alone he must wait for his death day to come.

"When he was a child, his parents forsook him.
They set him adrift, consigned to the dark whim
Of Fortune. He grew, and soon was a man.
'Twas then that his thoughts ran to vengeance and doom.

"He challenged his father and cut off his head.
He challenged the priesthood and left the priest dead.
He challenged the people, but they drove him out
Into exile. Now doubt plagues his mind and his soul.

"How diff'rent are we than he wand'ring there,
Forsaken by nature, forbidden the care
Of other poor mortals in trial after trial?
We are the exiles:
Amusements to angels and vermin to god."

As the song died away, sober applause rose in the room. The bard bowed low, then turned with finality toward Casimir's table.

"Quite the impassioned delivery," Casimir commented icily.

"Kind of you to notice, meistersinger," Lukas said with a sneer. He drew a chair out from the table and lowered himself gracefully into it. In the same motion, he extended his long arm, resting his hand on the back of Julianna's seat.

"What has brought you to my fair city, Casimir? Business . . . pleasure . . . political asylum?" Lukas broke into a brutal laugh, which Thoris and Julianna nervously joined.

At that moment, the tavernkeep arrived with the food.

Casimir sat in smoldering silence as the enormous man set plates in front of each of them. Pulling out his scrap of parchment, he peered questioningly at Lukas. The bard waved him off. The tavernkeep nodded and backed out of the alcove.

Lukas turned toward Julianna, studying her weary face. "My dear, you look positively spent."

Julianna glanced toward the bard and managed a smile. "We've ridden all night and can't get a room till noon."

"Noon!" Lukas said, "why, that's three hours from now! Do you plan to sit here and fiddle with those eggs until noon?"

"Have you an alternative?" Casimir asked, irritated.

The tall bard leaned luxuriantly back in his seat. "I'll make you an offer," he said with an infuriating grin. "I'll speak to the owner, a personal friend, and get two rooms immediately if I can guide one of you around my happy little city."

Lukas looked from face to face. Julianna could barely keep her eyes open, and Thoris looked rough about the edges. Only Casimir's eyes were keen, but he was as silent as his companions.

"No one agrees?" Lukas asked, frowning. "A pity, that. I hope you find these chairs comfortable." Lukas rose, brushing his hands together.

"Wait," Julianna said sleepily. "I'll go with you."

Lukas nodded graciously. "I'd be most honored, dear Ju—"

"No . . . I'll go with you," Casimir said, sinking a fork into his plate of eggs. "Arrange adjoining rooms for us while I finish breakfast."

"Agreed," Lukas replied. Nodding once to Julianna, he said, "I will return shortly."

*   *   *   *   *

The sun approached noon as Lukas and Casimir toiled up the eastern cliffs that overlooked Skald. The dark bard climbed steadily up the slope, his eyes scanning the craggy stone. Panting, Casimir followed behind, his temples growing dappled with sweat. He stopped, positioning his feet on a narrow ledge and peering up toward his guide. With relative ease, Lukas attained a rocky prominence that jutted some ten feet from the cliff's top. There he halted, turning back toward his young protégé.

"I know why you've come to Skald, Casimir."

After a few more strides, Casimir also reached the prominence. He stepped onto the ledge, refusing the hand held out to help him. "I'm sure you'll tell me."

Lukas looked out over the cliff and sighed. The city of Skald lay like a giant gem in the broad, forested valley below. Drawing a deep breath, Lukas said, "Rumor has it that Casimir of Harmonia is a werewolf—and an exile."

"Rumors are rumors," Casimir muttered darkly.

Stepping over to Casimir, the bard clapped him on the shoulder. "But don't worry; the bounty hunters won't find you here. I'll make sure of it."

"Small consolation."

"It's just as well," Lukas replied with a caustic laugh. "I told you a year ago your talents would be wasted as meistersinger. There are greater things in store for you now."

Pulling back from the cliff's edge, Casimir sat down on a boulder. "Yes . . . like vagrancy."

"No, like power," Lukas said, his eyes gleaming intently. "After all, *I'm* not meistersinger of Skald, but I rule this city."

A wry smile formed on Casimir's face. "The streets are your home, right?"

"Before you scoff," Lukas said, stepping toward the edge of the precipice, "let me show you the grandeur of my rule." He pointed toward the misty falls. "Do you see the water mill there below the falls? I receive all its profits. The owner is a puppet of mine. Now look farther down the river to where the toll bridges stand. I receive a share of that money as well. And at the bend in the river, you can see my sawmill. . . ."

"Another source of funds?"

"Yes," Lukas said, his eyes still on the city, "and also a place to stash . . . remainders. The wood chips and sawdust cover a multitude of sins," Lukas replied. He paused, drawing a deep breath. "Just below the sawmill lie the lower wharves. That's where I do some of my best hunting. I like to befriend visitors who've boated up the river, then take them to the inn for a nice meal," he said, clicking his teeth together.

Casimir studied the bard's face, noting the deep lines that ran across his forehead. "And the inn is yours, too?"

Lukas nodded and said, "It's filled with secret passages and trapdoors, and it houses many of my . . . associates."

Looking again toward the city, Casimir's eyes traced a field of toppled ruins that adjoined the southern wall. "What's that section of hexagonal ruins to our left?"

Lukas sighed, one side of his mouth hitching. "Dargacht Keep was its name. It was built many centuries ago to guard the fording point of the river. The city grew around it. It burned and toppled shortly after I arrived in Skald. I was only mildly responsible for the disaster."

For the first time in a full day, Casimir laughed. "What nonsense! That place has been in ruins for at least a century. You couldn't have been around when it burned."

Lukas gazed solemnly at the young meistersinger. "Yes, I could have."

Feeling suddenly uncomfortable, Casimir ran his fingers through his hair. "Look, I don't need to see any more of Skald. I believe you've got power—"

"And you can have it, too, Casimir. Your year in Harmonia was only a prelude to your true power," Lukas said.

"Yeah, yeah," Casimir said, shaking his head. "Doesn't it occur to you, Lukas, that we're monsters? I've denied that all my life, but now that my secret's out, I can't deny it anymore. I'm a murderer. I'm a monster.

I'm better off in exile, out of power. I'm better off weak or dead."

"You're a fool, Casimir," Lukas said, brushing a dusty spot from his cloak. "Why do you say we're monsters?"

An incredulous look crossed Casimir's face. "Maybe because we change into wolves and kill people."

Lukas paced across the precipice and started down the slope. "Yes, but we do so according to our nature and instinct. If our nature is evil, if our instincts are murderous, can we be blamed?"

"Semantics," Casimir said, following in the bard's dusty wake. "We're still more evil than any human could possibly be."

"No," Lukas replied. "We're evil by nature; humans are evil by *choice*. We act out of hunger, whereas humans act out of cruelty. Therefore they bring a peculiar genius to their evil deeds. Instead of killing a woman outright, a man will marry her and then beat her night after night until, years later, she is dead. Instead of killing a poor man outright, a ruler will slowly starve him until he's a living skeleton. Instead of killing a child outright, playmates will heap years of ridicule on him until he kills himself."

"I don't care what you say; you and I are more evil than anyone in this town," Casimir said bitterly.

"Follow me," Lukas replied, gesturing toward the city.

*   *   *   *   *

"Here lives a man more wicked than either of us," Harkon Lukas said, indicating the tidy house before them.

Casimir gazed dubiously at the cottage. Its windowsills, doorposts, shutters, and eaves had all been meticulously painted green. The half-timber walls were whitewashed, and not a shake was missing from the roof. "This isn't the house of a monster."

Lukas seized Casimir's chin. "This isn't the face of a monster either." Drawing his hand back, Lukas turned and strode to the sharp-edged cellar doors. "Come, Casimir—he's not home." Fiddling with the lock for a moment, Lukas pulled the doors open and descended into the darkness. Shaking his head, Casimir watched as the shadows closed over the bard. Glancing down the street to see if anyone was watching, Casimir followed, closing the doors behind him.

The cellar was dark and dank, with rubble-work walls and a floor of packed earth. Along the walls ran thick wooden shelves, which held hundreds of translucent jars. The contents of these containers were veiled by a film of dust. Similar containers also rested on the mismatched tables that filled the room. The tabletops were devoid of the dust that covered the rest of the cellar, but they were still not clean. A thick resin blanketed their cracked tops. Casimir sniffed it: unmistakably blood.

"What does this . . . friend of yours do down here?" Casimir asked irritably as he studied the cobweb-laced rafters.

"Oh, surely you can guess," Lukas said, gesturing broadly toward the tables. "Or perhaps we should wait here until he comes to explain."

"Obviously these tables have been used for butchering and dressing," Casimir noted as he spotted the pulleys and broad hooks embedded in the rafters. His attention shifted to the drain clinking beneath his foot. "But what's so heinous about butchering in a cellar rather than out in the open air?"

"You choose the right word when you speak of 'butchering,' " Lukas replied wryly. "But I think you haven't allowed yourself to draw the obvious conclusions. Perhaps this will help you." The bard pulled a polished case of brown leather from one of the shelves. The soft leather opened beneath Lukas's hand, spilling a pile of metal implements onto the table. Casimir moved forward, studying the oddly curved knives, sundry hooks and pins, toothed clamps, and blood-stiffened sponges.

"What's your point?" Casimir asked with a sigh.

"You still don't see?" Lukas replied, his eyes incisive.

"This man is among a new class of men. He believes in healing through knife and needle rather than salve and rest. The jars around us hold the fruits of his research."

Casimir peered about the dingy place. "Why is that evil? If he cuts open animals or people to heal them—"

"Not to heal . . . not anymore," Lukas replied offhandedly, gathering the glinting bits of metal back into the case. "He began his dissections on dead rabbits and raccoons, probing their small bodies for answers to human ailments. But health is a saucy mistress: She doesn't hide her mysteries in the bodies of the dead. My friend found no answers. Although he hungered for the knowledge to save lives, that knowledge eluded him.

"So I showed him a trick I'd learned as a boy. I showed him how to scramble a rabbit's brain with thin wire so that its body might be cut open while still alive. My friend learned much from the first rabbit he sliced open thus. He learned of the ceaseless pounding of the heart; learned of the pumping action of the viscera; learned of the presence of pain behind the creature's glassy eyes. He learned volumes in the eight hours he kept that creature alive.

"But most important, he learned he enjoyed it. He enjoyed the power, the domination. He could slice a creature open and run his fingers through its living body, and it had no power to stop him. That day, he ceased his healing practice and began his hurting practice. He's become quite skilled, learning to scramble the brains of higher creatures and keeping them alive for days or weeks on end. In fact, I believe that behind that door lies his latest—"

The words caught short in the bard's throat as a clanking sound came at the latch. Casimir shot a fearful glance toward Lukas, who remained in place and gestured for him to keep silent. The afternoon sun stabbed suddenly into the cellar as the doors rattled open. Down the mildewed steps came legs garbed in dun-colored linen trousers. All about the descending form swirled clouds of dust, illumined by the sunlight.

The man was middle-aged and muscular, with leathery skin. He squinted into the dark cellar, his expressionless eyes passing over the bard and his young apprentice. The man's mouth hinted at a smile as he began to speak. "I'm pleased to have guests here, though I can't yet make out who you are."

"Von Daaknau, it is I, Harkon Lukas. I've a friend along with—"

"This must be Casimir, whom you told me about," the man interrupted, descending the last step and shuffling slowly into the room. He extended his brawny hands to avoid running into any obstacles. In moments, he had reached Casimir. He settled his sun-cracked fingers warmly over the young meistersinger's hands.

"With that very hand," Lukas said, "Eiren has performed many, many surgeries . . . have you not, Von Daaknau?"

"With this very hand, some special powder, and a wire," the man said humorlessly, still clasping Casimir's hand. "Make no mistake, I'm not usually so candid with strangers, but Master Lukas has told me much about you." Ever since Von Daaknau's small, misaligned eyes had found Casimir in the dark cellar, they clung mercilessly to him. Casimir shivered and pulled his hand back.

"Would you like to come upstairs for some tea?"

"No, thank you, old friend," Lukas said cordially. "We've much yet to do."

Casimir rubbed his fingers, icy from the man's touch. "Do you really use those tools to—"

"Yes," Von Daaknau said placidly.

"I've heard about the wire, but what's the powder for?"

"Most of my . . . guests are unwilling," Von Daaknau said lightly. "The powder puts them to sleep."

"Why do you do it?" Casimir blurted, regaining his courage.

Von Daaknau shrugged and looked away from Casimir for the first time. An expression of musing—the

clearest manifestation of emotion he'd shown so far—
crossed his face. "I'm sure you know the aroma of fear,
Casimir. Pain is the wine, and fear is the wine's bouquet.
I enjoy those both, but I suppose, even more than fear
and pain, I enjoy the sound."

"The sound?" Casimir echoed, shifting his feet awkwardly on the crusted grating where he stood.

"Oh, there are lots of sounds," Eiren replied, running
his tongue lightly over his teeth. The man's voice was
maddeningly calm. "I bet you didn't know that bones
make different sounds. . . ."

"Enough," Casimir said, his stomach twisting into a
knot. "Lukas put you up to this, didn't he?"

Von Daaknau's pillowy face stretched into a gleaming
smile as he pulled a joiner's hammer from the wall. "Let
me introduce you to Anna," Eiren said simply.

Casimir turned away and plodded heavily up the
mildewed stairs. "I'm leaving," he announced. As he
rose from the dank cellar, he could hear Lukas apologiz-
ing. "Take no offense. He has a great deal to learn. And
don't worry . . . your secret's as safe as ever."

"Surely you'll come to watch?" Eiren replied, nodding
toward a doorway at the back of the cellar. He bounced
the hammerhead in his hand.

"Perhaps another time," Lukas said as Casimir passed
through the heavy doors.

SIXTEEN

Casimir emerged from the green cellar doors of Von Daaknau's cottage and stepped into the bustling street. He peered left and then right, scanning the cheery shops and houses that lined the cobbled road. "Which way to the inn?" he wondered aloud. He couldn't remember passing any of the bright-painted signs and cluttered windows of the shops; he remembered only Von Daaknau and his cellar of atrocities. "I just want to get out of here," he murmured. Turning left, he quickly merged with the flow of people on the street.

In moments, Lukas caught up to the fast-striding Casimir, matching his pace with long and regal steps. "Do you still think no human could exceed us in evil?"

"Von Daaknau's a freak," Casimir spat without looking up.

"A freak, yes," Lukas said, "but he embodies the evil latent in every man."

Casimir wheeled, halting in the street. He stabbed his finger against Lukas's chest and hissed quietly, "Don't be an idiot. What sane person would lure me down into a cellar, poison me, and cut me open like a hog? Name one."

"Thoris," Lukas said, his steely eyes unwavering. "Not only is he sane, but he's also a priest and your best friend. But given a chance, he'd kill you without blinking."

Casimir glowered in silence. His head was swimming with foul images, and he wanted only to return to the inn and get some sleep. "You're wrong."

Studying Casimir's face, Lukas said, "I showed you Von Daaknau because his evil is undeniable. But all humans are predators, Casimir. All of them seek to dominate and kill, and they do so with every weapon at their disposal: words, coins, laws, swords—even teeth and nails sometimes. They prey on each other every moment of every day."

Casimir raised a listless hand in front of his face, brushing away the idea as though it were an annoying fly. "Let's just go back to the inn."

Gesturing for Casimir to remain still, Lukas said, "Casimir, there's so much you must learn tonight, but where can I begin?"

"What are you talking about?" Casimir moaned, exhausted.

"Look," Lukas said, turning his young protégé toward the afternoon sun. "You see where the sun stands in the heavens?"

"Of course."

"It's still high in the sky," Lukas noted, then added offhandedly, "but I need for the day to be done."

Suddenly the golden beams of sunlight disappeared. The cobbled road was abruptly dark and empty. The people were gone. Cold shadows filled the street, and shutters closed off every shop and house. Overhead, a lacy cloud curled around the full moon.

"What happened?" Casimir gasped. "Where's the sun?"

Lukas waved off the question and said, "Our business lies in the forest."

As Casimir watched, the half-timber houses melted away, reshaping into broad-trunked trees and scrubby undergrowth. Spongy humus took the place of the cobblestones, and the starry sky above was supplanted by a breeze-tossed canopy of leaves and needles. The moon cast spectral shafts of light down through the treetops.

Reeling, Casimir clutched a nearby trunk to keep from falling. "What have you done, Lukas?" he gasped.

Harkon gazed intently toward Casimir, his profound

eyes glinting with dark excitement. "You've not even begun to glimpse the significance of this evening, have you, Casimir?"

"What have you done with the houses, with the day?" Casimir cried, his eyes wide with fear.

"I've marshaled my every power for this night, Casimir," Lukas said, his resonant voice pitched with pleasant anxiety. "I only hope my powers will prove strong enough."

"Strong enough for what?" Casimir shouted frantically, seizing Lukas's brocaded jacket in white-knuckled hands.

"Tonight is the night of your salvation," Lukas said in a hushed voice. "Salvation from your curse."

Casimir looked incredulous at the tall man, his eyes scanning the other's for some sign of insincerity. "How can you save me? Not even Milil could save me."

"And have you ever seen Milil end the day as I just did? Or lift you from a city and set you in a forest?" Lukas asked, prying Casimir's fists from his clothes. "Follow me now, and I will save you." With a sidelong glance, Lukas strode off into the forest. Stunned and wordless, Casimir fell in line behind the bard.

The rich scent of pine engulfed them as they passed through the woods. Beneath their feet, dry needles crackled with each step, and overhead, the wind moaned quietly through the swaying canopy. They marched in silence for some time, questions struggling to form in Casimir's mind. Before he could utter any of them, however, Lukas spoke.

"For twenty years, you've been neither a man nor a wolf."

"Yes," Casimir murmured distractedly.

Lukas continued. "All that time, you've tried to purge the wolf, not the man—and you have failed. That's because your true heart is the heart of a wolf."

"No . . . no, it isn't," Casimir said, his voice far away. "The wolf is like a disease in me."

"No—the *human* is the disease," Lukas said, shaking

his head grimly. "All these years, you've been mistaken. You're not a werewolf—a man cursed to change into a wolf; you're a wolfwere—a wolf cursed to change into a man."

"What?" Casimir gasped, his face pallid beneath the moon.

"The human side of you is only a mask," Lukas replied flatly. "Your true form is that of a wolf. You were born as a shapeshifting wolf who could assume a human form for the purpose of deception. Your human side is nothing more than that—a deception."

Casimir shook his head, the words whirling nonsensically in his mind. "It's all mere wordplay."

Lukas halted his heavy strides, letting the younger man curve around in front of him. "No, Casimir. It's not wordplay. Like men, werewolves have souls, but like wolves, wolfweres do not. You, Casimir, do not have a soul."

"How do you know?" Casimir cried, his eyes ringed with confusion.

"I know, Casimir, because I, too, am a wolfwere."

A shiver ran down the young meistersinger's back. "Maybe *you're* a wolfwere, Lukas, but I can't be. My father, Zhone Clieous, was a *werewolf.*"

Lukas shook his head and said calmly, "Yes, Clieous was a werewolf. But he was not your father."

"What?" Casimir said, shaking. "Of course he was my father! He was married to my mother. He killed her when he found out about me."

"Listen to me," Lukas said, pinning Casimir with his gaze. "Clieous knew you were a werebeast from birth. He was glad to have a son that shared his power. He didn't kill your mother because he discovered your curse. He killed her because he discovered that you were someone else's son."

Casimir's legs were growing weak again. "What? Whose son?"

"Mine," the bard said, his baritone voice rumbling quietly.

"That's impossible," Casimir whispered, remembering with dread that Lukas had been a friend of his mother's.

"No. It's true," Lukas assured him. "When Clieous became meistersinger of Harmonia, I decided to spread my influence by seducing his wife. She came to be with child—you, Casimir, my son. Clieous, of course, thought the child was his, but *I* named you, and *I* reared you. Clieous hired me to be your chaperon and tutor. I trained you to rely on the wolf within you, hoping someday you would kill Clieous and take his place.

"But Clieous discovered certain love letters to his wife, all of them signed 'Heart of Midnight.' The letters spoke of their son, Casimir. Enraged, Clieous tried to kill you, then only five years old, with silver daggers, but the silver didn't wound you because you are a wolfwere, not a werewolf. Desperate, Clieous ordered his guards to slay you and your mother by fire."

The whole time that Lukas spoke, Casimir studied his features mutely. Slowly, fearfully, he saw the resemblance between them: their height, their thinness, their raven hair, their dark complexions. . . .

"My gods, you *are* my father," he gasped.

"Yes," Lukas responded quietly.

"If this is all true," Casimir said, his eyes reddening, "why did you forsake me? Why did you leave me to wander, pitiful and afraid . . . leave me to become an orphan?"

"I didn't forsake you, my son," Lukas replied, his voice growing thick. "I searched for you for three years before I gave you up for dead. Nine years later, I encountered you at the meistersinger masquerade. I knew immediately that it was you."

"Why didn't you say something?"

"I wanted to test your mettle. I wanted to see what the decade had done to you, to see if any of my training remained. And it has," Lukas replied, smiling brutally. "So I sponsored your bid for the seat of meistersinger; I claimed you as student; I dispatched men to burn the poorhouse and awaken your wrath against Clieous; I killed Gaston for you; I revealed to you the attempted escape of Julianna and your priest; I whispered suspicions into Thoris's ears to show his treachery; I arranged for the woman to meet you beside the Longhorn Inn; I set up your downfall in Harmonia so that you might join me here; I even drove the carriage that brought you to Skald—to your salvation!"

"You—you're the one that destroyed me?"

"No, I saved you. The office of meistersinger was slowly killing you, and so were your friends," Lukas said with hushed excitement. "How many times did you try to kill yourself, Casimir? How many times did you scourge yourself for crimes you were destined by the gods to commit? I haven't destroyed you, Casimir. I've saved you."

With that, the tall bard turned and resumed his steps. "We've almost reached the ritual clearing, my son."

Confusion written across his face, Casmir stood stock still, staring after the retreating bard. The revelations had torn his mind apart. He couldn't think; he could hardly stand. But everything that Lukas had said rang true. Suddenly all the dark mysteries of his life were laid open. Clutching his robe over his chest, he yammered at the retreating bard, "What is this . . . this salvation for me?"

Lukas whirled about. "Come, Casimir. Embrace your evil nature. You can't escape it. You *are* the wolf within!"

"No," Casimir said hollowly. "I hate the wolf in me. I can still cling to my humanity."

"Your humanity is a sham, a stage face! Cling to it and watch as you decay and die. That's what you've done for the last year. You know you can't escape that way."

Casimir's heart pounded painfully in his chest. His hands were shaking. "How can I live believing I have no soul?"

"You can become a god," Lukas said simply. Turning, he strode deeper into the wood.

Biting his lip, Casimir watched him go. He wanted to

run away into the woods. He wanted to bundle up Julianna and escape from Skald and Thoris and Lukas. "But they're not the enemy," he muttered heavily to himself. "The enemy is me." Suddenly he could no longer hear the drumming of his heart. He set his jaw and took the first step after Harkon Lukas. Then, he took a second step and a third. Gritting his teeth, he rushed down the path on the heels of the dark bard.

On the heels of his father.

Reaching Lukas, Casimir fell in step beside him. Nodding to acknowledge his presence, Lukas walked with his hands clasped pensively behind his back and his hot breath rising wraithlike in the chill night air. They pushed forward in silence, passing larger and larger trees.

"We are children of darkness, my son."

Casimir risked a glance toward his father, then nodded his silent assent.

Lukas continued, "We are brothers to angels. They are born of pure good and we of pure evil, but both siblings act according to the plan of the gods."

"Is that how you perform your sorceries, Lukas . . . Father? Is that how you make the woods sing, or turn day to night?"

"Those sorceries will be yours as well," Lukas said, his quiet voice edged with encouragement. "But you must fully embrace your evil nature and fully purge yourself of humanity."

Casimir nodded, though he understood little. "What's going to happen when we reach the ritual clearing?"

"Many things, Casimir," Lukas replied. "Your heart will be purified for evil. Your hunger will be stoked, your humanity stripped away. And you yourself will become a god."

"But an evil god," Casimir noted in a hushed voice.

"Evil and good don't mean the same to gods as to men. Even good gods kill their people. Gods have the right to take away the life they've granted."

Casimir gazed up at the blue-black sky, just visible

through the maze of treetops. "I don't wish for godhood, Father."

"Do you wish to be free of your curse?"

"Yes."

"That is the first step."

* * * * * *

Lukas stepped through a narrow gap between trees and into a hilltop glade. Casimir followed, his breath catching short as he scanned the place. Moonlight blanketed the short, tufted grass of the glade, illumining also the columnar trees at the edge of the clearing. Above, the heavens were crowded with stars. A chill breeze greeted Casimir as he stepped up beside his father.

"This is a sort of temple, isn't it?" Casimir noted in a hushed voice. "A temple for the children of night?"

"I'm pleased you can sense it, Casimir," Lukas said genuinely. He moved reverently into the clearing. Reaching its center, he halted, his head bowing for a moment and his eyes closing to slivers. He breathed deeply thrice, filling his lungs with the thick scent of pine. "Casimir, since your birth, I've been training you for this moment. I've been readying you, shaping you. At last you're here. Come forward."

Casimir gazed blankly toward the center of the clearing. His head, which moments before had been filled with clamoring voices, was now quiet. Running both hands through his midnight hair, the young meistersinger stared at the star-cluttered sky and smiled. The stars had witnessed his birth, his rise to power, his fall, and now even his entry into darkness. They'll see my death, too, he thought, and still stare down implacid, unchanged.

Dropping his gaze, he stepped forward.

Lukas's rows of perfect teeth flashed pearly beneath the moon. As Casimir approached, he returned his father's smile.

Then he saw the eyes.

They were everywhere beyond the trees, reflecting the silvery light of the moon. The furtive eyes of a deer peered out from among ferny branches. Nearby hovered the hungry eyes of a wolf and the savage ones of a boar. Still other beasts stood close on hand: owls and bears, snakes and squirrels, falcons and badgers and rats. All had approached the glade in utter silence; all stood gazing toward the center, predator and prey alike standing shoulder to shoulder. Casimir sniffed the air, drawing in their mingling scents. These were no illusions.

"Behold, Casimir . . . the company of beasts!" Lukas said reverently. "They are soulless, just as we are. I've called them here to witness your passage into the wilds . . . and into evil."

Casimir stood now at the center of the clearing. His eyes shifted from the animals around him to the dark silhouette of his father. "Now you must shed your humanness. Change into your half-wolf form," Lukas commanded.

Stripping off his garments, Casimir triggered the transformation in his bones. His body willingly welcomed the change, as though it hoped never to don the human form again. Casimir's limbs began their heinous warping, the tendons and muscles and viscera twisting and realigning. The pain swept across his body in bone-crunching surges.

"Casimir, your passage tonight requires a costly toll, as does any passage of significance. But this toll is too great to be paid in silver or gold. The toll tonight will be paid in blood. You must kill a wolf, symbol of your dark curse, and drink its blood." Raising his hand in a grand gesture toward the black woods around him, Lukas said, "I've provided just such a sacrifice for you, Casimir."

A massive beast shifted in the shadowy underbrush. Then, with footfalls that sent a shudder through the ground, the creature paced out from the trees. It was a dire wolf, huge and graceful. It loped into the clearing, its muscled frame washed gray by the stony moonlight. The pony-sized wolf snorted as it lumbered to a spot between the dark bard and the transforming Casimir. There it settled on its massive haunches. At that moment, the last shuddering changes crossed Casimir's body. He rose on half-wolf legs and stared coldly at the sacrificial beast.

Lukas reached fondly toward the creature's grisled mane. "She is beautiful indeed. Swift, fierce, insatiable— avatar of the dark angels." For a moment more, the narrow fingers of the bard passed over the creature's muscle and fur.

"Kill her."

Casimir lunged like a striking snake. He buried his teeth into the beast's neck, and foamy blood sprayed out over his muzzle. The creature struggled to break free. With each convulsive movement, Casimir's razor teeth cut deeper into her neck. She tilted her head, and Casimir could see white terror in her eyes. He didn't relent. The dire wolf spun its legs hopelessly on the now-slick grass as Casimir drew the hot liquor from her throat. The wolf planted its forelegs on the beast-man, pushing fiercely to break free. The wound opened wider.

Abruptly the creature's movements slowed. She tumbled backward, pulling Casimir atop her. She was dying. He felt the resolve slide from her muscles.

Casimir unclenched his jaw, letting the wolf drop, limp, to the forest floor. He raised his blood-mantled face toward Lukas.

"So it begins," Lukas said, his eyes resting on the scarlet beast. "The wolf's blood has anointed you into the circle of night. The illusion of your soul has vanished."

A fiendish grin crossed Casimir's dagger-filled mouth. For the first time in his life, he felt true release. For the first moment in twenty years, he knew what and who he was. The pangs of conscience were gone. The chorus of remembered screams had been silenced forever. A wild howl of joy erupted from his lungs, a howl that sent the creatures scattering from the top of the knoll. Again he howled, and again, drawing the chill night air into his lungs and blasting it out toward the white-hot moon.

"Through the wolf's blood, you've given birth to the wolf within you. Now, to put to death the man in you, you must drink the blood of your dearest friend."

"What?" Casimir gasped through sanguine teeth.

Lukas stepped forcefully toward him. "To escape your humanity, you must destroy the sympathies of your life among humans."

Casimir staggered backward. Thoris's face flashed into his mind. Yes . . . he had said it only the day before: *Thoris must die.* Now no voice of conscience rose to oppose the thought.

Thoris must die.

The phrase echoed hauntingly through his soulless mind.

Thoris must die.

Casimir lowered his fiery lupine eyes. He studied the blood-spattered wolf before him. The body lay motionless beneath the brightly shining stars. The wolf had become part of the hill, soulless in life and in death.

Raising his eyes, Casimir rasped simply, "I go."

*   *   *   *   *

Through the dark doorway of the inn room, Thoris could hear the faint breathing of Julianna. She lay sound asleep in the adjoining suite. Along with her breaths, Thoris heard many other noises: every minute creak from the planking in the hall, every muffled laugh from some room somewhere. For the hundredth time, he rolled to his other side. The urge arose in him to check the latches on the hallway doors, but he had checked them three times already. Nor did he wish to pace: The creaking floorboards unnerved him. He could do nothing but lie there, keeping the thick covers drawn close beneath his chin.

"Tomorrow we escape," he promised himself.

A scrabbling noise arose at the window. Thoris froze. Again it came, like claws on glass. He cautiously rolled his head to peer out the rippled pane. No tree limbs showed against the moon-bright sky.

Again it came, undeniably now.

Something, or someone, was prying at the window.

It wasn't locked.

Thoris slid awkwardly out of bed, setting his feet on the creaking floorboards. More scratching. As he tiptoed across the complaining planks, he thought, What if it hears me? What if it springs through the glass? Another scrape. Thoris hurried to the sill and, with a desperate lunge, grabbed the lock mechanism. It was stuck. He struggled with it, rattling the window. The frame began to rise. He struck it closed with his free fist and yanked the lock shut.

Thoris leapt to the side of the glass, resting his back on the solid wall of wood. He panted heavily, and his palms ran with sweat. A tremor of fear moved through him.

Even the dark ones cry to thee, Milil. The words of the hymn broke into Thoris's mind unbidden, bringing with it some measure of relief. Mopping his sweat-speckled brow, Thoris listened again. No sound came but the gentle breaths of Julianna and laughter from some distant room.

"I should go back to bed," he moaned.

The scratching came again.

Thoris's body clenched tightly. He cast a sidelong glance down through the glass but could see nothing.

Scraaatch, screeeech.

Something had to be causing it. Thoris edged nearer the window, broadening his view. Still nothing came into sight. Closer still. He could see the empty ground below the window and the smooth clapboards on one side.

Scraaaaape, Scraaaaatch.

Mustering his courage, Thoris stepped in front of the window and shot a glance to the other side. There, too, he saw nothing.

Screeeeech, scraaaaape.

What's making that noise? Thoris wondered, panic rising in him. His hand had loosened the lock before he realized what he had done.

The window rose violently.

Clawed hands seized his throat before he could scream. A broad thumb choked off his breath. The arms yanked him forward, through the open window. His scrabbling hands caught a hold on the window frame, and he hung half out the window in the swirling fog. The head of a wolf hovered horribly before him.

"Casimir?" Thoris managed to rasp, though the sound was lost in the roar of the waterfall. The claws tightened, closing his throat entirely.

The wolfman's blood-red eyes didn't look like Casimir's. They showed no intellect. Only hunger filled them . . . brute hunger.

No mercy. No compassion. No shame.

Thoris's lungs ached for air. His eyes felt as if they would drop from his head. His arms trembled, their hold on the window frame slipping. Then he saw the vertical scar on the beast's forehead—a scar created when the mask of Sundered Heart was forced up on Casimir's face.

It *was* Casimir.

Thoris was dying. A tear streaked down his cheek, and his lips said soundlessly, "Good-bye, Casimir."

The beast's eyes changed; compassion momentarily flickered there. The beast's clawed fingers loosened on Thoris's throat, and its sinewy arms pushed him back through the open window. Then, over the deafening roar of the falls, came the creature's raspy voice:

"Beware, Thoris. Keep Julianna from Lukas. I'll return tomorrow night."

The claws were suddenly gone from Thoris's throat, and the beast was gone with it.

"What's happening?" came Julianna's fearful voice from the doorway.

Thoris stumbled back weakly, his breaths coming in huge gulps. "A . . . a nightmare," he gasped, slamming the window closed and locking it again. "It's the roar of those damned falls."

SEVENTEEN

Casimir's midnight visit haunted Thoris's dreams that night. He dreamt of children with fanged mouths where their eyes should have been, of women bathing in the blood of saints, of Milil as a deaf beggar. Each time Thoris sank fitfully into sleep, an imagined horror reared its head and startled him awake, more weary and desperate than before. At last he abandoned any hope of sleep and divided his attentions between the window and Julianna. He focused his mind on a simple imperative: Guard Julianna with your life.

Next morning, a bristling fog wrapped its catlike body about the Kartakan Inn—an even darker, denser fog than that of the morning before. Noting the muted daylight, Thoris arose sleepless from his sweaty mattress. Surely Julianna will be safe now that daylight has come, he told himself. And the sooner I arrange our escape, the safer she'll be.

After dressing and performing a minimal grooming, he headed down to the tavern. As he shouldered through the taproom's curtain, he saw once again the dense fog. It pressed menacingly against the glass of the tavern's windows. With reluctant steps, Thoris descended the short flight of stairs that led into the tavern. The patrons turned their darksome faces momentarily toward him. Seeing that he was neither familiar nor important, they one by one directed their eyes back toward their runny eggs and thick porridge.

Thoris pulled his clerical garb more tightly about his shoulders, then moved slowly through the gathered patrons to the long bar on the room's opposite side. Behind the counter stood the woman whom Lukas had kissed the previous morning. Her back was turned toward Thoris, and her tanned shoulders flexed as she dried and stacked glasses along the back wall. Thoris hovered at the bar for long moments, waiting for her to turn around. She did not. Finally he rapped softly on the counter.

"Excuse me, miss."

The woman shot a glance over her shoulder, a capricious half-smile forming on her lips as she studied Thoris. "What may I do for you, master priest?"

Thoris leaned toward her, dropping his tone. "Have you seen Harkon Lukas this morning?"

Turning fully about, the woman regarded Thoris dubiously. The saucy expression melted from her face. "He's not in any mood to be spoken to this morning. Particularly not by a priest."

Thoris's tone grew uncharacteristically harsh. "That's my business, not yours. Tell me where he is."

Her hand did not lift from the rumpled rag on the countertop, and her eyes narrowed. "He's there, in the third alcove."

Thoris nodded and smiled. "Thank you."

"I'll say a prayer for you, master priest," the woman finished sarcastically, her voice filled with warning as she turned back to drying the glasses.

Without further comment, Thoris swung about and waded through the crowd. As he approached the third alcove, his heart began an insistent pounding in his chest, as though to warn him away from the tightly drawn curtain. Four more footsteps across the creaking floorboards brought him to the alcove. He reached out for the curtain's edge and pulled it back slowly. The figure within raised his black mantle of hair. His monocle momentarily flashed with the light of the candle on his table. Eyes narrowed, he stared at Thoris.

"Good morning, priest," came the bard's rich voice—not inhospitable, but oddly bitter all the same. "I see that you survived the night."

Thoris smiled nervously, the comment unsettling him. "I have slept on far less comfortable beds than these."

"How is Casimir this morning?" Lukas asked flatly.

"Oh," Thoris responded, his voice betraying the lie he prepared, "he slept through the night, then awoke before dawn and went out on some errand or other." Nervously licking his lips, Thoris scanned the bard's face; clearly Lukas believed not a word. "Sir, I do not wish to impose, but—"

"Impose you shall," Lukas finished the thought. His tone softened. "Come within, good priest. Close the curtain and tell me what is so important."

Thoris ducked into the alcove, letting the thick curtains join silently behind him as he found his seat. Now the words failed him. He had spent the latter half of the night planning what he would say to Lukas this morning, rehearsing the traitorous words until he could have recited them in his sleep. But now, beneath Lukas's gracious malevolence, Thoris wondered if his treachery were merely the spawn of a sleepless night.

"Trouble at the temple?" Lukas prodded. "More sinners than saints?"

Thoris shook his head in irritation, averting his gaze from Lukas's merciless eyes. At last Thoris managed to speak. "What I have to say this morning, Master Lukas, will shock you, and you may not believe me at first. But I swear upon the voice of Milil that I speak the truth."

The sarcasm fled Lukas's voice as he spoke, "What is your news, priest?"

"It's Casimir. I know he's charmed you into friendship, much as he's charmed us all, but Casimir carries a deadly curse that threatens all our lives," Thoris began, mustering the courage to lift his eyes again toward Lukas. "Master Lukas, Casimir is a werewolf. He can't be cured; he was born with the curse. When I said that he slept through the night, I lied so that prying ears might be misled. No. He returned for mere moments last night and attacked me, nearly ripping my head from its shoulders. But he released me—the gods alone know why—and a moment later, he left. He told me to guard Julianna, to keep her safe . . . from you."

Lukas's expression was impenetrable. The darkness of the alcove deepened the lines of his forehead and shadowed his eyes in murky blackness. His eyebrows lowered slowly. Once again the candle flame played across the monocle as he spoke, "A werebeast, sharing my roof . . . ?"

"Forgive me, master, for failing to tell you before," Thoris said, his voice more pleading than he had intended. "I was myself uncertain as to his true nature until . . ."

Lukas held up a long, dexterous hand to silence Thoris. As the words fell away, the low rumble of the crowd seeped into the tiny alcove, bringing with it the ever-present roar of the falls outside. Thoris felt suddenly suffocated. He drew a long breath and turned his attention to the guttering candle at the table's center. When at last Lukas did speak, his words were mercilessly few.

"What shall we do?"

Thoris looked up, strangely surprised. Through the many hours he had rehearsed this betrayal, he assumed that Lukas would suggest a solution. Thoris hadn't the slightest notion of what to do now.

"Clearly," Lukas prompted, "he can't remain in this inn—in this town of mine."

"He won't leave of his own accord," Thoris responded, his voice edged in panic, "unless he can take Julianna. But if we let him do so, it would be like sentencing her to death."

"He loves his Julianna," the dark bard echoed, running his tongue across his lower lip as he thought.

"Yes, more than anything . . . more than even his life," Thoris replied urgently. "But I won't let her be bait for him."

"If she were stolen from him," Lukas conjectured, "he would be ruined . . . destroyed. Perhaps he would even take his own life."

"Yes, but it's not sure enough," Thoris said. "He might go mad and slay hundreds of people."

Lukas now leveled his deadly eyes toward Thoris. "If he can't remain here, won't leave without Julianna, and can't be trapped, then how will we get rid of him?"

Thoris's heart labored painfully in his chest, rebelling against the words that rose to his lips.

"I will kill him."

Lukas studied the rumpled priest. "How?"

Thoris dropped his gaze to the table. "He said he'll return tonight. I'll have a meal prepared and brought up for him in the room. When he comes, I'll close the door to Julianna's room and keep the lights off so as not to waken her. Then, distracting him with the meal and with cheerful talk, I'll circle around behind him and stab him through the heart." Thoris went very pale, and tears began to well up in his eyes. Setting his unblinking, red-rimmed eyes on the bard, Thoris continued. "But to do so, I'll need from you a blade that will strike into his heart. It can't be steel—werewolves turn steel. It must be magic or—"

"I'll secure such a blade for you before nightfall, good Thoris," Lukas interrupted. He reached out an icy hand and, setting the long-nailed fingers over Thoris's wrist, asked, "What will become of you and Julianna?"

"We'll escape. Twice before we've fled for Gundarak and twice been stopped. The first time, a magical enchantment put us asleep when we approached the border and deposited us in our beds. I studied this enchantment and learned that gypsies were immune to it. So next time, I hired a gypsy. We would have escaped, too, but Casimir found out and stopped us on the road."

"I've heard of this enchantment," Lukas said, nodding. "You can't escape by horseback, carriage, or foot, for the enchanted song will only snare you again. On the other hand, the gypsies failed you before."

"We've no other choice. Whether I kill him or not tonight, we'll flee as soon as possible."

* * * * * *

The green door of Eiren Von Daaknau's house was meticulously polished, unmarked by the soil and scars of habitual visitors. Casimir noted its perfection with a wry grin; those who visited Von Daaknau did so only once. Casimir knocked. Waiting for a response, he tugged at the collar of the yeoman's clothes he had stolen and dropped his gaze to the smooth-painted porch of green wood beneath his feet.

With a minute click of the latch, the green door slowly swung open. Casimir peered cautiously into the dark crevice before him. On the other side of that opening, Von Daaknau's intense and uneven eyes stared inquisitively out.

"Hello, Casimir. What may I do for you today?" came the smooth, self-possessed voice.

For a moment, Casimir couldn't speak. Even more so than on the previous day, Von Daaknau's perversity hung like a fetid smell about him . . . the smell of the grave. Shaking off his fear, Casimir summoned the speech he had rehearsed. "Knowing about your . . . hobby," he began with a nod toward the cellar door, "and knowing you had recently run shy of material, I thought you might be interested in a new prospect."

The door swung open farther to show an ingratiating smile. "Won't you come in and have some tea?"

"Thank you, but I am not interested in tea," Casimir responded, his grin showing his unease. "But I will come in."

Von Daaknau only nodded, bowing and backing away to allow Casimir entrance. The small sitting room within was as bright and meticulously cared for as the house's exterior. The floor was comfortably crowded with fine chairs, thin lampstands, and florid rugs—crystal and walnut, linen and silk. The air held the tart fragrance of *meekulbern* tea.

With a series of bobbing bows, Von Daaknau gestured Casimir toward the finely embroidered couch. "Please be seated. Please. Are you certain I cannot get you anything?"

Casimir sat down uncomfortably on the couch, his use-worn yeoman's clothes feeling out of place on the fine fabric. "Yes, I am certain," he said, his confidence growing. "I didn't have myself in mind for your next project."

Von Daaknau's uneven stare rested for a moment on Casimir, then dropped toward the planking as he backed away into the kitchen and larder. "I assume, then, that Master Lukas told you of my method for administering the drug?"

"Yes," Casimir lied. "But it's no matter. The subject I offer you will be far more enchanting than I."

Von Daaknau scuttled now into the room, a steaming cup of tea resting in one hand and a broad hammer in the other. He stooped at the parlor's entrance and leaned the hammer conspicuously against the wall, as though to warn off his lycanthropic visitor. Then he shuffled into the room and arrayed himself on a high-backed chair and footstool, placing his tea in a coaster on a nearby table.

"You do yourself an injustice, Casimir. Forgive me if I speak candidly, but I would find your dissection quite enchanting."

A chill proliferated across Casimir's back, and he straightened his posture before continuing. "If I understand correctly, you concentrated first on the dissection of animals, and then of . . . higher beings?"

The blank-faced man sipped his tea and, peering through the rising steam, nodded.

"Well, good sir, I am prepared to deliver into your hands the next higher step in the process," Casimir said, rallying his tone.

"What 'next higher step'?" Von Daaknau asked, blinking myopically.

"I can give you a god," Casimir said in a whisper.

"A god?" Von Daaknau asked, intrigued.

"Yes, a god," Casimir replied decisively. "I've seen him sing folk to sleep and make them awake twenty miles distant; I've seen him change day to night and city to forest; I've seen him command the creatures of the woods to perform his bidding; I've seen him change at will from his current form to that of a wolf, or that of a woman."

"You speak of Harkon Lukas, do you not?" Von Daaknau asked, leaning forward and setting his elbows on his knees. Casimir nodded, and the pillow-faced man continued. "He is a wolfwere, Casimir, not a god."

"He is a god in flesh . . . flesh that you can dissect," Casimir replied immediately. "I've never encountered a more powerful being . . . have you?"

Von Daaknau was silent for a moment, distracted by the pattern of leaves forming across the base of his cup. At length he muttered, "No, I have not."

"And whether Harkon Lukas is a god or not, he would still be the culmination of your work among beasts and men because he is, of course, both beast and man."

"True enough," Von Daaknau conceded after another sip. "But did you think I had not considered dissecting a werebeast before? Of course I have . . . but there are unlimited difficulties to the proposition—especially as concerns Harkon Lukas."

"What sort of difficulties?" Casimir prodded, leaning anxiously forward.

"The poison, for one," Von Daaknau stated. "He knows how my poison is administered, and where."

"That's why I'll deliver the poison, and do so at the Kartakan Inn."

Von Daaknau's lightless eyes narrowed. "Furthermore, there is the problem of the poison's strength. It is measured for humans, not werebeasts. I can't administer it in great enough potency to bring down a wolfwere. It would leave Harkon Lukas awake, as though drunken. It might, perhaps, block transformation, but it wouldn't wholly incapacitate him."

"Once again, that's why I'll administer the drug and then wrestle him to the ground. He'll be no match for me in such a state," Casimir replied, his voice now ringing with confidence.

Von Daaknau engaged Casimir with depthless eyes. The steam from his teacup circled hypnotically about his face, its tendrils reaching out and caressing the leathery skin. For a moment, the house was soundless but for the wary rise and fall of the madman's breath.

"Every act has its motivation, Casimir," Von Daaknau at last said, his eyes narrowing as he spoke, "and every motivation is a self-movement, a self-advancement. The meaning is inherent in the word *motivation* itself. So what strange self-advancement do you plan that you should want your mentor dead?"

"Quite simply, my motivation is revenge," Casimir said without hesitation, matching the man's brutal gaze. "Harkon Lukas brought me, irredeemable, into this world and has since plotted to wean from me any humanity I have. He's trapped me time and again, and plans now to take me down to the Nine Hells with him. But I'll not go." He paused, studying the man's inscrutable face. "Make no mistake—I'll *go* to the Nine Hells, Von Daaknau, but not with Harkon Lukas. No. I'll send him there ahead of me."

Von Daaknau had gained his feet. He stood before his chair with a saucer cradled in one hand and his teacup cradled in the other. "I appreciate an honest man, Casimir. Lies, like all petty sins, are unbecoming of great men. Murder and betrayal are more to our liking."

Casimir's gaze followed the stubby man as he retreated into the kitchen and set his clanking saucer and cup onto the counter. Von Daaknau paused beside the window, glancing out as though watching a child in play. Then he turned and moved from sight.

"I'll bring him directly to you, Von Daaknau—once he's incapacitated," Casimir said loudly.

Silence filled the room for a moment, then Casimir heard the bone-on-bone grinding of a mortar and pestle. From the kitchen came the man's satiny voice. "Leave him the ability to feel pain."

"Then we are agreed?"

"I'm grinding the poison now," Von Daaknau said matter-of-factly. "When can you deliver him?"

"Tomorrow," Casimir said with confidence. "Tonight I must go to be reconciled to my friends and warn them of Lukas's power."

Once again silence fell, except for the grating sound of the pestle and mortar. Then low, beneath the grinding noise, came a weak thudding sound followed by a sobbing moan.

The noise came from the cellar.

"Don't be disturbed," Von Daaknau said, as though reading Casimir's mind. "That's only Anna. I relented and did not finish her last night. I think she can hold on until tomorrow when you deliver Lukas."

Casimir ran his thumb in small circles on his fingertips, wishing he held the pouch of powder already. For a moment, he wondered why he would deliver his own father into the hands of the wickedest man who ever lived. Next moment, he closed off the thought and received the small bag into his anxious fingers.

* * * * *

The marketplace was a wind-blasted and mean-spirited square within the merchant district of Skald. The cloudy sky hung low over the straggling tents and makeshift stalls. Buyers and sellers moved about slowly beneath the heavy sky. Among the ragtag masses was Thoris, his priestly robes wrapped tightly about him as he shuffled through the dingy square. The young priest's eyes passed disinterestedly over the trinkets and baubles. He wasn't interested in merchandise, only in passage out of Kartakass.

"A sash for you, good sir?" asked a craggy female hawker from a tattered stall.

Thoris stopped, his thoughts jumbling to a halt in his head. He gazed down stupidly at the toothless woman as she dragged a faded scarf through her aged hand. At length, Thoris blurted awkwardly, "What use would I have for a scarf, good lady?"

"Oh, plenty of uses," she cackled. "Plenty of uses if you've got something to hide, like missing teeth—" she drew the limp fabric quickly over her mouth—"or crooked hands—" she wrapped the scarf about her gnarled fingers—"or moles, or warts, or blemishes . . . " As each category of defect was tolled, she found another site to cover. "I suppose even a young man like you has something he'd like to hide."

Thoris's eyes were unblinking. "No, thank you. You haven't any scarves for souls."

Turning, he moved away, out into the current of the marketplace. After shuffling through a few more aisles and stepping across the market's rank gutter, he spotted the cherry-red side of a gypsy caravan. A band of vistana sat before the clustered *vardos*, playing on their violins and tambourines and dancing in exuberant circles. The sound of the music rose warm on the chill air, and Thoris gazed in wonder at the spinning forms.

How strange, he thought to himself, to dance on a day like this. It's as if they don't even notice the weather. Pressing through the crowd, Thoris made his way toward the Vistana caravan. His resolute steps brought him quickly to the gypsies' circle of admirers.

A brown-eyed girl-child moved among the crowd, cupping her hands before her and gazing with longing into the faces of the onlookers. Thoris watched as a well-dressed nobleman conspicuously dropped a copper into the child's hands. She beamed, flashing her ragged teeth. Deftly slipping the copper into her already-bulging pocket, she moved on to the next crowd member. Thoris, amazed by her ingenuity, shouldered his way to the front of the group.

A few more choruses of the rousing dance brought the little girl to him, her hands cupped and her eyes imploring. Peering intently toward the ring of dancers, Thoris acted as though he didn't see the waif. She hesitated, intensifying her stare, but the priest was unresponsive. Setting her lips together in determination, she moved forward to the next person. Before she arrived, however, she found a shiny gold piece in her open palms. With undisguised shock, she stared up at Thoris, who still feigned oblivion. But the smile that crept into his features betrayed him, and his capricious wink sealed the identification.

Thoris knelt down and cupped his hands to whisper in the girl's ear. She hovered near, cautiously clutching her pocketful of coins next to her. As the stranger spoke, the nervous fear left her eyes. She nodded once, then again, then pulled back from the speaker, motioning him to follow. With twenty fast paces the child brought Thoris to the lead *vardo*, then clambered up its short steps and rapped heavily on the door.

"Madam Duccia, come out! Come out! A *giorgio* is here to see you!"

*   *   *   *   *

Julianna gazed worriedly out the window of her inn room. The gray mists beyond were growing sooty with the coming night. Something was definitely wrong. Casimir hadn't returned since the morning before, and Thoris had disappeared near noon today. She got up from the chair and began pacing toward the door. "I'll ask Harkon Lukas about them." She halted, the floorboards creaking into silence.

"No," she said to herself. "Thoris said to stay." Casimir had probably gotten himself into some trouble, and Thoris had gone to save him. She huffed and said sarcastically, "They're doomed."

A knock sounded at the hallway door of the adjoining room.

Julianna peered through the open passage between the rooms. Lamplight spilled beneath the hallway door, showing the shadow of someone's feet. Once more the rapping came. Julianna moved cautiously toward the door between the rooms, hoping to close it before the sound came again. She was halfway to the door when another noise caught her attention: the quiet rattle of a key in the lock. On tiptoe, Julianna reached the door between the rooms.

Suddenly the hallway door swung wide.

She froze.

The dark silhouette in the doorway was draped in a cloak that glistened with mist. He was a tall, angular man with one glistening eye. As he moved forward into the dark room, a triangle of light skipped across the dagger he carried.

Julianna swung the door beside her closed, shutting the man in the adjoining room. She groped in her pockets for the key, but it lay across the room and out of immediate reach. Throwing her back against the door, she heard heavy footstep approach on the other side. Her hand seized the doorknob and held it firmly. She could feel the man's hand settle on the opposite side of the knob. The smooth metal began to jiggle, turning slowly in her hand. Julianna tightened her grip. Still the knob turned. She planted her foot firmly against the door and braced herself.

The latch clicked.

With one firm push, the stranger forced his way through. Julianna sprawled heavily to the floor, and the man loomed over her.

"Julianna, my dear, please accept my humble apologies," said Harkon Lukas, already deep into a gracious bow. She clung to the foot of the bed, her heart racing. Lukas rose from the bow and continued. "I meant only to deliver this knife to Thoris. I didn't think the door between the rooms would be open."

Julianna could scarcely gather her breath. "The door wasn't open until you came through it."

The bard's face split into a disarming smile. "I couldn't let you think Thoris's room was being burgled, could I?"

"What would a priest want with a dagger?" Julianna

asked, her hand clutching her heaving chest.

"Some ritual of Milil," Lukas said by way of dismissal. His expression changed now to one of concern. "Why, you're trembling," he noted, moving toward her with arms open.

She rose, escaping his advance, and retreated toward the window. "Where is Casimir?"

Lukas shrugged boyishly. "After my tour yesterday, he stopped off at a *meekulbrau* house. I've heard some wild stories, none of which I should repeat in your presence."

As he approached her, she held out her hands to keep him back. "You may leave now."

"Again I ask your forgiveness, my lady," Lukas said, kneeling before her and kissing her hand. "If my little town has heaped offenses on you, please forgive me. How can I take back these wrongs done?"

Julianna had a sharp response poised on her tongue, but she bit it back, looking down into the face of Harkon Lukas. He could have been Casimir in twenty years. She stared into his profound eyes for long moments before she realized he still held her hand. Her face flushed and she withdrew to the window.

"How can you take back these wrongs?" she repeated, peering out into the mist. "Find Casimir and bring him back. Find Thoris, too. Something is very wrong here."

Lukas rose gracefully and, cupping her chin gently in his hand, said, "Don't worry. I'll find Casimir."

Then he spun about resolutely, paced to her bed, and set the barbarous dagger at the foot of it. Without turning to face her, he said, "You'll see that Thoris has this dagger in hand the moment he returns tonight?"

"I'll see to it," she replied nervously.

Lukas strode to the door. In one swift motion, he opened it, stepped through into the glowing hallway, and shut it behind him.

*   *   *   *   *

The gypsy *vardo* rocked slightly as its occupant moved toward the door. Over the jangling music of the violins and tambourines, Thoris heard the sound of light footfalls. A brassy doorknob turned, slipping the latch, and the top section of the caravan's bright yellow door swung slowly open.

A surprisingly young woman leaned her elbows on the lower half of the door, her black hair silky on her shiny tunic. She couldn't have been older than thirty-five. Thoris noted a natural grace in the disposition of her limbs and the coy tilt of her head. Despite her alluring beauty, though, the woman's green eyes held the wisdom of a person twice her age. She scanned Thoris casually from toe to crown.

"You seek passage from this place?" she asked.

Thoris was stunned. Neither he nor the Vistana child had spoken of his wishes. "Does my purpose show so clearly?" he wondered aloud, fetching her graceful hand from the half door and managing a light kiss on it.

"It does to me," she replied, pulling her hand back as a look of suspicion entered her eyes. "Perhaps you should better conceal it so that the one you flee might not discover you."

Thoris motioned toward the *vardo*. "May I enter your caravan to discuss terms?"

A fire flashed in Madam Duccia's eyes. "Let me see the girth of your purse before I let you enter my caravan."

Thoris reached into his robes and produced a jingling bag of coins. "Gold and silver, these—no coppers among them."

The second latch sounded, and the lower door swung open. "Come inside, good priest."

Thoris ducked his head and entered the *vardo*. The caravan seemed somehow larger within than it was without. Its four windows admitted ample light, even through the sheer veils that twined around them. A lamp that dangled from the low ceiling further illuminated the *vardo*. The lamplight fell warmly across the *vardo*'s small bed, meager stool, narrow desk, and canted shelves. Beads, veils, and feathers hung from every corner. Thoris settled onto the small stool while Madam Duccia closed the door and seated herself grandly on the bed.

"Where are you bound?" she asked, her silken voice firm and businesslike.

Thoris rubbed the sigil of Milil nervously. "Gundarak."

Madam Duccia stared into the lamp's fire. "I do not think you wish to flee there."

"I'm not fleeing *to* Gundarak so much as *from* Kartakass," Thoris said, his voice becoming grim. "Have you a better destination in mind?"

The gypsy woman's brow furrowed in thought, and she grew silent. At last she said, "No. These are strange lands, young priest. I've heard of better lands, but seen none."

"Then to Gundarak it is," Thoris said, "for me and a friend."

The green in Madam Duccia's eyes deepened, and she stared intently at him. "A lover or a sister?"

"Neither," Thoris snapped irritably, "though she is a woman. The lover of the one we flee."

"Hmmm," Duccia considered. "The lover of the one you flee. That'll cost extra. The danger is high."

"Ten gold each, and that's generous," Thoris said firmly.

"Twenty each, and that's a bargain," the gypsy woman said.

"I might as well take the forty gold and buy myself a horse," Thoris said, rising.

"Sit down," Duccia said, the firmness of her voice forcing Thoris back in his seat. "If you believed you could escape on a horse, you'd have done so already. Perhaps you tried to and fell asleep at the border. Don't make threats you won't carry out."

"Ten for me and twelve for the woman."

"I am to risk my whole tribe for twenty-two? Make it thirty-eight!"

"We shall each pay fourteen. That makes it twenty-eight and halfway between our marks."

"No, halfway is thirty, and I'll add five to that for your dishonesty. Thirty-five."

"Thirty-two."

"Thirty-five."

"Thirty-three."

"Thirty-five."

"How much will freedom cost us?" Thoris muttered to himself. "Thirty-four."

"Thirty-four it is."

"I'd like to leave tonight," Thoris said.

"Leave tonight?" Duccia cried, indignant. "We'll not leave tonight—or double your cost! We leave tomorrow!"

"Tomorrow?" Thoris said, disappointed. If I'm successful tonight, I won't need to flee by tomorrow, he thought. Still, it's best to keep my options open. "If not tonight, then I'll wait for tomorrow to pay you. I'll meet you here at noon."

"At dusk," Duccia said. "You'd filch from us half a day of selling? No, we sell when the people will buy and travel when they will not."

"Dusk then, tomorrow, on this very site," Thoris said with an angry sigh. He rose from the ragged stool where he sat and stepped toward the door. His hand settled on the doorknob, but he didn't open it yet. "Madam Duccia, how did you know I meant to flee? How did you know my companion was a woman?"

She smiled deeply and rose from the bed. "Your face has a look of betrayal about it . . . betrayal and fear. But the fear is not for yourself. And who else does a man fear for than a woman, even if she's stronger than he? So I knew your companion was a woman. The fear may well be for her, but the betrayal you feel for yourself. You'd rather sink a dagger into your own back than into the one you betray."

Thoris gazed darkly at her and, turning the doorknob, said, "If you're as skilled a driver as you are a reader of faces, I think my thirty-four gold pieces will be well spent."

EIGHTEEN

Standing in the hallway like a porter of the inn, Thoris peered down at the covered platter cradled to his chest. It rattled, as though sensing the beat of his heart. He drew a calming breath into his lungs, then fit a key into the lock of his inn room. Before turning the knob, he glanced one last time down the lantern-lit hallway. Curling tendrils of smoke and steam rose ghostlike through the floor from the tavern below. Otherwise, the hall was empty.

No guests. No clerks. No Casimir.

Thoris returned his attention to the smooth brass knob before him. Tightening his grip, he twisted the knob, or tried to. His sweating fingers slipped ineffectually on the metal.

"Thoris," came a raspy voice from the hall's end.

He lifted his bloodshot eyes toward the sound.

Casimir was rising from the dark stairwell, covered with blood, incorporeal, swathed in smoke and death.

Thoris spun about, almost upsetting the platter.

The specter was gone.

The miasmatic air was undisturbed.

Panting with fear, Thoris slumped backward against the door. "Just my nerves," he mumbled. Succulent steam rose from the platter of mutton, wreathing his head. He thought of the darksome fog surrounding the inn and of the long night just begun.

Casimir was out there somewhere.

Dear friend.

Deadly foe.

"Tonight I kill my oldest friend," Thoris said to himself, drawing the mutton's savory steam deep into his lungs. If Lukas had provided the dagger, tonight Thoris would sink it home. And more than he feared for Casimir's soul, he feared the blade might miss its mark.

Maybe the dagger won't be there, he thought. Maybe Julianna and I can escape tomorrow, leaving Casimir alive.

He wiped the sweat from his free hand, turned the doorknob, and pushed.

The door swung silently open. Returning the key to his pocket, Thoris shuffled across the threshold. The room beyond was as black as ink. Only the rectangular windowpanes, gray with the night mist, stood out in the blackness. Leaving the hall door open for light, Thoris shambled toward the bed, set the platter there momentarily, and groped on the bed table for his flint and tinder. It's on the other bedstand, he thought. He paused. If a lamp is burning when Casimir arrives, I'll have a hard time surprising him with the dagger. I'd better keep it dark.

Striding back toward the door, Thoris quickly closed it. With the latch's heavy click, the room became impenetrably black. Patiently Thoris waited for his eyes to adjust. In time, the blackness gave way to shades of gray-black. Then Thoris swept forward into the room, moving a small bed table into the center of the floor and fetching a chair to place before it. He lifted the steaming platter from the bed and placed it atop the table. Straightening his back, he surveyed the dull glint of silver on the platter cover. His eyes then shifted to the window. I wonder how Casimir will make his entrance.

Thoris wandered to the door that led to Julianna's room. By this time, his eyes had adjusted enough that he could clearly make out her sleeping form. He drew a long breath and sighed. As he gazed at her fragile, innocent body, resting so quietly, Thoris's resolve steeled.

Tonight's the last night of horror, he thought. Slowly he closed the door, taking care that the latch closed soundlessly.

"You've ruined a perfectly good view," came a cold, deep voice in the darkness.

For the second time that night, Thoris wheeled about. This was no ghost's voice. Words stumbled guiltily from his lips. "Casimir! When did you arrive?"

A shadow, deeper than the shadows around it, hovered with menace along the far wall. "Why did you close the door, Thoris?"

"I—uh," Thoris stammered, clutching onto the doorpost, "I thought it improper for me to see her asleep."

"You certainly got an eyeful," came the malevolent voice. "And the door was open when last I came calling."

"You could always see through me," Thoris flattered, hoping this time Casimir could not. "Yes, I was watching her sleep. But I closed the door because I knew you'd come. I've told her nothing about the curse, Casimir, and I knew we couldn't talk freely with her here," Thoris finished, regaining his nerve.

Casimir's laugh was hushed, but harsh all the same. "And why not light a lamp?"

"She'd wake up," Thoris replied quickly. "Even when this door's closed, enough light spills through to wake her," he lied.

"I see." The sound of boot heels scudding on the floor told Thoris that Casimir was moving forward—and that he was in human form. He paused, the silver platter ringing slightly as he lifted the cover from it. "Nice dinner, if my nose serves me."

"I brought it for you," Thoris said, edging in a wide arc around Casimir, hoping to glimpse his silhouette against the gray windows. "You said you'd return, Casimir, and I knew you'd be hungry."

"You knew I'd be hungry, did you?" Casimir began acidly. "You thought a luscious lump of lamb would dissuade me from eating you?" Again came that humorless laugh. The chair creaked as he sat down, and once again the platter cover rang.

Thoris laughed uneasily as he reached a spot where Casimir was silhouetted against the windows. He'd expected to be set at ease by the familiar silhouette, but instead Thoris was shocked by it. Casimir's hair stood in bristly clumps across his head, and ragged yeoman's clothes draped his shoulders.

"How's the mutton?" Thoris asked, his voice quivering.

With a full mouth, Casimir's voice sounded like a growl. "Excellent. A bit cool by now, but I've had colder meat," he noted seriously, then paused to swallow. "Thoughtful of you to bring me mutton, Thoris. Did you intend the dagger for me as well?"

"Dagger?" Thoris gasped, his heart leaping into his throat.

"Yes," Casimir responded, his incisive grin almost palpable in the darkness. "The dagger you left on the foot of your bed."

Swallowing hard, Thoris said, "Surely if I had any plans to use a dagger on you, I wouldn't have left it on my bed."

"Who's it for, then?"

Thoris bit his lip and said, "I got it in the marketplace today. I needed something to protect me and Julianna from Lukas."

Casimir's knife made a sawing motion across the porcelain plate. "A noble thought, Thoris, but probably thought in vain. You need a specially forged blade to wound Harkon Lukas."

The tension in Thoris's shoulders eased slightly. Keeping his eyes trained on Casimir, Thoris moved toward the bed. "Well, that dagger's better than none at all. Where is it?"

Casimir tilted his head toward Thoris. "On the bed, where I found it."

Thoris strode toward the bed, trying to walk casually on his stiff and shaking legs. "I'll stow it in the other bedstand in case he surprises us here," Thoris said, his voice shaking. Reaching the bed, he lifted the dagger. Its grip felt cold in his unsteady hand.

Turn and strike him down. Kill him now, or he'll kill you.

Thoris cradled the dagger against his chest. It certainly didn't feel like silver; it seemed too heavy and unrefined. Its long, narrow blade would require an exact stab for a kill.

Strike him to the ground. Unmake the beast.

He pivoted toward Casimir and began to pace forward. Casimir's dark-specked eyes fixed, immovable, on the keen dagger. Only two steps farther. Thoris veered away from Casimir. "Sorry. Didn't mean to scare you. My eyes are so poor in this darkness."

"Quite right," Casimir observed unconvincingly. His eyes followed Thoris all the way around his table and to the other side of the bed. There Thoris knelt beside the bedstand and slid the dagger loudly into a drawer. Taking a breath, he cautiously picked it up again and slipped the blade beneath the straw mattress. The dagger's handle protruded in easy reach. Smiling nervously, he stood up, dusted off his palms, and circled around to the front of Casimir.

"So what changed your mind?"

"Changed my mind?" Casimir asked, warily returning his knife to the meat.

"You were going to kill me last night."

"Yes." He lifted a few steamy morsels to his mouth and chewed. "It was a wretched night."

"What happened? Tell me," Thoris said, glad to forestall the inevitable task.

"It's too much to tell, Thoris," Casimir replied, with some measure of his old friendliness. "You'd probably think me crazy."

"I already do," Thoris said, managing a sweat-beaded grin.

"Where to begin," Casimir said, ignoring the comment. He drew a deep breath, then said, "Thoris, I know that over the last year I've become more an enemy than a friend. But now you must believe me when I say we have a far greater enemy than each other. Our true enemy is Harkon Lukas."

"Harkon Lukas?"

"Yes," Casimir replied. "He's a werebeast . . . like me." Thoris noted that the knife and fork had left Casimir's hands and now rested idly on the silver tray. His hands lay in his lap. "But he's worse than that. He doesn't really have a human side at all—it's just a mask, a facade."

Thoris leaned forward in his seat, setting his elbows anxiously on his knees. "How do you know?"

"Oh, I've known for some time," Casimir said, shaking his head. "I've known for over a year. But only last night did I find out the worst." His voice grew soft and distant, and he buried his face in his hands. "He's like a god, Thoris. He's been setting this up for twenty years. We're just . . . puppets."

Thoris shifted in his seat. "A god? What are you talking about?"

Casimir sat up, his eyes searching the darkness. "Think back to when you and Julianna first rode for Gundarak," Casimir said. He added gently, "Yes, I knew about that. I knew because of him."

"You knew," Thoris whispered, breathless.

When he spoke again, Casimir's voice trembled quietly. "I stood on the heights with Lukas, watching as you rode for the border. He brought me there. He made the forest sing to you . . . sing you to sleep. Then he spirited you away. Don't you remember?"

Thoris rose and began to pace uneasily. "That was . . . that was Harkon Lukas who did that?"

"Yes," Casimir replied, his voice growing urgent. "And remember when you heard Milil's voice in the temple? That, too, was Lukas."

Thoris paced around the table and over to the window. Casimir turned to face his friend, silhouetted black against the gray-black fog. Thoris clung to the window frame, his eyes buried in the dense mist. "How many werewolves are there, Casimir? How many? I thought you and Zhone Clieous were freaks. But now it's Harkon Lukas, too . . . and how many more?"

Casimir studied Thoris's silhouette. "Many, Thoris." He set his hand on his knee and said quietly, "They are legion."

Thoris was shaking. He slid his hands onto the windowsill and leaned heavily on it. "Tell me, Casimir . . . is Julianna infected?"

Silently Casimir rose. He stepped slowly toward Thoris. "No. On my life, I promise you she isn't. I've kept my distance. I've stayed away from her, even though it kills me. If I ever tainted her, I'd kill myself."

Thoris slumped against the window frame and sighed. "I'm glad."

Clasping his friend's shoulder, Casimir said, "Will you help me kill Lukas?"

Thoris shied away, retreating from the window. His voice grew cold. "This is too much, Casimir."

Feeling for the bed, Thoris sat down. His hands fluttered nervously about the straw mattress. Then, folding his arms across his midsection, he began to rock back and forth.

"You're asking me to kill someone—someone I hardly know."

Casimir stared toward Thoris, a wrinkle of pity creasing his brow. Then slowly he approached the bed, his arms extended. "No, Thoris. I'll do the killing. I just need your help." Pivoting, Casimir sat down beside Thoris, setting a consoling hand on his friend's knee. "It'll be like old times, Thoris. You and me, fighting together . . . like old times."

Casimir began to laugh. For the first time in months, he sounded like the old Casimir—like the boy Casimir, who gave Thoris his wooden sword to lure him from the plague house.

A salty liquid rose in Casimir's throat, sealing off the laugh. He sputtered for breath. It was blood, his own blood. Only then did he feel the sharp and disorienting pain below his left shoulder blade. It was a knife, lying just below his heart. Not a killing wound, but a deep wound all the same. The blade was heavy in the cut— heavy with iron, heavy with Thoris's fist. Thoris's other hand splayed across Casimir's chest, and the young priest leaned his head on Casimir's shoulder.

He was crying.

"Forgive me, Casimir, forgive me. I've finally killed you—killed you as you begged me to do long ago."

The words sounded hollow in Casimir's leaden ears. A shudder began in the cold blade. It moved through him in rippling waves. It grew larger as it reached his hands . . . reached his feet. The transformation had begun. How strange it felt to move again. The blade had seemed to sever Casimir from his body. But now he could move. He thrust his elbow brutally backward, striking Thoris's arm. With a bone-snapping thud, Thoris's hand flew from the wound, pulling the knife with it. The blade struck the far wall and rattled to the floor.

Thoris whimpered. He was cradling his arm. Casimir staggered up from the bed. He pivoted slowly, his heel greased with his own blood. Then another blow.

Craaaaack!

Now both of Thoris's arms lay limp and twisted beside him. Casimir balled his slick, salty fist. He hurled it downward. It buried itself in Thoris's chest. The priest's groan was punctuated by the pop of ribs. Casimir took a moment to laugh. Again, hammerlike, the fist fell. More ribs snapped. Casimir grunted his pleasure. Thoris fell back on the bed, rolling to get away. A brutal kick pulverized his hip, and another cracked his thigh across its center.

Thoris stopped squirming. His chest rose and fell in panicked gasps, and his eyes were lidless with terror. Casimir towered over him. His toothy leer looked strangely intoxicated. Reaching down with clawed fingers, Casimir tore the shirt from Thoris's back and he tied it over his wound.

"Forgive me, Thoris," he said, staring long moments at his victim. Turning with a shuffling gait, Casimir moved to the door. He threw Thoris's cloak over his shoulders and, casting a final glance at the broken priest, slipped away into the smoky hall.

*   *   *   *   *

Harkon Lukas strode heavily down the main corridor of the Kartakan Inn, his black cloak flapping winglike behind him. A man fiddling with the buttons of his waistcoat happened through a doorway into the main corridor and into Master Lukas's path. Hearing the bard's ominous footfalls, the man glanced up and stepped back hastily. Lukas marched past, unaffected. Nothing and no one would stand in his path this morning.

No one but the mousy desk clerk.

"Master Lukas?" the emaciated clerk called, his voice rising insistently above the dauntless footfalls. "Master Lukas?"

Lukas stopped in his tracks, five paces beyond the main desk. A blast of air sprayed from his nostrils.

"Master Lukas?" the unaffected man repeated.

The bard pivoted slowly about, growling, "This had better be damned important."

Apparently unaware he'd been threatened, the man produced a scrap of paper from the uppermost drawer of his desk and waved it. "An odd man stopped by last midnight. He dictated this to me and said to give it to you."

"Don't wave papers at me," Lukas snapped, striding forward and snatching the paper from the bony hand. He unfolded the crumpled parchment and said, "What *sort* of odd man gave this to you?"

"Well," the clerk said, leaning back dramatically in his chair, "the fellow's hair was most unkempt, and he wore a cloak that was far too small for him. He kept his hands buried in the folds of his clothes, and one shoulder had rather a hunch."

"Quite a lot to remember from a midnight," Lukas scowled. He glanced down at the paper and read:

Master Lukas,

The sacrifice is complete. Go visit Thoris and see. Meet me tonight at dusk in the tavern. We must celebrate before we hunt again.

Lukas looked up from the wrinkled page, his eyes narrowing in thought. Then, cramming the rumpled note in his pocket, he strode onward.

*   *   *   *   *

Thoris slowly surfaced from sleep. He felt little better than a corpse. The first sensation that entered his dazed mind was a numb throbbing, which he eventually recognized to be his heart. Next came the ache of his swollen lungs. With each breath, spiders of pain scrambled over his ribs. Now he realized his eyes wouldn't open, as though caked shut by thick mud. As the wave of wakefulness spread slowly across his body, a thousand subtle aches merged into pain.

Pain.

Pain from limbs he could sense in no other way. He suddenly wished that Casimir had finished him off. Perhaps I can fall asleep again, he thought.

Except for the voices. The room echoed with voices. The hushed words bit sharply into Thoris's ears. Who is that? he wondered. The higher, gentler voice belonged to Julianna, but he couldn't place the low, velvety rumble. The man's voice was smooth and practiced, as though he'd been perfecting the tongues of men for three or four lifetimes. A chill shivered through Thoris.

It was Casimir.

The memory of what had happened last night lingered all too clear in Thoris's mind. He tried to move his arm, tried to sit up, but his limbs felt like wood. He struggled, gritting his teeth with the effort, but he still couldn't move. A rising wave of nausea convinced him to lie still. Lie still and listen.

"I don't doubt"—it was Casimir speaking—"that tonight will open your eyes."

"You speak as though I'm blind," Julianna replied coldly.

"Not blind, just fooled by stage sets," came the silky response. "Yes, I'll take you to Casimir tonight, but you won't like what you see."

A jolt of pain shook Thoris's body. The velvety voice belonged not to Casimir but to Harkon Lukas.

"Where is he?" Julianna asked insistently.

"We'll go on a hunt, you and I."

Thoris struggled to sit up, his stiff arms shaking ineffectually.

"He's waking," noted Julianna. "You'd better leave."

Thoris's jaw clamped in determination, but still his arms wouldn't bend.

"I'll go," Lukas said, "but only if you promise to meet me tonight."

"Yes," came the impatient reply.

Thoris thrashed all the harder. Julianna's gentle hands settled on him. "Be still, Thoris dear. You'll be all right."

Thoris forced his blood-crusted eyelids open. Julianna sat at his bedside, concern filling her emerald eyes. She leaned over him, checking splints and bandages as the door closed behind her. Thoris gazed up toward Julianna through bruise-swollen eyes.

"Is he . . . gone?" Thoris rasped.

A sad smile came to Julianna's face. Her lips were as red as the silk chemise she wore. "Yes, he is gone."

"You must escape."

"Shhh, shhhh, shhh," Julianna soothed, gently rubbing his shoulders.

Thoris forced his swollen eyes open farther and spoke with painful clarity. "Listen to me, Julianna. You must . . . flee this place."

"No," Julianna replied, concern filling her eyes. "I haven't left your bedside since the thief came last night. I don't plan to leave you now."

"Julianna . . . you must leave," Thoris implored, his splinted arms straining hopelessly toward her. "You're in danger."

Julianna's brow knitted. "Do you know what's happened to Casimir? He's been gone three days and now this theft . . ."

Thoris's eyes closed as the pain rose in his legs.

"Don't worry," she said. "We've got protection. I put the thief's knife in a drawer and asked Harkon Lukas to post a guard."

Opening his eyes, Thoris asked, "How . . . badly off am I?"

Julianna peered into his cloudy eyes and bit her lower lip. She stroked his tangled hair. "Thoris, you should sleep."

"How badly off?" he insisted, the words gurgling in his throat.

She sighed, her lips pressed firmly together. "Your legs and arms are splinted. The local leech thinks your ribs are broken, too. Your face is bruised and swollen."

Thoris looked away from her. For a moment, his tear-ringed eyes wandered hopelessly across the blank ceiling. Tucking his lower lip beneath his teeth, he gasped, "You must go without me."

Julianna searched his face. "What are you talking about?"

"I've . . . arranged it all, Julianna," Thoris said, clamping his eyelids tight as a spasm of pain clutched his chest. "Take my bag of gold. Meet the gypsies . . . tonight in the market. Pay seventeen gold. They'll . . . take you away."

"But tonight I must meet Harkon Lukas."

"No . . ." Thoris insisted, his unsteady eyes gazing past her. "Lukas is a werewolf, Julianna . . . and Casimir, too."

"What?" Her brow wrinkled, and her hands lifted reflexively from him.

"I've no strength for proofs," Thoris stammered. Forcing his eyes to focus on Julianna, he muttered, "I'm your proof. It wasn't a thief who . . . who did this to me. It was . . . Casimir. Lukas and he are in league. . . ."

Julianna's face blanched; the color rushed even from her full lips.

"If you have any compassion for me . . . flee tonight."

Julianna stared blankly ahead of her. "I can't believe it."

"Love is blinding you," Thoris said, "love for Casimir. . . . It blinded me, too."

Standing, she shook her head in disbelief. Sorrow painted her pallid features. "How could this be?"

"Don't question it," Thoris choked out impatiently. "Just flee."

Her exquisitely green eyes were laced with red lines. "But, Thoris, I can't leave you here for them to—"

"I am already dead, Julianna," Thoris said with a labored sigh. "I'll die . . . whether you take me or not. . . . If you take me, you'll die, too."

She had begun to cry. "I can't leave you for dead!"

"You've got to."

Her chin quivered with the sobs she held back. Leaning over, she embraced him. Through the cloud of pain that encircled him, Thoris felt the warm press of Julianna's body against him. A tear rolled down his cheek. Then reluctantly Julianna let go.

"Good-bye, good priest."

Thoris knew in that moment he would never again look on her emerald eyes or her raven hair.

"What watch of the day is it?" he asked.

"Tail of the fourth watch," she said sadly. "One hour till sunset."

"Meet the gypsies at dusk. Take my gold and slip out now. Let no one see you leave. Ask for Madam Duccia."

She kissed him full on the lips.

"Farewell Thoris, High Priest of Milil."

"Farewell," Thoris replied. Julianna rose from his bedside and, in moments, was gone.

* * * * *

Perhaps minutes, perhaps hours later, Thoris awoke from a fitful sleep. One thought swept like a beacon through his mind: She forgot the dagger.

* * * * *

Harkon Lukas sat in darkness at the back of a curtained alcove. The flickering candle at the table's center seemed to draw the shadows in rather than dispelling them. Lukas brooded, stony and silent. His steely eyes were fastened on some unseen object far beyond the alcove's curtain. In his hand rested a single red rose, drawn from the vase at the table's center. A minute drop of blood sat in a red ball on one of his fingertips.

"Julianna," he mused quietly.

The curtains before him began to part, pushed back by a hand bearing a foamy stein. The hand was followed by a young man, whose red brocade jacket and ruffled ivory shirt were as fine as any Lukas had seen. Lukas's eyes flicked in subtle shock as he studied the black-haired intruder.

"Close the curtain behind you, Casimir," Lukas said.

With a cocky grin, Casimir slid a stein to his father and turned to pull the curtains closed. "Good evening to you as well, Lukas." Securing the curtains, Casimir dropped into a seat. He raised his foaming stein toward the bard and said, "How's the *meekulbrau* here, Master Lukas?"

Ignoring the question, Lukas droned, "I visited your priest today."

Casimir took a long draft from his *meekulbrau*. "What do you think of my handiwork, Father?"

"I think he's still alive, if that's what you mean," Lukas replied, setting the rose gently down on the table before him. His gaze shifted to the drop of blood on his fingertip.

"Still alive, but shattered like a wine goblet," Casimir said, peering at Lukas's untouched stein. "Alive and able to perceive his torture. I learned much from Von Daaknau."

Lukas's attention remained on the drop of blood, shifting it from his finger to his thumb. "You don't understand, Casimir. The torture of Thoris is not a sufficient sacrifice."

Casimir resolutely set his stein down and said in a hardening tone, "I thought perhaps you'd find some small pleasure in my ingenuity. I invited you here tonight to toast our future. . . . but also to watch me kill my priest," Casimir said, raising his stein to gesture a toast.

Rubbing out the blood on his fingertips, Lukas reluctantly took hold of his tankard. "We toast, then we kill the priest, then we hunt?"

Casimir flashed a brutal grin. "To our future as monsters, father and son! As deeply as we drink of our steins now, let us drink of our lives as beasts!"

Lukas began to smile. Lifting his stein, he rang it against Casimir's. Then both set the vessels to their lips, threw back their heads, and drank the liquor to its dregs. As their tankards clunked heavily to the tabletop, Casimir produced a loud belch. Lukas laughed heartily.

Casimir sprang capriciously up from his seat and threw back the curtains of the alcove. The light from the crowded tavern flooded painfully into the nook, and Lukas, eyes smarting and face white with shock, began to rise from his seat. Casimir seized Lukas's arm like a boy helping his grandfather stand.

"Come, my father," he said in a stage whisper loud enough to be heard by those nearby. "Why must we wait any longer? Let us up to the room and kill us a priest!"

A barrel-bodied woman with papery skin glanced toward the pair. Casimir gazed down at her, patting her on the back. Turning back toward his father, the youth raised a finger to his lips. "Guess I said that a little too loud." He leaned heavily on the bard, spewing alcohol breath into his face.

Lukas regarded the woman with a look of apology. "The enthusiasm of youth," he said, wrapping an arm about Casimir. He pushed his stumbling son from the alcove. "Did that *meekulbrau* run straight into your brain?"

Casimir laughed loudly, then whispered, "Should I change into a wolf or kill him as a man?"

Clamping a hand over Casimir's mouth, Lukas shouldered his way through the tavern. His eyes flashed warnings to any who might have overheard. Oddly, he himself felt a bit unsteady on his feet. Perhaps he'd judged Casimir too harshly.

The short flight of stairs that led from the tavern to the main hall proved too treacherous for Casimir's wobbly legs. Sighing, Lukas picked him up and slung him over one shoulder.

He didn't unload his cargo until they were some twenty paces down the hall. There he unceremoniously dumped Casimir, who thudded like a flour sack to the floor. Lukas peered down imperially, shaking his head in angry amusement. Casimir returned the gaze, a dopey grin spreading across his face.

Lukas whispered, "In your condition, you couldn't kill a sleeping child."

Casimir let out a wheezing laugh.

"Haven't you ever drunk *meekulbrau* before?"

Casimir extended a flaccid arm, seeking assistance in rising. His father seized the hand and yanked him upright. Casimir winced in pain and spent a moment rubbing his shoulder. Then, noting his father's severe expression, he straightened.

"Don't sell me short. I feel quite well enough for murder."

Lukas eyed the unsteady youth from head to foot. "You couldn't kill a half-poisoned rat."

"Really, I'm fine," Casimir insisted, an edge of insolence entering his eyes.

Suddenly Lukas staggered. He took a step back to regain his balance.

"How do *you* feel, Father?"

The dark bard was holding his stomach. "Suddenly . . .

not so well."

Casimir moved toward him, gracefully catching Lukas's arm. All sign of Casimir's drunkenness was gone. "What's wrong?"

The tall bard clamped his eyes closed. He swooned a second time, caught only by his son. He raised a hand to his brow, which was dotted with sweat. "I . . . don't know. The hall seems to be swaying beneath my feet . . . and I hear bells."

"Perhaps it was the *meekulbrau*," Casimir offered coldly.

Lukas rubbed his forehead, "Perhaps. How do you feel?"

"I feel fine," came the quick, sober response.

Lukas opened his eyes and peered toward his son. The first long hairs were sprouting across Casimir's leering face.

NINETEEN

"What are you doing?" Lukas hissed, stumbling backward into the wall.

Casimir's eyes glowed with a hungry orange light. "Transforming, dear father. I'm transforming," he replied, his flesh beginning to boil.

"You fool," Lukas spat, lunging toward Casimir and clutching his brocade jacket. "Not here! What's come over you?"

"The bloodlust," cried Casimir, the features of his face beginning to crack and shift.

Ignoring the stabs of pain that passed through his stomach, Lukas angrily hauled on the jacket, pulling Casimir toward the stairs. "Fight down the bloodlust, Casimir. Fight it! Your prey isn't even in sight!"

Beneath the long strands of hair that snaked from Casimir's brow, his eyes burned like embers. "My prey *is* in sight."

Lukas's legs, numb from the *meekulbrau*, shuffled to a halt. He stared, dumbfounded, at his son.

An odd leer, half lupine and half human, formed on Casimir's face. "*You* are my prey, Father."

The words ran like cold water down Lukas's spine. He searched his son's serious eyes.

No mercy, no compassion, no humanity.

Releasing Casimir's jacket, Lukas staggered backward. The blood drained from his face as he touched off his own transformation. "It's true, isn't it?" he stammered, still backing away from the towering youth. Sweat stood out across his brow. "It's true! You want to kill me!"

"I'm my father's son!" Casimir roared, his teeth sprouting in thick stalks. The bulging roots of the fangs cracked his jaw and the forward plate of his face. A canine muzzle began to jut violently from the front of his skull.

Lukas retreated farther along the wall, wondering why his own transformation hadn't begun. "You dare challenge me in this place . . . in *my* place?!"

Claws emerged from Casimir's fingertips. He stepped relentlessly forward and, with one grand swipe, tore away his own jacket and shirt. His heaving rib cage contorted, growing longer and thicker. Convoluted patterns snaked across his skin as muscles and bones shifted and multiplied beneath. From every pore, hair as thick as grass emerged.

"Stop this, Casimir," Lukas growled, marshaling his fury. "You know I'm the greater wolfwere!"

Casimir released a throaty howl from his fully lupine mouth. Behind him, shouts rang out from the tavern, and a stream of dark forms began to emerge. Heedless, Casimir rasped, "If you're greater than I, Lukas, then transform!"

Paces from the stairs, Lukas halted and gathered his will. He summoned the transformation, calling on every reserve of strength in his lethargic body. Nothing happened. There was no tingle of flesh, no fire of bone—nothing. The metamorphosis refused to begin. Again he tried to trigger it, but his bones felt like wet wood.

Casimir snarled, "You cannot change, can you?"

"What have you done to me?" Lukas roared.

"Poison," Casimir replied with a fiendish leer.

"Poison?" Lukas echoed, unbelieving. His gaze shifted to the crowd that had emerged from the tavern. "Whether or not I can transform matters little, Casimir, for I have an army who can."

Without turning to look at them, Casimir replied, "I

know of your army. I can smell them—their sweat, their fear. Ten of them are no match for me."

"We shall see," Lukas replied, motioning the dark forms forward.

Casimir lunged, seizing his father's throat in a razor-tipped hand. "Halt them! One more step and they'll have your head."

Lukas's eyes bulged, and veins stood out like snakes on his neck. Still he didn't motion them off. The claws tightened. Lukas's windpipe dimpled and closed. His face grew scarlet, then purple. The dark figures advanced another step.

With a stiff and yellowed hand, Lukas waved off his henchmen.

"Back farther!" Casimir demanded, the claws of his other hand slashing brutally across Lukas's midsection. With the shuffle of clawed feet, Lukas's minions complied.

Casimir's hold relented. Lukas gasped for air, the purple blood draining from his face. Only then did he feel the slashes across his stomach. They burned as though filled with acid. His doublet and shirt hung in blood-soaked ribbons. Lukas dropped a hand from his bruised neck to cradle the lacerations.

Roaring, Casimir flung his father backward like a rag doll. The dark bard landed in a sprawl at the base of the stairs. His son towered over him, scythelike claws poised for the killing blow. Clutching his stomach, Lukas drew a long breath and said resignedly, "My sword can't harm you. My minions are out of reach . . . and so, too, my wolfish power. . . . You've won, my son. Kill me."

The haughty anger that lined Casimir's face hardened into hatred. "Look at you, Lukas! Dead so soon? I've killed children with more fight than you. You're pathetic . . . worthless. A paper wolf."

"A fine soliloquy," the dark bard said with a sneer. "You've made your father proud. You're a more wicked beast than I, and you'll make a wondrous replacement for me." He peered about the room once, then shouted, "Now end this!"

"Don't preach to me," Casimir roared, his clawed hand quivering with rage. "I know what I am. I know what I've become—everything vile and detestable, everything to be hated by men, to be tracked down and slain. I know! I've become what I sought to destroy. But if I kill you, Father, my damnation will be worth it. Nothing can save you now."

The tight-strung muscles across Casimir's shoulder flexed, and his sickle-tipped fingers rose like a scorpion's tail.

A sound came on the stairs: descending footsteps.

"Stop there!" Casimir roared.

The approaching footfalls didn't slacken.

"Stop or die!"

The narrow shins of the intrepid desk clerk descended into view. He kept coming.

A scream of rage erupted from Casimir. He swung his lethal claws toward the neck of his father. Lukas turned sharply, seizing the desk clerk's calves. The gaunt man toppled over him. The sickle claws sunk deep into the man's back, dragging bony fingers in after them. The clerk screamed, perhaps for the first time in his life. Lukas rose beneath the thin man and flung him, flailing, onto Casimir. The clerk shrieked once again. His gangly body struck the wolfwere square in the throat. Casimir flung the hapless clerk to the ground and, with one swift stroke, dispatched him. Looking toward the stairs, he saw that Lukas was gone. The muscles of his legs bundled for a leap, but a swarm of claws and teeth descended on him.

Lukas's minions.

*   *   *   *   *

Otherworldly shrieks from the base of the stairs rose up into the long hallway above. Lukas, his hand clutching the lacerations across his stomach, shambled down the smoky passage. His free hand fished a ring of keys from the pocket of his doublet. Blood-sticky fingers fumbled through the clanking pieces of iron, selecting the proper key just as he reached the doorway. Fitting the key into the iron lock, Lukas pushed his way inside.

"Good evening, young priest," he said, stepping into the lightless room. A small whimper emerged from the bandaged body that occupied the bed. Lukas smiled, staggering wearily across the room and taking up a lantern. "How are you, good friend? I myself am doing fine this evening—or at least compared to you." Striking a spark with flint and tinder, he awoke a small flame in the lantern. Patiently trimming back the wick, Lukas added, "You needn't fear. My business tonight only initially deals with you."

Another hail of screams rolled in through the open door. Chuckling humorlessly, Lukas set the lantern on the bedstand and wandered back toward the doorway. "I almost forgot to secure the door. It wouldn't do for Casimir to barge in suddenly." Slowly, painfully, Lukas swung the door closed and locked it.

"Now to business," he said, turning to face Thoris and rubbing his blood-stained hands together. "Where is that dagger I brought for you?"

Thoris didn't move, his half-closed eyes peering emptily toward the ceiling.

The dark bard's hand dropped to his bloodied stomach as he approached the bed. His tone grew more insistent. "You remember the dagger, I'm sure—the one you failed to use."

Still the priest lay in silence.

Lukas sighed. "Let me phrase it this way. Casimir is fighting his way up here even as we sp—even as *I* speak. Withhold the blade, and he will kill us both."

"I don't . . . have it," Thoris muttered at last, pain gripping his face as he formed each word.

"Where is it?" came the quiet demand.

"I don't have it," Thoris insisted, breathless.

Lukas drew back from the bed and began to stroke his bearded chin. "Say that I had an iron dagger, good against wolfweres while nothing else is, and that my best friend were a wolfwere who wanted to kill me. And say, if I am not stretching the bounds of reason too far, that I were an invalid, bedded from injuries suffered in the last confrontation with said wolfwere. Granted, I would be a great fool to get caught in such a predicament. But objections aside, where would I put my iron dagger?"

With slow, deliberate steps, Lukas walked to the bedstand and drew open its single drawer. "Ahhhhhh! Just where I would have placed it. Thank you for your gracious assistance, young priest."

Thoris glowered silently.

Lukas turned his attention toward the door that adjoined Julianna's room. It was closed. "Well, then, my business with you is done. Thank you for your time, my little broken friend." He staggered toward the door, pulling the jangling ring of keys from his pocket. Finding the correct key, he fit it to the lock and swung the door open. The room beyond was utterly dark. The bard's bloodstained hand lifted the lantern from Thoris's bedstand and shined it through the room. The bed was empty, as was the chair, the settee, and the window seat. A cursory check of each corner of the room confirmed that no one was there.

Stepping back through the doorway, Lukas said to Thoris, "Where's Julianna?"

"Gone," Thoris said simply.

"I understand," Lukas said, setting the lantern down again. He turned, his mind still reeling with the poison. Slowly he began to pace. In the hush that fell, the distant clamor of the battle downstairs rose to Lukas's ears.

"Now the matter comes down to this," Lukas said at length. "Should I descend into the battle downstairs and plant this dagger in Casimir, or should I wait for him here? He will defeat my whole wolfwere guard. He is, after all, my son," Lukas said, nodding toward Thoris and allowing himself a sardonic smirk. He glanced toward the dark room beyond, and his thoughts returned to Julianna. Innocent and vulnerable Julianna.

And beloved by Casimir.

A light entered Lukas's eyes, a cold, gray, intense light. He lifted the iron dagger and studied it. "Death by this blade would be too merciful for my renegade son. No. There's a better way." Turning toward Thoris, he said, "She's fled for Gundarak, hasn't she?"

Thoris's mouth drew into a tight line, and his eyelids shut.

"That's answer enough for me, young priest," Lukas laughed. "You wanted to go with her, didn't you?" Still Thoris held his eyes closed. "Don't be so disconsolate, good priest. She won't reach Gundarak." With a raking laugh, Lukas staggered to the window, drew it open, and lowered his aching frame down to the dewy ground.

* * * * *

The lower hall had become a slaughterhouse.

The place was painted in blood, from its low ceiling to its rough-planked floor. Casimir's hands dripped with the stuff. He moved slowly through the ruin, choosing careful footsteps among the bodies. No matter what form they had died in, their bodies had all reverted to the full-wolf form. Their lupine flanks were ribboned with lacerations. Some lay in boneless sprawls, others drooped over chairs, and still more hung from coat hooks.

Casimir averted his eyes as he walked. He felt no honor in this slaughter, no exultation of defeated foes. Only a silent audience of the dead. Reaching the stairs, he began to climb, his feet leaving crimson claw marks. Then he spotted a thin line of blood spots leading toward the top of the stairs. Slowly his black canine lips drew back as his nose scented the blood.

"Harkon Lukas," he whispered, and the feverish light returned to his eyes.

Casimir bounded up the stairs, leaping five treads at a time. The smell of Lukas's blood poured fragrant into his nostrils. He topped the stairs and ran down the hall. He sniffed the dense air, separating from the myriad banal odors the exotic perfume of Lukas's blood. It smelled like fear—blood always did—and it was intoxicating. The telltale path continued forward, past door after closed door. Casimir's stomach began to rumble anxiously within him. At last the trail stopped.

Thoris's door.

They plotted together, Casimir realized with sudden anger.

"*Lukas!*" he shouted, his claws biting deep into the hardwood door. Splinters of wood cascaded to the floor or rammed deep beneath his nails. Again Casimir swung. A chunk of the door broke loose, exposing the lamp-lit room beyond. Clamping a brutal hand in the gap, Casimir wrenched backward. The thick door split lengthwise, like a thin plank. Hinges groaned and tore loose. A spray of wood chips littered the hall.

Casimir burst inside, vaulting toward the bed where Thoris lay. With one leap, Casimir reached the bed. He seized the invalid's shoulders, tilting his broken body up from the mattress. Thoris's eyes were wide and blank. Casimir stared him down, dreadful delight curling across his lips. Rearing back, he released a glass-shattering roar. The young priest winced as a blast of hot, putrid breath swept over him.

"In league with my enemy, are you, Thoris?" Casimir rasped, lines of streaming drool pooling across the bandages. The mirth fled from his face. "Where is Lukas!"

Thoris's eyes remained blank and staring. He offered not a word.

Casimir shook him violently. "*Where is he?*"

Only then did Casimir notice that the door to Julianna's room stood wide open. The room beyond was dark. Prying himself from the reticent priest, Casimir stalked slowly into Julianna's room. His nose told him immediately that she was gone.

Staggering back through the doorway, Casimir clutched Thoris's neck and growled, "What has Lukas done with her?"

Slowly the pale, swollen eyelids blinked. Through cracked and puffy lips, the words came.

"What . . . has he done to you?"

"Answer me!" Casimir demanded.

"Answer *me*," Thoris echoed breathlessly.

Casimir raised his wicked claws overhead. "Answer me, or by the gods, I'll kill you."

"You already have," Thoris replied. "You've worked your poisons into me . . . for a decade. Even . . . at the Red Porch . . . the most . . . happy memories . . . are filth and lies."

Disgusted, Casimir lurched up from the bed and began restlessly pacing the room.

"What happened to you . . . Casimir?" Thoris continued, choking.

Casimir loped into Julianna's room again. He rushed to the bed and sniffed heavily across it, then to the settee and chair to do the same. "The scent is old," he muttered distractedly as he tore drawers from the dressing chest and wardrobe. "The scent is old," he repeated, plodding back into Thoris's chamber.

"You search for . . . Julianna. But where is Casimir?" Thoris asked, his feeble voice straining. "Where is Casimir?"

Casimir wheeled, bloodied hands clutching the bedframe and shaking it. "He's dead, Thoris! Casimir is dead! You killed him last night! He still believed in you, still believed he could save you, if not himself. But you sank the blade in anyway. You killed him. And *I'm* all that's left!"

Thoris flinched, a tear coming to his eye. With the back of his clawed hand, Casimir struck Thoris across the face. "Don't cry for me, little priest. Save your tears for yourself." He backed away from the bedside, watching the blood and tears mingle on Thoris's face.

Stalking toward the window, he repeated to himself, "The scent is old. She didn't leave with Lukas. She fled on her own. But where?"

He remembered the night on the Gundarak road.

Already his limbs were realigning. In moments, the transformation to full wolf was complete. He rushed to the open window and hurled himself into the beckoning night.

*   *   *   *   *

Julianna sat on the edge of Madam Duccia's bed as the *vardo* labored along the Gundarak road. She hadn't spoken since the trip began, though she did have a traveling companion. A small gypsy girl named Delanya occupied a footstool across from her. But the sable-haired child had no interest in conversation; her job was to ensure that nothing was stolen. The *vardo* contained all manner of valuable items—jewels, chains of gold, exotic feathers, piles of books. Delanya's brown eyes were fiery and watchful. She reminded Julianna of herself as a child. A bemused smirk pulled at Julianna's lips. The girl didn't see it, though, for she turned her head to catch a sound.

"A horseman," she whispered, her eyes growing wide. The next instant, she was at the *vardo*'s window, her head tucked beneath the swaying curtains.

A sense of dread settled heavily on Julianna. "Perhaps it's just a messenger speeding north."

"He's riding to the front of the caravan."

"Did he keep going?" Julianna asked, sliding from her seat to kneel beside the child at the window. As though in answer to her question, the caravan rumbled to a halt. Julianna's hands grasped the windowsill. Her fingers were trembling. She could see nothing beyond the window, nothing but the nighttime forest.

"What could he want?" she worried aloud. Only then did she notice that Delanya was no longer at her side. Julianna pulled back from the curtains, wincing at the lantern light. Delanya was seated on her stool, a full-sized crossbow leaning against her knees.

"What are you doing with that?" Julianna asked in shock.

"Loading it," the girl replied, her voice ringing with gypsy haughtiness. She looped her feet through each side of the bow and fitted a small crank mechanism in place. In moments, she had notched the cord and set a quarrel in place. The child glanced up toward Julianna, a thoughtful expression on her dark face.

"Haven't you any weapons?" she asked.

"No," Julianna replied simply.

Delanya clucked and shook her head. "A *giorgio* without a weapon." Then she rose from the stool and crept again to the window, dragging the weighty crossbow behind her. Cautiously pulling back the curtain, she hefted the crossbow to the sill.

"He's coming this way with Madam Duccia."

Julianna's heart ached, and she clenched her hands on her legs. Footsteps approached. Delanya's finger settled on the crossbow's trigger. The door handle slowly began to turn. The gypsy child's finger tightened.

"Put away my crossbow, Delanya," came Madam Duccia's angry voice.

Delanya's shoulders slumped, and she lowered the unwieldy weapon to the floor. The doorknob turned, and the door swung wide. Into the caravan stepped a tall, bent figure, dark like a corporeal shadow.

But shadows don't bleed.

"Harkon Lukas," Julianna gasped, edging backward on the bed.

The bard's face was ashen and weary. His long black hair was filled with tangles and matted clumps, and his clothes were ragged. A bloodstained hand rested on his stomach, as though to hide the bloody tatters of his shirt. He bowed feebly. "Julianna . . . how good it is to find you here."

Julianna rose from the bed, unwilling to let him tower over her. "Please, Master Lukas, I'm on a pressing journey."

A polite smile spread across his features. "I know of your journey, my dear—fleeing a monster you haven't seen. Such journeys are common."

Julianna moved forward, gesturing for him to leave the *vardo.* "Please. Your wounds should be dressed by a leech or a priest. My journey must continue."

Warning flashed in Lukas's eyes. "Come, confront the monster. Epiphanies are too rare to pass up."

Her heart drumming in her breast, Julianna set a hand on Lukas and pushed him from the door. "Madam Duccia, I demand safe passage!"

Lukas clamped on to her arm and pulled her out of the *vardo*. The cold night swept over her. Lukas spun her around in front of him. His face was very close to hers as he began to speak. "Madam Duccia will provide you passage . . . but first I want you to know Casimir for what he really is. I want you to know his depravity. I want you to learn to hate him."

"Let me go!" she demanded, wrenching at his hands.

"No!" he shouted angrily. "It's too late to run, my dear. Even now Casimir approaches."

Julianna gasped, peering down the Gundarak road. Its rutted stone blocks were illuminated by shafts of moon-light slanting through the forest canopy. Stately trees rose like pillars to each side of the road, the darkness between them somehow deepened by the hypnotic vio-lining of crickets.

A black form topped a rise in the road.

It was moving at terrifying speed.

Its claws clittered on the cracked blocks of stone. Moonlight flashed frenetically over the galloping beast, its coat flapping in the wind. Even from this distance, its silvery eyes seemed to bore into Julianna. A small sound of dismay escaped her lips, and she pulled back toward the caravan, but Lukas swung a powerful arm about her waist. He held her before him like a shield. She struggled to break free, but suddenly she felt a dag-ger at her throat.

"Forgive my rough handling, my dear, but this is in your own best interest," Lukas hissed. "Behold! Your lover arrives."

The beast had closed to within a hundred yards. It plunged into a shadowy region of the road. Then it emerged, bearing down on Lukas and Julianna. Lukas

backed up a few paces, dragging Julianna with him. He
brandished the keen dagger of iron.

"Stop or she dies!"

The gray-grizzled wolf skidded to a halt some ten
yards away.

"Good, Casimir, good!" Lukas cried out, sweat rolling
down his regal features. "So a dagger at your lady's
throat can still sway you! I'm amazed."

Casimir snarled in reply, his deep-set lupine eyes
glowing blood-red. He turned and began to circle in a
wide arc around them.

Lukas pivoted slowly, keeping Julianna always before
him. "You see, Julianna? You see what he is? He's a
monster. See how his mouth runs red with blood? See
how his claws are stained?"

Julianna's eyes followed the circling wolf as she
spoke. "Thoris told me about you, Lukas. You're a werewolf, too."

The bard's voice came soothingly. "No, my dear. You
misjudge me. If I were a werewolf, wouldn't I transform
and fight him instead of hiding like this?"

"It looks to me as if you already lost a fight to him,"
Julianna said with a sneer.

"I can't prove my innocence," Lukas said, noting that
Casimir's circle had grown tighter. "Get back or she
dies!" he shouted. The hackles across Casimir's back
raised, but he backed away.

"Of course you can prove it. Let me go."

Again Casimir had begun to close the circle, his glowing eyes searching for an opportunity to attack.

"If I can convince you in no other way," Lukas began,
his voice rich and strangely sad, "then so be it."

The dagger dropped from Lukas's hand and clattered
to the stony road below. He released Julianna, pushing
her clear of him. The wolf's circling approach halted,
and his muscles bundled to spring.

"I'm a man, and nothing more," Lukas shouted to
Julianna. "Kill me, Casimir."

The wolf was already airborne. The distance fell cleanly

away. Lukas didn't flinch. Horrible, flashing teeth . . .

Impact.

The bard lurched backward, off balance. He landed with a bone-splintering thud on the stony road. Casimir fell on him instantly. Lukas clutched at the beast's throat, but the massive jaws dropped mercilessly on him. Teeth like plowshares cut furrows through the muscles of his stomach. Lukas shrieked in pain. His hands thrust the wolf back. His elbows locked. A brutal claw gouged into his wounded stomach, cutting a new track of lines. Lukas's legs kicked the creature's belly. He tried to squirm backward across the stones, but again the teeth fell, and again they rose dripping with blood. A scarlet spray spewed from each nostril as the wolf howled. Lukas screamed again, his fists pounding frantically on the creature's massive skull. The steaming maw opened and dropped. Teeth clamped hot about the bard's neck. Slowly they scissored together. Fangs broke through the skin and drove down into muscle and sinew. Still the jaws closed. A scream erupted from Lukas's mouth, hot blood rimming his lips. He pried at the beast's jaws. The forest canopy above began to fade.

Suddenly the jaws released.

Casimir's huge muzzle lifted, dripping, from Lukas's throat. A howl of pain rolled from the beast. The sound echoed mournfully through the cricket-filled wood. Then, with an odd gurgle, the howl ceased. Casimir's lupine legs locked up beneath him. The red fire that had filled his eyes dwindled and went out. The massive creature slumped to one side, its sightless face landing heavily on the stony ground.

Clutching his bleeding throat, Lukas edged away from the shuddering beast. Only then did he glimpse the iron dagger buried to its hilt between the wolf's massive ribs.

Julianna was standing there, her fist rimmed with blood and a tremble running through her. Lukas pulled himself backward to the *vardo* wheel and propped himself up against it. His hands were shuddering and his breaths spasmed. Even so, a brief smile of victory flashed across his face. His plan had worked.

With slow reverence, Madam Duccia approached Julianna and set a woolen blanket over her trembling frame. Tears began to stream down Julianna's cheeks. She gazed for a moment at the blood on her hand, then wiped it away on her scarlet chemise. The gypsy woman wrapped her in her arms, and they stood that way for long moments.

In time, Julianna pulled away from the embrace. She drew the blanket from her shoulders and draped it over the lower half of the now motionless beast. Stepping back, she watched the slow transformation come across Casimir. The muzzle shrank quietly into his face; the hairs faded and vanished across his cheeks and brow; muscles and bones slowly reshaped and realigned. The massive frame beneath the blanket contracted into the thin, curled body of a young man.

Lukas watched in amazement. "He shouldn't be changing to a man!" he whispered breathlessly. "He's a wolfwere. His human side was only a sham."

Julianna approached Casimir with slow and quiet steps. "Perhaps you thought so, Master Lukas." She knelt sadly beside the body. "Some who are born human make themselves beasts; perhaps some who are born beasts make themselves human." Her thin hand ran fondly across Casimir's smooth cheek. A trembling began in her chin. She looked away from the lifeless face, tilting her head back to the pitching treetops above. Tears welled unstoppable into her emerald eyes, and a low sobbing began in her breast. She took his battered hand in his and wept unrestrainedly.

When the tears at last were gone, she leaned over and kissed him. "Your lips are still warm," she said sadly. "Good-bye, Casimir, my once-loved. If there are gods in this world, let them judge you with eyes like mine."

Drawing a deep breath, she rose from the still corpse and stood there for a time. She stared blankly, as though somehow seeing beyond the forest. At length, she brushed the dirt from her dress and began to stagger toward Harkon Lukas.

"Madam Duccia," she said, "may I buy some linens from you?"

The gypsy woman turned her face quizzically toward Julianna. "What do you need them for?"

"For bandages," Julianna replied, kneeling beside Lukas.

"Bandages? For him?" Duccia scoffed. "We'd do better to run him through and be done with it."

"I want bandages," Julianna said, her voice firm despite its weariness.

"I'll fetch one sheet. For you, only four gold," Duccia said as she headed toward her *vardo.*

"Fine," Julianna replied, raking her hair with a shaking hand.

The dark bard studied her, an impish grin emerging on his lips. "*You* will bandage *me?*"

"Yes," she replied with a hint of irritation.

"What if I've lied to you? What if I *am* a monster?" he asked, his eyes prying into hers.

"If I knew you were, I'd kill you with the same blade that killed Casimir. But all I know is that you're a man— a wounded man. And good or evil, a wounded man should be tended."

"What if I were to confess to you that I'm a monster?"

"Don't," Julianna replied simply.

Madam Duccia arrived with the sheet. It was ragged and sloppily bundled, as though she'd pulled it off her own bed. She smiled as she handed Julianna the ball of linen. "I thought it a waste to give him a clean one."

"This will do," Julianna replied quietly. She took the sheet and began tearing long strips from it. "Madam Duccia, I want to bear the body of my love to Gundarak for his burial. How much do you ask?"

The gypsy woman set her dark hand on Julianna's shoulder. "I'll charge you nothing. You'll need money for the plot and the stone." Then her face darkened. "But no amount of money can convince me to carry *this* rogue

. . . dead or alive."

"What?" Lukas protested. "You'll bandage my wounds one moment and leave me here to die the next?"

Wrapping a strip of cloth around Lukas's neck, Julianna said, "We'll leave your horse here. Dawn will come soon. If you're a man, as you say you are, perhaps the gods will let you live."

"Letting him live is part of his sentence," Madam Duccia replied with a harsh laugh. "Here, I'll finish with the bandaging. You should go tend . . . Casimir."

With the mention of Casimir, Julianna stiffened. The linen strips fell from her hand. Madam Duccia knelt in front of the bard, screening his eyes from Julianna. Julianna sat back on her heels. Slowly, mustering her courage, she looked toward Casimir. He seemed almost curled in sleep beneath the blanket, his coal-black hair forming a dark halo about his face.

Never again would the wolf take hold of him.

Never again would he race beneath the howling moon.

Never again would Sundered Heart sing about his love.

"Yes, I must tend him."

EPILOGUE

Sunlight streamed warm through the dimpled window and soaked into the heap of blankets piled atop Thoris.

But still he shivered.

As cold as the grave, he was. As cold as death.

The splints had long since come off, and his legs, albeit crooked, were solid enough to stand on. But his soul was another matter. He had had enough heart to roll out of his deathbed at the Kartakan Inn, to crawl to the doorway and shout for a messenger. He had had enough heart to summon Valsarik and ask to be taken back to Harmonia. But when he finally arrived at Valsarik's doorstep, the panic he had mistaken for hope died within him.

Since that time, Valsarik had tended him well, with hot meals and hearthside stories. But nothing could warm Thoris's icy soul. With each passing day, his body healed, but his mind descended deeper into melancholy.

Today was like any other, spent shivering beneath the blankets. Thoris shifted the quilts atop him. His movement stirred up specks of dust, which rose and swirled into the rays of sunlight. The specks glowed like stars.

It had been an eternity since Thoris thought of stars.

They were said to be the minions of Milil, the stars were. They were said to be the chorus of his celestial voices. But perhaps they were only swirling points of dust, accidental and lifeless, caught in a meaningless puff of air. Thoris blew into the swarm of dust specks and watched the swirling particles spin and collide, then fall slowly to the blanket.

He pulled back the covers and swung his misshapen legs over the bed's edge. Slowly he eased his weight onto wobbly feet and slipped a robe across his shoulders. Bracing himself for a moment on the bed frame, he began to shuffle toward the door. It struck him that he didn't know why he had risen or where he planned to go. His feet pushed him forward, regardless. His hand settled on the door's metal latch, and he slowly opened it. A shaft of sunlight stabbed into the doorway. Once again the dust swirled like stars. This time, Thoris was heedless of the spinning specks. He stepped into the warm garden, pulling the robe tightly about him, and turned his eyes toward the savagely bright sky.

On many days, Thoris had seen Valsarik walk from the door stoop to the garden rail. The trip took mere moments. With Thoris's shuffling legs, though, it seemed a matter of days.

As he scuttled along the path, he realized why he had risen from the bed. He realized where he was going.

Gustav's grave lay along the cliff's edge, marking the spot where Casimir had jumped off almost two years ago. The statue of Gustav proved a perfect stepping-stone. Thoris's twisted limbs slowly climbed to the rail as the stone Gustav patiently watched. The statue held a flute in one hand and a book of song in the other. Blasphemous though it might have been, Thoris clutched the flute to pull himself the last few inches to the rail.

Then he stood, holding the stony hand of Gustav and peering out toward the wide valley below. At the cliff's base lay a boulder-strewn thicket. Beyond it stretched a long heath, reaching to a green-black rim of forest on the horizon. In places, farmers had fought back the heather, laying down wriggling rock walls or planting thorny hedges. Thoris's attention shifted to the glaring sky, vast and unconcerned, oblivious to the farms below.

"Gustav," Thoris muttered to the statue, "where is our Milil in this vast place? You are more present than he is." He sighed shallowly, his fingers clinging to those of the statue. "This is no place for priests—no place for children. Milil, if you're here, help me step from this cliff."

No answer came. Thoris had expected none. Only the balmy summer breeze spoke in his ear. Otherwise, there was silence. Thoris leaned over the rail, his hand loosening on the motionless fingers of Gustav. He closed his eyes, feeling the warm wind rush over him. Perhaps it would feel this way, his long fall to the rocky earth below. Perhaps if he closed his eyes, he'd only feel the warm wind billowing through his robes as though they were wings. Perhaps he could banish fear from his heart for those final seconds of life.

A warm hand settled on his ankle.

"Please, Valsarik," Thoris said tearfully. "Please don't stop me. This could be the one heroic act of my life."

"Do you think this frail old hand of mine could stop you?" came the manservant's gravelly voice.

"I'm sorry. I don't do this out of ingratitude. You've done so much to save me."

"Of course you do it out of ingratitude," Valsarik blurted. "I've labored long to save your life, but you don't care."

"I can't be saved," Thoris said.

"Nonsense," came the bitter reply. "No one—not even your friend Casimir—is beyond redemption if he clings to life."

"I'm too afraid to live," Thoris said, his voice far away.

"I have something here for you," Valsarik said. "I found it in the marketplace, and I remembered it was yours." Thoris looked momentarily over his shoulder. The old manservant held the wooden sword, the sword Casimir had given to Thoris on the day they met. Its battered edges were still keen. "Come now, Thoris," the man growled. "You shouldn't be afraid. Milil needs his priests."

"Milil is dead, or nearly dead."

"All the more reason he needs his priests," Valsarik observed. "You obviously fear to step over the cliff, just as much as you fear to step back from it," he said, releasing Thoris's ankle. "Otherwise you'd have leapt by now. Take hold of the sword, Thoris. You must ask yourself which you fear more, to live or to die, my friend. . . ."

Thoris heard none of these words. He was watching the fleecy clouds on the horizon. Among the veils and columns of white mist, there were angels dancing. They were whiter than the clouds, white like lightning. He could hear their singing, quiet on the wind. But it wasn't the song of Milil. It was fierce and strangely sad. The song grew louder. Suddenly the angels were winging toward him. A legion of them. Their radiance burned his skin, burned his eyes, poured like water through him. They filled the sky and stretched their hands out, beckoning. Their shouting song blared across the heath.

Deafening, it was.

Deafening and beautiful and horrible.

They'd almost reached him now, fangs glistening in their singing mouths. One flew straight for Thoris, its teeth the size of a crescent moon.

" . . . which you fear more, to live or to die."

"The angels have fangs," Thoris said.

And he stepped into the niveous jaws.

Coming in 1993

Webs of evil that trap the unwary . . .

Tapestry of Dark Souls   Elaine Bergstrom

The Gathering Cloth is a shimmering web in which some of the darkest evils in Ravenloft are trapped. It is up to Jonathan, son of the most powerful of the beings in the tapestry, to find a way to destroy the cloth before the evil breaks his will and binds him to the darkness forever. **On sale March 1993.**

Carnival of Fear   J. Robert King

A murder has occurred along the sideshow boardwalk of Carnival l'Morai. Three of the performers at the carnival attempt to track down the killer, but their investigation leads to more murders and the discovery of a great conspiracy. Before they can bring the killer to justice, they are themselves marked for death. **On sale July 1993.**

. . . and the epic tale of the Ebonacht family

The Screaming Tower   James Lowder
Ebonacht Trilogy, Book One

Captured by the ruthless Lord Ebonacht, Marius is forced to become a slave. His only hope for escape lies in uncovering the mystery of the Screaming Tower, which holds the key to the Ebonacht family's power. Though Marius is no stranger to magic or the dark creatures that stalk the mists of Ravenloft, he is unprepared for the horror he must confront to win his freedom. **On sale September 1993.**